"Let me make love to you, Demelza."

She began to trace figures in the sand. Her heart was beating as if there were a drum inside her. Her mouth was so dry she could not swallow. The nakedness of her body inside her frock seemed to have suddenly become more apparent to her, seemed to flower. She gave a slight groan which she tried to suppress altogether but could not quite.

Hugh sat back looking at her. "What is it?"

"Please let us go."

"May I just kiss you?"

She raised her head and pushed her hair back. "It would be quite wrong."

"But you will permit it."

"Perhaps I cannot stop you."

He moved toward her and knew the moment he touched her that something had won his battle for him. He took her face in his hands, held it like a cup to be drunk from, and then kissed her . . .

THE POLDARK SAGA
published by Ballantine Books:

THE FOUR SWANS

A Novel of Cornwall
1795-1797

Winston Graham

BALLANTINE BOOKS • NEW YORK

Library of Congress Catalog Card Number: 76-18347

ISBN 0-345-26005-8

This edition published by arrangement with
Doubleday & Co., Inc.

Manufactured in the United States of America

First Ballantine Books Edition: April 1978

Cover photograph credit: BBC-TV

To
Fred and Gladys

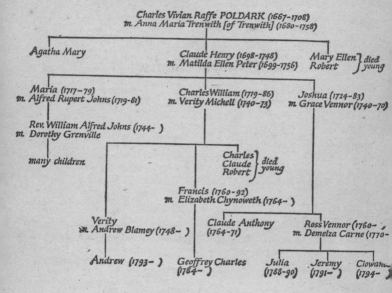

Charles Vivian Raffe POLDARK (1667-1708)
m. Anna Maria Trenwith [of Trenwith] (1680-1758)

Agatha Mary

Claude Henry (1698-1748)
m. Matilda Ellen Peter (1699-1756)

Mary Ellen } died
Robert } young

Maria (1717-79)
m. Alfred Rupert Johns (1719-81)

Charles William (1719-86)
m. Verity Michell (1740-73)

Joshua (1724-83)
m. Grace Vennor (1740-70)

Rev. William Alfred Johns (1744-)
m. Dorothy Grenville

many children

Charles } died
Claude } young
Robert }

Francis (1760-92)
m. Elizabeth Chynoweth (1764-)

Verity
m. Andrew Blamey (1748-)

Claude Anthony
(1764-71)

Ross Vennor (1760-
m. Demelza Carne (1770-

Andrew (1793-)

Geoffrey Charles
(1784-)

Julia
(1788-90)

Jeremy
(1791-)

Clowan...
(1794-)

Jonathan CHYNOWETH [of Cusgarne] (1690-1750)
m. Anne Tregear (1693-1760)

Jonathan (1710-77)
m. Elizabeth Lanyon (1716-50)

Robert (1712-50)
m. Ursula Venning (1720-88)

Jonathan (1737-)
m. Joan Le Grice (1730-)

Hubert (1750-93)
m. Amelia Tregellas (1751-)

Elizabeth (1764-)
m. (1) Francis Poldark
    (2) George Warleggan

Morwenna (1776-)
m. Rev. Osborne Whitworth

Garlanda (1778-)
Carenza (1780-)
Rowella (1781-)

Tom CARNE (1740-94)
m. Demelza Lyon (1752-77)

Luke WARLEGGAN (1715-)
m. Bethia Kemp (1716-44)

Nicholas [of Cardew] (1735-)
m. Mary Lashbrook (1732-)

Demelza (1770-)
Luke (1771-)
Samuel (1772-)
William (1773-)
John (1774-)
Robert (1775-)
Drake (1776-)

Cary Warleggan
(1740-)

George (1759-)
m. Elizabeth Poldark (1764-)
   (née Chynoweth)

Valentine (1794-)

BOOK ONE

CHAPTER I

Daniel Behenna, physician and surgeon, was forty years old and lived in a square, detached, untidy house in Goodwives Lane, Truro. He was himself square in build and detached in manner, but not at all unkempt, since the citizens of the town and district paid well for the benefit of his modern physical knowledge. He had married early, and then again a second time, but both his wives had died, and he and his two young daughters were now looked after by a Mrs Childs, who lived in. His assistant, Mr Arthur, slept over the stables.

Behenna had been in Truro only five years, having come direct from London where he had not only established a reputation as a practitioner but had written and published a monograph amending Smellie's famous *Treatise on Midwifery*; and since his arrival he had much impressed the wealthier provincials with his authority and skill.

In particular authority. When men were ill they did not want the pragmatical approach of a Dwight Enys, who used his eyes and saw how often his remedies failed, and therefore was tentative in his decisions. They did not want someone who came in and sat and talked pleasantly and had an unassuming word for the children, even a pat for the dog. They liked the importance, the confidence, the attack of a demi-god, whose voice was already echoing through the house as he mounted the stairs, who had the maids scurrying for water or blankets and the patient's relatives hanging on every word. Behenna was such a man. His very appearance made the heart beat faster, even if, as often happened, it later stopped beating altogether. Failure did not depress him. If one of his patients died it was not the fault of his remedies, it was the fault of the patient.

He dressed well and to the best standards of his profession. When he travelled far – as his mounting reputation more and more obliged him to do – he rode a handsome black horse

called Emir and wore buckskin breeches and top boots, with
a heavy cloak thrown over a velvet coat with brass buttons,
and in the winter thick woollen gloves to keep his hands
warm. When in town he used a muff instead of the gloves and
carried a gold-banded cane which had a vinaigrette in the
head containing herbs to combat infection.

In an evening in early October 1795 he returned from local
calls across the river where he had prescribed his heroic treatment for two patients suffering from summer cholera and had
drawn three pints of fluid from the stomach of a dropsical
corn merchant. It had been a warm month after the bad
summer and the deadly winter which had preceded it, and
the little town had been drowsing gently in the day's heat.
The smells of sewage and decaying refuse had been strong all
afternoon, but with evening a breeze had sprung up and the
air was sweet again. The tide was full, and the river had
crept in and surrounded the clustered town like a sleeping
lake.

As he reached his front door Dr Behenna waved away a
small group of people who had started up at his coming. In
the main the less well-to-do went to the apothecaries of the
town, the poor made do with what nostrums they could brew
themselves or buy for a penny from a travelling gypsy; but
sometimes he helped on odd case without charge – he was not
an ungenerous man and it ministered to his ego – so always a
few waited about for him, hoping for a moment's consul-
tation on his doorstep. But today he was not in the mood.

As he left his horse to the stable boy and entered the house,
Mrs Childs, his housekeeper, came out to greet him. Her hair
stood out, and she was wiping her hands on a soiled towel.

'Dr Behenna, sur!' Her voice was a whisper. 'Thur be a
gent to see ee. In the parlour. He've been yur some five and
twenty minute. I didn't know rightly 'ow long ye'd be gone,
but he says to me, he says, "I'll wait." Just like that. "I'll
wait." So I put'n in parlour.'

He stared at her while he set down his cloak and bag. She
was a slovenly young woman, and he often wondered why
he tolerated her. There was only one reason, really.

'What gentleman? Why did you not call Mr Arthur?' He
did not lower his voice, and she glanced nervously behind her.

'Mr Warleggan,' she said.

Behenna observed himself in the mildewed mirror, smoothed his hair back, dusted a freckle of powder from his cuff, looked his hands over to see there were no unpleasant stains on them.

'Where is Miss Flotina?'

'Gone music. Miss May be still abed. But Mr Arthur say the fever have remitted.'

'Of course it will have remitted. Well, see that I am not disturbed.'

'Ais, sur.'

Behenna cleared his throat and went into the parlour, a puzzled man.

But there was no mistake. Mr George Warleggan was standing by the window, hands behind back, square shouldered, composed. His hair had been fresh dressed; his clothes were of a London cut. The richest man in town and one of the most influential, there was yet something about his stance, now that he had passed his middle thirties, which was reminiscent of his grandfather, the blacksmith.

'Mr Warleggan. I hope I have not kept you waiting. Had I known   '

'Which you did not. I have passed the time admiring your skeleton. We are indeed fearfully and wonderfully made.'

His tone was cold; but then it was always cold.

'It was put together in my student days. We dug him up. He was a felon who had come to a bad end. There are always some such in a big city.'

'Not only in a big city.'

'Allow me to offer you refreshment. A cordial or a glass of canary.'

George Warleggan shook his head. 'Your woman, your housekeeper, has already offered.'

'Then pray sit down. I'm at your service.'

George Warleggan accepted a seat and crossed his legs. Without moving his neck his glance wandered round the room. Behenna regretted that the place was not in better order. Books and papers were jumbled on a table, together with jars of Glauber's salts and boxes of Dover's powders. Two empty bottles with worm-eaten corks stood among the medical records on the desk. A girl's frock was flung over a chair-back beside the dangling skeleton. The surgeon frowned: he did not expect his rich patients to call on him, but if they did this appearance could create a bad impression.

They sat in silence for a minute or so. It seemed a very long time.

'I called,' said George, 'on a personal matter.'

Dr Behenna inclined his head.

'Therefore what I have to say must be confidential. I imagine we cannot be overheard?'

'Everything,' said the surgeon, 'everything between doctor and patient is confidential.'

George looked at him drily. 'Quite so. But this must be more so.'

'I don't think I follow your meaning.'

'I mean that only you and I will know of this conversation. If it should come to the ears of a third party I shall know that *I* have not spoken.'

Behenna drew himself up in his chair, but did not answer. His very strong sense of his own importance was only just contained by his sense of the greater importance of the Warleggans.

'In those circumstances, Dr Behenna, I would not be a good friend.'

The surgeon went to the door and flung it open. The hall was empty. He shut the door again.

'If you wish to speak, Mr Warleggan, you may do so. I can offer you no greater assurance than I have already done.'

George nodded. 'So be it.'

They both sat quiet for a moment.

George said: 'Are you a superstitious man?'

'No, sir. Nature is governed by immutable laws which neither man nor amulet can change. It is the business of the physician to grasp the truth of those laws and apply them to the destruction of disease. All diseases are curable. No man should die before old age.'

'You have two young children?'

'Of twelve and nine.'

'You do not think they are likely to be affected by the bones of a felon hanging in their home day and night?'

'No, sir. If they appeared to be so affected, a strong purging would cure them.'

George nodded again. He put three fingers into his fob pocket and began to turn the money there.

'You attended my wife at the birth of our child. You have been a frequent visitor to our house since. You have, I assume, delivered many women.'

'Many thousands. For two years I was at the Lying-in Hospital at Westminster under Dr Ford. I may claim that my experience is not equalled in Cornwall – and seldom elsewhere. But . . . you know this, Mr Warleggan. You knew it when your wife, Mrs Warleggan, was with child and you retained my services. I presume that you have not found those services wanting.'

'No.' George Warleggan thrust out his bottom lip. He looked more than ever like the Emperor Vespasian being judicial on some matter of empire. 'But it was about that that I wished to consult you.'

'I am at your service,' said Behenna again.

'My child, my son Valentine, was an eight-month child. That's correct? Because of the accident of my wife's fall, my son was born prematurely by about a month. Am I right?'

'You are right.'

'But tell me, Dr Behenna, among the thousands of children you have delivered, you must have seen a great many infants prematurely born. Is that so?'

'Yes, a considerable number.'

'Eight month? Seven month? Six month?'

'Eight and seven. I've never seen a child survive at six months.'

'And those born prematurely that did survive, like Valentine. There were distinct and recognizable differences in them at birth? I mean between them and such as come to the full time?'

Behenna dared to allow himself a few seconds to speculate on the trend of his visitor's questioning. 'Differences? Of what nature?'

'I am asking you.'

'There are no differences of any importance, Mr Warleggan. You can set your mind at rest. Your son has suffered no ill-effects whatsoever from being prematurely born.'

'I'm not concerned with differences now.' Asperity had crept into George Warleggan's voice. 'What are the differences at the time?'

Behenna had never considered his sentences more carefully. 'Weight chiefly, of course. It is almost unknown for an eight-month child to weigh more than six pounds. Seldom the same loud cry. Nails . . .'

'I am told that an eight-month child does not have nails.'

'That's not correct. They are small, and soft instead of hard –'

'I am told the skin of such a child is wrinkled and red.'

'So is that of many at full term.'

'I am told that they do not have hair.'

'Oh, sometimes. But it is rare and very thin.'

A cart clattered down the lane. When it had gone George said:

'The purpose of my questions may by now have become clear to you, Dr Behenna. I have to put to you the final question. Was my son, or was he not, a premature child?'

Daniel Behenna moistened his lips. He was aware that his expression was being closely watched, and he was also aware of the tensions of the other man and what in a less self-possessed person would have been observed as suffering.

He got up and walked to the window. The light showed up the bloodstains on his cuff. 'On many physical questions, Mr Warleggan, it's not easy to return a definite yes or no. In this matter you must first give me leave to remember. I am sure you will understand that your son is now – what? – eighteen, twenty months old. Since I delivered Mrs Warleggan I have attended many women in parturition. Let me see, what day did you call me in?'

'On the thirteenth of February of last year. My wife fell on the stairs at Trenwith. It was a Thursday evening about six o'clock. I sent a man for you at once and you came about midnight.'

'Ah, yes, I remember. It was the week I treated Lady Hawkins for broken costae which she had sustained in the hunting field, and when I heard of your wife her accident I hoped she had not been a-horse; for such a fall –'

'So you came,' George said.

'. . . I came. I attended on your wife throughout the night and into the next day. I believe the child presented itself that following evening.'

'At a quarter after eight Valentine was born.'

'Yes . . . Well, I can only tell you on first recollection, Mr Warleggan, that there was nothing that appeared as strange in the circumstances of your son's birth. It did not, of course, occur to me to wonder, to speculate, or to observe closely. Why should it? I didn't suppose there would ever come a time when it would be necessary to pronounce one way or the other on such a matter. On the mere matter of a month. In view of your wife's unfortunate fall I was happy to be able to deliver her of a live and healthy boy. Have you asked your midwife?'

George too got up. 'You must remember the child you delivered. Did it have fully-formed nails?'

'I believe so, but I cannot tell if —'

'And hair?'

'A little dark hair.'

'And was the skin wrinkled? I saw it within the hour and I remember only a slight wrinkling'

Behenna sighed. 'Mr Warleggan, you are one of my wealthiest clients, and I have no wish to offend you. But may I be entirely frank?'

'That's what I have just asked you to be.'

'Well, may I suggest, in all deference, that you return home and think no more of this matter. Your reasons for this enquiry I'll not venture to ask. But if you expect to receive from me at this date — or indeed from any other person — a plain statement that your son was or was not a full-term child, you are asking, sir, for the impossible. Nature is not so to be categorized. The normal is only the norm — on which there are wide variations.'

'So you will not tell me.'

'I *cannot* tell you. Had you asked me at the time I should have ventured a firmer opinion, that is all. *Naturalia non sunt turpia*, as the saying is.'

George picked up his stick and prodded at the carpet. 'Dr Enys is back, I understand, and will soon be riding his rounds.'

Behenna stiffened. 'He is still ill and will shortly marry his heiress.'

''Some people think well of him.'

'That is their concern, not mine, Mr Warleggan. For my part I have only contempt for the majority of his practices, which show a weakness of disposition and a lack of conviction. A man without a lucid and well-proven medical system is a man without hope.'

'Just so. Just so. I have always heard, of course, that medical men do not speak well of their rivals.'

Nor perhaps bankers of *their* rivals, Behenna thought.

'Well . . .' George got up. 'I'll wish you good day, Behenna.'

The surgeon said: 'I trust that Mrs Warleggan and Master Valentine continue in good health.'

'Thank you, yes.'

'It's time almost that I called to see them. Perhaps early next week.'

There was a moment's pause, during which it seemed possible that George was considering whether to say, 'Pray do not call again.'

Behenna added: 'I have tried not to speculate, Mr Warleggan, on your reason for enquiring into the matter you have raised with me. But I would not be human if I did not appreciate how important my answer might be to you. Therefore, sir, appreciate how difficult that answer is. I could not, and indeed assuredly would not, make a statement which, for all I know, might be considered to impugn the honour of a noble and virtuous woman – that's to say, I could not and would not without a certainty in my mind which I emphatically do not possess. Did I possess it, I would feel it my duty to tell you. I do not possess it. That is all.'

George regarded him with cold eyes. His whole expression was one of distaste and dislike – which might have conveyed his opinion of the surgeon or only what he felt of a necessity which forced him to betray so much to a stranger.

'You will remember how this conversation began, Dr Behenna.'

'I am pledged to secrecy.'

'Pray see that you keep it.' He went to the door. 'My family is well, but you may call if you wish.'

After he had gone Behenna went through into the kitchen. 'Nellie, this house is a disgrace! You idle away your time gossiping and dreaming and observing the traffic. The parlour is not fit to receive a distinguished patient! See, have that frock taken away! And the shoes. Have a care for your position here!'

He went on rebuking in his strong, resonant voice for three or four minutes. She stood observing him patiently from under her hearthrug of brown hair, waiting for the storm to pass, sensing that he needed to restore his authority after having it briefly encroached on. It was rare for him ever to have it encroached on, for even when he visited his richest patients they were in distress and seeking his help. So he pronounced, and they waited on his words. He had never attended on George Warleggan himself, since the man enjoyed abnormally good health. But today, as always when meeting him, he had had to defer. It did not please him; it had made him sweat; and he took it out on Nellie Childs.

'Ais, sur,' she said, and 'no, sur,' and 'I'll see to'n tomorrow, sur.' She never failed to call him sir, even when he followed her into her bedroom; and this was the basis of their relationship. There was an unspoken *quid pro quo* between them. So she took his reprimands seriously but not too seriously; and when he had done she began quietly to tidy up the parlour while he stood by the window, hands under his coat tails, thinking of what had passed.

'Miss May'll be wanting for to see ee, sur.'

'Presently.'

She tried to gather up all the slippers, and dropped two. Her hair ballooned over her face. 'Reckon tis rare for the gentry to call on ee, like that, sur. Was he wanting for something medical?'

'Something medical.'

'Reckon he could've sent one of 'is men for to fetch something medical, don't ee reckon, sur?'

Behenna did not answer. She went out with the slippers and returned for the frock.

'Reckon I never seen Mr Warleggan come here afore like that. P'raps twas private like, not wanting his household to know?'

Behenna turned from the window. 'I think it was Cato who said: *"Nam nulli tacuisse nocet, nocet esse locutum."* Always bear that in mind, Mrs Childs. It should be a guiding principle of yours. As of many others.'

'Mebbe so, but I don't know what it d'mean, so I cann't say, can I?'

'For your benefit I will translate. "It is harmful to no one to have been silent, but it is often harmful to have spoken."'

II

George Tabb was sixty-eight and worked at the Fighting Cocks Inn as a horse keeper and porter. He earned 9s. a week, and sometimes received an extra shilling for helping with the cocking. He lived in a lean-to beside the inn, and there his wife, still an industrious woman in spite of ill-health, made about an extra £2 a year taking in washing. With the occasional pickings that come to a porter he therefore earned just enough to live on; but in the nine years since his friend and employer Charles William Poldark had died he had become too fond of the bottle; and now often drank himself below subsistence level. Emily Tabb tried to keep a tight hold on the purse strings, but with 5s. a week for bread, 6d. a week for meat, 9d. for half a pound each of butter and cheese, a shilling for two pecks of potatoes, and a weekly rental of 2s., there was no room for manœuvre. Mrs Tabb endlessly regretted – as indeed did her husband in his soberer moments – the circumstances in which they had left Trenwith two and a half years ago. The widowed and impoverished Elizabeth Poldark had had to let her servants go one by one, until only the faithful Tabbs were left; but Tabb in his cups had presumed too much on his indispensability and when Mrs Poldark suddenly remarried they had had to leave.

One afternoon in early October George Tabb was brushing out the cockpit behind the inn to make ready for a match that was to take place the following day, when the innkeeper whistled to him and told him there was someone to see him. Tabb went out and found an emaciated man in black, whose eyes were so close-set that they appeared to be crossed.

'Tabb? George Tabb? Someoné want a word with you. Tell your master. You'll be the half-hour.'

Tabb eyed his visitor and asked what it was all about, and who wanted him and why; but he was told no more. There was another man outside in the street, so he put away his broom and went with them.

It was no distance. A few yards down an alley, along the river bank where another full tide glimmered and brimmed, up a street to a door in a wall, across a yard. The back of a tall house.

'In here.' He went in. A room that might have been a lawyer's office. 'Wait here.' The door was shut behind him. He was left alone.

He blinked warily, uneasy, wondering what ill this summons foreshadowed. He had not long to wait. A gentleman came in through another door. Tabb stared in surprise.

'Mr Warleggan!' He had no forelock to touch, but he touched his wrinkled head.

The other George, the infinitely important George, nodded to him and went to sit down at the desk. He studied some papers while Tabb's unease grew. It was on Mr Warleggan's orders when he married Mrs Poldark that the Tabbs had been dismissed from her service, and his greeting today had shown no amiability.

'Tabb,' said George, without looking up. 'I want to ask you a few questions.'

'Sur?'

'These questions are questions that I'll put to you in confidence, and I shall expect you to treat them as such.'

'Yes, sur.'

'I see that you left the employment I obtained for you at Mrs Warleggan's request when you left her service.'

'Yes, sur. Mrs Tabb wasn't up to the work and –'

'On the contrary, I understand from Miss Agar that it was you who were unsatisfactory, and that she offered to retain Mrs Tabb if she would stay on alone.'

Tabb's eyes wandered uneasily about the room.

'So now you eke out a miserable living as a pot boy. Very well, it is your own choice. Those who will not be helped must take the consequences!'

Tabb cleared his throat.

Mr Warleggan put fingers in his fob pocket and took out two coins. They were gold. 'Nevertheless I am prepared to offer you some temporary easement of your lot. These guineas. They are yours, on certain conditions.'

Tabb stared at the money as at a snake. 'Sur?'

'I want to ask you some questions about the last months of your employment at Trenwith. Can you remember them? It's little more than two years since you left.'

'Oh, yes, sur. I mind it all well.'

'Only you and I are in this room, Tabb. Only you will know the questions I have asked. If in the future therefore I hear that the nature of these questions is known to others I shall know who has spoken of them, shall I not?'

'Oh, I wouldn't do that, sur –'

'Would you not? I'm far from sure. A man in his cups has an unreliable tongue. So listen, Tabb.'

'Sur?'

'If ever I hear word spoken of anything I ask you this afternoon, you will be driven out of this town, and I'll see that you starve. Starve. In the gutter. It is a promise. Will you in your cups remember that?'

'Well, sur, I promise faithful. I can't say more'n that. I'll –'

'As you say, you can't say more. So keep your promise and I will keep mine.'

Tabb licked his lips in the ensuing silence. 'I mind those times well, sur. I mind well all that time at Trenwith when we was trying, me and Mrs Tabb, to keep the 'ouse and the farm together. There was no more'n the two of us for all there was to be done –'

'I know – I know. And you traded on your position. So you lost your employment. But in recognition of your long service another position was found for you and you lost that. Now, Tabb, certain legal matters bearing on the estate wait to be settled and you may be able to help me to settle them. I first want you to remember everyone who called at the house. Everyone you saw, that is. From about April 1793 until June of that year when you left.'

'What called? To see Mistress Elizabeth, d'ye mean? Or

Miss Agatha? There was few what called, sur. The house was real bye . . . Mind, there was village folk. Betty Coad wi' pilchards. Lobb the Sherborner once weekly. Aaron Nanfan – '

George waved him into silence. 'For the Poldarks. Socially. Who called?'

Tabb thought a few moments and rasped his chin. 'Why *you*, sur. You more'n anyone! An' for the rest, Dr Choake to see Miss Agatha, Parson Odgers once a week, Cap'n Henshawe, the churchwarden, Cap'n Poldark over from Nampara, Sir John Trevaunance maybe twice; I believe Mrs Ruth Treneglos once. Mrs Teague I seen once. Mind I was in the fields half the time and couldn't hardly – '

'How often did Captain Poldark come from Nampara?'

'Oh . . . once a week. There or thereabouts.'

'Often in the evening?'

'Nay, sur, twas always avnoon he come. Thursday avnoon. Took tea and then off he'd go.'

'Who came in the evening, then?'

'Why no one, sur. Twas quiet – quiet as the dead. One widow lady, one young gentleman scarce ten years old, one rare old lady. Now if you was to ask me 'bout Mr Francis's time; thur was times then – '

'And Mistress Elizabeth – no doubt she went out in the evening?'

Tabb blinked. 'Went out? Not so's I know, sur.'

'But in the light evenings of that summer – April, May and June, she must have ridden abroad.'

'Nay, she scarce rode at all. We'd sold all the 'orses, save two which was too old to be rid.'

George fingered the two guineas, and Tabb stared at them, hoping that this was all.

George said: 'Come, come, you have earned nothing yet. Think, man. There must have been others about at that time.'

Tabb racked his brains. 'Village folk . . . Uncle Ben would be there wi' his rabbits. Thur were no outlanders nor – '

'How often did Mistress Elizabeth go to Nampara?'

'To Nampara?'

'That's what I said. To visit the Ross Poldarks.'

'Never. Not ever. Not's I know. No, not ever.'

'Why did she not go? They were neighbours.'

'I reckon – I reckon mebbe she never got on so well with Cap'n Poldark's wife. But tis merest guessingwork fur me to say.'

There was a long silence.

'Try to remember particularly the month of May. The middle or early part of May. Who *called*? Who called in the evening?'

'Why . . . why no one, sur. Not a soul I ever seen. I *said* so.'

'What time did you go to bed?'

'Oh . . . nine or ten. Soon as it went dark. We was out and about from cocklight to cockshut and – '

'What time did Mistress Elizabeth retire?'

'Oh . . . 'bout the same. We was all spent.'

'Who locked up?'

'I done that, last thing. Time was when we never locked, but wi' no other servants and all these vagrants about . . .'

'Well, you have earned nothing, I fear,' said George, moving to put the money away.

'Oh, sur, I'd tell ee if I knew what twas ye wanted for me to say!'

'No doubt you would. So tell me this. If someone called after you went to bed, would you hear the bell?'

'At night, d'ye mean?'

'When else?'

Tabb thought. 'I doubt. I doubt there'd be anyone t'hear. Twas in the lower kitchen, the bell was, and we all slep' well above.'

'Never? Would you have known?'

'Why – *yes*, I reckon. What would anyone want t'enter for except to steal? – and there was little enough to steal.'

'But is there any secret way into the house that you know of – one that would be known perhaps to a member of the family?'

'Nay . . . None's I know. An' I been there five and twenty year.'

George Warleggan got up. 'Very well, Tabb.' He dropped the coins on the table. 'Take your guineas and go. I enjoin you to say nothing to anyone – not even to Mrs Tabb.'

'Shan't tell she,' said Tabb. 'Else . . . well, sur, you know how tis. She'd want for to put this money away.'

'Take your guineas,' said George. 'And go.'

III

Elizabeth Warleggan was thirty-one, and had two children.
Her eldest, Geoffrey Charles Poldark, would soon be eleven
and was in his first term at Harrow. She had so far received
three grubby letters which told her that he was at least alive
and apparently well and getting into the routines of the school.
Her heart ached every time she looked at them, folded carefully in a corner of her desk; in imagination she read so much
between the lines. Her younger son, Valentine Warleggan, was
not yet two years old and making a slow recovery from a
severe attack of rickets he had suffered last winter.

She had been out to a card party with three old friends – it
was one of her pleasures in spending each winter again in
Truro; *everyone* played cards in Truro, and it was so different
from those dull and lonely winters at Trenwith with Francis,
and after Francis died. Life with her new husband had its
trials, particularly of late, but there was so much more
stimulus in it, and she was a woman who responded to
stimulus.

She was wrapping a small parcel in the parlour when
George came upon her. He did not speak for a moment but
went across to a drawer and began to look through the papers
there. Then he said: 'You should let a servant do that.'

Elizabeth said lightly: 'I have little enough to employ
my time. It's a present for Geoffrey Charles. His birthday
comes at the end of next week and the London coach leaves
tomorrow.'

'Yes, well, you may include a small present from me. I had
not altogether forgot.'

George went to another drawer and took out a small box.
In it were six mother-of-pearl buttons.

'Oh, George, they're very pretty! It is good of you to
remember . . . But d'you think he should have them at school?
May they not get lost?'

'No matter if they do. He is rather the dandy – a tailor there
will be able to make use of them for him.'

'Thank you. I'll include them with my present, then. And I

will add a note to my birthday wishes telling him they are
from you.'

In his letters home Geoffrey Charles had omitted any reference to or message for his stepfather. They had both noticed
this but avoided mentioning it.

George said: 'You've been out?'

'To Maria Agar's. I told you.'

'Oh, yes. I had forgot.'

'I so much enjoy Maria's company. She's so light and jolly.'

Silence fell. It was not a restful silence.

Elizabeth said: 'Valentine was asking for you today.'

'Oh? *Valentine?*'

'Well, he said repeatedly: "Papa! Papa! Papa!" You
haven't seen him for some days and he misses you.'

'Yes, well . . . tomorrow perhaps.' George shut the drawer.
'I saw your old servant today. I chanced upon him at the
Fighting Cocks.'

'Who? What servant?'

'George Tabb.'

'Oh . . . Did he seem well?'

'He tried to talk about the old times.'

Elizabeth re-folded the end of the parcel. 'I confess I have
felt a little conscience-stricken about him since he left.'

'In what way?'

'Well, he worked for us – I mean for my father-in-law and
for Francis for so many years. It's hard that he should lose
everything because he grew above himself in the end.'

'I gave him two guineas.'

'Two *guineas*! That was more than generous!' Elizabeth
stared at her husband, trying to read his unreadable expression.
'I've sometimes wondered, though, if we should not take him
back. He has learned his lesson.'

'A drunkard? Drunkards talk too much.'

'What could he have to talk about? I did not know we had
any secrets from the world.'

George moved to the door. 'Who has no secrets? We are all
vulnerable, aren't we, to the whispered calumny and the
scandalmonger.' He went out.

Later they supped alone. Elizabeth's father and mother had
remained at Trenwith, and his father and mother were at

Cardew. Recently they had been silent meals. George was an unfailingly polite man with narrow variables of behaviour. Her first husband, Francis, she had known high-spirited, moody, cynical, witty, urbane, coarse, punctilious and untidy. George was seldom any of these things; always his emotions were under a rein. But within those limits she had come to read much, and she knew that over the last two months his attitude had greatly changed towards her. Always he had watched her, as if striving to see if she were really happy in her marriage to him; but of late his watching had become hard to tolerate. And whereas in the old days if she looked up and met his glance his eyes would remain steady, openly brooding on her but in a way that caused no offence; now if she looked up he quickly looked away, taking his thoughts out of her reach before she could comprehend them.

Sometimes too she thought the servants watched her. Once or twice letters had reached her which looked as if they might have been opened and re-sealed. It was very unpleasant, but often she wondered how much her imagination was at fault.

When the servants had gone Elizabeth said: 'We still have not replied to our invitation to Caroline Penvenen's wedding. We must soon.'

'I've no desire to go. Dr Enys has airs above his station.'

'I suppose all the county will be there.'

'Maybe.'

'I imagine he will have quite a hero's wedding, having been just rescued from the French and barely survived the ordeal.'

'And no doubt his rescuer will be there too, receiving all the admiring plaudits for an act which was criminally rash and lost the lives of more men than he saved.'

'Well, people love the romantic gesture, as we all know.'

'And the romantic figure too.' George rose and turned away from her. She noticed how much weight he had lost, and wondered if his changed attitude was a result of some changed condition of health. 'Tell me, Elizabeth, what do you think of Ross Poldark these days?'

It was a startling question. For a year after their marriage his name had not been mentioned.

'What do I *think* of him, George? What do you mean, what do I think of him?'

'What I say. Just what I say. You've known him for what –
fifteen years? You were – to state the least of it – his friend.
When I first knew you you used to defend him against all
criticism. When I made overtures of friendship to him and
he rebuffed them, you took his side.'

She stayed at the table, nervously fingering the hem of a
napkin. 'I don't know that I took his *side*. But the rest of
what you say is true. However . . . in the last years my feelings
for him have changed. Surely you must know that. Surely
after all this time. *Heavens! . . .*'

'Well, go on.'

'My change of feelings towards him began, I think, over
his attitude to Geoffrey Charles. Then when I married you,
that was clearly not to his liking, and his arrogance in forcing
his way into the house that Christmas and threatening us
because his wife had got at cross with your gamekeeper – it
seemed to me *intolerable*.'

'He did not force his way in,' George said quietly; 'he
found some way in that we did not know of.'

She shrugged. 'Does it matter?'

'I do not know.'

'What d'you mean?'

They listened to a tapping on the cobbles outside. It was a
blind man feeling his way along, his stick like an antenna
plotting out the path. The window was an inch open and
George shut it, cutting out the sound.

He said: 'I sometimes think, Elizabeth; I sometimes
wonder . . .'

'What?'

'Something that you may consider an unsuitable thought for
a husband to have of his wife . . .' He paused. 'Namely that
your new enmity for Ross Poldark is less genuine than your
old affection . . .'

'You are *right*!' she said instantly. 'I *do* consider it a most
unsuitable thought! Are you accusing me of hypocrisy or
something worse?' Her voice was angry. Anger to drive out
apprehension.

In their married life they had often had differences of
opinion but had never quarrelled. It was not that sort of a
relationship. Now on the verge he hesitated, drawing back

from a confrontation for which he was not fully prepared.

'How do I know?' he said. 'It may not even be hypocrisy. Perhaps it is self-deception.'

'Have I *ever* – have I *ever* at any time in these two years given you reason to suppose that I have warmer feelings for Ross than my words suggest? Name a single time!'

'No. I can name none. That's not what I mean. Listen. You are a woman of enduring loyalties. Confess that. Always you stand by your friends. In those years when you were married to Francis your friendship with Ross Poldark never wavered. If I mentioned his name you froze. But since we married you have become as unfriendly to him, as unwelcoming as I. In all controversy you have taken my side –'

'Do you complain?'

'Of *course* not. This has pleased me. It has gratified me to feel that you have – changed your allegiance. But I'm not sure that it is in your character so to change. It's more in your character to support me with reluctance against an old friend – because as my wife you feel it your *duty* to support me. But not with the strong feelings that you appear to show. Therefore at times I suspect them. I say to myself: perhaps they're not true. Perhaps she is deceiving me because she thinks it pleases me. Or perhaps she is deceiving herself into mistaking her own feelings.'

She got up at last from the table and went towards the fire, which had only recently been lit and was burning low.

'Have you seen Ross today?' She tucked a wisp of hair into the comb she was wearing, making the movement as cool as her words.

'No.'

'I wonder, then, what makes you bring this charge upon me now?'

'We were talking of his certain presence at Caroline's wedding. Is that not enough?'

'Not enough to justify these . . . imputations. I can only assume you've long felt this suspicion of me.'

'It has crossed my mind from time to time. Not frequently. But, I have to tell you, I have wondered.'

There was a long silence, during which Elizabeth with an effort took control again of her fluctuating emotions. She was learning from George.

She went across and stood beside him like a slim virgin. 'You are unduly jealous, my dear. Not just of Ross but of all men. D'you know, when we go out to a party I can scarce smile at a man who is under seventy without feeling you are ready to run him through!' She put her hand on his arm as he was about to speak. 'As for Ross – you thought I was turning the conversation but you see I am not – as for Ross, I do sincerely care nothing for him. How can I convince you? Look at me. I can only tell you that I once had feeling for him and now have *no* feeling for him. I do not love him. I would not care if I never saw him again. I scarcely even *like* him. He has come to seem to me a – a braggart and something of a bully, a middle-aged man trying to assume the attitude of a young one, someone who once had a – a cloak and a sword and does not know they have gone out-of-date.'

If she had had longer to choose her words she probably would never have found any so suitable to convince him. A declaration of hatred or contempt would have carried no conviction at all. But those few cool, destructive sentences which put into words very much his own opinions, though in phrases he would not have been perceptive enough to use himself, these brought a flushing reassurance to his soul.

He did flush in the face, an exceedingly rare symptom with him, and said: 'Perhaps I *am* unduly jealous. I can't tell, I can't tell. But you must know why.'

She smiled. 'You must not be. You have no one to be jealous of. I assure you.'

'You assure me.' Doubt flickered across his face again, darkening it, making it ugly. Then he shrugged and smiled. 'Well . . .'

'I assure you,' she said.

Dr Dwight Enys and Miss Caroline Penvenen were married on All Hallows' Day, which in 1795 came on a Sunday, at St Mary's Church in Truro. Killewarren, Caroline's house, was in the parish of Sawle-with-Grambler; but Sawle Church would hardly have been big enough, Truro was more central for most of the guests, and November with its heavy rains was not a time for country travel.

It was a big wedding after all. Dwight had objected from the start, but she had over-ridden his protests while he was still too feeble to be emphatic about anything. Indeed his recovery from his long imprisonment was not yet sure. He had long spells of listlessness and inertia and he could not get rid of a troublesome cough and a breathlessness at night. His personal inclination had been to postpone the wedding until the spring, but she had said:

'Darling, I've been an old maid long enough. Besides, you must consider my good name. Already the county is scandalized because we're living in the same house without the benefit of chaperone during your convalescence. The grannies are insisting that you hasten to make an honest woman of me.'

So the date had been agreed, and then the nature of the wedding. 'It is no good being ashamed of me,' Caroline had said. 'It's embarrassing that I have so much money, but you knew that all along, and a big wedding is one of the consequences.'

As Elizabeth had predicted, most of the county, or that part of the county within reasonable travelling distance, was there. Heavy rain in the night had been followed by a bright day with the puddles in the streets glinting like eyes where they reflected the sky. Caroline wore a gown of white satin with the petticoat and facings covered with a rich gold net, her hair held with a coronet of seed pearls. Her uncle from Oxfordshire gave her away, and after the wedding a reception was held at the Assembly Rooms in High Cross.

Elizabeth's persuasions had finally resulted in George's agreeing to go with her, and he very quickly spied his old enemy standing with his wife near to the bride and groom. In his present mood it was almost more than he could bear to go up and pass close beside them, but only Elizabeth noticed his hesitation as they went on.

Ross Vennor Poldark, owner of 100 acres of rather barren and unproductive farmland on the north coast, sole proprietor of a small but highly profitable tin mine, one-time soldier and perpetual non-conformer, was dressed in a black velvet coat cut away at the front to show the grey suede waistcoat and the tight grey nankeen trousers. The waistcoat and the trousers were new but the coat was the one his father had bought him for his twenty-first birthday and which he refused to replace, even though he could now well afford to. Perhaps there was a subtle pride behind his refusal, pride that in fourteen years he had neither fattened nor grown more lean. Of course the cut was out of date, but those who observed that, Ross thought, had no claim on his opinion or consideration.

Nevertheless he had insisted that his wife, Demelza, should have a new gown, even though she herself protested it unnecessary. Demelza Poldark was now twenty-five, a young woman who had never been a raving beauty but whose eyes and smile and walk and general exuberance of spirit always drew men's attention like a magnet among iron filings. Childbearing had not yet coarsened her figure, so she was still able to wear a tight-waisted frock of green damask embroidered with silver trimmings. It had cost more than she could bear to think, but which she still constantly thought about. In it she looked as slight as Elizabeth, though not as virginal. But then she never had.

The two neighbours and cousins by marriage bowed slightly to each other but did not speak. Then the Warleggans passed on to the bride and groom to shake their hands and wish them a happiness which George at least begrudged. Enys had always been a protégé and a creature of Ross Poldark, and while still a struggling and impecunious mine surgeon had turned away from the rich patronage of the Warleggans and made it plain where his loyalties lay. George observed today how sick Dwight was still looking. He stood beside his tall radiant red-haired wife, who topped him by an inch and who looked the picture of youth and sophisticated happiness, but himself thin and drawn and grey at the temples and seemingly devoid of muscle and flesh within his clothes.

They moved on again and spoke for a while with the Reverend Osborne and Mrs Whitworth. Ossie as usual was dressed in the extremity of fashion, and his bride of last July had got a new outfit of a snuff brown, which did not suit her because it made her dark skin look darker. For the most part she kept her eyes down and did not speak; but when addressed she looked up and smiled and answered politely, and it was really not at all possible from her expression to perceive the misery and revulsion that was burning in her heart, nor the nausea caused by the cellular stirrings of an embryonic Ossie in her womb.

Presently George moved away from them and drew Elizabeth towards a corner where Sir Francis and Lady Basset were talking. So the pleasant conversazione of the wedding reception went on. Two hundred people, the cream of the society of mid-Cornwall, squires, merchants, bankers, soldiers, fox hunters, the titled and the landed, the untitled and the moneyed, the seekers and the sought. In the mêlée Demelza became separated from Ross, and seeing Mr and Mrs Ralph-Allen Daniell, went to speak to them. They greeted her like an old friend which, considering they had only met her once, was gratifying, and, considering that on that occasion Ross had refused to oblige Mr Daniell by accepting a magistracy, even more pleasing. Standing near them was a sturdy, quietly dressed, reserved man in his late thirties, and presently Mr Daniell said: 'My Lord, may I present to you Mrs Demelza Poldark, Captain Ross Poldark's wife: the Viscount Falmouth.'

They bowed to each other. Lord Falmouth said: 'Your husband has been very much in the news, ma'am. I have yet to have the pleasure of congratulating him on his exploit.'

'I am only hoping, sir,' Demelza said, 'that all the congratulations will not go to his head and induce him to embark on another.'

Falmouth smiled, a very contained smile, carefully poured out, like a half measure of some valuable liquid and not to be wasted.

'It is a change to find a wife so concerned to keep her husband at home. But we may yet have need of him and others like him.'

'Then,' Demelza said, 'I b'lieve neither of us will be lacking.'

They looked at each other very straightly.

Lord Falmouth said: 'You must come and visit us some time,' and passed on.

The Poldarks were staying the night with Harris Pascoe, the banker, and over a late supper in his house in Pydar Street Demelza said:

'I'm not sure that I've done good for you with Lord Falmouth, Ross,' and told of the interchange.

'It's of no moment whether you pleased or displeased him,' Ross said. 'We do not need his patronage.'

'Oh, but that is his way,' said Pascoe. 'You should have known his uncle, the second Viscount. He had no appearance but was arrogant withal. This one is more easy to treat with.'

'He and I fought in the same war,' said Ross, 'but did not meet. He being in the King's Own and a rank superior to me. I confess I do not take greatly to his manner but I'm glad if you made a good impression on him.'

'I do not at all think I made a good impression,' said Demelza.

Pascoe said: 'I suppose you know that Hugh Armitage is a cousin of the Falmouths? His mother is a Boscawen.'

'Who?' Ross said.

'Hugh Armitage. You should know Lieutenant Armitage. You rescued him from Quimper gaol.'

'The devil! No, I don't know. I suppose we spoke little on the way across.'

'It should make the family feel somewhat in your debt.'

'I don't really see why. We didn't at all set out to rescue him. He was one of the lucky few who made use of our entry to escape.'

'Nevertheless you brought him home.'

'Yes . . . we brought him home. And useful enough in navigation he was on the way . . .'

'Then we are in each other's debt,' said Demelza.

'Did you speak with the Whitworths?' Ross asked her.

'No. I have never met Morwenna, and I did not ever very

much care for Osborne.'

'At one time he appeared to have a distinct taking for you.'

'Oh, that,' said Demelza, wrinkling her nose.

'I spoke with Morwenna,' Ross said. 'She's a shy creature and answers yes and no as if she thinks that makes a conversation. It was hard to tell whether she finds herself unhappy.'

'Unhappy?' said Harris Pascoe. 'In a four-month bride? Would you expect it?'

Ross said: 'My brother-in-law, Demelza's brother, had a brief and abortive love attachment for Morwenna Whitworth before she married. Drake is still in deep depression over it and we are trying to find some sort of life for him that he will accept. Therefore it is of interest to know whether his loved one has settled comfortably into a marriage Drake says she bitterly opposed.'

'I only know,' said Pascoe, 'that for a cleric he spends f-far too much on this world's attire. I don't attend his church but I understand he is careful about his duties. That at least makes a welcome change.'

After Demelza had gone to bed Ross said:

'And your own affairs, Harris? They prosper?'

'Thank you, yes. The bank is well enough. Money is still cheap, credit is readily available, new enterprises are growing up everywhere. In the meantime we keep a careful watch on our note issue – and lose trade thereby – but as you are aware I am a cautious man and know that fine weather does not last for ever.'

Ross said: 'You know I am taking a quarter interest in Ralph-Allen Daniell's new tin smelting house?'

'You mentioned it in your letter. A little more port?'

'Thank you.'

Pascoe poured into each glass, careful not to create bubbles. He held the decanter a moment between his hands.

'Daniell is a good man of business. It should be a useful investment. Where is it to be built?'

'A couple of miles out of Truro, on the Falmouth road. It will have ten reverberatory furnaces, each about six feet high by four broad, and will employ a fair number of men.'

'Daniell cannot have w-wanted for the money himself.'

'No. But he has little knowledge of mining and offered me

a share and a say in the design and management.'

'Good. Good.'

'And he does not bank with the Warleggans.'

Harris laughed, and they finished their port and talked of other things.

'Speaking of the Warleggans,' Pascoe said presently. 'Something of an accommodation has been reached between their bank and Basset, Rogers and Co., which will add to the strength of both. It is not of course anything like an amalgamation, but there will be a friendly co-ordination, and that could be of some disadvantage to Pascoe, Tresize, Annery and Spry.'

'In what way?'

'Well, their capital strength will be five or six times ours. It is always a disadvantage to be much smaller than one's competitors – especially in times of stress. In banking, size has a curious magic for the depositor. It's some years now, as you know, since I took my three partners, because of the danger of being overshadowed by the other banks. Now we are a l-little overshadowed again.'

'You have no one to call in to redress the balance?'

'Not in the neighbourhood. Outside, of course . . . but the distances are too great between here and, say, Helston or Falmouth for the easy or safe transport of gold or notes.' Pascoe got up. 'Oh, we shall stay as we are, and come to no hurt, I am sure. While the wind blows fair there is indeed nothing to hurt anyone.'

II

In another part of the town Elizabeth was combing her hair at her dressing table and George, sitting by the fire in a long lawn robe, was as usual watching her. But now, in this last week or so, since that talk, there seemed to be some easing of the nature of the surveillance. The screws were off. It was as if he had been through some nervous crisis, the character of which she barely dared to guess, and had now emerged from it.

'Did you notice,' George said, 'did you notice how Falmouth avoided us?'

'Who, George Falmouth? I didn't. Why should he?'

'He has always been unwelcoming, cold, grudging.'

'But that is his nature! Or at least his appearance, for he is not really so in truth. I remember when we were first married I met them at that ball and he looked so cold and forbidding that I wondered what I had done to offend. And all he did was chide me that now we all had the same names – two Georges married to two Elizabeths – and we might become confused as to our bed-mates!'

'Oh,' said George, 'he approves of *you*; but nothing I or my father may do will gratify him. He is perpetually antagonistic and has become worse of late.'

'Well, his wife's death has hit him hard. It is sad to be left with so young a family. And I don't believe he is the re-marrying kind.'

'He would only need to crook his finger for a hundred girls to run. Such is the lure of a title.'

The contempt in his voice made Elizabeth lift an eye to him and then look away. The Warleggans were hardly insusceptible to such a lure, if one ever came their way.

'He's not content to be lord of his lands beside the Fal but wishes to be lord of Truro also. And none may be allowed to stand in his light!'

Elizabeth said: 'Well, he *is* lord of Truro, isn't he – so far as possessions and influence are concerned. No one disputes it. It all works very peaceable, I believe.'

'Then you believe wrong,' said George. 'The town and the borough are very tired of being treated as a rich man's chattels. We have never been a corrupt borough in that the voters receive payment, but his behaviour makes the corporation a laughing stock.'

'Oh, you mean in elections,' Elizabeth said. 'I never did understand elections.'

'There are two Members, and the corporation elect them. Hitherto, this corporation has been glad to elect the Boscawen nominees – indeed until recently two minor Boscawens held the seats – there's nothing amiss with that, for we are all of much the same political complexion, but it is essential that for their self-respect the burgesses should be given the *appearance* of choice – indeed that they should be given the actual choice, however unlikely it is that they would in the event choose to run counter to Falmouth's wishes.'

Elizabeth began to plait her hair. 'I wonder that George gives this unnecessary offence. His uncle, I know, was a great autocrat but – '

'They all are.'

Elizabeth thought she had some idea why George Evelyn, the third Viscount, and indeed the Boscawens generally, kept the Warleggans at a distance. She knew the infinite pains to which Nicholas, George's father, and indeed George himself, had been to ingratiate themselves with the Falmouths; but apart from the natural prejudice which an old and now titled family could be expected to have against a thrusting new one, their interests covered too much of the same ground. The Warleggan influence increased constantly; it might not obviously clash with Boscawen interests but it ran alongside them. Also the Boscawens were used to treating either with their equals or with their inferiors; the Warleggans were neither: they represented the new rich who did not yet fit into a recognizable sector of society. There were, of course, other new rich, especially in London, but some adapted more quickly than others. In spite of all their efforts, Elizabeth saw that the Warleggans did not adapt quickly.

George said: 'There is much discontent in the town, and Sir Francis Basset could well become the figure round which this discontent might centre.'

'Francis? Oh, I'm sure he is very important in his own way and very rich and very busy, but – '

'Of course you have also known *him* all your life, but my acquaintance dates only from last February. We have found much in common. As the proprietor of the third bank in Truro, he has been able to put business in my way and I in his. We are in fact collaborating in a number of matters.'

'And how does this – '

'He has been buying property in the town for two years and recently has been elected a capital burgess. He is MP for Penryn himself and controls several other seats. Well, I know him to be looking at the Truro seats with interest.'

Elizabeth tied the end of her plait with a piece of corn-flower-blue ribbon. Dressed thus for bed, she would have passed for a girl of eighteen.

'Has he said as much?'

'Not yet. We are not yet that intimate. But I can see where his thoughts are leading. And I have a thought that if our friendship grows I might be one of his nominees.'

Elizabeth turned. 'You?'

'Why not?' he asked sharply.

'No reason at all. But – but this borough *belongs* to the Boscawens. Would you have a chance?'

'I think so. If things continue as they are. Would you object?'

'Of *course* not. I believe I should like it well enough.' She got up. 'But Basset is a *Whig*!'

The Chynoweths had been high Tories for generations.

'I like the label no more than you,' George said. 'But Basset has disavowed Fox. If I went into the Commons it would be as one of his men, and as such I should support the present government.'

Elizabeth blew out one of the candles. A wisp of smoke drifted towards the mirror and was gone.

'But why this interest now? I have heard no talk of an election.'

'Nor is there. Though Pitt's mandate is growing old. No . . . there is no talk of an election but there is a possibility of a by-election. Sir Piers Arthur is gravely ill.'

'I did not know.'

'They say he cannot pass water and obstinately refuses to submit to the operation of the catheter.'

Elizabeth pulled back the curtains of the bed. 'Poor man . . .'

'I am simply telling you my thoughts and showing you which way my friendship with Sir Francis Basset may lead.'

'Thank you, George, for taking me into your confidence.'

'Of course, it is essential that nothing of this should get out, for the ground has yet to be prepared.'

'I will say nothing about it to anyone.'

George said after a moment: 'Do I not always take you into my confidence?'

'I hope you always will,' Elizabeth replied.

III

In yet another part of the town Ossie Whitworth, having been about his nightly exercise upon his wife, rolled over, pulled down his nightshirt, adjusted his cap and said:

'This sister of yours, if I decided to have her, when could she come?'

With a muffled voice, hiding the nausea and the pain, Morwenna said: 'I would have to write to Mama. I do not think Rowella has any commitments, but she may have engagements that I do not know of.'

'Mind,' he said, 'we couldn't afford to have her about the house eating her head off and just companioning you. She would be expected to see to the children, and when you have a child to help generally with household duties.'

'I'll make that clear when I write.'

'Let's see, how old is she? You've so many sisters I can never remember.'

'She was fourteen in June.'

'And healthy? Educated in home crafts? We cannot afford a young lady who's afraid to soil her hands.'

'She can sew and cook and has a little Greek. My father said she was the best pupil in the family.'

'Hm . . . I don't see that an ancient language is of value to a woman. But of course your father was a scholar, I'll give him that.'

Silence fell.

Osborne said: 'The bridegroom today looked tedious sickly. I would not give him long for this world.'

Morwenna did not reply.

'It's a question of "physician heal thyself", eh, what? . . . Are you asleep?'

'No, no.'

'The bride I've met often at the meets.' He added reflectively: 'She's mettlesome. I'll wager she'll be a handful, with that red hair.'

'She remembered me, although we have only met twice.'

'That's surprising. You have a tendency to make yourself perfectly unnoticeable, which is a great pity. Remember always that you are Mrs Osborne Whitworth and entitled to hold your head high in this town.'

'Yes . . .'

'It was a fair enough company today. But some of the

fashions were unbearably dated. Did you see the Teague girls? And that man Poldark, his coat must have been cut half a century ago.'

'He is a brave man.'

Ossie settled more comfortably in the bed and yawned. 'His wife keeps her looks uncommon well.'

'Well, she's still young, isn't she?'

'Yes, but usually the vulgars go off more quick than those who are gentle bred . . . She used to make quite an exhibition of herself a few years ago at the receptions and balls – when he had first married her, that was.'

'Exhibition?'

'Well, flaunting herself, attracting the men, I can tell you. She wore low-cut frocks . . . She greatly fancied herself. Still does, I suspicion.'

'Elizabeth never mentioned that – and I do not think she greatly cares for her sister-in-law.'

'Oh, Elizabeth . . .' The Reverend Mr Whitworth yawned again, snuffed out the solitary candle and drew the curtains together. Rounding off the evening in his customary way produced a pleasant and customary sleepiness after. 'Elizabeth speaks no ill of anyone. But I agree, there's no love lost.'

Morwenna sighed. The worst soreness was subsiding, but she had no sleep in her. 'Tell me about that. What is the cause of the feud between the Poldarks and the Warleggans? Everyone knows of it but no one speaks of it.'

'You angle for a fish that is not in my pond. All I know is that it's something to do with some jealous rivalry. Elizabeth Chynoweth was promised to Ross Poldark and instead married his cousin Francis. Some years later Francis was killed in a mining accident and Ross wanted to throw over his kitchen maid, whom he'd married in the meantime, and take Elizabeth. But Elizabeth would have none of it and married George Warleggan, who had been Ross's sworn enemy . . . ever since they were at school together . . .' Like someone retreating down a tunnel, Ossie's voice was fading fast.

Through a nick in the bed curtains Morwenna looked at the spears of moonlight falling into the room. Inside the canopy of the bed it was so dark that she could hardly see her husband's face; but she knew that in a few moments he would be asleep and would be unconscious on his back with his mouth wide open for the next eight hours. Mercifully, although his breathing was heavy, he did not snore.

'And I loved Drake Carne, Mrs Poldark's brother,' she said in an undertone.

'What? What's that . . . you say?'

'Nothing, Ossie. Nothing at all . . . Why were Ross Poldark and George Warleggan such enemies before?'

'What? Oh . . . I don't know. It was before my time. But it's oil and water, ain't it. Anyone can see that . . . They're both stiff-necked, but for opposing reasons. I expect Poldark despises Warleggan for his low origin and hasn't always hid it. And you can't do that safely with George . . . Did I say my prayers tonight before? . . .'

'Yes, Ossie.'

'You should be more assiduous about yours . . . And remind me in the morning,' he said. 'I have a christening at eleven . . . and it is the Rosewarnes . . . substantial family.' His breathing became deep and steady. Body and mind relaxed together. Since his marriage to Morwenna he had been in supreme good health. No more of those frustrations of a lusty widower, in holy orders in a small town.

'I *still* love Drake Carne,' she said, aloud now, in her soft gentle voice. 'I love Drake Carne, I love Drake Carne, I love Drake Carne.'

Sometimes after an hour or two this repetition lulled her into sleep. Sometimes she wondered if Ossie would wake and hear her. But he never did. Perhaps only Drake Carne awoke and heard her, many miles away.

IV

In the old house of Killewarren bride and bridegroom were in their bedroom together. Caroline was sitting on the bed in a long green peignoir; Dwight in loose silk shirt and breeches was idly stirring the fire. Horace, Caroline's little pug and the agent of their first meeting, had been banished from the room and taken far enough away for his protests not to be heard. In the early months he had shown an intense jealousy of Dwight, but with patience Dwight had won him round, and in the latter weeks he had come to accept the inevitable, that there was going to be another claimant for his mistress's attentions.

They had come home, for there seemed nowhere better to go. It had been their common home since Dwight returned an emaciated wreck from the prison camp of Quimper. Caroline had insisted that he stay where she could best look after him. In these months, while flouting the overt conventions, they had observed a separateness of establishment which would have satisfied the most prudish of their neighbours.

It had not altogether been moral considerations which had influenced them. Dwight's life had flickered and wavered like a candle with a thief in it; to introduce the demands of passion might have seen it flicker out.

Caroline said: 'Well, my dear, so we are here together at last, unified and sanctified by the church. D'you know, I find it very difficult to detect any difference.'

Dwight laughed. 'Nor I. It's hard not to feel adulterous. Perhaps it's because we have waited so long.'

'Too long.'

'Too long. But the delay has been outside our control.'

'Not in the first place. The fault was mine.'

'It was no one's *fault*. At least it has come right in the end.'

He put down the poker, turned and looked at her, then came to sit on the bed beside her, put his hand on her knee.

She said: 'D'you know, I heard of a doctor who was so earnest in his study of anatomy that he took a skeleton away on his honeymoon and the wife woke to find him fingering the bones in the bed beside her.'

Dwight smiled again. 'No bones. Not at least for the first two days.'

She kissed him. He put his hands to her hair, pressing it back from either cheek.

She said: 'Perhaps we should have waited longer until you were quite recovered.'

He said: 'Perhaps we should not have waited so long.'

The fire was flickering brightly, sending nodding shadows about the room.

She said: 'Alas, my body has no surprises for you. At least so far as the upper half is concerned, you have examined it thoroughly in the harsh light of day. Perhaps it is fortunate that I never had a pain below the navel.'

'Caroline, you talk too much.'

'I know. I always shall. It is a fault you have married.'

'I must find ways of stopping it.'

'Are there ways?'

'I believe so.'

She kissed him again. 'Then try.'

CHAPTER III

Except in one particular Sam Carne was a happy man. A few years ago, while still in the arms of Satan, he had been half persuaded, half bullied by his bullying father into attending a Methodist prayer meeting. There his heart had suddenly warmed within him, he had wrought deeply and agonizingly with his spirit and had come to experience the joy of sins forgiven: thereupon he had embraced the living Christ and his life had been utterly transformed. Now, having moved far from his home in search of work at the mine of his brother-in-law, Captain Ross Poldark, and having found the neighbourhood of Nampara a dry and barren wilderness in which regular meetings had been discontinued and all but a very few had long since fallen back into carnal and sinful ways, he had in less than two years re-formed the Society, inspirited the few faithful, wrestled with Satan in the souls of many of the weak and erring, and had attracted several newcomers, all of whom had been prayed for, had discovered for themselves the precious promise of Jehovah, and had in due time been sanctified and cleansed.

It was a notable achievement, but it did not end there. Acting without the sanction of the leaders of the Movement, he had caused to be raised on the edge of Poldark land a new Preaching House which would contain fifty people seated and which now was nearing completion. Furthermore he had recently walked in to Truro and met the stewards and the leaders there, who had now conferred on him the official title of Class Leader and had promised to send out one of their best Travelling Preachers for the opening of the House in the spring.

It was all wondrous in his sight. That God had moved through him, that Christ had chosen him to act as his missioner in this small part of the land, was a source of constant wonderment and joy. But every night he prayed long on his knees that this privilege which had been awarded him should never lead him into the sin of pride. He was the humblest of all God's creatures and would ever remain so, serving Him and praising Him in time and through all eternity.

But perhaps some weakness and wickedness still moved in him and had not been rooted out, and this was why he had a cross to bear in the shape of a fallen younger brother.

Drake was not yet quite twenty, and, while never so ardent, had laid hold of the Blessing at an earlier age than Sam and had achieved a condition of real and true holiness of heart and life. The two brothers had lived together in that perfect unity which comes from the service of Jesus; until Drake had taken up with a Woman.

Marriage with a suitable wife was a part of God's holy ordinance, and not at all to be discouraged or despised; but unfortunately the girl Drake had become enraptured with came of a different class from his own, and although, being a clergyman's daughter, she no doubt dutifully and sincerely worshipped God, her whole upbringing and the authoritarian beliefs with which she had been instilled made her an unsuitable partner for a Cornish Methodist. They had been separated – not by Sam, who could not have controlled his brother had he so wished, but by the girl's cousin, Mr Warleggan, and by her mother; and she had been married off very suitably to a rising young clergyman in Truro.

It was certainly the best thing that could have happened for all concerned, but Drake would not see it that way; he could not be so persuaded; and although all those around him were convinced that this was a case of broken first love and that within a year he would have forgotten his infatuation and be as bright and cheerful as before it happened, there was no such improvement yet, and some months now gone.

It was not that he went about letting everyone see his hurt; he worked well and ate well; the French musket ball in his shoulder had left no permanent impairment, he was quick as ever up a ladder or a tree. But Sam who knew him so well knew that inwardly he had quite changed. And he had almost left the Connexion. He scarcely ever came to the evening meetings, and often would not even go to church with them on Sundays, but would stride away across Hendrawna Beach and be gone for hours. He would not pray with Sam at nights and would not be reasoned with.

'I know I'm in the fault,' he said. 'I d'know that full well. I know I'm yielding to unbelief, I know I'm not exercising faith in Jesus. I know I've lost the great salvation. But, brother, what I just lost on *this* earth seem to me *more* . . . All right, tis blasphemy as you d'say; but I cann't change what's in my very own heart.'

'The things of this world – '

'Yes, ye've telled me, and no doubt tis true, but it don't change my heart. If Satan've got me, then he've got me, and he be too strong to fight. Leave me be, brother, you have other souls to save.'

So Sam had let him be. For a few weeks Drake had lived with his sister and brother-in-law at Nampara, and Demelza had told him that he need not leave; but presently he had moved back into Reath Cottage with Sam. For the first time it was an uneasy relationship. Ross brought it to an end in the January of '96.

Drake was still working on the rebuilding of the library, and one day in early December he was summoned into the parlour of the house.

Ross said: 'Drake, I know you have been wanting to leave the district for long enough. I know you feel you can never settle here after what has happened. But, however bad you feel about that, neither Demelza nor I are content to watch you waste your life in vain regrets. You are a Cornishman with a good trade to your name, and there are better prospects for you in an area where we can help you than up-country where you would have to take menial work to survive at all . . . I have said all this to you before, but I say it again now because there is a prospect just come to my notice – a reasonable prospect – of setting you up in business on your own.'

He picked up the latest copy of the *Sherborne & Yeovil*

Mercury & General Advertiser and offered it to the young man. It was folded with the back page outwards, and an advertisement had been marked. Drake frowned down at the printing, still only just able to spell out the words. He read:

'To be sold by Auction on Wednesday the ninth of December at the King's Arms Inn, Chacewater. That Blacksmith's Shop, House and Land, situate in the parish of St Ann's, property of the late Thos. Jewell, consisting of: House of four rooms, brew house, bake house, barn; Commodious shop with contents thereof, to wit: 1 anvil, 1 pair bellows, hammers, tongs, 2 doz. new horse shoes, Stable with 1 mare, 1 colt, one parcel of old hay. In all six acres including one acre and a half of winter wheat, two and a half acres ploughed, 6 store sheep. Book debts £21.

'For sale thereof a survey will be held, preceding auction.' When he had finished Drake moistened his lips and looked up. 'I don't rightly see . . .'

'There are advantages and drawbacks,' Ross said. 'The chief of the drawbacks is that St Ann's is no more than six miles from here, so you would be only "getting away" to a minor degree. Also you would be even nearer to the Warleggans, when they are in residence at Trenwith. And two of the four mines at present working in the district are Warleggan owned. But it is the most important village along this piece of coast; trade generally is recovering, and there might be opportunities for later expansion – for someone who worked hard and had initiative.'

Drake said: 'I've two pound two shilling in all the world. I reckon with that I could buy the horse shoes!'

Ross said: 'I don't know what it would cost, but you know well I could afford to buy this on your behalf. If you agree, that's what I propose to do. In July on our adventure in France you suffered a serious wound that near killed you. Although you have denied it, I believe you incurred it at least partly in an attempt to save my skin. I don't like being in debt – especially to someone young enough to be my son. This would be a way of discharging it.' He had spoken without warmth, hoping to head off equivocation or thanks.

'Did Demelza –'

'Demelza has had nothing to do with this idea, though naturally as your sister she approves it.'

Drake fingered the newspaper. 'But this here says six acres and . . . it would be a big property.'

'So we shall have to pay for it. It's fortunate that the chance has come up, for such shops and smallholdings most often descend from father to son. Pally Jewell, who died last month, was a widower with two daughters, both married to farmers. The girls want the money to divide.'

Drake looked at Ross. 'Ye've asked about it?'

'I've asked about it.'

'I don't rightly know what to say.'

'The auction is on Wednesday week. The survey will be the same day; but I think we should ride over before. Of course it is a matter for you to decide.'

'How do you mean?'

'You are still scarcely twenty. Maybe it's too much for you to tackle. You have never been your own master. It would be a responsibility.'

Drake looked out of the window. He also looked over the grey vista of his own heart, the lack of zest, the long years without the girl he loved. Yet he had to live. Even in the darkest hours suicide had been outside the scope of his consideration. The project he was now being offered was a challenge, not merely to his enterprise and initiative but to the life force within him.

'Twould not be too much for me to tackle, Cap'n Poldark. But I'd dearly like to think it over.'

'Do by all means. You have a week.'

Drake hesitated. 'I don't rightly know whether I *could* accept all that. It don't seem right. Twill be too much for ee to pay. But tis not for lack of appreciation . . .'

'From reports I have, the place will likely fetch two hundred pounds. But allow me to decide about that. You decide your own part. Go home and talk it over with Sam and let me know.'

Drake went home and talked it over with Sam. Sam said it was a great opportunity which God had been pleased to put in his way. While the bonds of this temporal life still contained them they had every justification for trying to improve themselves materially as well as spiritually. Serve the Word in all things, but be not idle or slothful in work or business. It was right to pray for God's blessing on any enterprise undertaken in honesty, charity and humble ambition. Who knew but that through such industry the black cloud on Drake's soul might not be lifted and that he would once more find a full and abiding salvation?

Drake said, supposing he went to see this property and supposing Captain Poldark bought it for him – or loaned him the money to buy it, which seemed to him something he could more properly accept – then would Sam come with him and enter into a partnership so that they could work together and share in any trials or prosperity the enterprise might bring?

Sam smiled his old-young smile and said he had thought he might be so asked and was glad he had been so asked, but he had been thinking about it while they had been talking and he felt that his duty must keep him here. With the divine inspiration of Christ's love working through a poor sinner such as himself, he had recreated new men and women around him and brought many to the throne of Grace. He had just been appointed Class Leader here; the new Meeting House was almost completed; his work was coming to blessed fruition; he could not and must not leave it now.

Drake said: 'I still don't rightly know if I should take this from Cap'n Ross. It seem to me too much.'

'Generosity be one of the noblest of Christian virtues and it should not be discouraged in others. Though it be more blessed to give than to receive, yet tis noble to know how to receive with a good grace.'

'Yes . . . yes . . .' Drake rubbed his face and his chin rasped. 'Tis a poor living and a hard one you make, brother. And ye'd be little more'n six mile off. Many d'walk that far to work. Why not to pray?'

Sam said: 'Later maybe. If . . .' He stopped.

'If what?'

'Who's to say in a year or more when ye're stablished there you may not best to alter your condition in life? And then not wish for me.'

'Don't know's I follow.'

'Well, by exchanging your single state for a wedded one.

Then you'd be raising your own family.'

Drake stared out at the dank driving rain. 'Twould not be in me, as you well d'know.'

'Well, that's as mebbe. I pray for ee every night, Drake, every night and day, that your soul should be relieved of this great burden. This young woman –'

'Say no more. Ye've said 'nough.'

'Aye, mebbe.'

Drake turned. 'D'ye think as I don't know what other folks d'think? And d'ye think as I don't know as they may be right? But it don't help. It don't help here, brother.' Drake touched his chest. 'See? It don't help! If . . . if-twas said – if twas said as Morwenna had passed away and I knew I should never see her the more it would be hard, hard, hard. But I could face'n. Others have lost their loved ones. But what I cann't face up to and never shall face up to is she being wed to that man! For I know she don't like him, Sam. I know she can't abide him! Be that Christian? Be that the work of the Holy Spirit? Did Jesus ordain that a man and a woman should lie together and be of one flesh when the woman's flesh d'turn sick at the man's touch? Where be *that* in the Bible? Where do it say *that* in the Bible? Tell me, where do God's love and mercy and forgiveness come in?'

Sam looked very distressed. 'Brother, these are only *thoughts* you d'have about the young woman's prefer-ences. Ye cann't know –'

'I know 'nough! She said little, but she showed much. She couldn't lie to me over a thing like that! And her face could not lie! That is what I cann't bear. Understand me, do you?'

Sam walked up and stood beside his brother. They were both near tears and did not speak for a few moments.

Sam said: 'Mebbe I don't understand it all, Drake. Mebbe some day I shall, for some day I shall hope with God's guidance to choose a wife. But tis not hard to see how you d'feel. I can only pray for you as I've done ever since this first ever happened.'

'Pray for she,' said Drake. 'Pray for Morwenna.'

II

Pally's Shop, as it was called, was in a small deep valley on the main track from Nampara and Trenwith to St Ann's. You went down a steep winding hill to it, and had to climb a steep winding hill on the other side to reach the little sea town. There was about a mile and a half of flat stony fields and barren moorland separating it directly from the sea; with one of the Warleggan mines, Wheal Spinster, smoking distantly among the gorse and the heather. Behind the shop the land rose less steeply, and here were the fields representing the six acres for sale. The property was separated from anything else actually belonging to the Warleggans by Trevaunance Cove and the house and land of that elderly bachelor, Sir John Trevaunance. On the hill going up to St Ann's were a half dozen cottages in ruinous condition, and the only cluster of trees in sight sheltered the blunt spire of St Ann's church just visible over the brow of the hill.

Demelza had insisted on riding with Ross and Drake to see the property, and she darted about and examined everything with far greater zest than either of the men. To Ross the purchase of this would be the discharge of a debt, a satisfactory good turn, the sort of use to which money could healthily be put. To Drake it was a dream that he could not relate to reality: if he came to possess this he became a man of property, a young man with something to work for, a skilled tradesman with a future. It would be blank ingratitude to ask to what end. But Demelza went over it as if it were being bought for her private and personal use.

A low stone wall surrounded a yard inches deep in mud, with an accumulation of old metal, bits of rusty ploughs and broken cart shafts littered around it. Behind that was the 'shop', open to the yard, with its central stone post for tethering horses, its forge, its pump emptying into a water barrel, its anvil and its wide chimney. Horse dung was everywhere. Backing on the shop was the cottage, with a narrow earth-floored kitchen and two steps up to a tiny wood-floored parlour with a ladder leading to two bedrooms in the roof above.

Demelza had everything to say on the way home, how this should be cleared out and that repaired and the other improved; what could be done with the fields and the barn and the yard, and how Drake could employ cheap labour to have the place cleared and done up. For the most part the men were silent, and when they reached home Drake handed her down, squeezed her hand and kissed her cheek, smiled at Ross and then went striding away to his cottage.

Ross watched him go. 'He says little. The place has possibilities, but he needs bottom to shake himself out of that mood.'

'I think "the place" as you call it, will help, Ross. Once he owns it he cannot let it go to pieces about him. I can see so much that can be done with it.'

'You always can. I suppose I'm gambling that he is sufficiently like you.'

So two days later Ross and Drake rode over to the King's Arms Inn at Chacewater and stood among twenty other people and presently Ross nodded for the last time and Pally's Shop was knocked down to him for £232. And seven weeks later Drake Carne left Reath Cottage for the last time, giving his brother a hug and a kiss, and mounted the pit pony lent him for the occasion, and with another pony following behind carrying panniers stuffed with all the food, utensils and spare furniture and curtain material Demelza had been able to gather together, he rode off to take possession of his property. It was going to be a lonely life to begin, but they had arranged for a widow from the nearest cottage to go in once in a while to prepare a meal, and two of her grandchildren would work for him in the fields when work got out of hand. He would never need to be idle himself while the light lasted; but at this time of year dark fell early and lasted late; and Demelza wondered sometimes if it had all been wisely timed. Ross said: 'It's no different from what I went through thirteen years ago. I don't envy him. It's an ugly way to be when so young. But he must work it out for himself now.'

'I wish Sam had gone with him.'

'I expect Sam will go over often enough.'

Sam went over often enough throughout those early months, and sometimes when the weather was bad spent the night there; but his own flock made many claims on him. And those outside his flock too. It was necessary, in Sam's view, always to practise what you preached. One must follow Christ by ministering to the sick of body as well as of soul. And although this winter was benign compared to last, con-

ditions in some ways were worse. The price of wheat was
110 shillings a quarter and still rising. Half-naked children
with tumid bellies sat crouching in fireless dripping windy
hovels. Hunger and disease were everywhere.

One morning, a brilliant clear cold morning of late February, Sam, having slept at Pally's Shop, left with an hour to
spare to reach Wheal Grace in time for his core, so he stopped
in Grambler at an isolated and run-down cottage where he
knew almost all the family was ill. The man, Verney, had
worked first at Grambler Mine, then when that closed at
Wheal Leisure, on the cliffs. Since that too closed he had been
on parish relief, but Jim Verney had refused to 'go in', which
meant separating from his wife, or to allow any of his boys
to be apprenticed as paupers, knowing that that could mean
semi-slavery.

But this morning Sam found that the fever had separated
them where man, could not. Jim Verney had died in the night,
and he found Lottie Verney trying to get her man ready for
burying. But there was only the one room and the one bed,
and in the bed beside the corpse of his father the youngest
boy lay tossing and turning, sick with the same fever, while
at the foot the eldest boy was lying weak and pale but on the
way to recovery. In a washing tray beside the bed was the
middle boy, also dead. They had no food, nor fire, nor help;
so although the stench was unbearable, Sam stayed with them
a half-hour doing what he could for the young widow. Then
he went across the rutted track to the last cottage in the village
to tell Jud Paynter there were two more for the paupers' grave.

Jud Paynter grunted and blew through his teeth and said
there were nine in this one already. One more and he'd fill it
in whether or no. Leave it too long and the gulls'd get in, spite
of the lime and spite of the boards he plat down acrost the
hole. Or dogs. There was a dirty hound been on the gammut
these last weeks. Always sniffing and ranting around. He'd get
him yet. Sam backed out of the cottage and went to leave a
message with the doctor.

Dr Thomas Choake's house, Fernmore, was back on his
tracks barely a half mile, but one moved in that time from
desperate poverty to quiet plenty. Even ten paces from the
foetid little shack made all the difference; for the air outside

was biting clear and biting cold. There had been a frost in the night but the sun was quickly thawing it. Spiders' webs spangled the melting dew. Seagulls screamed in the high remote sky, partly in control of themselves, partly at the behest of the wind. Surf tumbled and muttered in the distance. A day to be alive, with food in your belly and youth in your limbs. 'Glory be to the Lord Jesus!' said Sam, and went on his way.

He knew of course that Choake did not concern himself much with the poor, but this was a neighbourly problem and such dire distress merited some special attention. Fernmore was little more than a farmhouse but it was dignified by its own grounds, its own drive, its group of wind-blown and elderly pine trees. Sam went to the back door. It was opened by a tall maidservant with the boldest, most candid eyes he had ever seen.

Not at all abashed – for what had shyness to do with proclaiming the kingdom of God? – Sam smiled his slow sad smile at her and told her what he wished her to tell the doctor. That two people, two of the Verneys, were dead in their cottage hard by, and that help was much needed for the youngest, who ran a hectic fever and coughed repeatedly and had blotches about the cheeks and mouth. Would surgeon have a mind to see them?

The girl looked him over carefully from head to foot, as if assessing everything about him, then told him to wait while she asked. Sam pulled his muffler more tightly round his throat and tapped his foot against a stone to keep warm and thought of the sadness of mortal life but of the power of immortal grace until she came back.

'Surgeon says you've to carry this back, and he'll come see the Verneys later in the morning. See? So off with you now.'

Sam took a bottle of viscous green liquid. She had the whitest skin and the blackest hair, with tinges of red-copper in it as if it had been dyed.

'To swallow?' he said. 'Be this for the lad to swallow or –'

'To rub in, lug. Chest an' back. Chest an' back. What else? An' surgeon says t'ave the two shilling ready when 'e call.'

He thanked the girl and turned away. He expected the door to slam but it did not, and he knew she was standing watching him. All down the short stone path, slippery with half-melted frost, he was wrestling with the impulse which by the time he had made the eight or nine paces to the gate had grown too strong for him. He knew that it would be wrong to resist this impulse; but he knew that in yielding to it he risked misunderstanding in speaking so to a woman of his own age.

He stopped and turned back. She had her hands on her elbows and was staring at him. He moistened his lips and said: 'Sister, how is your soul? Are ee a stranger to divine things?'

She did not move, just looked at him with eyes slightly wider. She was such a handsome girl, without being exactly pretty, and she was only a few inches shorter than he was.

'What d'you mean, lug?'

'Forgive me,' he said. 'But I got a deep concern for your salvation. Has the Searcher of hearts never moved in ee?'

She bit her lip. 'My dear life and body! I never seen the likes of you before. There's many tried other ways but never this! Come from Redruth fair, av ee?'

'I'm from Reath Cottage,' he said stolidly. 'Over to Mellin. We been there nigh on two year, brother and me. But now he –'

'Oh, so there's another like you! Shoot me if I seen the equal. Why –'

'Sister, we have meetings thrice weekly at Reath Cottage where we d'read the gospel and open our hearts t' each other. Ye'd be welcomed by all. We'd pray together. If so be as you're a stranger to happiness, an unawakened soul, wi'out God and wi'out hope in the world, we would go down on our knees together and seek our Redeemer.'

'I'll be seeking the dogs to come after you,' she said, suddenly contemptuous. 'I wonder surgeon don't give folk like you rat's bane! I would an' all –'

'Mebbe it d'seem hard for you. But if once your soul be drawn out t'understand the promise of forgiveness and –'

'Cock's life!' she shouted. 'You really think you can get me to a praying feast?'

'Sister, I offer ee this only for the sake of –'

'And I tell ee to be off, lug! Tell your old wives' fables to them as wishes to hark to them!'

She slammed the door in his face. He stared at the wood for a moment, then philosophically began to walk back to the Verneys with his bottle of lotion. He would have to leave 2s. with them to pay the surgeon when he called.

Having done this, he quickened his pace, for the height of the sun told him it was time he was at the mine. His partner, Peter Hoskin, was waiting, and together they climbed down the series of inclining ladders to the forty fathom level, and stooped through narrow tunnels and echoing caves until they reached the level they were driving south-west in the direction of the old Wheal Maiden workings.

Sam and Peter Hoskin were old friends, having been born in the neighbouring villages of Pool and Illuggan and having wrestled together as boys. They worked together now as tut men; that is on a constant wage per fathom excavated, paid by the mine owner; they were not tributers who struck bargains with the management to excavate promising or already discovered ground and received an agreed share of the proceeds of the ore they raised.

Their work at present, driving away from the main excavations, was made more difficult because, as the distance from the air shafts increased, it became harder to sustain a good day's work without moving out of the tunnel every hour or so to fill their lungs with oxygen. This morning, having picked away all that had been broken yesterday, and having carried it away and tipped it in the nearest cave or 'plot', they had recourse to more gunpowder.

They put in the charge and squatted on their haunches until the explosive went off and sent reverberatory echoes and booms back along all the shafts and tunnels and wynds, with shivers and wafts of hot air from which they had to shelter their candles. As soon as the echoes died away they went back, climbed over the debris and fallen rubble and began to waft the fumes away with their shirts to peer through to see how much rock had come down. Inhaling this smoke was one of the chief causes of lung disease, but if you waited until the fumes dispersed in this draughtless hot tunnel it meant twenty minutes wasted every time you used explosive.

During the morning as they worked Sam thought more than once of the bold, defiant but candid face of the girl who had come to the door at the doctor's. All souls, he knew, were equally precious in the sight of God; all must kneel together at the throne of grace, waiting like captives to be set free; yet to one who like himself sought to save a few among so many, some seemed necessarily more worth the saving than others. She, to Sam, seemed worth the saving. It might be a sin so to discriminate. He must pray about it.

Yet all leaders – and he in his infinitely small way had been appointed a leader – all leaders must try to see into the souls of those they met, and in looking must discern so far as he was able the potentiality of the person so encountered. How else did Jesus choose his disciples? He too had discriminated. A fisherman, a tax collector, and so on. There could be no wrong in doing what Our Lord had done.

Yet her rejection had been absolute. One would have to pray about that too. Through the power of grace there had been convulsions of spirit and conversions far more dramatic than might be needed here. 'Saul, Saul, why persecutest thou Me? . . .'

At croust they moved out of the bad end into the cooler and less contaminated air of a disused cave which had been worked three years ago for copper before tin was discovered in the sixty level. Here they put on their shirts, took off their hats, sat down, and by the smeeching light of the tallow candles spent a half-hour over their meal. Munching his thick cold pasty, Peter Hoskin began to chaff Sam about Drake's new property and asked politely if he could have the grass captain's job when Captain Poldark bought Sam a mine of his own. Sam bore this equably, as he often had to bear jokes about his religious life from other miners who were hardy unbelievers and meant to stay that way. His even temper had stood him in good stead many times. With an abiding conviction of the redemption of the world, it made little difference to him that some should scoff. He smiled quietly at them and thought no worse of them at all.

But presently he interrupted Peter's mouth-filled banter by saying he had been to surgeon's that morning to get aid for the Verneys, and that a maidservant had opened the door, tall and handsome but bold looking, with white skin and blackish hair. Did Peter know who twas?

Peter, having been in the district a year longer than Sam, and having mixed in different company, knew well enough who twas. He sputtered some crumbs on his breeches and said that without a trace of doubt this would be Emma Tregirls, Lobb Tregirls's sister, him that worked a stamp in Sawle Combe, and daughter of that old scoundrel Bartholomew Tregirls who had but recent found himself a comfortable home at Sally Chill-Off's.

'Tholly went wi' your brother Drake and Cap'n Poldark on that French caprouse. You mind last year when Joe Nanfan were killed and they comed back wi' the young doctor – '

'Aye, I mind well. I should do!'

'Tholly went on that. Old devil 'e be, if ever I seen one. 'E'd not live long round these here parts if some folk 'ad their way.'

'And – Emma?'

Peter wet his forefinger and began to pick up the crumbs he had spattered on his breeches. 'Cor, that's better now. I were nation thurled for that. I 'ad scarce a bite for supper last eve . . . Emma? Emma Tregirls? Reg'lar piece. You want to be warned, you do. Half the boys of the village be tail-on-end 'bout she.'

'Not wed?'

'Not wed, nor like to be, I'd say. There be always one man or another over-fanged 'bout Emma; but gracious knows whether they get what they come for. She d'go mopping around but she never had no brat yet, not's I know. Bit of a mystery. Bit of a mystery. But that d'make the lads all the more randy . . .'

Sam was silent then until they resumed work. He thought quietly about it all. God moved in a mysterious way. He would not presume to question the workings of the Holy Spirit. Nor would he attempt to direct them himself. In due course all would be revealed to him. But had there not also been Mary Magdalen?

CHAPTER IV

On a sunny February afternoon which, although fine and bright, had all day had a hint of frost lingering in it like a chill breath, the stage coach, on the last leg of its journey from Bodmin to Truro, stopped about a mile out of town and deposited two young girls at the mouth of a lane leading down to the river. Waiting to meet them was a tall, graceful, shy young woman who in the last months had become known to the inhabitants of the town as the new wife of the vicar of St Margaret's.

The young woman, who was accompanied by a manservant, embraced the two girls ecstatically, tears welling into her eyes but not falling; and presently they began to walk together down the steep lane, followed by the manservant with a trunk and a valise belonging to the girls. They chattered continuously, and the manservant, who was accustomed to his mistress being excessively reserved and silent, was astonished to hear her taking a full part in the conversation and actually laughing. It was a surprising sound.

As sisters they were not noticeably alike – except perhaps in the fancy names which their father, an incurable romantic, had given them. The eldest and married one, Morwenna, was dark, with a dark skin, beautiful soft short-sighted eyes, of moderate looks but with a noble figure, just beginning to thicken now with the child she carried. The second sister, Garlanda, who had only come to bring her youngest sister and was returning to Bodmin on the next coach, was sturdy, country-built, with candid blue eyes, thick irrepressible brown hair growing short, a vivid way of moving and speaking and an odd deep voice that sounded like a boy's just after it had broken.

The youngest of the family, Rowella, not yet fifteen, was nearly as tall as Morwenna, but thin, her general colouring a mouse brown, her eyes set close together over a long thin nose. She had very fine skin, a sly look, sandy eyebrows, an underlip that tended to tremble, and the best brain in the family.

At the foot of the hill was a cluster of thatched cottages, a lych gate, the old granite church which dated from 1326, and beyond that the vicarage, a pleasant square house looking on to the river. They went in, dusted the mud and melting frost from their skirts and entered the parlour for tea. There the Reverend Osborne Whitworth joined them. Ossie was a big man with a voice accustomed to making itself heard but, in spite of the fashionable extravagance of his clothes, clumsy in the presence of women. Although he had had two wives, his understanding of the opposite sex was limited by his lack of imagination. He saw women mainly as objects, differently attired from himself, suitable to receive unmeant compliments, mothers of children, static but useful vehicles for perpetuating the human race, and frequently but only briefly as the nude objects of his desire. Had he known of Calvin's remark that women are created to bear children and to die of it, he would probably have agreed.

At least his first wife had so died, leaving him with two small daughters; and he had taken speedy steps to replace her with a new one. He had chosen one whose body appealed to him physically and whose marriage portion, thanks to the generosity of her cousin-by-marriage, Mr George Warleggan, had helped him wipe off past debts and improve his future standard of living. So far so good.

But it had been borne in even upon his obtuseness over the last few months that his new wife was not relishing her marriage or her new position. In a sense he was prepared for a 'going off' in women after marriage; for his first wife, though welcoming their physical union to begin with, had shown a decreasing willingness to receive his attentions; and although she had never made the least attempt to refuse him there had been a certain resignation in her manner which had not pleased him too well.

But with Morwenna it had never been anything else. He had known – indeed she had declared before marriage – that she did not 'love' him. He had dismissed this as a female quibble, something that could easily be got over in the marriage bed: he had enough confidence in his own male attraction to feel that such maidenly hesitations on her part would be soon overcome. But although she submitted to his large attentions five times a week – not Saturdays or Sundays – her submissiveness at times came near to that of a martyr at the stake. He seldom looked at her face when in the act, but occasional glimpses showed her mouth drawn, her eyebrows contorted; often afterwards she would shiver and shudder uncontrollably. He would have liked to believe that this came from pleasure – though women were not really supposed to get pleasure out of it – but the look in her eyes, when he caught it, showed all too clearly that this was not so.

Her manner annoyed him and made him irritable. Sometimes it led him into little cruelties, physical cruelties, of which afterwards he was ashamed. She performed her simple duties about the house well enough; she attended to the calls of the parish, frequently being out when he expected her to be in; she was fond of his daughters and they, after a probationary period, of her; she attended church, tall and slender – well, fairly slender anyhow; she sat at his table and ate his food; she wore in her own undistinguished way the clothes he had had made for her; she discussed church affairs with him, sometimes even town affairs; when he went to a reception – such as the Penvenen wedding – she was at his side. She did not chatter at meals like Esther, she did not complain when she was unwell, she did not fritter money away on trivialities, she had a dignity that his first wife had quite lacked. Indeed she might have been the sort of woman he would be thoroughly pleased with, if the unfortunate but necessarily main purpose of matrimony could have been ignored.

It could not. Last week when performing the wedding ceremony in his own church he had allowed his mind to wander from its immediate task and ponder a moment on his own marriage and the three purposes for which the Prayer Book said matrimony had been ordained. The first, the procreation of children, was already being fulfilled. The third, for the mutual comfort and society, etc., was fair enough; she was there most times and did his will. It was the second which was the stumbling block. '. . . a remedy against sin, and to avoid fornication; that such persons as have not the gift of continency might marry, and keep themselves undefiled members of Christ's body.' Well, he had not the gift of continency, and she was there to save him from fornication. It was not for her to shiver and shudder at his touch. 'Wives,' St Paul had said, 'submit yourselves unto your own husbands as unto the Lord.' He had said it both in his Epistle to the Ephesians and in his Epistle to the Colossians. It was not for her to look on her husband's body with horror and disgust.

So at times she goaded him into sin. Sometimes he hurt her when he need not. Once he had twisted her feet in his hands until she cried out; but that must not happen again. It had troubled him in the night. He blamed her for that.

But today in the presence of three young women he was at his best. Secure in his dignity – he had told Morwenna before they came that they must call him Mr Whitworth to his face but must always refer to him among others as the Vicar – he could unbend and be clumsily genial. He stood on the hearth-rug with his hands behind his back and his coat-tails over his arms and talked to them of parish affairs and the shortcomings of the town, while they sipped tea and murmured replies and laughed politely at his jokes. Then, unbending still further, he told them in detail of a hand of cards he had played last night, and Morwenna breathed again, for to confide in this way was always a sign of his approval. He played whist three nights a week: it was his abiding passion, and the play of the previous night was his customary topic at breakfast.

Before leaving them to their own devices he clearly thought it necessary to correct any impression of lightness in his manner or conversation and so launched into a summary of his views on the war, England's food shortage, the dangerous spread of discontent, the debasement of money, and the opening of a new burial ground in Truro. Thus having done his duty, he rang the bell for the servant to clear away the tea – Garlanda had not quite finished – and left them, to return to his study.

It was a time before normal conversation broke out again between the three girls, and then it was centred wholly upon the affairs of Bodmin and news they could exchange of friends in common. The sunny-tempered, outspoken, practical Garlanda was aching to ask all the questions she would normally have asked, all about preparations for the coming baby, and was Morwenna happy in her married life, and how did it feel

to be a vicar's wife instead of a dean's daughter, and had she
met many people socially in the town and what new dresses
had she had made? But she alone of the other sisters knew
something of Morwenna's troubles, and she had seen as soon
as they met this afternoon that they were not over. She had
hoped and prayed that a few months of marriage, and
especially the coming child, would have made her forget 'the
other man'. Whether it was thoughts of her lost love that were
troubling Morwenna or merely that her gained love was not
to her liking, Garlanda did not yet know, but having now met
Ossie she could see some of the problems her sister had to
face. It was a pity *she* was not staying, Garlanda thought; she
might have helped Morwenna more than any of the others.
Morwenna was such a soft gentle creature, easily hurt but
temperamentally intended to be happy; in the next few years
she would *have* to harden herself to deal with a man like Ossie,
to stand up to him, otherwise she would go under, become
as much like a white mouse and as much in awe of him as
those two little girls who crept around. She *had* to be given
strength.

As for the sister who was staying, Garlanda did not know
what *she* thought and probably never would. For whereas
Morwenna's quietness and reticence were really as open as the
day and came only from shyness, so that anyone could soon
penetrate to her thoughts and feelings and fears, little Rowella
with her thin nose and narrow eyes and fluttering underlip had
been inscrutable from the day she was born. Little Rowella,
already three inches taller than Garlanda, was taking only a
minor part in the conversation, now that, haltingly, it had
broken out again. Her eyes travelled around the room, as they
had been doing from time to time ever since she came into it,
assessing it, forming her own conclusions, whatever they might
be, as no doubt she had formed her own conclusions about her
new brother-in-law.

Presently, while the other two were chatting, she rose and
went to the window. Darkness had almost fallen, but light
still glimmered on the river, which shone like a peeled grape
among the stark trees.

The servant came in with candles and drove the last of the
retreating daylight away.

Seeing Rowella so silent, Morwenna got up and went to the window and put her arm round her.

'Well, darling, do you think you will like it here?'

'Thank you, sister, I shall be near you.'

'But far from Mama and your home. We shall need each other.'

Garlanda watched her two tall sisters but said nothing.

Presently Rowella said: 'The vicar dresses his hair in a very pretty manner. Who is his operator?'

'Oh . . . Alfred, our manservant, looks after him.'

'He is not at all like Papa, is he?'

'No . . . no, he is not.'

'Nor is he at all like the new dean.'

'The new dean is from Saltash,' Garlanda volunteered. 'Such a little bird of a man.'

Silence fell.

Rowella said: 'I do not suppose we are so near revolution as the vicar suggests. But there were bad riots at Flushing last week . . . How far are we here from Truro?'

'About a mile. A little more if one goes by the carriage road.'

'There are some shops there?'

'Oh, yes, in Kenwyn Street.'

A pause. 'Your garden looked pretty. It runs right to the river?'

'Oh, yes.' Morwenna made an effort. 'We have great fun, Sarah and Anne and I. When the tide is half in there is a little island that we stand on and pretend we are marooned and waiting for a boat. But if we don't choose *just* the right time to escape, our feet sink in the mud and we get wet . . . And we feed the swans. There are just four of them and they are quite tame. One of them has a damaged wing. We call her Leda. We steal scraps from the kitchen. Anne is terrified, but Sarah and I – they will feed out of our hand . . .'

The darkness was now so complete that they could see only the reflections of themselves in the glass.

Rowella said: 'I have brought a pincushion to stick for you. It is of white satin and quilted curiously, the upper and undersides to be of different patterns. I think you will like it.'

'I'm sure I shall. Show it me when you unpack.'

Rowella stretched herself. 'I think I should like to do that now, Wenna. My shoes are pinching and I long to change them. They belonged to Carenza, who outgrew them and so they were passed on. But I believe they are now too small for me.'

II

Ross Poldark had known the Bassets more or less all his life but it had been the acquaintance that all landed people in Cornwall had of each other rather than friendship. Sir Francis Basset was too big a man to consort familiarly with the small squires of the county. He owned the Tehidy estate about eleven miles west of Nampara and his vast mining interests gave him a greater spendable income than any other man in the county. He had written and issued papers on political theory, on practical agriculture and on safety in the mines. He was a patron of the arts and sciences and spent half of each year in London.

It was therefore a surprise to the Poldarks to receive a letter from him in March inviting them to dinner at Tehidy; though not so much of a surprise as it would have been a year ago. To Ross's great irritation he found himself a hero in the county since his Quimper adventure; people knew his name who had never heard of him before, and this was not the first unexpected invitation they had received. To some of them he had successfully negotiated a refusal – the negotiation being with Demelza, who on principle never refused an invitation anywhere. During the winter Clowance had been out of sorts with teething troubles and this had given him a lever to get his own way, for Julia's death was still vivid in Demelza's mind, and the fact that their new child was a girl seemed to make her specially vulnerable. But now Clowance was better, so there was no excuse.

'Oh, I like him well enough,' said Ross, driven into a corner. 'He's a different mould from my more immediate neighbours; a man of sensibility, though a trifle ruthless in his own affairs. It is just that I don't relish an invitation which so clearly arises from my new notoriety.'

'Notoriety is not a good word,' said Demelza. 'Is it? I thought notoriety meant a kind of ill fame.'

'I imagine it can mean all kinds of fame. It certainly applies to undeserved fame, such as mine is.'

'Perhaps others are a better judge than you are, Ross. It is no shame to be known as a brave and daring person.'

'Daring and foolhardy. Losing as many men as I saved.'

'Not unless you guess at those that may have died trying to escape on their own.'

'Well,' Ross said restively, 'the objection holds. I have no love for being thought highly of for the wrong reasons. But I give in, I give way, I surrender; we'll go and beard Sir Francis in his den. His wife is Frances too, you know. And his daughter. So it will become very confusing for you if you take too much port.'

'I know when some ill word is coming from you,' Demelza said. 'Your ears twitch, like Garrick's when he has seen a rabbit.'

'Perhaps it is the same impulse,' said Ross.

Nevertheless Demelza would have been happier if this had been an evening party and she could in fact have fortified herself with a glass or two as soon as she arrived. To Ross it meant nothing that she had been born within a mile or so of Tehidy Park and that her father had worked all his life in a mine of which Sir Francis Basset owned the mineral rights. Four of her brothers had at times worked on mines in which he had a controlling interest. The name of Sir Francis Basset carried as much weight in Illuggan and Camborne as the name of King George, and it had been daunting even to be introduced to him at the wedding. Did Sir Francis know, or did he not, that Mrs Ross Poldark had been a miner's brat dragged up in a hovel with six brothers, and a drunken father who belted her at the least excuse? And if he did not, might not her accent – in spite of her greatly improved English – inform him? To a trained ear there were very noticeable differences of tone between one district and another.

But she said nothing of this to Ross because it might have given him another lever to refuse, and she did not feel that *he* ought to refuse, and she knew he would not go without her.

It was a Thursday they had been asked for, and the time one o'clock, so they left soon after eleven in light rain.

Tehidy Park was by far the largest and most affluent seat

anywhere along the north Cornish coast from Crackington to Penzance. Although surrounded at a short distance by moorland and all the scars of mining, it was pleasantly wooded, with a fine deer park and a pretty lake overlooked by the house. Seven hundred acres insulated it from the industry that brought its owner an income of above £12,000 a year. The house itself was an enormous square Palladian mansion sentinelled at each of its corners by a 'pavilion' or smaller house, one of which was a chapel, another a huge conservatory, and the other two accommodation for the servants.

They went in and were greeted by their hosts. If they knew anything of Demelza's origins they did not betray it by so much as the flicker of an eyelid. All the same, Demelza was greatly relieved to see Dwight and Caroline Enys among the guests.

Among others there was a Mr Rogers, a plump middle-aged man from the south coast, who was Sir Francis's brother-in-law, two of Sir Francis's sisters, his fourteen-year-old daughter, and of course Lady Basset, an attractive, elegant little woman whose diminutive size nicely matched her husband's. Making up the company was a florid gentleman called General William Macarmick and a young man called Armitage, in naval uniform, with the epaulet of a lieutenant on his left shoulder.

Before dinner they strolled about the house, which inside was so luxurious as to make the big houses round the Fal seem modest by comparison. Handsome pictures hung on the walls and over the marble chimney-pieces, and names like Rubens, Lanfranc, Van Dyke and Rembrandt were bandied about. On introduction Lieutenant Armitage had not meant anything to Demelza, until she saw him greet Ross, and then she realized that this was the kinsman of the Boscawens whom Ross had liberated from the prison camp of Quimper. He was a striking young man whose pallor, still possibly the result of his long imprisonment, accentuated his large dark eyes, with lashes that any woman would envy. But there was nothing girlish about his keen sharp-featured face and quiet brooding manner, and Demelza caught a gleam of something in his eye when he looked at her.

By the time they sat down it was three o'clock. Demelza was opposite Lieutenant Armitage and between Dwight and

General Macarmick. The latter, in spite of being elderly, was cheerful and outgoing, a man with a lot of opinions and no lack of the will to voice them. He had at one time been Member of Parliament for Truro, had raised a regiment for the West Indies and had made a fortune for himself in the wine trade. He was polite and charming to everyone, but in between courses when his hands were not engaged he repeatedly felt Demelza's leg above the knee.

She sometimes wondered what there was about herself that made men so forthcoming. In those early days when she had gone to various receptions and balls she had always had them two or three deep asking for the next dance – and often for more besides. Sir Hugh Bodrugan still lumbered over to Nampara hopefully a couple of times a year, presumably expecting that sooner or later persistence would have its reward. Two years ago at that dinner party at Trelissick there had been that Frenchman who had larded his entire dinner conversation with improper suggestions. It didn't seem right.

If she had known herself to be supremely beautiful or striking – as beautiful, for instance, as Elizabeth Warleggan, or as striking as Caroline Enys – it might have been more acceptable. Instead of that she was just friendly, and they took it the wrong way. Or else they sensed something particularly female about her that set them off. Or else because of her lack of breeding they thought she would be easy game. Or else it happened to everybody. She must ask Ross how often he squeezed women's legs under the dinner table.

Talk was much of the war. Mr Rogers had had the most recent dealings with French émigrés and was of the opinion that the newly formed Directory was on the point of collapse, and with it the whole republic.

'Not only,' said Rogers, 'is there moral and religious decay; this has become a decay of will-power, of a desire to accept any duty or responsibility whatever, of a willingness to take any action on behalf of the few Godless fanatics who cling to power. You, sir – ' to Ross ' – will I am sure bear me out in this.'

Ross's nod was one of politeness rather than agreement. 'My contact with the French republicans has been slight – except for the very few I met in – in what I suppose could be called combat. Alas, my experience of the French counter-revolutionaries has been such that I would apply most of your description to them also.'

'Nevertheless,' Rogers was undeterred, 'the collapse of the present regime in France can't be long delayed. What's your view, Armitage?'

The young lieutenant took his eyes off Demelza and said: 'D'you know, although I was nine months in France, I saw no more of it than the first nine days when I was moved from prison to prison. Did you, Enys?'

'Once inside Quimper,' Dwight said, 'and you could as well have been in purgatory. True, one heard the guards talking from time to time. The cost of many things had multiplied twelve times in a year.'

Rogers said: 'In 1790 you could buy a hat in Paris – a good one, mind you – for fourteen livres; now, I'm told, it is near on six hundred. Farmers will not bring their produce to market, for the paper money they are paid for it has lost value by the following week. A country cannot wage war without a sound financial basis to support it.'

'That's Pitt's view too,' said Sir Francis Basset.

In the silence that followed Ross said: 'This young general who crushed the counter-revolutionaries in Paris, has he not now been put in charge of the French Army to Italy? This month. Some time this month. I always forget his name.'

'Buonaparte,' said Hugh Armitage. 'It was he who captured Toulon at the end of '93.'

'There's a whole group of young generals,' Ross said, 'Hoche the most gifted of them. But while they live and command troops and are undefeated in battle it's hard to believe that the dynamic of the Revolution is altogether dead. There's a risk that, by ignoring the orthodox view of war and finance, they may keep up the momentum a while longer. For years the army has been paid only from the pickings of conquered countries.'

Basset said: 'This Buonaparte put down the counter-revolutionaries by firing *cannon* at them – he cleared the streets of Paris with grapeshot, killing and maiming hundreds of his own countrymen! Obviously such men have to be reckoned with. And their Directory of Five, who deposed those other blood-stained tyrants, these five are criminals in any sense of the word. They cannot allow the war machine to stop. In them, as much as for the young generals, it is conquer or die.'

'I'm relieved to hear you say so much, sir,' said Lieutenant Armitage. 'My uncle speculated that in dining with so prominent and distinguished a Whig I might hear talk of peace and references favourable to the Revolution.'

'Your uncle should have known better,' said Sir Francis coldly. 'The true Whig is as patriotic an Englishman as anyone in the land. No one loathes the Revolutionaries more than I, for they have broken every law of God and man.'

'As a lifelong Tory,' observed General Macarmick, 'I could not have expressed it better myself!'

Demelza moved her knee.

'A whiff of grapeshot,' he went on, cheerfully finding it again, 'a whiff of grapeshot would not come amiss in this country from time to time. To fire at the King's coach when he went to open Parliament! Outrageous!'

'I believe it was but stones they aimed,' Dwight said. 'And someone discharged an airgun . . .'

'And then they overturned the coach on its way back empty — and near wrecked it! They should be taught a lesson, such ruffians and miscreants!'

Demelza looked at the boiled codfish with shrimp sauce that had been set before her, and then glanced at Lady Basset to see which fork she was picking up. Despite the austerity of the times, when the consumption of food was being voluntarily restricted and it was patriotic to reduce one's style, this was still a handsome meal. Soup, fish, venison, beef, mutton, with damson tarts, syllabubs and lemon pudding; and burgundy, champagne, Madeira, sherry and port.

For a time talk was the gossip of the county: of the sudden death of Sir Piers Arthur, one of the Members of Parliament for Truro, which would require a by-election there, and whether the Falmouths would choose their new MP from inside the county to companion Captain Gower in the House. When they looked at him Lieutenant Armitage smiled and shook his head. 'Don't ask me. I'm no candidate, nor have I any idea who may be. My uncle does not use me as his confidant. What of you, General?'

'Nay, nay,' said Macarmick. 'I am past all that. Your uncle will be looking for a younger man.'

And of the earnest discussion in the county as to the need for a central hospital to deal with the widespread sickness among miners; and of the argument put forward among others by Sir Francis Basset and Dr Dwight Enys that such a central hospital should be sited near Truro.

And of how Ruth and John Treneglos's eldest, Jonathan, had taken the smallpox, and that Dr Choake had pronounced them of a good sort; and of his three sisters who had been brought into the sickroom at a proper stage in the disease and had all received the infection and were doing very favourably.

Demelza was relieved when dinner broke up. Not that she so much minded General Macarmick's intimacies, but his hand was growing progressively hotter, and she was afraid for her frock. Sure enough when she was able to look at herself upstairs there were grease stains.

While they dined the clouds had altogether cleared, the wind had dropped and a warm yellow sun was low in the sky, so the Bassets suggested they should take a stroll in the gardens and walk up through the woods to a terrace from which one could see all the North Cliffs and the sea.

The women took cloaks or light wraps and the party started off, to begin with in a strolling crocodile, led by Lady Basset and General Macarmick, but splintering up as this or that person stopped to admire a plant or a view or wandered down a side way as the fancy took him.

From the beginning Demelza found herself partnered by Lieutenant Armitage. It was not deliberate on her part, but she knew it was on his. He was silent for the first few minutes, then he said:

'I am under a great obligation to your husband, ma'am.'

'Yes? I'm that happy that it turned out so.'

'It was a noble adventure on his part.'

'He does not think so.'

'I believe it is his nature to deprecate the value of his own acts.'

'You must tell him so, Lieutenant Armitage.'

'Oh, I have.'

They walked on a few paces. Ahead of them some of the others were discussing the birth of a child to the Prince and Princess of Wales.

Armitage said: 'This is a delightful prospect. Almost as beautiful as that from my uncle's house. Have you ever seen Tregothnan, Mrs Poldark?'

'No.'

'Oh, you must. I hope you both will soon. While I'm staying there. This house, of course, is much finer. My uncle speaks sometimes of rebuilding his.'

Demelza said: 'I think I disfancy so large a house for so small a family.'

'It's expected of great men. Look at that swan flying; she has just come up from the lake, how her wings are gilded by the sun!'

'You are fond of birds?'

'Of everything just now, ma'am. When one has been in prison so long all the world looks fresh minted. One observes it with wonder – with a child's eyes again. Even after some months I have not lost that appreciation.'

'It's good to enjoy a little compensation for that ill time.'

'Not little compensation, believe me.'

'Perhaps, Lieutenant, you would recommend it for us all.'

'What?'

'Some months in prison to sharpen our savour for ordinary life.'

'Well . . . life is contrast, isn't it? Day is always the more welcome after a long night. But I think you joke with me, ma'am.'

'Not so. Not at all.'

Ahead of them Miss Mary Basset said: 'Well, it is a pity it is a girl; for at the rate Prinny topes on one wonders if he will survive his father.'

'He's deserted Princess Caroline altogether,' said Mr Rogers. 'It happened just before we left Town. Almost so soon as the child was delivered he deserted them both and went to live openly with Lady Jersey.'

'And Lady J. so flagrant about it all,' said Miss Cathleen

Basset. 'It would matter far less if it were done in a decent discreet fashion.'

'I'm told,' said Caroline Enys, 'that my namesake stinks.'

There was a brief silence. 'Well she does!' Caroline said with a laugh. 'In addition to being fat and vulgar, she smells to high heaven. Any man would spend his wedding night with a bottle of whisky and his head in the grate if he were expected to couple with such a creature! However handicapped by her humours, I do not think a woman ought to be offensive to a man's nose.'

'Else it might be put out of joint, eh?' said General Macarmick and broke into a guffaw. 'By God, you're right, ma'am! Not to a man's nose – ha! ha! – not to a man's nose – else it might be put out of joint! Ha, ha, ha, ha, ha!'

His laughter echoed back from the young pine trees and was so infectious that everyone joined in.

Hugh Armitage said: 'Shall we walk to the lake first? I think Lady Basset told me there were some interesting wild fowl.'

Demelza hesitated, and then went with him. Their interchange so far had been pleasant, formal and light. A pleasant post-prandial stroll in a country garden in the company of a pleasant polite young man. Compared to the predatory conquerers she had kept at bay in the past, such as Hugh Bodrugan, Hector McNeil and John Treneglos, this was completely without risk, danger or any other hazard. But it didn't feel like it – which was the trouble. This young man's hawk profile, deeply sensitive dark eyes and gentle urgent voice moved her strangely. And some danger perhaps existed not so much in the strength of the attack as in the sudden weakness of the defence.

They walked down together towards the lake and began to discuss the water fowl they found there.

Sir Francis Basset said: 'I have thought for some time, Poldark, that we should know each other better. I remember your uncle, of course, when he was on the bench, but by the time I was old enough to take an active part in the affairs of the county he seldom left his estate. And your cousin – I think he was not of a mind for public life.'

'Well, after Grambler Mine closed he was impoverished, and this disinclined him for much that he might normally have done.'

'I am glad to learn Wheal Grace is now so productive.'

'It was a gamble that came off.'

'All mining is a gamble. I only wish conditions were better in the industry as a whole. Within a three-mile radius of this house there used to be thirty-eight mines open. Now there are eight. It's a grim picture.'

There seemed to be nothing to say to that, so Ross said nothing.

'You have, I know, been something of the non-conformer yourself, Poldark,' Basset said, looking up at his tall companion. 'I, too, though in less drastic ways, have been – unorthodox – intolerant of precedent. Some of the more conventional families still look on me as an obstreperous young man – as indeed I was a few years ago.'

Ross smiled. 'I have long admired your concern for the conditions in which miners work.'

Basset said: 'Your cousin was financially embarrassed. Until two years ago you were in a like condition. Now that has changed.'

'You seem to know something of my affairs, Sir Francis.'

'Well, you may remember I have banking interests in Truro and many friends. I think my estimate is probably right?' Ross did not dissent. 'So have you not time for some public service? You are now a well-known name in Cornwall. You could put it to account.'

'If you refer to the possibility of my going on the bench . . .'

'I know that. Ralph-Allen Daniell told me you'd refused it, and why. They don't seem to me valid reasons but I imagine they haven't changed?'

'They haven't changed.'

There was more laughter from the main group, of which Caroline was the centre. Basset said: 'I have planted all these conifers. Already they are acting as a protection against the worst winds. But they will not be fully grown until I am dead.'

'Have patience,' Ross said. 'You may still have a long way to go.'

Basset glanced at him. 'I hope I have. There is still much to do. But no one approaches forty . . . Are you a Whig, Poldark?'

Ross raised his eyebrows. 'I'm little inclined either way.'

'You admire Fox?'

'I *did*.'

'I still do, in a qualified way. But reform must come by able administration from above, not revolution from below.'

'On the whole I would agree with that – provided it comes.'

'There is much, I think, on which we should find ourselves in agreement. I take it you don't believe in Democracy?'

'No.'

'Some of my erstwhile colleagues – a few only, I'm glad to say – still nourish the most extravagant ideas. What would be the consequences of these measures they propose? I'll tell you. The executive power, the press, the great commoners, would lose all their proper interest and be forced to acquire power by the baneful means of bribery and corruption, and this –'

'I would have thought there was ample bribery and corruption in the electoral system today.'

'Indeed, and I don't condone it, although I am obliged to make use of it. But equal representation would increase corruption, not diminish it. The Crown and the House of Lords would become cyphers, and all power would centre in the House of Commons which would, as in France, be chosen from the dregs of the people. Our government would then degenerate into the worst of all governments, namely that democracy that some people pretend to see as the ultimate goal. To be governed by a mob would be to see the end of civil and religious liberties, and all would be stamped down to a common level in the sacred name of equality.'

'Men can never be equal,' Ross said. 'A classless society would be a lifeless society – there would be no blood flowing through its veins. But there should be far more traffic between the classes, far more opportunity to rise and fall. Particularly there should be much greater rewards for the industrious in the lower classes and greater penalties for those in the upper classes who misuse their power.'

Basset nodded. 'All this is well said. I have a proposition to put to you, Captain Poldark.'

'I'm afraid I may offend you by refusing it.'

II

Hugh Armitage said: 'Shall we climb up to join the others? I think there is a prospect of a handsome sunset.'

Demelza rose from where she had been crouching, trying to encourage a little mandarin duck to swim nearer. 'We have no pond or pool in our place. There is but a stream, and that more often than not flows discoloured with the tin washings.'

'Perhaps some time I might be permitted to call on you – both? You are some miles farther north?'

'I'm sure Ross would be pleased.'

'And you?'

'Of course . . . But we do not have an estate, nor even a mansion.'

'Nor I. My father's family come from Dorset. We have a manor house hidden in the steep small hills near Shaftesbury. Do you travel up-country much?'

'I have never been out of Cornwall.'

'Your husband should bring you. You should not hide your light – either of you.'

Twice it seemed Lieutenant Armitage had included Ross in his remarks as an afterthought.

They began to climb the hill, wending a way along a part-overgrown path through holly, laurel and chestnut. The others were now out of sight, though their voices could be heard.

Demelza said: 'Shall you return to the Navy soon?'

'Not immediate. I cannot yet see at distances. The surgeons say it is a matter of time for my eyes to right themselves, but it has been brought on by trying to read and write in semi-darkness.'

'. . . I'm sorry.'

'Also my uncle would like me to stay at Tregothnan for the time being. Since his wife died his sister, my aunt, has taken over the management of the house, but he lacks company and has become morose.'

Demelza paused and looked back towards the house. It might have been a great square mosque guarded by its four pavilions. A group of deer bounded across a patch of sunlight falling through the trees. She said: 'Were you able to write letters home? Dwight was not. At least Caroline only received one in near a year.'

'No . . . I was writing for my own satisfaction. But paper was so short that every scrap was covered both ways, horizontal and vertical, and in a tiny script that sometimes now I cannot read.'

'Writing? . . .'

'Poetry. Or perhaps verse would be a more modest estimate.' Demelza blinked. 'I've never met a poet before.'

He flushed. 'It is not to be taken serious. But you asked. At the time it helped to keep me sane.'

'And shall you do more of it?'

'Oh, yes. It becomes, in however small a way, a part of one's life.'

They began to climb again, and presently came out on the terrace from which they were to observe the sunset, but still ahead of the others who had stopped somewhere on the way. The terrace was brick floored, with two stone lions guarding the steps up to it, and as its centre piece a small Grecian temple with a statue of Bacchus stared towards the sea.

The sun was already flaring behind a ridge of cloud. It was as if someone had opened a furnace door and the red-hot glow was showing behind unburnt coal. Cliffs jutted black and jagged into a porcelain sea. Seagulls whirled like scimitars, silently cutting the afternoon air.

Hugh Armitage said: 'Captain Poldark has now conferred two great favours on me.'

'Oh?'

'My liberty, and the opportunity of meeting his wife.'

Demelza said: 'I'm not skilled in such courtesies, Lieutenant, but thank you. Is it not . . .'

'What were you going to say?'

'I was going to say, is it not wrong to mention such different matters in the same breath? As if . . .' She stopped again. The others were now mounting the steps behind them.

'I was not trying to be courteous,' he said. 'Only truthful.'

'Oh, no –'

'When may I see you again?'

'I will ask Ross when he can invite you.'

'Pray do.'

'Ho, there!' said General Macarmick, coming up the steps like a sun himself, his round jovial face inflamed by the sunset. 'Ho, there! So you were here before us!'

III

Sir Francis Basset had to take almost three steps to Ross's two. He said: 'I have two farms in hand – the one of about three hundred acres, the other a bare fifty. The land is not good – there is much thin soil and spar stone; and overall it is not worth more than twelve shillings an acre. Does yours exceed that?'

'No. Nine to ten, I would guess, when it is worked.'

'I intend to try some experimental crops – turnips, cabbage, artificial grass – things not yet known in this part of the country, so that the farmers in the neighbourhood may see what answers best without going to personal expense. Also I have a deal of waste ground, where I have encouraged the poor to build cottages, and I have allotted three acres to each. They pay two and sixpence an acre as rent; often good land is made of it, the tenants being chiefly miners who cultivate their ground in their spare hours.'

Ross said: 'You are suggesting, Sir Francis – you are suggesting something of a revolt in the pocket borough of Truro, is that it? Whereby, at this by-election now pending, the corporation of the town should fail to vote for Lord Falmouth's nominee and should instead vote for the candidate you put forward? That is the proposition?'

'Roughly that is the proposition. As you may know, the

voting rests with the aldermen and the capital burgesses, who total twenty-five in all. I believe I may count on enough of them now. They are heartily sick of their treatment at the hands of Lord Falmouth, whose manner of choosing Members to represent the borough in Parliament is so high-handed as to make the burgesses feel corrupt and prostituted to the sale of their votes at his absolute direction.'

'Would that not be a fair approximation to the truth?'

Basset smiled thinly. 'I think you are trying to provoke me. Compared to many boroughs, their record is not an ill one. They receive favours for their votes but no money changes hands. It is understandable that they should feel insulted by being treated as lackeys.'

'And this – palace revolution. Who would lead it?'

'The new mayor, William Hick.'

'Who no doubt made protestations of loyalty to Falmouth before he was elected.'

'No doubt he meant them. There is a difference between wishing well of a man and allowing oneself to be trampled on by him.'

They paused in their walk. A flock of jackdaws was chattering in the trees.

Ross said: 'I am honoured by your thought. But I would be quite the wrong man.'

'Possibly. That would remain to be seen. Before you say more, allow me to be explicit. If your name went forward it would do so free of all cost to yourself. This is exceptional, as you must know. If you were elected you would serve until the end of the present parliament, however long that might be. At that stage you would consider whether you wished to continue – or whether I wished you to continue. It might be one year, or of course it might be several yet. I am not in Pitt's confidence.'

'But you would expect me to vote as you directed.'

'Not directed. I am not a Falmouth. But generally as Pitt's supporter. Naturally there could be occasions when I and my colleague at Penryn, together with several others – and yourself – might wish to take an independent line.'

'Individually or collectively?'

Sir Francis looked at him. 'Collectively.'

They walked on. They had not taken the direct route up to the terrace and were walking parallel to the rise of the hill.

Basset said: 'My proposition comes unexpectedly to you. Take a week to consider it before you reply.'

Ross inclined his head in acknowledgement. 'My father used to quote Chatham, who said that the rotten boroughs of England were excrescences which must be amputated to save the whole body from mortification. I have accepted his view without bothering to verify it; but I suspect that this prejudice will be hard to dislodge.'

They broke off the main path, and Basset led the way through some undergrowth until they reached another and narrower path climbing upward. For a time they were in single file; then Sir Francis paused to get his breath and to look back at the house. He said: 'Thomas Edwardes of Greenwich designed it – he who added the steeple to St Mary's in Truro. Considering how comparative new the house is, it has all merged into the countryside very well . . .'

'Did you tell me the ceiling in the library had been done recent?'

'Re-done. I did not like the previous design.'

'I am making a small extension to my own house and shall need a plasterer soon. Is he a local man?'

'From Bath.'

'Oh . . . then hardly so!'

'Remind me, I'll give you his name when we return to the house. He might come into this area again and combine a number of engagements.'

'Thank you.' They moved on.

Basset said: 'You have a son, Poldark?'

'One son, one daughter, so far.'

'You're fortunate. We have only Frances. A gifted girl; musically gifted; but not a son. It seems likely now that she will inherit all that I have. We are not a prolific family.'

'Yet enduring.'

'Oh, yes, since the time of the Conqueror. Whoever marries Frances I hope will take the name.'

They were near the steps up to the terrace.

He said: 'Think of what I've said, Poldark. Return me your answer in a week. Or if you have other things to ask about it, come over and see me before.'

IV

Ross and Demelza and Dwight and Caroline rode part of the way home together. Since the track was narrow Ross and Dwight rode ahead, Demelza and Caroline following, with Caroline's groom bringing up the rear. There was the soft clop of hooves on muddy ground, the creak of saddles, the click of reins, an occasional snort from a horse punctuating the murmur of voices rising into the empty dusk. Bats fluttered against the star-lit sky.

Caroline said: 'D'you know, all this talk about the war and the Frenchies, I believe my husband has some sneaking sympathy for 'em, in spite of his treatment at their hands. He has sympathy for all sorts of strange things. D'you know he does not believe in the death penalty for *any* crime; he believes the criminal should be made to work off his misdeeds! Well, I believe I shall never make him into an English squire.'

'Don't try,' said Demelza.

'No, it would be a pity, wouldn't it? He has no real concern for his estate; he has no interest in guns and will not even shoot a rabbit; horses he mounts occasionally for the convenience of getting more rapidly from place to place; he will not go near the hunt; he never drinks himself under the table; he never bawls at the servants; I think our marriage has been a great mistake.'

Demelza looked at her.

Caroline said: 'Almost the only consoling feature of my married life is that Horace, who viewed Dwight at first with sick resentment, has now taken to him in a most amazing fashion. Dwight can make the fat little beast do *tricks* – believe it or not, at *his* age! He will sit up and beg for a sweet and, when given it by Dwight – but only by Dwight – will hold it in his mouth while he rolls over on his back, until he's given permission to eat it!'

Demelza said: 'Dwight has a habit of being able to induce people to do what he wants.'

'I know. I have to be constantly on my guard. What do you

make of his looks?'

'A little more better. But he is still pale.'

'And as thin as a shotten herring. He ministers to his own needs, of course. But even if he consented to be doctored by another, I know no surgeon or apothecary within the Duchy that I'd trust him to.'

'When the warm weather comes it will make a difference. This summer –'

'He's so vilely conscientious, Demelza. It was after Christmas before I could get him to apply for his discharge from the navy. Though he sympathizes with the Frenchies, he is still prepared to fight them! . . . And now, in spite of anything I say, he's preparing to resume his doctoring at full stretch. I *hate* to see him going among the sick and think of what putrid infection he may chance to pick up from among them!'

'Surely it is only a little time he needs, Caroline. He has only been out of the prison a few months and will recover his strength in a while. I know how you must feel but there is no way out for you, is there? Men are headstrong.'

'Like horses that have never been broken,' said Caroline.

They clopped along while a chill night breeze soughed around them.

Demelza said: 'It must take time.'

'What?'

'For someone like Dwight to recover. He is lucky to be alive. Lieutenant Armitage suffers from his sight, he tells me. Trying to read in the half dark –'

'His poor sight did not seem to prevent Lieutenant Armitage from looking at you today. If I were Ross I should keep you under lock and key for a while.'

'Oh, Caroline, what nonsense you do talk! It was nothing more than –'

'My dear, I verily believe that if you and I walked together into a roomful of eligible men, they would immediately all look at me; but in five minutes they would all come to be clustered round you! It is an enviable complaint, for which I think there is no remedy.'

'Thank you, but it's not so. Or only with some . . .' Demelza gave a brief laugh which came to have a tremor in it. 'Sometimes I don't have half enough influence with those that matter to me.' She pointed with her crop at one of the figures riding ahead.

'They're a plaguey couple,' Caroline agreed.

'But Dwight – I will try on Dwight. Next time he comes to see Jeremy or Clowance. It's not right that he should risk too much too soon. You have so recent come to harbour. If you think – '

'He knows what I think. But another still small voice might help to impress him with its importance . . .'

A shooting star moved lazily across the sky and some night bird twittered as if alarmed at the sight. Dwight's horse shook its head and shivered in its nostrils, anxious to be home.

Dwight said: 'You will tell Demelza?'

'Of course.'

'What will she think?'

'If there is one unpredictable thing in the world it is what Demelza will think about anything.'

'You're sure refusal is the right course?'

'How could it be anything else?'

'Such a position could offer you great opportunities.'

'For self-advancement?'

'For exercising an influence in the world. And in you I know it would be a moderating influence.'

'Oh, yes. Oh, yes. If I could call my soul my own.'

'Well, hasn't Basset said – '

'Besides, I don't fancy being elected for Truro as a sort of puppet, representing Truro's resentment at George Falmouth's treatment of them. If the revolt were successful and I went in, I should feel that any personal merit I may possess was not involved at all. If it were unsuccessful I should feel even more humiliated. Of course I owe nothing to the Boscawens; whether I offend them is neither here nor there. But I would owe something to a patron who would not be above driving a hard bargain in the end.'

'Basset is the most enlightened of the landed gentry around here.'

'Yes, but he uses his power for his own ends. And he is strangely nervous about his own countrymen.'

'It goes a long way back,' Dwight said drily. 'Magna Charta was designed to free the barons from tyranny, not ordinary folk.'

They jogged on in silence. Ross was pursuing thoughts of his own. He said: 'Demelza tells me I sentimentalize about the poor. It is a dangerous habit in one who has always had a full belly. I doubt not that good and ill are evenly spread throughout the classes . . . But that riot at Flushing which someone – Rogers – mentioned this afternoon, last month, you remember?'

'I remember.'

'D'you know what happened there? Verity, my cousin, wrote me about it. Some four hundred turned up in Flushing in a desperate temper and armed with sticks and clubs, all set to seize a cargo of grain just discharged from a ship, and looking very ugly about it. There were no warships in and no one to let or hinder them except a few men storing the grain – and well-furnished houses and genteel women ripe for the picking. But someone set a child with a fine voice upon a sack of corn and told him to sing a hymn. This he did, and presently one by one the men began to uncover their heads and join in the hymn with him – most of them being Methodists anyway. After it was done they all quietly turned about and tramped away, carrying nothing but their sticks and staves, home to Carnon or Bissoe or wherever they came from.'

After a moment or two Dwight said: 'When the history of this time comes to be written, I wonder if it will be looked on as the history of two revolutions. The French Revolution and the English – or Methodist – revolution. One seeks liberty, equality and fraternity in the eyes of men; the other seeks liberty, equality and fraternity in the eyes of God.'

'That's an even profounder remark than it seems,' Ross said. 'And yet I find myself fighting one and suspicious of the other. Human nature is abominable, even one's own.'

'I think the truth,' Dwight said, 'is that man is never perfectable. So he fails always in his ideals. Whichever way he directs his aims, Original Sin is there to confound him.'

They were approaching Bargus, where four parishes met. Ross said irritably: 'I could no more be Basset's creature than kiss a Frenchman! It's not that I think myself in any way better than the next — only that my neck is stiffer. As a petty squire I am my own man. As a Member of Parliament under the patronage of a great landowner, I could never be that, say what you will.'

'Sometimes, Ross, one accepts compromises in order to achieve a small part of a desired end.'

With a change of mood, Ross laughed. 'Then let me put your name forward to Sir Francis in place of mine. After all, you are now a larger landowner than I, and much richer!'

Dwight said: 'I know that everything of Caroline's now belongs to me, but that is a quirk of law I intend to ignore. No, Ross, I shall argue no longer. I was simply trying to put the other side. There are good men in the House as well as venal ones — Basset himself, I would say, Pitt too, Burke, Wilberforce, many others. In any event . . .'

'What were you going to say?'

'This is where we part. Would you like our man to come with you the rest of the way?'

'Thank you, no, I have a pistol. What were you going to say?'

'It was but a passing thought . . . I understand when you refused the bench, George Warleggan was offered the seat in your place. I was going to say that happily there can be no risk of its happening in this instance, George being so interested in keeping in with the Boscawens.'

CHAPTER VI

An itinerant tinker selling and repairing pots and pans came round Wheal Grace Mine one day and said he had a message for the brothers Carne. He had been in Illuggan last week and brother Willie had had an accident and was like to lose both legs. Widow Carne had asked him to pass on the word. When Sam came up the message was given him, so he asked for the following day off to go and see them.

When he left he bore with him not only a few things for his own family but some for the Hoskins too. Peter entrusted him

with three shillings – asking Sam not to tell his wife – half a
pound of butter and six eggs. Sam reached Illuggan by mid
afternoon and found, as perhaps he should have expected,
that the message had become garbled on its way from mouth
to mouth. It was not Willie but Bobbie Carne who had been
injured; Bobbie had fallen from a kibble or bucket as it was
going down a shaft, and he was suffering from head and chest
injuries, his legs having no hurt at all.

Sam ate a meagre supper with them listening to his stepmother's tiring voice – it was a voice made for complacency
but driven by circumstance into complaint. Her nest-egg was
steadily being encroached on by the needs of the family she
had married into. Luke was wed and away, but three of the
brothers were still home, and she had one child of her own.
Moreover John, the fourth boy, had recently married – the
new, rather sulky and very pregnant wife was there – and who
knew how many extra mouths there might yet be to feed?

Sam slept on the floor beside his injured brother and spent
the following morning with him, then started for Poole on his
other mission, having left his last week's earnings for the
widow.

A rabble of Hoskins lived in a cottage in a scarred valley
between two disused chimney stacks on the track between
Poole and Camborne. They were an average family, none of
them shiftless but lacking the capacity to make the best of
bad conditions. Poverty can be endured if it is endured with
pride. They worked where and when they could and were
good workers, but they had no initiative. Sam sat for a while
in the kitchen talking to the older ones while the half-naked
children played on the floor, which was inches thick in dirt
and cinders. Then, having passed on Peter's presents, and
having said a prayer, he was about to leave, when John,
Peter's eldest brother, came in with another man from a
meeting. Sam knew the other man – who was called Sampson:
'Rosie' Sampson was his nickname because of his florid face –
and thought him something of a malcontent.

To Sam's mild questions, after the greetings, John Hoskin
said, no, they had *not* been to a prayer meeting, and grinned
and looked at his friend and added no more. But 'Rosie'
Sampson said:

'Well, tis no secret! There's no reason to be secret wi' Sam. We been to a meeting 'gainst the millers and the corn factors. Wi' wheat at two guineas the bushel they'm still holding on to it, waiting for it to climb higher! While folk be in want and starvation, the millers d'live in plenty, the corn stacked in their 'ouses! Tis wicked, wicked, and we d'need to do something 'bout'n!'

Peter's father said: 'Ye'll get no good outcome from taking measures into your own hands, Rosie Sampson. Nor you, John. Tis danger, that way. Two year back—'

'I know, I know, two year back, the soldiers,' said 'Rosie'. 'But they're gone and bye. There's no soldiers in the county to speak of. And what do we want? Not revolution but justice. Food at a fair price. Work at a fair wage. So's to keep our wives and our young alive. What's wrong wi' that?'

'Naught wrong wi' it,' said Peter's father, 'tis but right 'n proper. But ye d'need to keep within the law, whether or no. Soldiers may be gone. But these yur Volunteers, all over the county; mebbe they was formed to keep out the Frenchy, but there's other uses for they. They'd like as not ride to save the millers.'

'And d'you know what?' John Hoskin said to his father. 'D'you know what? Miners of St Just be talking of the forming of a *miners'* army to keep the Volunteers quiet. See? One 'gainst th'other. Not for revolution. Nay, but for justice. Justice for all!'

Being a man to whom the next world was all-important and this a transitory life of less significance, Sam had little in common with people who talked of breaking the law. But he walked home troubled, sympathizing with the distress though believing that their way of attempting to alleviate it was wrong. Yet he knew he could not have said so in that company without exciting derision. They were in the gall of bitterness and in spite of their professed religion were yet estranged from God. 'Through hidden dangers, toil and death, Thou, Lord, hast gently cleared my way.' He prayed aloud as he walked that all people should be saved from the hidden dangers of riot and violence and that the way should be clear for them to a new realization of the mercy and forgiveness of Christ.

II

When Sam went in Drake was shoeing a horse for Mr Vercoe, the Preventive man, and Sam sat on a log by the gate watching the scene until it was done and Vercoe rode off. Each time Sam called at Pally's Shop he noticed that more had been accomplished to improve the place, to tidy the yard, to repair the fences and to clean up the fields. As the days were lengthening more could be done. Sam wished he could see a similar improvement in the new blacksmith. Drake worked without stop from dawn to dusk, but there were still too many lonely dark hours to endure, and he had not yet found a pleasant way to endure them. Nor did he show any interest in the local girls or the bal-maidens, most of whom would have been all too happy to marry a good-looking young tradesman. Indeed with a small but unencumbered property and an old and honourable trade at his finger-tips, he had become the 'catch' of the neighbourhood.

Sam worked the bellows while Drake hammered out an iron stave. Among the clanging and the sparks he told his brother where he had been.

'Poor Bobbie! D'you think he'll come brave and well again?'

'They believe he have come to no mortal hurt, thanks be to God.'

'I thought you were early from core. Twas good of you to go but you should have left me know. I'd have come with you.'

'You've customers to tend,' Sam said, looking around. 'Be away a day, someone'll call, think that's no good and go else-where.'

With a forearm which remained obstinately pale Drake wiped the sweat from his forehead. 'Ye've missed a core at the mine? Leave me pay you for that. I've more'n I need here.'

'Nay, I make do, boy. You'll need all you make here for a while yet . . . But the good Lord has set you in pleasant places – '

'Cap'n Poldark done that . . . I got a letter last week, Sam . . .'

A shadow passed across Sam's face, for he dreaded always that Morwenna might write.

'. . . from Geoffrey Charles.'

This was close home but to be preferred to the other.

'He say he's doing brave at Harrow, and he's longing to see me when summer come.'

'I doubt his father will give him leave.'

'Stepfather. They've not been back at Trenwith yet. The less truck I have with they the better, but Geoffrey Charles may come and go as he pleases – '

Among Drake's earliest purchases was an old cracked ship's bell that he'd bought for a few pence in St Ann's; it now hung over the entrance to the yard so that a customer might draw attention to himself if Drake were working in the fields. Someone now started drawing attention to themselves in no uncertain fashion. Drake went to the door. Sam, following more slowly, heard a woman's laugh that he instantly and painfully recognized.

'Wheelwright Carne! Finished that job for us, have ee? Two weeks gone since I brought'n in . . . My dear life and body, Parson Carne too! Did I break in on a praying feast? Shall I call again Friday?'

Emma Tregirls, black hair shredding in the breeze, pink cotton frock caught at the waist with a red velvet belt, heavy black shoes smeared with mud; skin glinting in the sun, eyes alive with animal vitality.

'Tis all ready for ee,' Drake said. 'I made a new arm. Twas no dearer than to repair the old, and there'll be a longer life to him.'

She came in and stood arms folded while Drake lifted out a heavy wooden bar with an iron crook on the end. Sam said nothing to her, and after her first taunt she said nothing to him, but watched Drake.

She was a little piqued at finding the older brother there. Two weeks ago, on her afternoon off, she had visited her brother Lobb who ran his tin stamp at the bottom of Sawle village near the Guernseys and found him with part of a broken lifting bar, and about to put it over his shoulder and carry it to the blacksmith in Grambler for repair. But as usual he was coughing hard and worried about his old rupture, so she had said she would take it instead. At the top of Sawle Combe she had turned right instead of left. It was a deal

farther to Pally's Shop but she had heard Pally had sold out
and a handsome young wheelwright now worked there on his
own, so she thought she would look him over.

This she had done, though not with noticeable effect so far
as he was concerned. She was quite impressed with his looks
but piqued that for once in her young life her own looks
seemed to go unnoticed. He treated her with courtesy, and
soberly, walking with her to the gate when she left; but there
was no 'look' in his eye at all; she might have been thirty.
It didn't please Emma.

Now she was back to test out the temperature of the water
again; and here was his bible-spouting brother to spoil it all!
Indeed the bible-spouting brother was looking at her with
more interest, she was certain, than the wheelwright, though
how much concern was for her body and how much for her
soul she couldn't be sure.

She took out her purse and paid, the coins clinking and
glinting as she put them in Drake's hand. Then she gave a
heave and hoisted the heavy bar on her shoulder and prepared
to leave.

'You be going Sawle, mistress?' Sam said. 'I'm going that
way. I'll carry him for you. That's too great a weight for a
maid.'

Emma hooted with laughter. 'I brought'n here! What's the
difference?'

'Tis time I left, Drake,' Sam said soberly. 'I mustn't miss
Meeting tonight. There's none to carry on if I be away.'

Emma said: 'Giss along! I'm so strong as you any day of
the week. Reckon I could wrastle you down, if twas not
considered unladylike to take hold of a man. Dear life!'

Sam said: 'I'll come over next week, Drake. There'll be
little done feast day. I'll be over then.'

'Yes, Sam. When you please. I'm here all day and all night.'

Sam said: 'Leave me take him from you, mistress. Tis no
weight for a maid.'

Wide-eyed with amusement, Emma put her shoulder against
Sam's and allowed him to transfer the weight. Then she rubbed
her shoulder where the weight had rested and looked at Drake.

'Reg'lar gent, your parson brother, edn ee. Think he'll convert me, eh? What do *you* think, Wheelwright?'

Drake said: 'You may laugh at Sam, mistress, but you'll never make him shamed of his goodness.'

Emma shrugged. 'There, now. There's words for ee. Well, come 'long, Parson, now. We'd best be off home.'

III

Neither spoke for a while as they went. The tall sturdy girl walked beside the taller sturdier man. The strong breeze was from the north-east so that it blew the hair away from her face showing the clean bold lines; it also made her frock cling to her so that you could see the fullness of her breasts, the tightness of the waist, the curving swell of her thighs. After one startled glance Sam kept his eyes averted.

She said: 'Don't Brother have any taking for girls, Preacher?'

'Ah, tedn't that.'

'I reckon he has no taking for me.'

Sam hesitated, wondering whether to say more. But it was well known. She had only to ask elsewhere.

'Drake had a great taking for another young woman. But she were not for him.'

'Why not?'

'They weren't – matched. She was of a different station in life. She's wed now.'

'Huh? Still grieving, is he?'

'That's so.'

'What a brock! I'd see no man weeping long over me! Hah! Nor me over they! Life's too short, Preacher. Well . . . so he d'want no girl but the one he cann't have, eh? Well . . . Tes a pretty picture, I'll say that. And you?'

'Me?' said Sam, startled.

'God didn't say ye couldn't marry, did he?'

'No . . . When the time comes, mebbe . . . Er – that's not the way, Emma. That's over Warleggan land.'

She looked at him. 'Oh, so ye d'know what I'm named . . . This is the short cut. It d'cut off all Grambler village.'

'I know. But they don't like folk on Trenwith land. I been stopped before.'

Emma smiled, showing her teeth. 'I always d'go this way. Have no fear. Whilst you're wi' me, Parson, I'll protect ee.'

Sam still wanted to protest, but she had already climbed the stile and was walking on. He followed, with her load on his shoulder. It was odd, he thought, the last time he'd come this way he'd been shouldering another load with Drake, and in the copse ahead they had first met Morwenna Chynoweth and Geoffrey Charles Poldark. The commencement of all that trouble.

'D'you know my other name?' Emma asked.

'Tregirls.'

'And d'you know Father? A rare old lickerish devil, he be. Found a cosy nest wi' Sally Chill-Off now, he has. Hope he rots.'

Sam was shocked and wasn't quite sure how to answer. True, he had never liked or admired his own father but he had tried dutifully to love him, which was a different thing, and would certainly never have uttered words like these.

Emma looked at him and laughed. 'Don't hold wi' that talk, eh? Honour thy father and thy mother . . . I know. But this father deserted us when Lobb were twelve and I were six. We was brought up in Poor House, Lobb and me. Then Tholly come back looking to be a father again after leaving us fend for ourselves for thirteen year. We toldn' to go drown his self.'

'Forgiveness in Christ is a noble virtue,' Sam said.

'Aye, no doubt. D'ye know he laid hands on me behind a hedge last month, Tholly did. What d'ye think on that, Parson? Want me to show that sort of forgiveness, do ee? I says, no, Father, I says, when I want that there's young men in plenty about; betterer than an old devil wi' one arm, I says, as deserted Mother and we, when we was all young!'

Sam shifted the lifting bar to the other shoulder. Emma was not even seeking the shelter of the wood but was skirting it to take an even shorter cut which would bring them within sight of Trenwith House. There were two men in the distance. This was trouble, and it was the sort of trouble Sam had particularly wanted to avoid after all the upsets of last year. He recognized one of the men coming towards them as Tom Harry, the younger of the two Harry brothers, who were not only gamekeepers but particular creatures of Mr Warleggan.

Emma said: 'Lobb is always ailing. He was sent prison when he was seventeen for stealing apples, and the treadmill double ruptured him, so he d'look athurt at the world. And what wi' five childer I go over now'n then on my off day t'see how they be . . . Well, Tom, ye old hummock, been working hard all day watching the pheasants, 'ave ee?'

Tom Harry was a burly man with a heavy red face, the less ugly of the two brothers, but for all that formidable in a blunted unreasoning way, a brute force controlled by an intelligence that only recognized absolutes. He grinned at Emma, his eyes prepared to ogle, but sharply frosting as they glanced at Sam.

'Ere,' he said. 'What d'ye want? Be off afore I have ee throwed off. Jack, get this labbat off of our land and see 'e stays off.'

'Sam Carne's carren that lifting bar for me!' Emma said sharply. 'It belong to brother Lobb, and if Sam hadn't carried it I'd've had to!'

Tom looked her up and down, his eyes appreciating what the wind was doing to her frock.

'Well, Emma, ye'll need 'im no longer, for I shall carry it for ee from 'ere right into Lobb's 'ands. Now off with you, Carne.'

Emma said: 'Sam's brought'n this far, Tom Harry, and he'll go the rest of the way. Why should you have the good for it?'

Tom stared at her and then at his companion, and then at Sam, his brain working slowly.

'Off with ee, Carne. Or I'll give ee a hiding. Time's finished when worms like you can crawl over Warleggan land. Jack! –'

'Lay hand on him,' said Emma, 'and I'll never speak to you again. So ye may take your choice!'

Another pause while the matter was thought over.

Tom Harry said: 'You still my girl?'

'So much as ever I was, no more'n no less. I'm not your property yet, nor never will be neither if ye say I can't come acrost your land . . .'

'I always said *you* could! Mind that, I always said *you* could. But this . . .'

A short wrangle ensued, during which the second man glanced vacantly from one speaker to the other. Throughout the whole encounter Sam had remained unspeaking, staring out towards the sea. Presently it was over and the girl and her new escort were allowed to pass on. They walked away in silence until they reached Stippy Stappy Lane which led down to Sawle. Then Emma laughed.

'See? It was easy, see? They do what I tell 'em to do, see?'

'That true, what he said?' Sam asked.

'What?'

'You be his girl?'

'We-ll . . .' She laughed again. 'Just what I said. More or less. He d'want me to wed him.'

'What shall you say?'

'Ah, that depend, don't it. Tedn't the first offer ever I had.'

'Nor like to be the last.'

She glanced at him. 'As I see 'n, Sam, girl's only strength be when she have men dandling on a string. Once they get her, then she's got. String be round *her* neck then. Come 'long, do's you're told, bear the childer, moole the bread, sweep the planchin, teel the ground; tes like that all the time from bedding night to burying night. So I don't see's I can improve my lot by wedden anyone just yet awhile.'

Sam thought of the rumours current about this girl. He felt deeply drawn towards her, both as a woman and as a soul worth saving. Yet he knew that if he spoke of his spiritual interest in her it would be greeted with her usual derisive laughter. They went down the steep hill until they reached the broken-down cottages and the fish sheds at the bottom. There was a tremendous stink of decaying fish, though pilchards never came till summer. Some lads had been out fishing, and a quarrelsome flutter of seagulls marked where offal and bones had been left. But the smell was never absent; nor was it wholly of fish.

To the right of the gravel track a last tin stamp made use of the final trickle of water called Mellingey Leat, and it was towards this that Emma led the way.

Sam had been here before, for it was here that Betty Carkeek lived, who was a recent convert to his flock; but Lobb Tregirls, who lived in the next hut, Sam had never met, and he was startled when he saw a pale, wizened man, bent from the waist, hair thin and greying, who looked nearer fifty than the twenty-six or seven he must be if Emma was to be believed. Around him a brood of young children worked or grovelled according to their ages, half clothed, with stork-like legs and arms. Their mother was out on the beach gathering seaweed.

Emma arrived like a breath of laughter and good health, indicating Sam and telling of his help; and Lobb shook his hand and nodded and went to stop the stamp and asked Sam right away to help him fit the rod. While this was being done Lobb spoke hardly a word, and Sam did as he was told, while occasionally lifting a glance at the pink cotton frock and the fluttering black hair as it moved across the beach to greet a sister-in-law.

In about half an hour the rod was in place and Lobb pulled over the lever to divert the water back to the water-wheel. Sam watched interestedly to see the frail fall of water gradually bring the great wheel into motion again. The wheel activated a metal drum which had raised keys on it at intervals, for all the world like a musical box, but these keys instead of creating music lifted and let fall at varying intervals a series of twelve giant rods which when they fell helped to crush the crude ore-bearing ground tipped into the chute from above as it slithered or was shovelled down. Below this the water was utilized again to work a sweep which allowed the tin to settle and brushed away the lighter earth as it turned.

Lobb said: 'Reckon I'm obliged to ee, Carne. Are ee one of Emma's men?'

'No,' said Sam.

'Reckon she's besting what man t'ave. Tes wise. She'll get caught if she don't. Many a maid's forced put for less'n she's done.'

Sam stared out to sea. 'Reckon tis time I was going.'

Seldom in late years had he felt so awkward as he had done among these Tregirls. With the Hoskins there could be disagreement over the rights of miners to take the law into their own hands, but if they had so argued they would have been arguing from the same basic beliefs, differing as to how they should be applied. Not so here. Seldom had his language in a single afternoon so noticeably lacked the rich and colourful phrases of the Testaments to which he subscribed his life. It was not that they were not pertinent – rather was it as if he might have spoke the English language to people who

knew only Chinese. He was among heathens to whom the
word of the Gospel signified nothing at all. The sentences
meant nothing, the phrases meant nothing, the words meant
nothing. For the time it was better to save one's breath.

'Ullo,' said Lobb, glowering. 'Look oo's 'ere.'

A man on a donkey was coming down the hill. He wore a
wide-brimmed hat; his legs dangled so low that they reached
the floor; the reins were gathered in one skinny powerful hand,
the other arm lay across the saddle and ended in an iron hook.
His face was lined but twinkling.

'Fathur,' said Lobb with great contempt. 'I want no truck
with he.'

'Even if ye can't abide him,' Sam said, 'should ye not go
down and greet him?'

'Look,' said Lobb, 'tis no business of yourn.'

'I know he deserted you. Emma told me.'

'When he left, we all went Poor House. Know what that's
like, do ee? That's what he left Mother to. Now he d'come
round here smarming and bringing his presents . . . I can't
bear to speak with un. Go if you've the mind, Carne. I'm
obliged for the 'elp.'

When Sam got down Tholly was already off his donkey
and holding a bag with his hook while he delved into it with
his good hand.

'See, I had a morsel of luck Redruth this morn, so I brought
ye a few little things, like. Now how 'bout these here.' He
pulled out a pair of leather breeches and held them up. 'Won't
fit me. Thought they'd do for Lobb. Three shillings and sixpence I paid for 'em. Mint of money, that. They got years of
wear yet, years of wear.'

'Thank ee, Uncle Tholly,' said Mary Tregirls, a bedraggled
thin woman who might have been pretty not so long ago.
'I'll tell Lobb when he come down from the wheel.'

'Lo, Lobb!' shouted Tholly, undeterred by the enmity. 'I
brought something for Mary too!' He glanced at Sam. 'Drake
Carne's brother, ain't it? Peter, ain't it?'

'Sam,' said Sam.

'Sam Carne, eh? Been helping Lobb, have ee? We all try
to help Lobb when he'll leave folk help him. Emma, me little
apple-bird; looking as docy as ever, I see.'

'I'd best be going, Emma,' Sam said. 'I did ought to be home 'fore six. You're – you not coming yet?'

'No,' said Emma. To her father: 'What ee got for Mary?'

He delved in. 'See here. Warm petticoat. Four shilling it cost! That's seven and six for the two! Don't say your old father never give you nothing, now! I near bought a bonnet for you, Emma, but twas more'n I could run to.' He coughed horribly into the air, fine spray glinting in the sunlight. 'Peter!' he said as Sam turned away.

'Sam,' said Sam.

'Course. I'm absent as a fool. Sam, you a wrastler?'

Sam hesitated. 'Nay. Why?'

'Feast day next week there's to be wrastling. I'm getting up a match. You're big and handsome. Never wrastled?'

'Only as a lad.'

'Well, then!'

'Nay. Tis not my style. No longer.' He smiled at Tholly to soften his blunt refusal. 'Goodbye, Emma.'

'Goodbye,' said Emma. 'You should've brought *food*, Fathur, not clothes for their backs!'

'Aye, aye, is that all the thanks I get? Next time I'll buy something for my own back! Sam!'

'Yes?' Sam stopped again.

'You interested in bull pups? I got two proper little beauties. Handsome, handsome. Last of a litter. I'd let one of 'em go cheap to a friend. Fine for the baiting! In a year –'

'Thanks.' Sam shook his head. 'Thanks, no,' and walked on.

As he retreated he could hear them arguing among themselves about Tholly's gifts, while Lobb remained obstinately aloft tinkering with his water-wheel.

They were all Tregirls he had left behind, he thought – all nine of them: a mixed bag of heathens; quarrelsome, vital, grudging, grasping, noisy and ragged, and altogether unawakened in their sins. While all were worth the saving, since every soul was precious in the sight of Heaven, yet to Sam only Emma seemed to show a gleam of hope. And that gleam might as yet be more within his own soul than hers.

Although she was a sinner, as all creatures were, he found it difficult after their walk and talk today to believe the worst that was said of her. She was so straightforward, so direct, so bright and clear of eye and manner, that he found it hard to believe she was any man's game. But even if she were, the Biblical analogy that had occurred to him in the mine that day still held good.

But how to bring her to repentance? How make a person aware of sin when their unawareness was so complete? It was something for which he must pray for guidance.

CHAPTER VII

Another man who was praying for guidance at this time, though on matters very unrelated to those concerning Sam, was the Reverend Osborne Whitworth. He had two problems exercising his mind, one moral and one temporal.

It was eight weeks now since Dr Behenna had told Osborne that he must forgo intercourse with Morwenna until after the baby was born.

'You're a heavy man, Mr Whitworth, if I may say so, and every time this happens now you risk crushing the child to death. I am not altogether satisfied with Mrs Whitworth's health, and certainly she needs extra rest and care at this time.'

Ossie had reluctantly acceded. He saw the point, of course, and he did not want to injure the child in case it happened to be a son; but this imposed a restraint on him that irked more with every week that passed. He had, of course, suffered the same deprivation during the confinements of his first wife; but those disentitlements had been of a shorter duration than this one was likely to be, and somehow the loving and kissing and petting which had still been permissible had made the time bearable.

But the idea of kissing and petting with a woman who shrank from his touch and shrank from touching him was clearly an impossibility. So he was deprived of the normal routine association with a woman that a married man had a right to expect, and he found continence a heavy cross to bear. He found it more hard to bear than he would otherwise have done because of the presence of another woman in the house.

Rowella, of course, was a child. She would not be fifteen until May. All the same she was as tall as a woman and walked and spoke like a woman and sat at his meals like a woman, and sometimes smiled secretly at him like a woman. He didn't particularly fancy her looks – the long nose, the sandy eyebrows, the thin shapeless figure. Indeed, merely to consider her in a physical sense was nonsense and sinful nonsense at that. But the two maids in the house were elderly women, his wife a quiet sad figure with a bulging belly, and Rowella shone in this company with a youthful attraction.

Of course there were places in Truro down by the river where he could buy his pleasure – where he had been several times during his widowerhood – and these he patronized once or twice. But it was a dangerous game in a town of three thousand inhabitants; however disguised by heavy cloak, by taking off the clerical collar, by walking swiftly through the dark streets after nightfall. Someone might recognize him and report him to his wardens; someone might even *rob* him and then what redress? The woman herself might recognize him and attempt some sort of blackmail.

It was an increasingly difficult time for him.

His second problem was a matter of advancement, and could be discussed more appropriately with others. Eventually he took it to George.

He found Mr Warleggan in his counting house discussing some matter of credit with his uncle, Mr Cary Warleggan, and it was some half-hour before George was free to attend to him. Thereupon Osborne put his case.

Two weeks ago the Reverend Philip Webb, vicar of the parish of St Sawle-with-Grambler, had died of an impostume of the kidneys; and so the living had become vacant. This living Osborne desired for himself.

The living, Osborne pointed out, was worth £200 a year. Mr Webb, as they all knew, had lived in London and Marazion and had seldom visited the church, the Reverend Mr Odgers having been installed as a curate at £40 a year to conduct the business of the parish. Osborne felt that this was an excellent opportunity for him to add to his own income and had written to the Dean and Chapter of Exeter, in whose gift it lay, applying for the living. He had also written to his uncle, Godolphin, who was an influence at court, to put in a word for him. What Osborne thought was that if George were to write to the Dean and Chapter also it might be just enough to sway their choice.

George considered this unemotionally while Ossie was speaking. It was a natural enough ambition and a natural enough request, yet he resented it. Although the marriage of Elizabeth's cousin to this young man had been his idea and he had pushed it through in spite of various obstacles, not to mention Morwenna's objections, yet he found himself holding the young man in some distaste. His manner of dressing was too flamboyant for a parson, his voice too assertive, too important; George remembered the long haggling they had had over terms. Ossie had to keep in mind – and didn't seem sufficiently to realize – that although his marriage into the family linked the important name of Godolphin with that of Warleggan, he, financially, was small fry, as all the Whitworths – and indeed the Godolphins – were these days. A greater deference would have been suitable on the part of the younger man towards an older and much richer man who had befriended him.

Also Elizabeth, George knew, was not pleased with Morwenna's looks; the girl had gone more sallow than ever and her eyes were specially dark these days as if brooding on an inner tragedy. Most girls when they had made a loveless but advantageous marriage quickly adapted themselves and made the best of things. So Morwenna should. George had no patience with her. But Elizabeth blamed Ossie. Elizabeth said Ossie was a nasty young man, not an ornament to the church at all. When challenged to go into detail she shrugged her pretty shoulders and said it was nothing definite she knew – for Morwenna would never say anything – it was just a general feeling that had been growing in her bones over the last year.

So, when Osborne had finished, George said nothing for a time but turned the money in his fob and stared through the lattice window.

Eventually he said: 'I doubt that my influence with the Dean and Chapter is as great as you suppose.'

'Not great,' said Osborne practically. 'But as the owner of the old Poldark estate at Trenwith you are the biggest landowner in the parish, and this will count with the Dean, I'm sure.'

George looked at the young man. Osborne never phrased his sentences well. 'Not great'. 'The old Poldark estate'. If he wrote in this fashion to the Dean it was not likely to commend him. Yet Ossie was now part of the family. George did not like to think he had made a bad choice. And if things went as they now appeared to be going, a fashionable friend in London, one specially with an entrée at court, such as Conan Godolphin had, could be of considerable value to a new Member of Parliament, groping his way at Westminster, not quite sure of his social position or friends.

'I'll write. You have the address?'

'I just address my letters to the Dean and Chapter at Exeter. There's no need for more.'

'How is Morwenna?'

Ossie raised his eyebrows at the diversion. 'I could wish her better. It will be good when it is out of the way.'

'When is it to be?'

'About another month, she thinks. But women so often make mistakes. George, when you write, will you point out to the Dean that from my residence in Truro it will be easier for me to oversee Odgers than ever it was for Webb to do so, and even to preach there occasionally when I stay at your house.'

George said: 'Osborne, it is possible that I may be going to London later this year. When you next write to your uncle you might inform him that I shall expect to give myself the pleasure of waiting on him then.'

Ossie blinked, shaken out of his preoccupation by the steeliness of George's Warleggan's tone.

'Of course, George. I'll do that. Shall you be going for a prolonged stay?'

'It depends. Nothing is decided.'

There was silence for a moment or two. Ossie got up to go.

'The extra income would be more than useful now there is another mouth to feed.'

'I believe little Odgers had not had his stipend raised for more than ten years,' George said.

'What? Oh, no. Well . . . It is a matter I should be prepared

to consider – though in the country he is on very little expense,
I would have thought.'

George rose also and glanced back into his office, where
two clerks were working, but he did not speak.

'I'm writing to Lord Falmouth too,' Ossie said. 'Although he
has no direct interest he is generally so influential. I also considered approaching your friend Sir Francis Basset, although
I have not actually had an opportunity of meeting him. At the
Enys's wedding – '

'I think both those gentlemen will be too preoccupied over
the next weeks to have the time to pay attention to your
request,' George said shortly. 'You are better to save your ink.'

'D'you mean over this by-election? Have you heard whom
Lord Falmouth is favouring?'

'None of us will know until much nearer the time,' George
said.

II

That night Ossie made a very distressing discovery.

After Morwenna had gone to bed he went up to the lumber
room to find an old sermon which he thought would serve as
a basis for the one he had to deliver on Sunday. He found it
and was about to leave the room when a gleam of light
showed that there was a flaw in the wooden partition dividing
this room from the one where Rowella slept. He tiptoed across
and peered through, but the blue flock paper on the other
side blocked his view. Taking a pin out of the sheets of the
sermon, he inserted it and very carefully made a hole. Through
it he saw Rowella in a white nightdress brushing her long
lank hair.

Hastily dropping the pin, he tiptoed from the lumber room
and crept down to his study, where he sat for a long time
turning over the pages of his sermon without reading it.

III

Wednesday was the day on which Ross made a weekly inspection of Wheal Grace, along with Captain Henshawe. Since
the accident of May '93 he had never left anything to chance
or to the reports of other people.

This morning before they went down they had been intro-

ducing a surface change at the mine. Tin ore was loaded on
to mules for carting away to the stamps, and it had long been
the custom in the industry to fill one large sack with the ore-
bearing ground, which was lifted on the shoulders of one man
by two others, and the one man then carried it and threw it
across the back of the mule. But these sacks when filled
weighed about 360 lb., and twenty-five such mules were loaded
in such a way, often twice a day. Ross had known men
crippled as a result of bearing this weight, and proposed that
the new sacks when bought should be half the size and the
old ones as they wore out abandoned.

To his own surprise he met with opposition from the carriers
themselves, who were proud of their strength and suspicious
that if the new sacks were introduced more men would be
employed to earn less. It took Henshawe and himself the
best part of two hours to convince them that the change
would be for their own good. So it was past eleven before
the inspection of the mine got under way and nearly twelve
before they reached the tunnel that Sam Carne and Peter
Hoskin were driving south on the 40-fathom level.

Ross said: 'Neither of them working today?'

'Carne asked for the day off to visit his brother who has
injured both legs in a fall, so Hoskin is helping with the south
adit.'

'Sam's work is good? He does not let his religion interfere?
. . . Well, no, give them their due, they never do that. How
much further have they gone?'

'Twenty-two yards when I measured last week. They're in
hard ground and making little progress.'

Bent double, hat candles flickering in the dubious air, they
crawled to the end of the tunnel, where a shattered end and a
pile of rubble showed the extent of the digging.

Ross squatted down, staring at the rock, rubbed it here and
there with a wet finger. 'There's mineral veins enough here
and spots of ore.'

'There's been that all along. You can see the stockwork
farther back.'

'Problem is you could open this up twenty feet west and
twenty feet east and still miss a lode channel by a fathom or
so. Think you it's worth going on with?'

'Well, we can't be too far now from the old runs of Wheal Maiden, sur. Since that was worked by your father, and profitable for a time, we can't be too far from some of those old lodes.'

'Well, yes, that was why we drove in this direction in the first place. But were any of the Maiden lodes as deep as forty fathoms?'

'Tis doubtful. And Maiden being on a hill . . .'

'Quite . . . This is hard, bitter ground. I don't like these vugs. I don't want to risk another fall.'

'Oh, there's small risk of that. You could chop a church out here and twould hold.'

'Is there anything better we can put them on if we take them off this?'

'Only shoring up Gradient Alley behind Trevethan and Martin.'

'Then leave them be for another month or so. I take it there's no risk of unwatering Maiden?'

'God forbid! Tis little likely. She was always a dry mine.'

They made their way back slowly the way they had come, and began to climb up the stepped, slanting ladders. A pinpoint of light slowly enlarged itself until it was a great mouth in the darkness; then they were out into the startling brilliance of a rainy day.

Ross stood talking with Henshawe for a few minutes more, noticing as he spoke that a horse was tethered near his house. A visitor? He narrowed his eyes but could not recognize the horse. Its colour was pale roan and it was finely groomed. Some new acquisition of Caroline's? Sir Hugh Bodrugan out courting again?

From here the fine rain was blowing across the beach like smoke. The waves were lifeless, the landscape without colour or form. Two of the three tin stamps in this valley were working; ears were so accustomed to the clatter and rhythmic thump that one had to make a conscious effort to hear them; the hay in the Long Field was thin this year. He must keep in touch with Basset about these farming experiments. That was if Basset wished to continue the friendship after his refusal of the nomination. It had gone off yesterday.

He had talked the matter over with Demelza first, and, true

to his prediction to Dwight, her reaction had been unexpected. She had been against his accepting the offer. Although he had already wholly made up his mind to refuse, her definite stand against it had, naturally if irrationally, irritated him.

He had said: 'You were so disappointed that I turned down a seat on the bench, which is a small thing, but you applaud my wish not to attempt to become a Member of Parliament, which is a great.'

A curl had fallen across her forehead as she wrinkled it.

'Ross, you must not expect always reason from me. Often it is what I feel, not what I think, and that sways me. But I'm not one for words.'

'Try,' he said. 'I have found you very much one for words most times.'

'Well, it is like this, Ross. I think you live on a knife edge.'

'A knife. Whatever do you mean?'

'A knife. The knife is what you think you ought to do, what your – your conscience or your spirit or your mind thinks you ought to do. And if you move away from that, stray from that – what's the word? – then you cut yourself.'

'Pray go on. I am wholly fascinated.'

'No, you must not laugh. You asked me to say what I meant, and I'm trying. As a justice you would have been on the bench and sat in judgement – isn't that right? – and helped with local laws. That I thought you could do – should do – and if you failed sometimes you yet would not have to bend. And it is the *duty* of a gentleman to help in this way. Isn't it? I would still like you to be that. But in Parliament, if what you say is true, would you not often, quite often, be asked to bend? . . .' She impatiently pushed back her hair. 'By bend I don't mean bow; I mean bend from what you think you ought to do.'

'Deviate,' Ross said.

'Yes. Is that it? Yes, deviate.'

'You make me sound very stern and noble.'

'I wish I could say it better. Not stern. Not noble. Though you can be those. But you oftentimes make me feel you're like a judge in court. And who's in the dock? *You.*'

Ross laughed. 'And who better to be there?'

Demelza said: 'Most men as they grow into middle life, it

appears to me, get more and more self-satisfied. But you every year get more and more unself-satisfied.'

'And is that your reason?'

'My reason is I want you to be happy, Ross, and doing things you enjoy doing – and working hard and living hard. What I don't want is to see you trying to do things you can't do and having to do things you don't agree with – and cutting yourself to pieces because of what you think is failure.'

'Give me a coat of armour and I'll be all right, eh?'

'Give you a coat of that sort of armour and I'd say accept!'

He had finished the conversation off by adding in some exasperation: 'Well, my dear, your summary of my virtues and failings may be quite correct; but in honesty I must confess it is not for any of *your* reasons, nor really for any of the reasons I have yet stated that I'm sure I'm right to refuse. The real crux of it is that I am not willing to be *anyone's* tame lapdog. I don't *belong* in the world of pretty behaviour and genteel fashion. For most of the time I'm happy enough, as you know, to observe the courtesies – and as I grow older and more of a family man and more prosperous, the impulse to – to kick against the traces becomes less and less. But – I reserve the *right*. I *want* to reserve the right. What I did last year in France is little different from what I did a few years before in England; but for one I am named a hero and for the other a renegade! Put me on a bench dispensing laws or in a parliament making them and I should feel the biggest hypocrite on earth!'

When he drew near the house he thought he remembered seeing the roan horse once before – last week – and he was correct.

As he went in Lieutenant Armitage rose. 'Why, Ross, I hoped to see you but feared I would not. I must leave shortly.'

They shook hands and made polite conversation. Demelza, looking slightly flushed – a circumstance so rare that Ross couldn't fail to notice it – said:

'Lieutenant Armitage has brought me over a plant from his uncle's garden. A rare new plant which he says should go against the library wall. It's a mag – what did you say?'

'Not strictly from my uncle's garden,' said Hugh Armitage. 'He ordered three and they came in pots and I persuaded him to part with one as a gift to the wife of the man who saved his nephew from a hellish captivity. I was talking to your wife of them when we met at Tehidy last week. They are best against a wall, being rather tender and coming from Carolina in the Americas.'

Ross said: 'Any new plant to Demelza is like a new friend, to be cosseted and cared for. But why must you go? Stay to dinner. It has been a long ride.'

'I have been invited to dine with the Teagues. I said I would be there by two.'

'Mrs Teague still has four unmarried daughters to dispose of,' Ross said.

Armitage smiled. 'So I have been told. But I think she'll be disappointed if she entertains hopes of that sort. Having just escaped from one prison I'm the less likely just yet to want to enter another.'

'A sour view of marriage,' Demelza said, smiling too.

'Ah, Mrs Poldark, I take a sour view of marriage only because I see so many of my friends bound in unions they find tedious and restricting. I don't take a sour view of love. For the overwhelming love of an Heloise, a Chloe, an Isolde. I would if need be jettison everything, even life. For life is a trumpery thing at best, isn't it? A few movements, a few words, between dark and dark. But in true love you keep company with the Gods.'

Demelza had coloured again. Ross said: 'I don't think Mrs Teague will be thinking along those lines.'

'Well,' Hugh Armitage said, 'I shall hope at least for a passable dinner.'

They went chatting to the door, examined again the fleshy, dark green, heavy-leafed plant standing in its cloam pot beside the step, admired his horse, promised they would come and see him some time when he could get his uncle free of this election nonsense, watched him mount and clatter over the bridge and wave at a turn of the valley.

When he was no more to be seen Ross looked round and found Demelza examining the plant.

'I forgot to ask its name again.'

'Mag, you said.'

'Mag something. Mag – was it lina?'

'Magdalen perhaps.'

'No. I shall never remember it now.'

'It looks much like a laurel to me. I wonder if it will flourish on this coast.'

'I don't see why not. Against a wall, he said.'

'Vegetation is different on the south coast. The soil is darker, less sandy.'

'Oh, well,' she stood up; 'we can try.'

As they went into the parlour Ross said: 'Does he touch you, my love?'

She half glanced up at him, with a glint of embarrassment. 'Yes . . .'

'Deeply?'

'A little. His eyes are so dark and sad.'

'They light up when they look at you.'

'I know.'

'So long as your eyes don't light up when you look at him.'

She said: 'Who were those people he mentioned? Heloise, was it? Isolde?'

'Legendary lovers. Tristan and Isolde I know. I can't remember who loved Heloise. Was it Abelard? My education was more practical than classical.'

'He lives in dreams,' Demelza said. 'Yet he isn't a dream. He's very real.'

'I rely on your wonderful common sense always to remember that.'

'Well . . . yes. What I try to remember is that he's so young.'

'What? Three, four years younger than you? That at most. I wouldn't look on it as an unbridgeable gap.'

'I wish twere more.'

'You'd like to be old? What an ambition!' He put his arm round her shoulders, and quickly she leaned against him. 'I see,' he commented. 'A tree in need of support!'

'Just a small matter shaken,' she said.

CHAPTER VIII

A week later two gentlemen were pacing slowly up and down the great parlour of Tregothnan House. It was a big room, rather shabby, panelled in cedar, the chairs Jacobean and uncomfortable; the coats of armour needed a polish, the battle flags, hung high up, had been the prey of moths. Four small Elizabeth cannon guarded the high, carved mantelshelf.

The two gentlemen had now been waiting nearly three hours. Regularly at each hourly interval a butler appeared with canary wine and biscuits. The two men were Mr William Hick, the mayor of Truro, and Mr Nicholas Warleggan, the smelter and banker. Both were in a nervous state, though it manifested itself in different ways. Mr Hick sweated, though the night was cool and the room cold. His handkerchief could well have been wrung out; he smelt of unwashed sweat which had been started into life by new excretions. Mr Warleggan preserved an exaggerated calm which was only betrayed by the clicking of his fingers.

'This is disgraceful,' said Hick, for the tenth time. He was not a man for original remarks, and the situation had long since exhausted his invention. 'Quite disgraceful. To be invited here for seven-thirty and him not here at ten! And no word! And the election tomorrow! It is altogether too bad!'

'It serves to implement and confirm our decision,' said Warleggan.

'What? Eh? Oh, yes. To be sure. Our decision.' Hick sweated afresh. 'To be sure.'

'You must calm yourself, my friend,' Warleggan said. 'You know what to say. There is nothing to fear. We are all free men.'

'Free men? Yes. But a person of the Recorder's stature and influence. This waiting makes it all so much worse.'

'It is not a question of the Recorder's stature or influence, Hick. It is a question of your being here to communicate to him a decision arrived at by us all. You are only the mouthpiece, communicating to him – Ah . . . I think perhaps we shall not now have to wait much longer . . .'

There were sounds outside – the neigh of a horse, footsteps, doors opening and shutting, footsteps and more voices. Presently another door slammed and silence fell on the house again.

They waited another quarter of an hour.

Then a footman appeared at the door and said: 'His Lordship will see you now.'

They were led across a high echoing hall into a smaller parlour where Lord Falmouth, in stained travelling clothes, was eating game pie.

'Ah, gentlemen,' he said, 'you have been kept waiting. Pray sit down. Join me in a glass of wine.'

Hick glanced at his companion, then uneasily took a seat at the far end of the table. Nicholas Warleggan followed suit, but waved away the wine with a polite gesture.

Falmouth said: 'I have come in some haste from Portsmouth. Last night I was with friends near Exeter. Business delayed my departure this morning, and I have had no time to sup on the way.'

'Well,' said Hick and cleared his throat noisily. 'Your Lordship will no doubt wish to discuss – '

'As you've both been kept waiting a considerable time,' Falmouth said, 'I need not delay you longer.' He then kept them waiting while he finished his mouthful of chicken and cut up another. 'Your new Member is to be Mr Jeremy Salter of Exeter. He comes of an old and distinguished family and he is the cousin to Sir Basil Salter, the High Sheriff of Somerset. He has some links with my family and was at one time Member for Arundel in Sussex. He is in every way suitable and will make an admirable stable mate for the other, sitting, Member, Captain Gower.' The next mouthful went in, and, following a gesture to the footman behind his chair, another slice of pie was put on his plate.

'The burgesses,' Hick began. 'The burgesses have been meeting several times during your absence, and – '

'Yes.' Falmouth felt in a pocket. 'Of course they'll want to know his full name. I have it here. Pray convey it to the burgesses first thing in the morning. They'll want it in time for the election.' He handed a sheet of paper to the footman, who passed it to Hick, who picked it up with fumbling fingers.

'And what of Mr Arthur Carmichael?' Warleggan said quietly.

'I saw him in Portsmouth. Yes, he might have been of advantage to Truro in his handling of naval contracts, but he was unsuitable in other ways.'

There was silence. Hick sweated into his wine.

Warleggan said: 'You may be surprised, Lord Falmouth, at my presence here with Mr Hick. Normally –'

'Not at all. You are most welcome. Now, gentlemen, I am, as you will understand, very tired, and you both have an hour's ride home –'

'Normally,' said Nicholas Warleggan, his voice persisting; 'normally Mr Hick would have come alone; but it is necessary to communicate to your Lordship a decision which was reached at a meeting of a group of the capital burgesses last night; and therefore it was felt that at least one other person should accompany the mayor this evening in order to confirm what he has to tell you.'

George Evelyn Boscawen, the third Viscount, poured himself another glass of wine and sipped it. He did not bother to raise his eyes.

'And what, Mr Hick, do you have to tell me that cannot wait for tomorrow?'

Hick sputtered a moment. 'A meeting, your Lordship, was convened at my house on Tuesday, and again last night, being attended by a large number of the burgesses of the town. At which, at which meetings considerable, considerable disagreements and dissension were expressed as to the method of choice by which a candidate was – was selected. As your Lordship will know, the corporation of Truro has for a vast number of years placed the most unreserved confidence in the Boscawen family and treated them with – with the highest marks of friendship and esteem. You, my Lord, and your esteemed uncle before you, have been the Recorder for the borough, and two gentlemen of your family were for several parliaments chosen as their representatives – chosen, I may say, in the most noble and disinterested manner, they being elected freely and uncorruptedly in a way which was honourable both to the voters and to themselves. But of late years – during the last parliament and before – '

'Come, Mr Hick,' Falmouth said curtly. 'What is this you are trying to tell me? I am tired and the hour is late. You have a very good candidate in Mr Jeremy Salter and there can be no conceivable obstacle to his being elected.'

Hick gulped at his wine. 'Had you – you, my Lord, been content with having two of your own family returned to parliament without expense or trouble, your influence would have remained as great as ever. Nor would it have been in the power of any person to put an end to it – '

'Who,' said Lord Falmouth, 'is suggesting – or indeed daring to suggest – that my influence has abated?'

Hick coughed and struggled with his voice. He preoccupied himself with wiping his face on his sodden handkerchief.

Nicholas Warleggan said: 'What Mr Hick is trying to say, my Lord, is that the corporation can no longer be treated like a chattel to be disposed of at your Lordship's will. It was so resolved last night and it will be so confirmed at the election tomorrow.'

There was a moment's dead silence. Lord Falmouth looked at Warleggan, then at Hick. Then he resumed his meal.

After no one had spoken for a while Warleggan went on: 'With due respect, my Lord, I will venture to affirm that nothing but your own strange, and, I make so bold as to say, improper and ungrateful treatment of the borough has caused this change in our feelings. The borough has always endeavoured to preserve its reputation for openness and independence; how can this be maintained if it is virtually sold by the Recorder to the highest bidder and the borough not informed until the night before the election whom it has to vote for? This is a prostitution of the corporation's rights and makes us the laughing-stock of the whole country!'

'You are making laughing-stocks of yourselves coming here in this way.' Falmouth turned to the footman. 'Cheese.'

'M'lord.'

'Apart from which, you do not, I am sure, represent the whole or a majority of the corporation. A small dissatisfied junta . . .'

'A majority, my Lord!' Hick put in.

'That we shall see. That we shall discover tomorrow. Then
we shall know who there are, if any, that, having become
burgesses after expressing the profoundest loyalty to the
Boscawen family, now turn and for some venal prize dis-
honour those expressions – '

'No venal prize,' said Mr Warleggan warmly. 'The venality,
sir, is all on your Lordship's side. We learn on the highest
authority that in attempting to sell these seats to your friends
you constantly complain that it costs you a great deal of
money to maintain the borough. It has been said that your
Lordship claims he has paid for the new burial ground and
the new workhouse. Not so. You contributed not a farthing
to the workhouse and gave the ground for the cemetery, of
a value of about fifteen pounds, with a subscription of thirty
guineas – My own subscription was sixty. Mr Hick's fifteen.
Others gave the like. We are *not* a venal borough, my Lord.
That is why we are determined to reject your candidate
tomorrow.'

The table had been cleared of the pie, and cheese had been
put before their host, together with a jar of preserved figs.
Lord Falmouth took a fig and began to chew it. He said:
'Do I assume from this that you have some candidate of your
own to oppose him?'

'Yes, my Lord,' said Hick.

'May I ask his name?'

There was a pause. Then the bigger man said: 'My son,
Mr George Warleggan, has been asked to stand.'

'Ah,' said Falmouth. 'Now perhaps we detect the worm in
the bud.'

At that moment the door opened and a tall good-looking
dark-eyed young man half entered. 'Oh, I beg your pardon,
Uncle. I heard you had returned and did not know you had
guests.'

'These gentlemen are just leaving. Two minutes and I shall
be free.'

'Thank you.' He withdrew.

Falmouth finished his wine. 'I think there is nothing more
to say after *that*, gentlemen. All is clearly explained. I will
wish you good night.'

Nicholas Warleggan got up. 'For your information, sir, I

did not put my son's name forward. Nor did he. It was a choice made by others, and I resent your implication.'

'So I suppose Sir Francis Basset has been flexing his muscles again, eh? Well, we shall see tomorrow. Tomorrow I shall discover who are my friends and who are my enemies. It is a matter I shall take particular note of.'

'If your Lordship sees the contest on that level we cannot prevent you,' said Warleggan, preparing to take his leave.

'As for you, Mr Hick,' Lord Falmouth said. 'No doubt you will remember the contract you received for your carpet manufactory for furnishing the naval building in Plymouth. Your letters on this matter, which I have in my desk, will make illuminating reading.'

Hick's face swelled and he looked as if he was going to burst into tears.

'Come, Hick,' said Warleggan, taking the mayor by the arm. 'We can do no more.'

'Hawke, show these gentlemen out,' Falmouth said. He took a slice of cheese.

'Viscount Falmouth!' said Hick. 'I really must protest! —'

'Come, my friend,' said Warleggan impatiently. 'We have done as we were instructed to do and no good can be served by remaining.'

'Commend me to your friends,' said Lord Falmouth. 'Many of them have received favours. I will remind them when I see them in the morning.'

II

News had percolated that there was likely to be a contested election, and the Reverend Osborne Whitworth, as a prominent citizen of Truro, was naturally interested in the outcome. More particularly so when it transpired that his cousin by marriage, Mr George Warleggan, was to be a candidate.

He was therefore most especially irritated when his wife began to experience her first birth pains at about six o'clock in the morning of the day of the election. Mr Whitworth, not being a councillor, would not have been admitted to the chamber where the election was in progress, but he hoped to be one of a number who might collect outside, observe the comings and goings, and be the first to learn the result. But at ten-thirty – half an hour before the election was due to take place – Dr Daniel Behenna, who had been with Morwenna for more than an hour, sent Rowella to call him. They met in the small upstairs sitting-room that the girls had tended to make their own when Ossie was playing cards with his friends below. There was a spinning wheel in the room, work baskets, a frame for a sampler, baby clothes that Morwenna had been making.

Behenna waited until Rowella had left, then he said: 'Mr Whitworth, I have to inform you that there are complications in this *accouchement* which no one could have foreseen. I have to inform you that although the presentation was normal in the first stages of labour, your wife has now become gravely ill.'

Ossie stared at the other man. 'What is it? Tell me. Is the baby dead?'

'No, but I fear there is serious danger to both.' Behenna wiped his hands on a dirty cloth he carried. 'As the child's head descended Mrs Whitworth fell into a convulsion and although this ceased, as soon as the labour returned so the convulsions have recommenced. I may tell you it is a very rare condition in childbirth. *Musculorum convulsio cum sopore.* In all my experience I have only met with it three times before.'

Osborne's feelings were a mixture of anxiety and anger. 'What is to be done? Eh? Can I go and see her?'

'I would advise not. I have administered camphor, and also *tartaris antimonii*, but so far the emetic effect has not reduced the epilepsy.'

'But now? What is happening now, while you're here talking to me now? Can you save the child?'

'Your wife is insensible after the last attack. Mrs Parker by her bed will summon me at any sign –'

'Why, I can't understand it at all. Mrs Whitworth kept in goodish fettle right to the end, right until early this morning. A bit low, a bit low, but you told her to keep herself low. Eh? Didn't you? So what has caused this? She's had no fever.'

'On the previous occasions when ladies have suffered this I have observed them to be of a delicate and emotional nature.

The nervous irritability which can give rise to this condition appears to be brought on by an unstable emotional state, or excess of fear, or in one case of grief. Mrs Whitworth must be of a high-strung disposition – '

A choked scream came from the next room, followed by a more high-pitched and gasping sound that made even Ossie's face blench.

'I must go to her now,' said Dr Behenna, pulling a spatulum out of his pocket. 'Have no fear, we shall do all we can, we shall attempt all that physical and surgical skill and knowledge can achieve. I have sent your maid for Mr Rowe, the apothecary, and when he comes we shall open the jugular vein and draw away a substantial amount of blood. It should help to alleviate the condition. In the meantime – well – perhaps a prayer for your wife and child . . .'

III

So Ossie missed the election. He went down to his study, and then he went out into his garden to get out of earshot of the unpleasant noises that came from upstairs. It was a cheerful day, sunlit and cloud-gloomed by turns, and the tide was full. In this part of the river such water only occurred at full and new moon; for the rest of the time there were greater or lesser mud banks from which terns and lapwings called. There were also some swans that Morwenna and the children fed with scraps. They came towards him now, necks craning, waggling their tails, supposing that *he* had something for them. He drove them away with a fallen branch and stared across the river at the thick lush trees on the other side, considering his ill-luck.

His first wife had died this way – not in childbed but in the fever which followed. But she had experienced no difficulty, not the slightest, in bringing forth her child. He had not supposed that Morwenna would either. Her hips were of a sensible size. He wanted a boy to carry on the name. Of course death was a hazard any woman faced so soon as she began bearing children; as a vicar officiating at funerals he was very accustomed to the sight of young husbands and tiny children weeping at a graveside. It was not long, not so very long, since he had done this himself.

But there were many women, any number of women – and those he could number all too well – who produced one child after another, year in year out, with no trouble at all. They had ten or fifteen children, more than half of whom survived, and they themselves lived to a good age – often indeed outlasting their husbands who had worked unceasingly all their lives to maintain the mounting family. It was too bad if Morwenna were going to go the way of Esther, and with a dead child into the bargain. And in that case it was *certain* to be a boy.

About half an hour after he went into the garden he saw Mr Rowe, the apothecary, arrive. He looked at his watch. It was twelve noon and the election would be over. It did not take long for twenty-five people to cast their votes. He considered a quick visit. It was little more than a mile to the hall and he could be there and back in half an hour. But he decided against it. It would look bad to be so seen by his parishioners. It would look worse if Morwenna died while he was away.

Rowella came out of the house hurriedly; pattered down the steps, tying her bonnet as she went, and hurried off towards the town. What now? He watched her retreating figure and then turned back towards the garden. That rascal Higgins had not done the edges of the lawn well: he must be told of it. Ossie looked up at the vicarage. Twice since that night he had gone into the attic in search of a sermon, but he had not been so lucky; the girl had been moving out of range of the peephole, and although he had ventured to enlarge it a little he had seen nothing.

If Morwenna died, what of his association with the Warleggans? He had possession of the money but he would regret the loss of their interest. Suppose he transferred *his* interest to Rowella? She too was Elizabeth's cousin. But would George be so generous a second time? It seemed unlikely. So Rowella would have to go back to Bodmin and he, a man of thirty-two, widowered for the second time, a distinguished young cleric with a fine church and an income of £300 a year – £460 if the application for St Sawle were successful – he would be very much of a catch – son of a judge, related to the Godolphins, connected with the Warleggans – many a mother's eye would be cast enviously towards him. He would take his time, take a thorough look round, see who and what was on the marriage market. He thought of one or two who were eligible at least so far as money was concerned. Betty Michell? Loveday Upcott? Joan Ogham? But this time he must try to find a girl who not only was right financially, not only appealed to him as a woman, but also found him fascinating as a man. It could not be such a tall order. When he looked at himself in the mirror he saw no reason to doubt his own attraction for women. Only Morwenna failed. Why even Rowella, he suspected by some of her sly looks, was not unimpressed.

He stayed out by the river until he saw Rowella returning. She was coming in great haste, and he had to stop her by blocking her way.

'What news of your sister? What have you been for? How is she, tell me?'

She looked at him and her lip trembled. 'Dr Behenna sen. me to his house for this.' She showed a bag. 'Morwenna wat quieter when I left. But I am not allowed in now.' She insinuated herself past him.

Ossie walked across his garden to the church. Near the path was Esther's grave and a bunch of wallflowers were fresh in the pot. He wondered who had put them there. He went into the church and as far as the altar. He was proud of his parish, which extended far enough to include three of the main street. of Truro. In this district had lived Condorus, the last Celtic Earl, who had perished soon after the Norman Conquest. Men of influence and property from neighbouring estates came to worship here every Sunday. Though the stipend was not great, it was a warm living.

The church was empty today. Dr Behenna had suggestea, most presumptuously, that he, Osborne, should offer up a prayer for the survival of his wife and child. But he did this every night before retiring. Did this emergency entitle him to suppose that God in His infinite wisdom had not heard and harkened to his nightly prayers? Was it right that he should, as it were, call God's further attention to something that He might have overlooked? That hardly seemed right. That hardly seemed a religious thing to do. Far better to kneel a moment and pray that he should have the strength to bear any burden that God in His mercy should choose to place upon his shoulders. A second widowerhood so young – two tiny children bereaved of a mother for the second time. An empty house. Another grave.

So it was in an attitude of prayer, head bowed before the altar, that his physician found him some twenty minutes later, most appropriately posed, as if in the two hours since the beginning of the crisis the vicar had spent the whole time interceding with his God for the survival of his beloved wife and child.

Osborne started and looked round in irritation at the foot-step, as if impatient at being so surprised. 'Dr Behenna! Well?'

Behenna had pulled on his velvet coat carelessly and his shirt was stained and loose at the collar.

'Ah, Mr Whitworth. When they could not find you I suspected that I might myself discover you here.'

Ossie stared at him and licked his lips but did not speak.

'You have a son, Mr Whitworth.'

'Ecod!' said Ossie. 'Is that so? Alive and well?'

'Alive and well. Of six and a half pounds.'

'That's small, isn't it?'

'No, no, very satisfactory.'

'Both the girls were heavier. Eight pounds each, I believe. But of course that was another mother. Ecod, how pleasing! A son! Well, upon my word! D'you know I have always wanted a son to carry on the line. We Whitworths trace our ancestry a long way, and I was an only son – and difficult, I am told, to bear. I'm told I was ten pounds at birth. My mother will be pleased. Is he sound in every respect? I have chosen his name. John Conan Osborne Whitworth. It marks our blood connection with the Godolphins. Er – and? . . .'

'Mrs Whitworth has been through a great ordeal. She is now sleeping.'

'Sleeping? She will recover?'

'There is good reason to hope so now. I may tell you I was greatly disappointed in her, greatly disappointed, when last I saw you. The puerperal convulsions were an imminent hazard both to her life and to the child's. Had they continued another fifteen minutes they both must have died. But my operation upon the jugular vein was successful. Almost as soon as we had drawn sufficient blood from her she quieted, and after a while the child was presented. The placenta required aid, which naturally had to be effected with the utmost care lest my action should irritate the uterus, which could well have brought on a return of the convulsions or even a prolapse. But all was well. Your prayers, Mr Whitworth, have been answered, and a surgeon's skill has been rewarded!'

Ossie stared at Dr Behenna penetratingly. The sudden end to the crisis left him a little stupefied; emotionally he was not at all volatile, and the switch from expecting to find himself a doubly bereaved widower to that of happy husband and father was too much for him to accomplish in a moment. The thought flickered across his mind that physicians sometimes magnified the gravity of an ailment in order to squeeze a greater gratitude for themselves when they cured it. The thought brought a frown to his face.

'The boy. When can I see him?'

'In a few minutes. I came quickly to relieve your mind, and there is a little more yet to do.' Behenna was put out by the manner of the relieved parent, and he too frowned. 'But I would warn you, Mr Whitworth, about your wife.'

'Eh? You said all was well.'

'All *appears* to be well, but she has been through a great ordeal. She is sleeping heavily now and must on no account be disturbed. I shall leave, of course, full instructions with the midwife. But when your wife finally wakes she will likely remember nothing of her ordeal, particularly of the convulsions. She must on no account be told of them. In a sensitive woman it would have a very deleterious effect upon her emotions and might well result in a grave disorder of the nerve force.'

'Ah,' said Ossie. 'Well, then. She had best not be told, had she. That's simple. I'll issue orders in the house.'

Behenna turned away. 'In ten minutes, Mr Whitworth, you may see your son.'

He stalked out of the church in a manner that showed his lack of approval of the man he left behind.

Ossie followed him. The sun was shining again, and he narrowed his eyes as he looked down the lane. John Conan

Osborne Whitworth. He'd arrange to do the baptizing himself as soon as ever Morwenna was about again. Might have something of a party. His mother would be glad. His mother had never been quite sure about the match, thought he might have done better. Invite George and Elizabeth; other influential people: the Polwheles, the Michells, the Andrews, the Thomases.

He was about to go in when he saw a tall thin man coming up the lane past the church and towards the house, carrying a small parcel. The man, who wore spectacles and was in his late twenties, made for the front door of the house.

'Yes, what is it you want?' Ossie said sharply.

'Oh, beg your pardon, Vicar, I didn't see you what with the sun in my eyes. Good afternoon to you, sir.'

'Hawke, is it?'

'No, Solway, sir. Arthur Solway. From the County Library.'

'Oh, yes. Oh, yes.' Osborne nodded distantly. 'What is it you want?'

'I brought these books, sir. Miss Rowella asked for them. For herself and Mrs Whitworth. She said as – she said that I might bring them up.'

'Oh, indeed.' Ossie extended his hand. 'Well, it is not convenient for you to call now. I will take them in.'

Solway hesitated. 'Thank you, sir.' He handed over the parcel, but reluctantly.

'What are they? Romances?' Ossie held the parcel with distaste. 'I don't at all think – '

'Oh, no, sir. One is a book on birds and the others are histories – one of France and one of Ancient Greece.'

'Huh.' Ossie grunted. 'I will give them to Miss Chynoweth.'

Solway half turned. 'Oh, sir, will you tell Miss Chynoweth, please, that the other Greek book has not been returned yet.'

Mr Whitworth nodded dismissively and moved to go in. This library had been opened four years ago in Princes Street, and some three hundred volumes were available to be borrowed. Volumes on all sorts of subjects. He had never approved of it, for there was no real check upon what might be found in the books, three-quarters of which were secular; and it exposed unformed and uninstructed minds to thoughts and ideas outside their scope. This fellow was the librarian –

he remembered now. He must warn Morwenna – and also Rowella – of the bad habits they were getting into. He was tempted to throw the books in the river. Then he remembered something else.

'Wait,' he said to the young man, who by now was moving off.

'Sir?'

'Tell me. Perhaps you know. There will have been gossip no doubt in your library. Has the election taken place today?'

'Oh yes, sir, about two hours agone. In the Council Chamber, it was. Great excitement – '

'Yes, I know, I know. Who was elected?'

'Oh, Vicar, there was great excitement, fur it was a very close shave, I'm told. Thirteen votes to twelve. Thirteen to twelve. As close as a whisker!'

'Well? . . .'

'They say Lord Falmouth's candidate was turned down. What was his name now? An odd name, Salter, I believe – '

'So you mean – '

'Sir Francis Basset's candidate was elected by one vòte. Everyone's been talking about it! Mr Warleggan it is, you know, sir. Not the father but the son. Mr George Warleggan, the banker. It's been a real excitement! A close shave! As close as a whisker!'

'Thank you. That's all, Solway.' Osborne turned away and walked slowly up to the house.

On the steps to the front door he stood a minute, watching the young man trudge away. But his thoughts were not on what he was seeing at all.

The wind ruffled his hair. He went inside, remembering that he was hungry.

CHAPTER IX

In the month that John Conan Osborne Whitworth was born rumours reached Cornwall, soon to be followed by the firm news, that that general whose name Ross Poldark could never quite remember had performed prodigious feats of arms in northern Italy. At the head of a rabble of forty thousand Frenchmen, ill-equipped, ill-clad, ill-shod and ill-fed – their staple diet bread and chestnuts – he had crossed the Alps and fought six battles, had defeated the Austrians and the Piedmontese and on the fifteenth of the month had captured Milan. It was said it was a plan he had been pressing on his masters for two years; at last they had given him his head, and against all the odds of terrain and the rules of ordinary warfare he had succeeded. An English naval officer called Commodore Nelson, cruising in the Mediterranean, had observed the rapid march of the French along the Ligurian coast road, had discovered from spies the nature of the force, and had urged a small British landing in their rear, a manœuvre which would have stopped the invasion in its tracks by cutting its lifeline. But now it was too late, and the fame of General Buonaparte echoed through Europe.

And the rest of Italy lay unprotected before him. True the Austrians, it was said, were massing a great new army behind the Alps, but for the moment there was nothing to stop his march into the rich cities of central and eastern Italy. The coalition of England, Austria, Russia, Prussia, Sardinia and Spain had been incohesive for a long time. Holland had already gone over to the enemy. Who next? A French naval squadron was already in Cadiz blatantly refitting in the royal dockyards. If France succeeded in Italy, Spain would be the first to join the winning side. And Spain had eighty ships of the line.

Harris Pascoe said: 'I don't mind t-telling you, Ross, the whole election was a source of great embarrassment to your friends in Truro. Not least to me, I assure you, not least to me.'

'How did you vote?' Ross asked.

'N-need you ask?'

'Well, yes . . . I fear I must. I beg your pardon. You are nothing if not a Whig. And much more a Basset than a Falmouth man. And you have said more than once . . .'

'And would say it again. At the previous election the burgesses were not informed whom they were to vote for until ten minutes before they entered the hall. That time, bitterly though they resented it, there was no way of expressing their discontent. This time Sir Francis provided the focus. So Lord Falmouth has been taught a very salutary lesson – but at what a cost!'

'George may be very useful to Truro. He has the rare virtue of living here.'

'All this trouble need not have arisen if you had accepted Basset's invitation.'

Ross looked at his friend, startled. Pascoe took off his spectacles and polished them. His eyes looked bland, and rather blind.

'Who told you that?'

'In the narrow confines of this county, Ross, it is almost impossible to keep anything private.'

'Well, God's life, I did not think that would get about! . . . Well, I'm sorry; it was an impossible suggestion, as you know, knowing me, you must realize. I'm sorry if it has set you unexpected problems of conscience!'

Pascoe coloured. 'It was your choice. I cannot tell you different. But Basset's nomination of George Warleggan set me problems – and others beside me – problems I never expected to face as a burgess of this town. I have always been on friendly terms with Basset – so far, that is, as a mere banking man *is* on terms with a landed gentleman of such distinction. Basset, Rogers, & Co., the bank of which Basset and his brother-in-law are the principals, has always tended to have friendly relations with ours – though, as I think I told you, they have recently drawn much closer to Warleggan's Bank and undertaken a number of interlocking schemes which will draw them closer still. As for Lord Falmouth, he has, I think, an account with all three banks, but keeps his substantial capital in London. I have nothing against the present Viscount except his high-handed and arbitrary manner when dealing with the city council; but on those grounds I have spoken up against him in the chamber and I have been one of those fully supporting Basset's growing influence in the borough. But when it came to voting for the man Basset nominated, that was a pill I *could* not swallow!'

'D'you mean you –'

'And so on the morning I found myself disavowing all my

principles and political professions and casting my vote for this Salter man – Lord Falmouth's candidate!'

'Good God . . . I did not expect you to say that!'

Ross got up and looked out into the street where the rain was splashing the mud from between the cobblestones. 'And yet Salter did not get in even so.'

'No, but that was why the voting was close. There were others who voted as I did – against the candidate, although they were really Basset men. George is not popular among some sections of this town, you know.'

'I had always thought George a Boscawen crony.'

'He has always *sought* their friendship, but I think never received it. That was why he changed sides when such a favourable opportunity presented itself. I must say Falmouth behaved most reprehensibly on the morning.'

'Falmouth did? In what way?'

'He seemed utterly determined to defeat this revolt. And quite unscrupulous about it. He publicly canvassed among the burgesses immediately before the election – and he carried a file of papers – letters, private letters they were, written to him by one or other of the corporation over the last few years – and threatened to publish them unless they voted for his candidate! I was not able to hear all that was said; but he seemed to be threatening some of the electors with the withdrawal of trade and monetary support!'

'Then it's remarkable he didn't succeed.'

'I think the corporation acted under a quite uncontrollable impulse to prove they were not just puppets of the Recorder. In this I'm glad. I only regret the outcome.'

Ross was thoughtful. 'A pity that Sir Francis's second choice should be even more ill-judged than his first . . . I hope your vote will not affect your good relations with the Bassets.'

'It remains to be seen. I endeavoured to explain my reasons to Sir Francis afterwards, but I don't think he found them satisfactory. My chief fear is that he will think I changed sides because of his bank's new links with Warleggan's.'

'You should have voted for George.'

Pascoe shut the ledger in irritation. 'For you, of all people, to tell me that!'

Ross smiled. 'I'm sorry, dear friend, I shouldn't have said

so much. But you have always asserted that it is no business of a bank to take sides in any family feud. Your friendship with me is, alas, too well known to deny; but your dislike of George has always been concealed behind the diplomacy of commerce. I grieve that it should have come out now when it might affect your association with Basset. If it does that, your loyalty to me may prove expensive.'

Harris Pascoe opened the ledger again and impatiently turned the pages. 'Look, sign this now, else I shall forget.'

Ross signed at the bottom of his account. It showed a credit balance of nearly two thousand pounds.

Pascoe said: 'For once you esteem yourself too high, Ross.'

'Oh?'

'My vote was not cast out of loyalty to you but out of loyalty, if that is the w-word, to my own conscience. Happily for yourself, you see a good deal less of the Warleggans than I do. Over the last few years I have developed an antipathy for them that can be second only to yours. They are not dishonest men – not at all – but they exemplify the new style of commercial adventurer who has emerged in England this last decade or so. To them business and profit is all, and humanity nothing. A man who works for them is of exactly the same value as a figure on their ledger sheet. And there is something extra dangerous about them in that their only contentment is in their lack of contentment with their present size. To be healthy they must ever expand like a m-multiplying toadstool. They grasp and grow and grow and grasp . . .' Pascoe stopped for breath. 'Perhaps we who dislike them are old-fashioned. Perhaps this is to be the new way of the world; but I do not wish to change and I could not bring myself to cast my vote for such a one whatever good or harm it might do me!'

Ross put a hand on his friend's shoulder. 'I beg your pardon again. That's a line of reasoning I find altogether more respectable . . . I wonder how well Basset and George know each other.'

'They must know each other well.'

'Oh, in a business way, yes. But that is not all there is to friendship.'

'Don't go yet,' Harris said. 'You must stay a while until this rain is over.'

'In that event you'd have a lodger: I don't think it will stop today. No . . . Rain never hurt no one. But thank you.'

II

When Ross got outside the rain was fairly jumping off the cobbles, and the rivulet down the side of the street was in spate. Yellow puddles among the mud bubbled like boiling water. There were few people about, and in Powder Street the blocks of tin glistened unattended. The coinage was due to begin tomorrow, but no one worried about theft since the blocks, though of a value of ten or twelve guineas each, weighed over 300 lb. and were not likely to be carried away unnoticed.

More weight of tin left Truro for overseas than from any other port in the land. Its wharves were big and convenient and the river comfortably took vessels of 100 tons. Just at the moment Powder Street and its neighbour were in greater disorder than usual because the block of houses known as Middle Row was being pulled down, and a large new street was soon to be opened which would give space and air to the huddled buildings surrounding it.

Tomorrow at noon the controller and receiver would begin to weigh and assay the blocks of tin as they were brought into the coinage hall, and if their quality was up to standard they would have the Duchy arms stamped on them as a guarantee of their purity and having paid the toll. The coinage might last a week and would be attended by the tinners, by London and foreign traders, by middlemen and pewterers and all the necessary officials of the occasion. The coinages were held quarterly, which was far too seldom, for it meant that tin could not be sold before it was stamped, and the mines, particularly the small ones, had to run up credit in the intervals to pay their working expenses. So they borrowed money from the tin merchants at high rates of interest; and the larger mines obtained similar expensive credits from the banks, particularly from Warleggan's, who were prepared to take more risks than the others. Hence when a mine failed, whatever was saleable of land, stores or property fell in to these creditors.

It was a system that needed to be changed. Cromwell had

abolished the coinages, to the great benefit of the industry, but
when Charles II was restored to his throne the coinage system
had been restored with him and it had remained ever since.
Ross had sometimes been tempted to begin a campaign for its
alteration; but he had painful memories of his attempt to
break the stranglehold of the copper smelters, a campaign that
had resulted in near bankruptcy for himself and disaster for
many of his friends; so once bitten twice shy.

The fact that he had such a balance to his credit at Pascoe's
just before a coinage was proof enough of the extraordinary
richness of the lodes he had uncovered at Wheal Grace. But
he was not staying for the coinage. Zacky Martin, who had
been ill for eighteen months but had been brought back to
health by Dwight Enys since his return, was staying instead.

Splashing through the mud and the rain, Ross reached the
Red Lion Inn – which would benefit considerably from the
new light and space that was going to be given to its back
door. He found it crowded. The heavy rain had driven everyone indoors, and a lot of hard drinking was in progress.
Almost the first person he saw in the crowded tap room was
the innkeeper, Blight, with his pigtail and his red waistcoat.
The little man bustled anxiously across and Ross, shaking the
water from his hat, said:

'I'm looking for my manager, Martin.'

'Oh, sur. I haven't seen sight nor sound of Mr Martin all
day. Maybe he's over to the King's Head.'

'But you have seen him today. We were in together this
morning. And he has a room here.'

'Ah, yes, sur, I misremember. Well, he's not in just now.
I reckon he's over to the King's Head. Or maybe the Seven
Stars.'

There was a note of unwelcome in the innkeeper's voice that
Ross did not quite comprehend. The fracas he had had in this
inn with George Warleggan was years ago, and Ross had been
in and out many times since.

'I'll see if he's in his room. What is the number?'

'Oh, I'll send a boy.'

'No, I prefer to go myself.'

'Er – it's number nine, then. But I assure you he's not in.'

Ross pushed through the crowd, exchanging a word of greeting here and there. In the lobby of the hotel it was very dark and still very crowded. On the way to the stairs were two private rooms used for personal meetings, and the door of one of these was ajar and he saw several men in the room drinking and talking. He passed on to the stairs, but after he had mounted the first half dozen a voice said:

'Captain Poldark.'

A small grey man wearing a clerk's bob-wig. Thomas Kevill, Basset's steward.

'Pardon me, sir, Sir Francis is in the private room and would esteem it a favour if you joined him.'

Ross turned and came down. He was not sure that he wanted conversation with Sir Francis just at this time, but it would be churlish to refuse. Maybe, he thought, as he went into the room, it would be an opportunity to try to straighten out any resentment Basset might feel towards Harris Pascoe. Then as he got in he stopped. Basset had three companions, Lord Devoran; a middle-aged well-dressed man whom he did not know; and George Warleggan. It was small wonder that Innkeeper Blight had been nervous.

'Captain Poldark,' Basset said. 'I caught sight of you as you passed the door, and thought you might drink with us.' It was half a pleasant invitation, half a command.

'Thank you, I must return home this evening,' Ross said. 'But gladly for a brief space.'

'You know Lord Devoran, I imagine. Perhaps not Sir William Molesworth of Pencarrow. And Mr George Warleggan.'

'Lord Devoran, yes.' Ross bowed slightly. 'Sir William I do not, I think. Sir.' Another bow. 'And Mr Warleggan, yes. We went to school together.'

'Indeed, I didn't know you were such old friends.' Had nobody ever *bothered* to tell Basset, or did he feel himself important enough to sweep aside such petty quarrels between underlings? 'We are drinking Geneva, but if you have a different taste . . .'

'Thank you, no. That's what I'd choose to keep the rain out.'

Ross seated himself between George and Sir William Molesworth – there was no other chair – and accepted the glass that Kevill passed him.

'We were talking of the projected hospital, the infirmary that we hope to site near Truro, and I have been attempting to convert both Lord Devoran and Sir William Molesworth to my views.'

So that was it. Sir Francis was not a man to let an idea rest once it had taken hold of him. Sir William, whose estate was near Wadebridge, thought a hospital so far west would be useless to the eastern half of the county; Lord Devoran took the view that centralization was wrong and what they needed were a half dozen small but efficient dispensaries in different parts of the county.

George's face had set into rigid lines when he saw Ross enter, but now he was behaving as if there were nothing unusual in the encounter. Ross thought he had lost a good deal of weight – it had been noticeable at Dwight's wedding – but it did not look a particularly healthy loss. George did not so much look leaner as older. Lord Devoran was a fussy little man who had been associated with Ross in the copper smelting venture and had lost money over it. At the time he had seemed to resent this, but later he had been sufficiently generous to stand bail for Ross when he was to be tried for his life at Bodmin. He had a notorious daughter called Betty. Sir William Molesworth, a plump man with a grey moustache and a healthy outdoor complexion, was a person of altogether more importance than Devoran, and his opposition to Basset's proposal would count for a good deal in the county.

'What is your opinion, Poldark?' Basset said. 'I know you favour the scheme in a general way but you have not expressed yourself as to detail.'

Ross had no particular views of his own on this, but he knew Dwight's.

'The ideal would be to have the central hospital *and* the dispensaries. That being unlikely of achievement, I would say the hospital must come first and must be sited somewhere in this area. We are equidistant from Bodmin, Wadebridge and Penzance.'

Basset nodded approval for the opinion he had expected,

and general discussion broke out. Ross noticed some difference in George, in the way he spoke. Never in his life had he lacked confidence; and he had always been careful in his actual speech to exclude the accents of his childhood, to avoid the long R's, the vowels becoming diphthongs, the lifted cadences; but equally he had been careful not to *assume* an accent which might seem that he was trying with only partial success to ape his betters. He had kept his speech as carefully neutral as he knew how. Now it had moved on. Now it came distinctly nearer to the accent of Basset or Molesworth, and was more refined than Devoran's. Already. It had happened in only a few weeks. He had become a Member of Parliament.

Ross said to him: 'I believe we have to congratulate you, George.'

George smiled thinly, in case the others had heard, but he did not reply.

'When do you take your seat?'

'Next week.'

'You'll rent a house in London?'

'Possibly. In part of each year.'

'We shall not be neighbours on the coast this year, then?'

'Oh, for August and September, no doubt.'

'I presume you do not intend to sell Trenwith?'

'I do not.'

'If ever you thought of selling it I might be interested.'

'It will not come on the market – ever – to you.'

'We have been thinking, Captain Poldark,' Basset interposed, 'that those of us who are of like mind in this matter might put our names to a subscription. I do not think the time is yet ripe actually to subscribe money – we have far too much to do; for instance – ' with a smile – 'to convince those who think the project should begin otherwise. But the names of fifty influential men, with a promise of assistance when the scheme is moving forward, would I believe be a help at this stage to convince many who at present waver and hesitate. Do you agree?'

'Certainly, I agree.'

'Sir Francis,' said George, licking his lips, 'has put his name for a hundred guineas to start the subscription off, and I have done the same.'

A flicker of annoyance crossed Basset's face. 'I am specific-
ally not asking for a figure, Poldark, not at this stage. It's your
name I want.'

'And can have,' Ross said. 'And a hundred guineas with it.'

'That's very good of you. I hope you don't feel that you
are being Impressed into Service at a difficult time.'

'The metaphor does you an injustice, Sir Francis. I am not
too drunk to refuse the King's shilling. I'll give you a draft
on Pascoe's Bank.'

Basset raised his eyebrows, not liking the abrasiveness that
had come into the conversation. 'That will not be necessary,
as I have already said. But thank you, I'm grateful. I take it
that you two gentlemen are not sufficiently convinced yet of
the rightness of our cause?'

Devoran was hedging, but Sir William Molesworth remained
unconvinced. Ross looked at George: it was the first time
they had been together like this for years, when they could not
quarrel openly and could not move away.

He said: 'I hear nothing of Geoffrey Charles these days.
I trust he's doing well at school?'

'It is too early to say. I think he has some of his father's
idle habits.'

'At school, you may remember, his father was cleverer than
either of us.'

'It was a promise he did not fulfil.'

Silence fell between them while Molesworth spoke.

George said: 'I pay, of course, the whole considerable costs
of Geoffrey Charles's schooling. When he should by rights
have a sufficient income of his own.'

'From what?'

'From the shares in your mine.'

'Elizabeth sold the shares in my mine.'

'Back to you, at a fraction of what they were worth. You
were able to over-persuade her.'

Ross said: 'I wouldn't advise you to promulgate that twisted
version of events. Even your wife would call you a liar for it.'

Lord Devoran said: '. . . and the whole question of finding
suitable patients would be sifted through the dispensaries
instead of depending upon the patronage of individuals. If . . .'

'And necessarily,' said Sir William Molesworth, 'if the

central hospital were sited farther east . . .'

Ross said: 'What of Aunt Agatha's grave?'

'What of it?'

'I presume you have a stone on order.'

'No.'

'Surely, although you resented her existence, you can hardly deny the old lady some record of her having existed.'

'It is for Elizabeth to decide.'

'Perhaps I could call and see Elizabeth and we could discuss it.'

'That would not be desirable.'

'On whose part?'

'On hers. And on mine.'

'Can you answer for her on such a family matter?'

'Elizabeth is not a Poldark.'

'But she was, George, she was.'

'It is something she has long since had cause to regret.'

'Who knows what she will have cause to regret before our lives are ended—'

'Damn you and God damn your blood to all eternity—'

'*Gentlemen,*' Basset said, having heard only the last part, 'this does not become *either* of you—'

'It does not become us,' Ross said, 'but we do it. We bicker from time to time like playmates who see too much of each other. Pray excuse it and take no notice.'

'I am happy to take no notice of what does not occur in my presence. But ill will is not properly vented when we are here to discuss a charity.'

'Unfortunately,' Ross said, 'they both begin at home.'

There was a silence. Sir Francis cleared his throat irritably. 'Sir William, as I was about to say, the question of the hospital site is one that could be reviewed in committee . . .'

III

Ross was late reaching Nampara that night. It had been a head wind all the way, and he was drenched.

'My dear, that's not clever!' Demelza said. 'Have you supped? Let me have your boots. You should have stayed the night with Harris!'

'And knowing you imagining me drowned in a ditch or set

on by footpads? How is Jeremy?'

Jeremy was recovering from his inoculation against small-pox. They had given him a book to read so that he should not see any of the preparations, but all the same he had let out a piercing scream when Dwight made the deep incision. Demelza had felt as if the knife were in her own guts.

'The fever has gone and he has eaten today. Thank God Clowance can be spared the ordeal for a while. I doubt even if I shall ever consent. I am – what is the word? – immune; so why should not she be?'

Ross stripped off his shirt and bent to peer out of the bedroom window towards the sea. It had been so dark all day that the long evening was only just beginning to show the fall of night. The gusty wind was spinning webs of rain, weaving them in and out of each other across the wide and darkening stretches of sand. The sea had not been blown up by the wind, it had been deadened by the rain, and it curled over at the edge in listless green caterpillars.

They talked the gossip of the day while he changed. Then she went down to tell Jane to bring on the roasted neck of mutton, though he protested he wasn't hungry.

'We have another invitation, Ross! They fall thick now you are famous.'

He took the letter. It was headed Tregothnan, and ran:
'Dear Mrs Poldark,

'My brother and I would consider it a pleasure if you and your husband could visit us on Tuesday the twenty-sixth of July, dine and sup with us and spend the night. My nephew, Hugh, will be leaving the following day to rejoin his ship and would like to have the opportunity of seeing you both again before he leaves. I too should enjoy the opportunity of making your acquaintance and of thanking Captain Poldark for bringing my nephew safely away from the dreadful camp where he was imprisoned.

'Believe me, most cordially yours,

Frances Gower.'

Demelza was examining one of Garrick's ears, which she suspected of harbouring some parasite. There had been a number of years when Garrick was forbidden this room altogether, but as age lessened his tendency to sudden violent movement and thereby made the furniture and crockery a little safer, he had been allowed to insinuate himself into the parlour. As Demelza had said when Ross made a half-hearted protest: 'Every other gentleman has his dogs about him in his parlour.' To which Ross had replied: 'Every other gentleman doesn't have Garrick.'

Ross took a drink of beer and picked up the letter again.

'How did it come?'

'By the Sherborner.'

'Our friend Lieutenant Armitage didn't ride over with it, then?'

'No, no.'

'All the same you're looking a morsel wide-eyed about the whole thing.'

Demelza looked up. 'What *do* that mean?'

'Well . . . stirred . . . emotional, is it?'

'Dear life, your ideas are some funny, Ross. I have – you know I have some gentle feelings for Lieutenant Armitage; but you must think me a holla-pot to get emotional all just because of an invitation.'

'Yes . . , well, maybe I imagine things. Maybe it's worrying about Jeremy that gives you that look . . .'

He went on with his food. Garrick, who enjoyed every attention paid him, had continued to lie on his back waiting for more, one front paw half bent, one eye showing white and, wild among the straggling hair. Now he snuffled loudly to regain Demelza's attention.

'What a day,' Ross said. 'It has never stopped since dawn.'

'Our hay looks like Jeremy's hair before it has been combed in the morning.'

'I saw George Warleggan after dinner.'

'Oh! . . . Oh?'

Ross explained the circumstance. 'So in a sense it was peaceable. But disagreeable none the less. There is some element in the composition of his character and mine that immediately sets off a physical reaction. When I saw him sitting there I disliked being asked to sit down beside him, but I had *no* intention whatever of saying anything to provoke him! Possibly he feels the same.'

'At least they'll not be at Trenwith for so long this year.'

'And I shall put up a stone myself for Agatha without bothering them further.'

Demelza bent her head again over Garrick, and Ross looked at the acute curve of her figure: small firm buttocks and thighs, soles of slippers showing light like the palms of a negro's hands, blue silk blouse and holland skirt, dark hair falling over and touching the dog, a glimpse of neck with wisps of hair curling.

Presently he said: 'What are we going to do about this?'

'About what? Oh . . . well, I cannot say this time, can I?'

'Why not?'

'If I press to go this time you will think I am pressing for my own special reasons.'

'*I* certainly don't wish to go.'

'Well, then, it's better we should not.'

Ross got up from the table and stirred Garrick with his foot. Garrick coughed with delight and rolled over and hoisted himself on to his considerable legs.

'There,' Demelza said, 'you've spoiled it now. I think it's the rabbits he's catching these crawlers from.' She sat back on her heels and dodged Garrick's attempt to lick her face.

Ross began to fill his pipe. 'Devil knows what we can say to this woman without giving offence.' He was so used to being pushed into accepting invitations that he felt the sudden lack. His distaste for company – high company – was completely genuine, but with the perversity common to human nature, his reason began to list the difficulties of a refusal here. If he had sprung Hugh Armitage from his prison – however inadvertently – Hugh Armitage in turn had probably saved Dwight's life by his superior knowledge of navigation (another night at sea might have killed him). To refuse this invitation, unless he could think of some cast-iron excuse, would be churlish and unmannerly. And although he knew Demelza was affected by this young man, it hardly seemed likely that the friendship would burgeon uncontrollably at a final meeting.

He said: 'I quail at the thought of a day and a night in the company of George Falmouth. Harris tells me he behaved disgracefully at the election.'

'There must be hard feelings between them now, Ross. If we went, should it be thought that we were, you were running with the hare and – and – '

'Hunting with the hounds? Oh, you mean . . . I see no reason why. What Basset and Falmouth think of each other is their concern. I take no sides – still less so as Basset chooses in such a cavalier fashion to ignore my quarrel with George Warleggan.'

'D'you know what I'm always afraid of when you meet George, Ross? That you'll quarrel – as you usually do – and then the next thing is you'll be set to fight a duel.'

Ross laughed. 'There I think you can set your mind at rest. George is a man of business, with a very level head and a very good brain. I know we have come to blows twice or thrice in our lives, but that is in the heat of the moment – and the last time was several years ago, and we are growing older and a little wiser every day. He would gladly fight a commercial duel with me on any ground on which I care or dare to challenge him. But pistols – they are in his view the melodrama belonging to aristocrats and squireens and military men who know no better.'

'What a small matter concerns me,' she said, 'is when you meet him in the company of these great men you are now mixing with. Isn't there the danger that he might find himself drove into a corner where he would be forced to challenge you because they expected it of him?'

Ross was thoughtful. 'I know no woman whose conversation is so much to the point.'

'Thank you, Ross.'

'But it is really George you should be warning, since I am the soldier and he the trader. He would be much more greatly at risk from such a challenge, so I suspect his good sense will keep him safe.'

'And I trust you'll not have to meet too often in such high company.'

A few minutes later Ross went out to look at two newly-born calves, and Betsy Ann Martin came in to clear the table. When this was done Demelza pushed Garrick out of doors and was alone. She went upstairs to peer at the children. Jeremy was breathing noisily; the fever had left him with a blocked nose. Clowance slept like an angel, clenched fist against lip, thumb not quite in mouth.

Demelza went into their own bedroom and dug into the inside pocket of her skirt. She took out a second letter which had also been delivered.

It came from the same address as the other but had a separate seal and was written in a different hand.

It said simply at the top: 'D.P. from H.A.' and it went on:

To D.

She walks as peerless Dian rides
In moonlight and in rain,
As sea-bird gently windward flies
O'er wave and watery main.
Thus heavenly light and earthly tides
Combine in her as twain.

She smiles as sunrise on the wave
In summer and at dawn,
As daylight enters darkling cave
To bring the breath of morn.
Thus day and night in joy behave
With ardour newly born.

She walks like air and smiles like light
'Mong sinners yet unshriven,
But one among them knows his plight
Excluded yet from Heaven.

CHAPTER X

In mid-June it was Rowella's birthday: she was fifteen, and her mother, by the coach, sent her a cake. Morwenna gave her a little silver crucifix which she had ordered from Solomon, the gold and silversmith. Mr Whitworth gave her a book of meditation on the Revelation of St John the Divine.

It was also a month to the day since John Conan Osborne Whitworth was born.

He was prospering mightily, but his mother was still unwell. She had been able to attend the christening and got up each afternoon for about three hours, but she was so pale and listless, could not feed the baby, and her former gentle good looks had utterly faded. Dr Behenna said she was suffering from an excitability of the blood vessels pertaining to the womb, and bled her regularly. The infection, he warned Osborne, might spread to the pelvis, and to counteract this Morwenna was wrapped for two hours each morning in blankets saturated in warm vinegar. The nurse they had engaged for John Conan was also instructed to rub mercurial ointment into Morwenna's thighs and flanks. So far the treatment was bringing no improvement.

It was a mild damp Friday and after supper Osborne was in his study writing out the notes of his sermon, with the door of his study ajar – he believed it kept the servants up to scratch to know their master was not quite shut away – when he heard a footstep and a clink of metal and saw Rowella carrying the grey tin bath-tub up the first flight of stairs. Returning to his seat after having assured himself that he was not mistaken, he reflected that both Sarah and Anne were in bed by now. Apart from that, it was the larger tin bath which he used himself, on the rare occasions when he used it at all. This information registered in his mind while he tried to concentrate on his sermon. But after another rounded paragraph he heard Rowella come down, and about five minutes later a procession of Rowella and his two maids went up the stairs again, each carrying a pitcher; and a waft of steam was left behind them as they went.

He put his pen on his desk and ruffled the end of it with his thumb. Had he not preached rather on this subject once before, and if this were so would not the notes be filed away in the box in the attic? His mouth went very dry as he thought of this; it was as if all the saliva had suddenly disappeared. He walked to a side table and quickly drank two glasses of mountain, and while he was doing this he heard the two maids come down. But not Rowella.

In spite of his clumsy figure he could move quietly when need be, and he went silently up the first flight and listened outside his wife's door. He heard her cough once but he knew she was not likely to get up again today. Then, like a good father, he peered in at his two little daughters and kissed them good night. They wanted him to stay but he said he could not, as he had much work to do. Then he went up the second flight.

The latch of the attic lifted as if it were recently oiled, and he went in and stole across the room, sat gently on the wooden box beside the wall and applied his eye to the hole.

At first the fact that it was still daylight put him off slightly, and he was afraid that not only was she out of sight but that the light from the window would make it hard to see. But after a moment he focused properly and saw her sitting on a chair combing her hair. In front of her was the tin bath, from which steam was rising. While he watched she put in more water out of one of the ewers and felt the result with her hand. She was really a very plain girl with her mousy eyebrows and long thin nose and tremulous underlip. She pulled up her skirts and began to drag off her garters and black stockings. This done, she sat with her skirts above her knees and tried the water with the toes of one foot.

Her legs didn't have much shape but her feet fascinated him. They were long and slender and excellently proportioned, with good regular nails and very fine pale skin, through which a few blue veins showed like marks in alabaster. As she flexed them in and out of the water, the bones appeared and disappeared, revealing the delicate bone structure. Feet had always fascinated him, and these were the most perfect he had ever seen.

She got up and put a towel on the floor and stood on it and took off her two skirts and stood in her long white drawers. She looked very silly standing there while she began to take off her blouse. Under the blouse was another blouse and under that was a vest. In vest and drawers she walked away and disappeared from his sight. Osborne closed his eyes and leaned his head against the wall in desperation. Then she came back with two green ribbons and began to plait her hair. All this time her lips were moving and he realized she was humming a little tune. He did not think it was a hymn but some catchy silly little tune she had picked up in the town.

The light was fading a little now, but the day had cleared around sunset and an afterglow lit the sky. This fell softly in the room. Somebody made a noise downstairs and she stopped in her plaiting to listen, head on one side, thin fingers momentarily still. He too listened. It was that fool Alfred, his manservant, who had upset something. The man deserved a whipping.

Silence settled and she went on with her plaiting. He waited, with no saliva to swallow.

She stood up, long and scrawny, and pulled her vest up over her head and was naked to the waist. He almost exclaimed aloud when he saw her breasts; for it was the greatest surprise of his life. She was just fifteen and they were ripe and beautiful. They were bigger than her sister's, rounder than his first wife's, whiter and more pure than those of the women in the jelly houses of Oxford. He stared quite unbelieving, not crediting what he saw. How could they have been so hidden away under the lace of blouses, the pleats of frocks, the disguises of linen and cotton, the illusion of thin arms and narrowness of back?

Then Rowella raised her arms to pin back her hair, and her breasts stood out like full fresh fruit suddenly discovered growing upon some all too slender tree. After a moment she slipped her drawers down, pulled them off and stood and then crouched in the narrow tin bath and began to wash herself.

II

Morwenna was reading when Ossie came in. Reading had become her one escape, an escape from the debility of her own body, the miseries of her daily treatments, the claims of a child she could not feed and could not quite begin to love, and her sense of imprisonment in this house with a man whose very presence oppressed her. Thanks to Rowella and the new library she had a constant supply of new works to read, mainly history, but some geography and a little, but only a little, theology. Her deeply-ingrained religious beliefs had been under a severe strain this last year, and somehow books on the Christian virtues of humility and charity and patience and obedience did not move her any more. She had prayed about it but could not yet feel that her prayers had been answered. She was bitter, and ashamed of her bitterness, and unable to lift herself out of that state.

As soon as she saw Ossie she knew he had been drinking. It was rare for him; normally he drank copiously but knew when to stop. She had never known him unsteady on his feet or slurred in his speech. He had his standards.

Now he came in in his thick pleated silk canary-yellow dressing-gown, his hair awry, his eyes suffused.

He said: 'Ah, Morwenna,' and sat heavily by her bed.

She put the bookmark in her book.

He said: 'These weeks, these months, during which you have been the pr-proud bearer of our child, it has been a trying time for you. I know it well, don't deny it. Pray don't deny it. Dr Behenna says you are much recovered now but still need care. That as you know, I will endeavour to give you. Have done and will continue to do. Care. Great care. You have given me a fine child, from which you are now much recovered.'

'Did Dr Behenna say that?'

'But I think you must give a thought – a thought to the strain it has been – all these weeks and weeks and weeks – on me. On me. D'you understand, on me. That is the other side of the coin. During your pregnancy there was much patient, anxious waiting. At the birth, at the parturition, there was more anxiety, more waiting. At one time your life, I may say, was despaired of. Though one never knows how much Behenna exaggerates the seriousness of a disease in order to gain credit for its intermission. But be that as it may. Since then a month has passed – four long weeks – still of anxiety for me, still waiting.'

A little touched in spite of herself, Morwenna said: 'I shall be better in a while, Ossie. Perhaps if these treatments do not have effect Dr Behenna will essay something different.'

'It cannot go on,' Ossie said.

'What cannot go on?'

'I am a cleric, a clerk in Holy Orders, and I endeavour to perform my duties in accordance – in acc-accordance with my oaths of office. But I am also a man. We are all people of this earth, Morwenna, don't you understand that? I sometimes wonder if you understand.'

She looked at him and saw with horror that it was not only

drink that made him tongue-tied. Perhaps it was not drink at all.

She said: 'Ossie, if you mean . . .'

'That is what I do mean –'

'But I am not well! It is too soon! –'

'Too *soon*? *Four weeks!* I never waited so long as this with Esther. Do you wish me to be ill too? You must know that it is not in human nature –'

'Ossie!' She had raised herself in the bed, her plaited hair reminding him maddeningly of other plaited hair he had just seen. And all else that he had just seen.

'It is a husband's right to desire his wife. It is a wife's duty to submit. Most wives – Esther among them – she was always gratified by the resumption of her husband's attentions. Always.' He seized her hand.

'Ossie,' she said. 'Please, Ossie, do you not know that I am still –'

'Say no more,' he said, and kissed her on the forehead and then on the lips. 'I will just say a little prayer for us both. Then you must be a wife to me. It will soon be over.'

III

Nampara Meeting House had been opened in March, and a leading preacher of the circuit had been there to speak to the faithful and to give it and them his blessing. It had been a notable triumph for Sam, for in addition to the twenty-nine of his flock, all of whom he could sincerely and devoutly vouch for as having found Christ, there had been another twenty-odd cramming into the tiny chapel, most having come out of curiosity, no doubt, but some having been deeply moved by the preacher, and Sam's total flock had afterwards risen to thirty-four, with a number of others still wrestling with their souls and ripe for conversion. Afterwards the preacher had congratulated Sam and had eaten with the elders of the class before leaving.

But in June another man came, and his attendance did not bring with it the same warmth and the same joy. His name was Arthur Champion and he was a circuit steward. He preached ably but without the uplifting emotion one expected, and after the meeting he spent the night with Sam at Reath Cottage, eating the bread and jam Sam offered him and sleeping in Drake's old bed. He was a man of about forty who had been a journeyman shoemaker before he felt the call, and after supper he went politely but firmly into the finances of Sam's little class. He was interested to know if all the attending members paid their dues, and what record was kept and whether Sam had a good and reliable assistant to keep the money safe. Also, how the little chapel had been raised, what it had cost and what debts had been incurred. Also, whether seats were more expensive at the front of the chapel than at the back, and by how much. Also, who kept a record of the activities of the class, and who planned the weekly meetings. Also, what contribution could be made towards the visits of travelling preachers and full-time workers in the cause of Christ.

Sam listened with patience and humility and answered each question in turn. Most of the attending members paid their dues when they could, but, poverty in the area being so bad, these payments did not always come in as regular as maybe in a town. 'I reckon they should, Sam, just same,' said Champion with a gentle smile. 'No society's worth b'longing to that's not worth sacrificing for, d'ye see, specially one founded as a community that's discovered salvation.'

Sam said he had a number of good assistants but he did not bother anyone to keep a record and hold the money safe. He took it down himself in a little black book and the money, when there was money, was kept under the bed that his visitor would sleep on that night. 'Brave,' said Champion. 'You do brave and well, Sam, but I reckon wi' two or three elders in a group, like, tis desirable to spread the responsibility. Indeed, tis necessary in a well-run society.'

Sam said the chapel had been raised on ground given by Captain Poldark and the stones to build it had been taken from the ruined engine-house of Wheal Maiden right alongside; the roof'd been made of wreck wood which had washed in on Hendrawna Beach, very timely; and the thatch'd been come by at little cost. All the benches inside had been knocked up local and the altars and pulpit had been made by his brother Drake, who was handy with his carpenter's saw, out of wood taken from an old library Captain Poldark was having rebuilt. So, as the building had cost almost nothing but men's time, working as faithful servants for the divine Jehovah, Sam had not thought it proper to ask payment to enter the Lord's House from those who had built it. 'Right, Sam, right,' said Champion gently. 'Right and proper. But soon, maybe, a small charge, else ye'll not be able to contribute to the great wide brotherhood to which you now b'long. Much work is being done from the centre, d'ye see, by travelling preachers and those who give their lives fully to God. Tis the widow's mite from every soul we need, from every soul that's found salvation.'

Sam admitted his error and they went on to discuss organization, how the classes should be asked to meet and how mix and what instructions should be given and whether there was another who could act as deputy leader if Sam were ill or away. It was all very necessary, Sam fully understood, and all part of becoming active and permanent members of the great Wesley Connexion. It was no doubt as necessary to have organization as it was to have revelation. Yet he had an uneasy sensation of being brought down to earth. To Sam the spirit that moved within him and the spirit that had moved like summer lightning among the great concourse at Gwennap last year were the very fount of redemption, and, although he was quite capable of being practical in other things, he felt that to be practical in matters so vital to the very soul was like leaping a chasm and then being asked to go back and build a bridge across.

They talked and prayed together for nearly an hour and then Arthur Champion said:

'Sam, I d'wish to have word with ye on another and more closer matter. I'm certain sure that ye b'lieve all be well twixt you and your Redeemer, for there's few I've met more fully imbued wi' the joy of salvation. But tis my need and duty to give report to the circuit that all is proper and right, and I would ask ye to search your soul and answer me that ye have no sinful thought nor temptation that ye wish to discuss with me.'

Sam stared at him. 'We all need to be purified every moment of our lives, brother. But tedn in me to say as I feel in greater

risk today than I did last year or any time since I were saved.
If you have cause to suppose that Satan be nigh me, then I
would ask you to instruct me in my peril.'

'I refer,' said Champion, and cleared his throat. 'It have
been told me that you are consorting wi' a woman who is of
ill repute in the neighbourhood.'

There was silence. Sam loosened his neckerchief. 'Would ee
be meaning Emma Tregirls?'

'I b'lieve that were the name.'

Sam said: 'I thought twas part of a leader's holy task to try
to bring lost souls to Christ.'

Champion cleared his throat again. 'So tis, brother, so tis.'

'Well then. Where do I err?'

'Mind, I know nought of this myself, Sam. Less than
nought. But I'm telled as she is a wicked, sinful woman, but
young and of carnal attraction. The evil, I'm telled, has not
yet wrought 'pon her face. You too are young, Sam. Purity
and impurity d' sometimes become mixed in a man's impulses.
Therein lie the veriest dangers of Hell.'

Sam got up and his tall sturdy body blocked off some of the
failing light. 'I seen her five, nay six, times, brother leader. Be
she less valuable to the living God 'cause she have erred and
sinned like a lost sheep? 'Cause she have followed in her own
heart the devices and desires of Satan? There be greater joy
in heaven over one sinner that repenteth . . .'

'And do she show sign of repentance?'

'. . . Not yet. But with prayer and with faith I have the
hope.'

Champion got up too, rubbing his stubble of beard. 'They
d'say she have been seen drunk, drunk in the street after leaving an ale-house. And that you went into an ale-house last
week in search of her.'

'Christ in his time on earth walked among publicans and
sinners.'

'They d'say she be a whore. Horrible, horrible! That she
d'flaunt her loose body afore men, offering it to whoever care
to beckon.'

Sam frowned, his mind in some torment. 'That I don't
rightly know, brother leader. There be *rumour*; but rumour be
a wicked, evil, corrupting thing too. I know naught of that for

certain. But if tis true, Christ had such a one at the foot of His cross . . .'

Champion held up his hand. 'Peace, brother. I do not come to judge but only to warn. Although we d'follow the Divine Master, we do not have his sublime wisdom. D'ye see? As class leader tis bad for ye to be mixed up wi' a loose woman. There be many others to save. Christ was so pure that he *couldn't* be defiled. There's none of us so pure as that. So *safe* as that.'

Sam bowed his head. 'I'll pray about'n. Not's I haven't already. Many's the time. I'd dearly love to bring her to glory.'

'Pray to give her up, Sam.'

'That I could *not* do! She has a soul, and her soul has the right and the need of the Message –'

'Let others try. Tis not meet that ye should be talked about.'

'That may be, brother. I will pray over that.'

'Let us pray together, Sam,' Champion said. ' 'Fore we retire. Let us spend a little longer on our knees.'

IV

That week George Warleggan left to take his seat in the House of Commons. Elizabeth did not go with him.

All this year their relationship had fluctuated; sometimes icy, sometimes approaching the cool but companionate marriage of the first few years. George's success had delighted him; it had delighted all the Warleggans; it had delighted Elizabeth, for she was as ambitious as the next one and to be married to a Member of Parliament, even though one in trade, must raise her prestige. She was very glad for George because she felt this distinction must help him to throw off the sensation of inferiority which she knew clung to him like a hair shirt in spite of all his successes. From most people he was well able to disguise it, but not from her; though she had scarcely realized it, certainly not the extent of it, when they first married.

They had dined at Tehidy both before and after the election; Sir Francis had been at his most charming. Later he and Lady Basset had dined with them in Truro; the mayor and mayoress were there and George's father and mother and, to dilute them, as many people of eminence as could be summoned from the district round. It had been a great success; the house looked better than it had done since the ball celebrating the King's recovery in '89. The Bassets had spent the night with them; and George's pride in his wife had led to his sharing the same bed with her.

But a week later he had come back with white nostrils and a pinched taut look about his mouth, and from then until his departure there had been no kindness in his heart at all. He had been out to meet Sir Francis to discuss some project for building a hospital in the district, and Elizabeth could not understand what had occurred to change him. Her polite questions brought no response, so in the end she gave it up. There had certainly been talk of her going to London with him; she would have welcomed it for she had not been since she was a girl; but after this date it faded away. He made some excuse of wanting to find his feet, of inadequate lodgings, of taking her next time. She acquiesced, knowing that in this mood there would be little pleasure for her in the trip.

And George's unkindness to his son continued. Unkindness, that is, by neglect. Instead of being his pride and joy, Valentine now seemed disregarded. George could scarcely be persuaded to go and see him. It was unnatural and unfair. Even his mother noticed it and gently chided him

Elizabeth had no one to confide in. Her mother-in-law was a simple soul whose counsel would be impossible to seek on anything deeper than how to embroider a waistcoat or when to take a rhubarb powder. Her own mother was on the coast at Trenwith, and with one blind eye, one lame leg, and an impediment in her speech, had lapsed into an invalidism little better than her father, who now never dressed at all.

With a sick feeling Elizabeth realized that her married life was disintegrating, and she shuddered to suppose the cause. So when George left, with a formal kiss on her cheek, a promise to write, and no fixed date for his return, she felt a sense of relief that for the moment at least all her tensions would be allowed to ease. She was now complete mistress of the house, she could make arrangements to play whist with her friends every afternoon, she could chat with them and take tea and go shopping and live a quiet and comfortable town life without having to defer to her husband's fitful moods.

About a week after he had left she was in the library one day when she saw her cousin Rowella talking to the librarian and she went across and asked after Morwenna.

Rowella blinked and moved over to a private corner, a pile of books under her arm.

'She is no better, Cousin Elizabeth; that I can assure you. You saw her at the christening; well, she is no better than that – possibly worse. I was thinking of writing for Mama.'

'I should have been over, but have been so busy with Mr Warleggan leaving . . . I will come this afternoon. Will you tell her?'

She went about six, hardly bothered now for knowing that George's servant, Harry Harry, kept distant sight of her all the way. She took tea with Morwenna and then sought out Mr Whitworth, whom she found in church trying out a new crimson velvet cloth with a gold fringe for the communion table.

'Osborne,' she said, 'I think Morwenna is very sick. I believe you should consult another doctor.'

Ossie frowned at her. 'She's none too special, I agree, but she's better in bed. Seems to tire her, this getting up in the afternoon. Eh? Behenna's been very regular. He'd not like it.'

'Nor did he neither when Valentine had rickets last year. But we could not consider his feelings when it was perhaps life and death.'

Ossie looked at the cloth. 'This has just been presented to the church by Mrs Thomas. It's a thought gaudy for my taste. In this church, that is. We have not enough windows to light it up. There's no one rich enough round here to give windows. I wonder if – '

'I think you should have another opinion.'

'What? Well . . . Whom did you engage?'

'Dr Pryce of Redruth. And a very good knowledgeable man he was. But he died last winter.'

'Well, then, he's farther away than Redruth by now, eh? What? Ha! Ha! They say this apothecary who's set himself up in Malpas has a very good idea of physics. I could ask Behenna about him.'

'Ossie, I think you should ask Dr Enys to come and see her.'

'Enys?' Ossie's frown deepened. 'But he's a sickly man him-

self. Maybe married life doesn't suit him. Doesn't suit everybody, you know. Had a man in the parish called Jones; farrier;
married one of the Crudwells; swealed away like a candle after
it.'

'Dr Enys would come if I sent word. I have known him for
some years. After all, you went to his wedding.'

'Yes . . . He looked down-in-the-mouth then, if I remember.
But I also conceit that Dr Behenna does not at all like him.
I recall one or two very slighting remarks Behenna has made.
Very slighting indeed. He spoke of a case he had heard of
when Enys was called to the bedside of an old man with tooth-
ache and Enys dug out the tooth and cracked the jaw and the
old man died! . . .'

The contours of Elizabeth's face were losing their softness.
'Osborne, I believe Morwenna is very sick. If you do not send
for Dr Enys, I shall.'

'Oh . . .' He blew out a long breath and tried to stare her
down. But Elizabeth was not one of his parishioners. 'Very
well. It's a matter on which, of course, I feel the gravest
concern. Will you write, or shall I?'

'I would like to, if you'll permit me. But I would like you
to add a note.'

That was on the Wednesday. Dwight rode over on the
Friday. Dr Behenna had been told, but refused to be present.

Dwight sat by Morwenna's bed for a few minutes talking to
her before asking any medical questions. They talked about
Trenwith and George's election and Caroline's pug dog. He
led the talk round to the birth of John Conan and her ailments
after, and presently he invited the baby's nurse to come in
while he made an examination. The nurse was shocked at the
thoroughness of the examination. Ladies had to have preg-
nancies, but it was not customary to interfere with them after
the child was born. Then the bedclothes went back and the
nurse was ushered out.

So they sat talking for another ten minutes while Morwenna's flush died and came again and died away, leaving
the skin of her face sallow and dark. Then Dwight shook
hands with her and went downstairs to where Ossie was talking
to Rowella. After Rowella had gone Dwight said:

'I am not at all sure what is amiss with your wife, Mr Whitworth.' (This preliminary sentence at once damned him in Ossie's view.) 'I am not at all sure, but I don't think your wife is suffering from a puerperal infection of the tissues of the womb, such as has been suggested. Superficial signs may indicate that, but had that been the case I would have expected other and gouty symptoms to develop by now. That they have not is a good foretoken; but Mrs Whitworth is very weak and in a highly nervous condition. One thing I am convinced of is that the loss of blood at the time of her delivery has not been sufficiently made good. If this is due to a morbid condition of the blood then remedies may not avail. But for the time, as an experiment, I would advise no blood-letting and a strengthening, not a lowering, diet.'

Ossie stood with his hands behind his back looking out of the window.

Dwight said: 'She must take at least six raw eggs every day. It matters not how they go down, how she takes them, so long as they be taken. And two pints of porter.'

'Two . . . Two pints of – Heavens, man, you'll turn her into a toper!'

Dwight smiled. 'That is what she said. But many people drink more than that and come to no harm.'

'She is entirely unused to such drink!'

'Let her persevere with it for a month. She may leave it off then, for by then it will have done her much good or no good according to whether my diagnosis is correct.'

Ossie grunted and flipped his coat-tails. 'Mrs Warleggan is here; she came ten minutes ago; so you had best instruct her in the niceties of your treatment, since she entertains the notion that she knows best.'

'There is one thing, Mr Whitworth,' Dwight said, as he put the strap around his bag, 'and this I may not say to Mrs Warleggan.'

'Oh?'

'I gather that you have resumed marital relations with your wife.'

'Good God, sir, what is that to you! And what right has Mrs Whitworth to mention it to you?'

'She did not mention it. I asked her.'

'She had no right to tell you!'

'She could hardly lie to me, Mr Whitworth. And since I am her doctor it would have been very ill-advised, surely. Well . . .'

'Well?'

'It must stop, Mr Whitworth. For the time being. I would say at least for the month during which she takes this new treatment.'

The Reverend Mr Whitworth seemed to swell. 'By what *right*, may I ask? By what *right* – '

'By right of the love you bear your wife, Mr Whitworth. Her body is not properly healed. Nor are her nerves. It is essential that she be allowed complete and absolute freedom from any marital claims until they are.'

Osborne's eyes strayed to the lanky figure of Rowella as she walked past the window towards the vegetable garden.

He laughed bitterly. 'Who is to tell, who is to say, how can it be known, when she is or is not well enough to assume her full duties as a wife? *Who*, I ask you?'

'For the time pray accept my guidance,' Dwight said coldly. 'If in a month my treatment has brought no improvement you may dispense with my services and look elsewhere.'

CHAPTER XI

Although it had not been put into words between them it had been understood that Elizabeth should not go to Trenwith until George returned. But the week after George left Geoffrey Charles came home from Harrow, returning two weeks before the prescribed end of term because of an epidemic of scarlet fever at the school. All his puppy fat had gone, he was desperately pale, and he had grown three inches. She thought him ill but the weighing machine contradicted it. As she had feared, he was half a stranger to her, as tall as she though not yet twelve; and there was some darkness in his eyes that suggested he had been through the mill. His delightful spontaneity had disappeared, yet when he smiled he had a new and more adult charm. She thought he looked fifteen.

He did not want to stay in Truro. Truro was tedious. He had no friends here and no freedom. After a couple of visits to Morwenna and a day or two on the river he said he wanted to go to the coast. He could ride there more easily, swim there, take off his stiff collar and enjoy the summer. That week Elizabeth received a letter from her father saying that her mother was acting queerly, that the staff generally were misbehaving, that he was none too capital himself, and that he'd be glad to see her to discuss the inadequacies of Lucy Pipe who, since Aunt Agatha's death, had been looking after them.

Mr Chynoweth wrote monthly, and always on a note of illness and complaint, but this together with Geoffrey Charles's demands, and her own annoyance at finding all her movements in Truro tracked by one or other of George's personal servants, was enough. She left on the Saturday morning after Geoffrey Charles had returned, taking with her only her two sons, Valentine's nurse Polly Odgers, and the coachman. Harry Harry and his fellows were instructed to stay behind.

It was a teeth-rattling journey over tracks gone suddenly hard and rutted after ten days of fine weather. They reached the old Poldark home in glistening sunshine and a heat rare so near the coast. Bees hummed in and out of nodding Canterbury bells, Tom Harry's terrier barked excitedly, the leather trappings creaked as the coach came to a standstill, and startled servants peered out of windows at the unexpected arrival.

Once she was here she was glad she had come. Although the house had mixed memories for her, this was much less a Warleggan property than the house in Truro and the mansion of Cardew. The servants, once they realized no severe reprimands were coming, were genuinely pleased to see her. Even her parents seemed less tiresome after the separation. And she was free of surveillance.

She had a moment of doubt when the first morning Geoffrey Charles took a pony and rode off to see Drake Carne. It was what she had feared; you could not break affection by decree; yet Geoffrey Charles came back to dinner looking happier than he had done since he returned from school, and this pattern continued for several days. After all, now that Morwenna was wed, the only bar to a friendship between the young man and the boy was that Drake was too low in class and that he was Ross Poldark's brother-in-law. But now that he was living on the *other* side of Trenwith he seemed less likely to involve them with Nampara, and his trade and his new little property gave him a small enhancement of status. She, Elizabeth, had a number of cottager friends in Grambler and Sawle whom she was accustomed to call on and chat to, and most of these were ex-servants who remembered Francis and his father or village women connected with the church. It wasn't very different.

One of the families for which she had always taken some responsibility – from the days when she had been newly wed and prosperous, through the long years of indigence and again in the much greater prosperity of her new marriage – was that of the Reverend Clarence Odgers and his wife and brood. Polly, Valentine's nurse, was the eldest child; but by now most of the others were grown-up enough to work. Three of the children had died in recent years but there were still seven to be accounted for. So, after sending for Mr Odgers on the first afternoon and exchanging greetings and news with him, she invited them to supper on the Tuesday and when they were leaving, the evening being warm and splendid, she said she would walk back with them to their tiny overburdened cottage that passed for a vicarage. As they reached it Mr Odgers went off into a dead faint.

There was nothing wrong with him except that, after a spring of malnutrition, he had eaten altogether too much at Trenwith, his trousers had become very tight and he was ashamed to unbutton them in front of his hostess, so that the constriction round his middle together with four glasses of canary wine brought his feeble body to a state where it opted out of the struggle.

His eldest son, who acted as verger and did most of the kitchen garden work for his father these days, and a sturdy child of about twelve carried their father up to bed, where he recovered consciousness and was all eagerness to hurry downstairs again to apologize to Elizabeth for the embarrassment he had caused her.

She waited twenty minutes to be sure that all was well, and then had to wait another twenty while a sudden rain shower pattered upon the leaves and the uneven stones outside. In a brilliant lambent sky with the setting sun orange-tinting the moorland, a few bags of cloud had gathered and were dropping their load. A vivid rainbow faded as the rain stopped and the sun sank.

'Paul will come with you, Mrs Warleggan,' said Maria Odgers. 'Paul will just walk with you so far as the gates. Paul – '

'Let him see to his father,' Elizabeth said. 'It's ten minutes and I shall enjoy the cool of the evening.'

'It might be better if Paul were to go with you, Mrs Warleggan. Mr Odgers would never forgive me if – '

'No, no, thank you. Good night. I'll send over in the morning to enquire.' Elizabeth slipped out, not anxious to have an escort.

As she went off, a few spots of rain, reluctant to cease altogether, fell on her hair, so she put on the white bonnet she carried. On the way from Trenwith Mr Odgers had talked anxiously with her about the vacant living of Sawle-with-Grambler. He would dearly have liked the living for himself; after all he had administered the parish and conducted the services for eighteen years, and such a plum, quadrupling his income at a stroke, would make him virtually a rich man for the rest of his life. This son could be apprenticed here, that son, who showed rare promise in the ancient languages, sent to the Grammar School, this daughter, who was ailing, provided with special food, that daughter, who had all the looks of the family, given an opportunity of spending a year with their cousins in Cambridge. His wife Maria would be saved the endless anxious scraping to make ends nearly meet, and, as for himself, well one hardly needed to look at him to see what such preferment would do for him.

But he had no friends in high places, so he had really little hope of the living coming to him. But now that Mr Warleggan had become a Member of Parliament, was there perhaps *just* a chance that he would speak for him to the Dean and Chapter, or even write a letter, or otherwise intercede for him among his influential friends?

Elizabeth had heard him out and had promised to do what she could.

As she reached the church the rain became heavier again so she ducked into the porch and took off her bonnet and shook it and peered up at the sky. She had been so impatient to be on the move that she had not properly observed the manœuvres overhead. The rain fell in slanting rods which were splintered into brilliance by the afterglow. It could not last long. The church was locked, so she had no choice but to stand in the porch and wait.

'The parson knows enough who knows a duke.' Who had said that? She would mention Mr Odgers's hopes to George if when he returned he was in an approachable mood. A word to Francis Basset? She might attempt that herself. Too far to ride on such a small matter, but she might write a letter. Would Mr Odgers make a suitable incumbent? The poor little man was so anxious, so down-trodden, with his horse-hair wig and his dirty nails. He seemed doomed to be subservient to others. Yet how better would the parish be served by having another absentee vicar? She could not even remember the *name* of the man who had just died. Odgers had given his life to the parish in his own unkempt unscholarly way. Indeed, she had noticed recently he sometimes put SCL after his name. Student of Civil Law, a non-existent degree that non-graduates sometimes used in an attempt to improve their status.

By the time the rain stopped the light was fading and she stepped into the churchyard, trying to avoid the puddles with her white buckram shoes. The quickest way from here was diagonally across the churchyard by a path among the grave-stones to a stile at the corner. She took it, knowing it would lead her past Aunt Agatha's grave.

Many families as important to a church as the Poldarks had been to Sawle would have had a family vault; but, except for an old Trenwith vault at the other side of the yard, long since full and crumbling with neglect, all the Poldarks were buried in this area of the graveyard, individually or at the most in pairs. A few were commemorated by plaques inside the church. This was the only part of the graveyard not grossly over-full. In many parts, as Jud Paynter complained, it was hardly possible to thrust in a spade without jarring it on a bone. Jud, of course, complained at anything, but it had been the same story from the sexton before him. She must try to persuade

George to give a new piece of land. The scars of mining came like a tide right up to the churchyard wall.

Just near Aunt Agatha's grave, as Elizabeth had noticed at the time of the funeral, were three stunted hawthorn trees, so bent and slanted by the wind that they might have been clipped into their distorted shape by giant shears. Coming on them now, silhouetted against a sky gone sallow with the fall of evening, they produced a replica of Aunt Agatha herself, etched and magnified in black against the chalky light. Bending forward, cloak drooping, nose and chin thrust out, cap on head. A long-handled shovel someone had leaned against the trees provided the stick.

Elizabeth hesitated and stared, smiled to herself: then the smile turned to a shiver and she stepped past. As she did so a part of one of the trees moved and came to life and became a figure, and she stopped.

She turned to walk back quickly the way she had come, and a voice said: 'Elizabeth!'

She stopped again. It was Ross's voice, and sooner than meet him she would have been more willing to have confronted some long-dead corpse dragging the rotted remnants of its winding sheet.

He moved a few steps away from the trees, and she could see rain glistening in his hair.

'I had come to look at Agatha's grave and was sheltering from the shower. Were you in the church?'

'Yes.'

He had changed little over the years, she thought, the same restless, bony face, the same heavy-lidded unquiet eyes.

'You were going – returning to Trenwith?'

'Yes.'

'You'd be safer with an escort. I'll walk with you that far.'

'Thank you, I'd prefer to walk alone.'

She went past him to the stile but he followed, and followed her over.

When he spoke his voice was again without expression: 'I've been considering the size of stone to put up for Agatha. I gather from George that he has no plans for doing this, so I thought to do it instead.'

After a bit of rough ground they rejoined the path and so

could walk side by side. Short of returning to the Odgers, there was no way of preventing his accompanying her.

'I thought a granite surround and cross in the style of her brother's but smaller. Nothing but granite will stand the weather here.'

Choking anger welled up in her against this man who had done her such a monstrous, an unforgivable wrong. Anger especially that he should be walking beside her and talking in this apparently casual tone, as if they were two uninvolved cousins-by-marriage discussing a simple matter of the headstone of a deceased great-aunt. Had her anger not been so fierce she might have realized that his calm was a surface calm hiding the emotions that her appearance had stirred in him. But it was too great. He seemed at that moment the cause, the fount, the initiator of all her present and past miseries.

He had been speaking again but she sharply interrupted him. '*When* did you see George? *When* did he tell you that we did not intend to erect a headstone?'

These were the first words she had really directed at him, and he could hear the anger trembling in her voice.

'When? Oh, last Tuesday sennight it would be. I was in Truro, and Francis Basset called me in to discuss a charity hospital.'

She had stopped. 'So *that* was it.'

'What? What is wrong, Elizabeth?'

'What do you – you suppose is wrong?'

'Well, I know all that has been amiss between us all these years, but what new is there?'

'New?' she laughed. 'Nothing, of course! How could there be?'

He was startled by the harshness of her laugh. 'I don't understand.'

'It's nothing. A mere nothing. Except that every time George meets you it transforms him from a reasonable man into an unreasonable one, from a kind husband to a bitter one, from – from . . .'

Ross digested this in silence for a while.

'I'm sorry. Our antagonism has not softened over the years. I confess it seems even to have sharpened again of late. I spoke a few words with him that afternoon and as usual we rubbed each other the wrong way, but I was not conscious of special enormity. Still less, since you married him and threw in your lot with him, would I wish to say anything or do anything to make your life a more dislikeable one or to spoil the happiness you should be enjoying.'

Against his intentions a bite had come into the last sentence.

She stood there in her white frock in the deepening twilight. He thought exactly what she had thought, what little change the years had made. He might have been back in Trenwith thirteen years ago, looking at the girl who had then meant everything in life to him and on whose word his whole future hung.

This was practically the first time they had spoken directly to each other since May '93. He was only too aware of the indefensibility of his actions then and the probably greater indefensibility of his non-action of the month following. He knew it was something for which Elizabeth would never be willing to forgive him: she had made this clear in their brief meetings since in the company of George. Ross did not altogether blame her; if their positions could possibly have been transposed he thought he might have felt the same himself. So he expected coldness. But he did not expect this trembling anger. It startled him and shook him. As he grew older his own tendencies were to try to repair the breaches that past enmities had made.

'Why should my meeting George turn his disposition against you? I say nothing about you. I never mention your name . . . Though, stay, on that occasion I did suggest I might discuss Agatha's stone with you. But it was a simple suggestion that he brusquely turned down. Is he still jealous of our one-time attachment?'

'Yes, he is! Because he now appears to suspect the nature of that attachment!'

'But . . . how can he? What do you mean?'

'What do you think I mean?'

They stared at each other.

'I don't know. But whatever is past is long past.'

'Not if he suspects that Valentine is not his child!'

It was something she could not have said to any other

person. It was something that for a long time she had not even said to herself.

'Oh God,' Ross said. 'God in Heaven!'

'If you think God has been concerned in this!'

Over the land it was almost night now but, seawards, sea and sky lent a luminous light to the dark.

Ross said. 'And is he?'

'What?'

'Is he George's child?'

'I cannot say.'

'You mean you will not say.'

'I will not say.'

'Elizabeth . . .'

'Now I'll go.'

She turned to thrust past him. He caught her arm and she wrenched it away. She said: 'Ross, I wish you would *die* . . .'

He stared after her stupidly while she walked rapidly away. Then he ran after her, caught her arm again. She pulled with real violence but this time his grip held.

'Elizabeth!'

'Let me go! Or are you still so much the brute and the bully?'

He released her arm. 'Hear me out!'

'What have you to say?'

'Much! But some of it cannot be said.'

'Why? Are you the coward as well?'

He had never seen her like this, or remotely like it. She had always been so composed – except on that one occasion when he had broken her composure. But this was different, this corroding hysteria and hatred. Hatred of *him*.

'Yes, the coward, my dear. It's impossible to dredge up all the memories of fifteen years. It would hurt you the more and I'm sure do my cause with you no good. Three years ago, mine, no doubt, was the crowning injury, the insult you can never forgive and forget. I only ask you when you're of quieter mind to think over the events that led to my visit that night. Injury until then was not all on one side.'

'Do you mean – '

'Yes, I *do* mean. Not to excuse myself, but to tell you to think over the ten years before. Wasn't it the tragedy of a woman, a beautiful woman, who couldn't make up her mind, and so ruined the lives of all of us? . . .'

She appeared about to speak again but did not. Her hair and frock gleamed, but there was not enough light now to show her face. She turned slowly and walked on. They were near the gates of Trenwith.

He said: 'But that's past. Even my offence is three years past. It's the *present* that shocks me.' He hesitated, groping for words. 'How could he *ever* know?'

'I thought perhaps you had hinted . . .'

'Great God, you must have thought me a monster!'

'Having done the rest, why should you not do that?'

'For the very good reason that I loved you. You were – the love of my life. Love can't turn to *that* much hate.'

She was silent. Then in a voice somewhat changed, as if his words had at last made a difference. 'Someone else, then.'

'Who could there be?'

'Demelza?'

'She knew, of course. It nearly broke up our marriage, but now I believe the break is healed. But she would say *nothing*, nothing ever to anyone. It – it would destroy her to speak of it.'

They walked on for a few paces.

'Was he – like this when Valentine was born?'

'George? No.'

'He accepted him as a premature child?'

'I am not saying that Valentine was not. I am only speaking of George's suspicion.'

'Very well. So he must have learned something more recently or have been given reason to suspect since.'

'Oh, what is the *use* of talking!' Elizabeth said with great weariness. 'It's all – destroyed. If your purpose in what you did was destruction, then you altogether succeeded.'

But he would not be sidetracked. 'Who was in the house that night? Geoffrey Charles? He slept soundly in the turret room. Aunt Agatha? But she was almost bedridden. The Tabbs? . . .'

'George saw Tabb a few months ago,' Elizabeth said reluctantly. 'He mentioned it to me.'

Ross shook his head. 'How could it have been Tabb? You

complained to me in those days that he never went to bed sober. And I came through no door – as you know.'

'Like the devil,' said Elizabeth. 'With the face and look of the devil.'

'Yet you did not treat me so after the first shock.' He had not intended to say it but she had provoked him into it.

'Thank you, Ross. That's the sort of taunt I should have learned to expect.'

'Possibly. Possibly. But this meeting between us – after these years. I can't see the beginning or end of it.'

'The end of it's now. Go on your way.'

They were at the wicket gate. 'This meeting itself is a shock, Elizabeth – but what you tell me is the greater shock. How can we separate – just at this moment? There must be more said. Stay for five minutes.'

'Five years would make no difference. It's all finished.'

'I'm not trying to revive something between *us*. I'm trying to see what you have told me in some believable shape . . . Are you quite certain that George has these suspicions?'

'How else would you explain his attitude towards his son?'

'He's a strange man – given to moods that might give you the wrong impression. The fact that you have a natural fear . . .'

'A guilty conscience, you mean.'

'Never that, for the guilt was all mine.'

'How generous!'

With the first hint of impatience he said: 'Have it how you will. But tell me what makes you so sure.'

They were so silent for some moments that an owl flew by them, almost between them, and Elizabeth put up a hand to guard her face.

'When Valentine was born George could not make enough of him. He doted on him, spoke constantly of his prospects, his schooling, his inheritance. Since last September he has changed. His mood varies, but at its worst he has not visited the child's room for days at a time. After your last meeting with him I carried Valentine into his room and he refused to look up from his desk.'

Ross frowned into the dark, thinking all round what she said.

'God in Heaven, what a pit we've dug for ourselves! . . .'

'And what a pit has been dug for Valentine . . . Now if you will let me pass.'

'Elizabeth—'

'Please, Ross. I feel ill.'

'No, wait. Is there nothing we can do?'

'Tell me what.'

He was silent. 'At the worst—why don't you have it out with him?'

'Out with him?'

'Yes. It's all better to be spoken than unspoken.'

She gave a hard laugh. 'What a noble suggestion! Would you not like to have it out with him yourself?'

'No, because I should kill him—or possibly he me—and that would not help your dilemma. I don't suggest you should tell him the truth. But challenge him—make him say what he suspects and then deny it.'

'Lie to him, you mean.'

'If it's necessary to lie, yes. If you cannot find some way of denying what you have to deny less directly. But I don't know what is the truth. Perhaps you do not. Or if you do, only you do. He can have no proof because there is no proof. If anyone knows who is Valentine's father it can be only you. And as for the rest—what happened between us—that's known only to us. All else is speculation, suspicion, whispers and rumour. What can he have heard since September to destroy his peace of mind? You say his mood varies. That means he has no certainty—only some evil has been breathed into his ear and he can't rid himself of it. You are the only one who can free him.'

'How bravely you solve the problem. I should have come to you before!'

He refused to be provoked. 'I solve nothing, my dear, but I think it's what you should do. I've known George for twenty-five years. And you fifteen. And I know in this you underrate yourself. Face him with his suspicions. Possibly because of this fear within you, you have come to magnify it all. But you are the one person in his world, perhaps the only one, who has no need, no possible reason to fear him.'

'Why?'

'Because you're still precious in his eyes—as in the eyes of many other men – and he couldn't *bear* to lose you. His very passion about this . . . I tell you, I know him, he'd do anything to keep you, to know you love him and to be told you have eyes for no other man. He has wanted you since he first saw you; the very first time I saw him looking at you, I knew. But I never dreamed that he had a chance. Neither did he.'

'Neither did I,' said Elizabeth.

'No . . .'

The owl was screeching now in the denser blackness of the trees.

He was not sure, but some of the bitterest anger seemed to have gone out of her. He said: 'Can you imagine how I felt when I learned that he was to have you?'

'You left me in no doubt.'

'It was ill done, but until now I have not regretted it.'

'I had supposed that you might have done – almost at once.'

'You supposed wrong. But I could not come to you again – break up everyone's life afresh.'

'You should have thought of that before.'

'I was mad – mad with jealousy. It's not easy to reason with a man when he sees the woman he has always loved giving herself to the man he has always hated.'

She looked at him. Even in this dark he caught some questing look.

'I have thought many ill things of you, Ross, but not that you were – devious.'

'In what respect do you suppose I am now?'

She sheered away from what had been suddenly growing between them. 'Is it not devious now to try to save a marriage you did your best to prevent?'

'Not altogether. Because now there is a third person to consider.'

'It would redeem your conscience if –'

'Good God, my conscience is not at issue! What is, is your life and the life of – your son.' He stopped. 'In all this I'm assuming that you don't wish your marriage to George to founder?'

'It is already foundering.'

'But you speak as if you wish to save it.'

She hesitated. 'Yes . . . I wish to save it.'

'Most of all you must save Valentine. He above all is worth fighting for.'

He saw her stiffen. 'Do you think I'm not prepared to fight?'

'Whatever else,' he said harshly, 'he is your son. I *hope* he is George's. I want to have produced no cuckoo in the nest who shall inherit all the Warleggan interests. But he is *your* son, and as such he should grow up free of the taint of suspicion . . . And, Elizabeth . . .'

'What?'

'If it should happen – if so be that you should ever give George another child . . .'

'What are you trying to say?'

'If so be that you should, would it not put a seal upon the marriage that no one could dispute?'

'It could not alter anything that had gone before.'

'But it could. If you were to contrive . . .' He stopped again.

'Well – go on.'

'Women can get confused as to the months of their conception. Perhaps you did with Valentine – perhaps not. But let there be confusion next time, however arranged. Another seven-month child would convince George as nothing else would.'

She was examining something on her sleeve. 'I think . . .' she said: 'can you get this off me, please?'

A July-bug, or cockchafer, had landed and attached itself to the lace of her sleeve. They were harmless insects but enormous, and most women were afraid of them getting in their hair. He took her arm and held it; with a sharp sweep he tried to knock it off; it clung, and he had to get hold of the fat yielding body between his fingers and pull it away before it would fall.

At last it was gone, somewhere in the dark grass where it buzzed helplessly, trying to take to the air again.

'Thank you,' Elizabeth said. 'And now goodbye.'

He hadn't released her arm and though she made a movement away from him he did not let go. Quietly he pulled her towards him and covered her face with kisses. Nothing at all violent, this time; five or six brushing kisses, loving, admiring; too sexual to be brotherly yet too affectionate to be altogether resented.

'Goodbye,' Ross said. 'My dear.'

CHAPTER XII

Dwight and Caroline had been invited to Tregothnan too, so Ross and Demelza called for them at Killewarren on the way. They drank chocolate together before setting out in procession. Ross had recently bought two new horses, called Sheridan and Swift, from Tholly Tregirls, so he and Demelza were not so greatly outshone in the quality of their mounts, and since they had to carry night clothes and evening clothes they had brought John Gimlett with them on old Darkie. It had been a long time since Gimlett had had an outing, and Ross thought it suitable that he should eat and sleep at Boscawen expense. Caroline had brought a maid as well as a footman.

On the way down into Truro, down the long steep dusty lane, with its sheds and its hovels and its pigs rooting in the road, Dwight said that they must excuse him for half an hour, as he had a patient to visit.

Caroline said: 'He is going to call on the vicar's wife. Dwight can never dissociate his duty from his pleasure. Though I truly believe he makes a pleasure of duty, especially when it is some pretty young woman he has to attend!'

'Caroline, please,' Dwight said, half smiling.

'No, no, don't deny it! All the young women adore you. Even, I blush to confess it, your own wife, who takes her place in the crowd humbly hoping for a little attention!'

'Caroline,' Dwight said, 'loves to pillory me for neglect because I venture to pursue my own trade. But don't put on this pretence among your friends, my love. They know how much I neglect you.'

Ross said: 'Is it Whitworth's wife? Morwenna Whitworth? I didn't know she was ill.'

'Yes ... ill,' said Dwight.

'She had a baby some months ago,' Demelza said. 'Is all not well because of that?'

'She's a little on the mend.'

'Dwight,' said Caroline, 'will not discuss his patients. It all differs greatly from my uncle's doctor in Oxford who chatters freely about how this lady has benefited from his grated rhubarb powders and how that gentleman has caught the French pox and is responding to treatment. And always by name, of course, always by name. It makes for an entertaining visit and keeps one abreast of local gossip.'

'Whitworth,' Ross said. 'Do you find him an agreeable fellow?'

'He's seldom about when I call.'

'I have always wanted to throw him in some stinking pond.'

Caroline said: 'I admire you for your subtlety, Ross. What has the poor man done to deserve such dislike?'

'Except that he used at one time to come sniffing round Demelza, very little to me personally, but–'

'Well, I trust you don't dislike every man who takes a fancy to Demelza, or you would be hard pressed to find a friend!'

'No, but Whitworth has such an intolerable, loud conceit of himself. I'm sure Demelza has no fancy for the fellow either.'

'Sniffing,' said Demelza. 'I don't recollect him sniffing. It was the way his tail wagged I didn't greatly care for.'

The spire of St Mary's Church lofted itself above the huddle of the town. Water wrinkled under the crouching clouds. The convoy threaded through the narrow streets, hooves slipping and clattering over the cobbles and the mud. Ragged children ran after them, and Caroline opened her bag and threw some ha'pence in a scattering fan. Immediately the urchins fell on them, but they were beaten away by men and women nearly as ragged who had been sitting in doorways.

They turned a corner, and the noise of the struggle and of the shouts and cries and the yapping dogs was left behind. They made for Malpas, and here Dwight left them. A drop or two of rain fell. The way was narrow, and they went in single file to avoid the cart ruts.

Ross looked at Demelza's straight back jogging ahead of him. She hadn't the 'seat' of Caroline, but considering how little she rode it was pretty good. He had not told her of his meeting with Elizabeth. However carefully he explained, she would be liable to misunderstand it. Not surprising in view of their history. Yet he would have liked very much to tell her. Elizabeth's news of George's suspicions worried and shocked him, and Demelza's wisdom would have been specially welcome. But this was the one subject on which Demelza's wisdom could be drawn off course by the lode star of her emotions. You could expect no other. It was a dangerous and nasty situation that he saw ahead, but he had no right to bring Demelza into it further than she already was.

But more particularly he would have liked to tell her again of his feelings for Elizabeth. He had tried to do this once before and it had nearly led for the second time to a break-up of their marriage. The good news that he then tried to convey to her, namely that his love for Elizabeth was no longer to be compared to his love for her, had somehow in the telling become pompous and condescending, and the terrible quarrel that ensued had led to her saddling her horse and being almost away before a last appeal from him and a bathetic domestic crisis had stopped her.

So nothing good, certainly, would come of his reopening the wound after it had been healing for three years. Yet, riding towards the ferry on that oppressive July afternoon, with bees buzzing in the hedgerows and butterflies flickering at the water's edge and thunder spots falling, he would have liked to say: 'Demelza, I met Elizabeth and we talked for the first time for years. At first she was bitter and hostile. But towards the end she softened and when we parted I kissed her. I'm still fond of her, in the way a man is for a woman he has once loved. I'm grieved for her predicament and would do much to help her. I tried deliberately to show my affection for her because it sears me to find her so hostile. I have an uneasy conscience about her for the two misdeeds I committed against her. One, I took her against her will – though in the end I do not believe it was *so* much against her will. But, two, I never went to see her thereafter and I believe to the first injury added a much greater injury for which it would be far more injurious to apologize. I would *like* to be friends with her again – so far as is possible considering whom she has married. The other evening I *tried* to make her think I still loved her –

for in a way I truly do. But not in any way you need fear, my dear. Fifteen years ago I would have given the whole earth for her. And *she* hasn't changed much, aged, coarsened, or become less lovely. Only I have changed, Demelza. And it is your fault.'

He would very much have liked to say all this to Demelza; but one attempt to explain his feelings for Elizabeth was enough. Once bitten twice shy. Somehow in the telling the confidence would have got itself twisted up and turned inside out and become an attempt to reassure his wife of something he didn't believe himself. His witty, earthy, infinitely charming wife would for once in her life employ her wit and earthiness to unseat his reason and his good-will, and in no time they would be saying things to each other that they neither thought nor meant. And there would be Hell to pay.

So all must be kept secret. And all must be left unsaid.

II

The drive to the house from the entrance gates above Tresillian was four miles, but by crossing at the ferry they cut this out and in a few minutes they were approaching Tregothnan. It was, Demelza found, an older and altogether more shabby house than Tehidy. Nor had it the singular Elizabethan elegance of the far smaller Trenwith. It was built of some sort of white stone with a pale slate roof, and it stood on rising ground looking down the river. Inside the rooms were gaunt and rather gloomy, being hung with flags and war trophies and full of suits of armour and small cannon.

'I had no idea you were such a warlike family,' she said to Hugh Armitage. 'It seems – '

'Some of these things belonged to my grandfather, the great admiral,' Hugh said, 'whose widow still lives in London. But as for the rest, I suppose they have accumulated. As individuals we take part in most wars, but as a family we have chiefly prospered by minding our own business.'

He had come down the steps to greet them, and Mrs Gower, a pleasant plump woman in her forties, had been just behind him. Lord Falmouth's two children were in the hall, as was Colonel Boscawen, an uncle, but of the viscount himself nothing was yet to be seen. Half a dozen other guests had arrived

about the same time, and in the bustle Demelza was able to
withdraw her hand from Hugh's without Ross noticing how
long he had held it.

'I think I have offended you, Mrs Poldark,' Armitage said.

'If you have I didn't know it,' she replied.

He smiled. In spite of his tan he still contrived to look pale.
'I know no woman so witty without any element of malice.
Nor one so beautiful without any element of conceit.'

'Kind words . . . If they were deserved they couldn't hardly
fail to spoil what they try to praise.'

'That I cannot believe, and will not believe.'

'I suspect you build something, Lieutenant Armitage, that
isn't really there at all.'

'You mean I set up an ideal woman which cannot be
attained of? On the contrary. On the *very* contrary. Let me
explain – '

But he could not explain because a footman came to show
them the way upstairs. They changed and supped at a long
table at which, apart from the family, there were twenty guests.
After supper another twenty-odd people arrived, and they
danced in the great parlour, that room in which, not so long
ago, Mr Hick and Mr Nicholas Warleggan had had their
protracted and uncomfortable wait. But now much of the
furniture and armoury had been removed and a three-piece
band played in the corner by the empty fireplace with its large
caryatids supporting the wooden chimney piece.

His Lordship had come to dinner, and his manner was
gracious; but there was a reserve about him that made high
spirits seem out of place in his presence, and no one complained when he disappeared as dancing began.

Most of the other guests were young, and it made for a
lively party. Lieutenant Armitage acted the part of host, and
behaved very circumspectly towards Demelza; and it was half
through the evening before he approached Ross and asked if
he might dance with his wife. Ross, who had just done so and
found the evening warm, smilingly agreed. He stood by one
of the double doors and watched them go on to the floor: it
was still a formal dance, this, a gavotte, and he saw them
talking to each other as they came together and separated and
met again. Demelza was one of those women who usually

contrive to retain some element of attractiveness under the most adverse conditions; and he had seen her in plenty; hair lank and sweaty with fever, face twisted in the pains of child-birth, dirty and unkempt from taking some nasty job out of the servants' hands; bitter from that long disastrous quarrel. But perhaps her greatest asset was an ability to bloom with excitement at quite small things. Nothing ever seemed to stale. The first baby wren to hatch was as fascinating this year as last. An evening out was as much of an adventure at twenty-six as it had been at sixteen.

So he must not take too much account of the way she was blooming tonight. But he suspected there was something different about it; some look of serenity he had not noticed before. Of course any woman likes admiration, and new admiration at that, and she was not different. They had quarrelled once on a ballroom floor – God knew how long ago it was – that time, if he remembered, he had angrily accused her of leading on a pack of undesirable and undeserving men, and she had retorted that he, Ross, had been neglecting her.

This time he was not neglecting her, and only one man, the man she was dancing with, was in any way being led on. Armitage was an honest, charming and likeable chap, and there was nothing whatever to show that Demelza was more than the passive recipient of his admiration and attentions. Ross hadn't really very serious doubts about Demelza; he and she had been so close so long; but he hoped she didn't allow Armitage – almost by default – to imagine something different.

A throat was cleared behind him, and he turned. A white-wigged footman.

'Beg pardon, sir, but his Lordship says would you be kind enough to wait on him in his study.'

Ross hesitated. He had the least possible desire to talk with his Lordship, but as he was a guest in the house he could hardly refuse. As he walked through the hall Caroline was coming down the stairs and he said:

'Will you tell Demelza, if she should come off the floor, that I'm in his Lordship's study. I shall not, I trust, be long.'

Caroline smiled at him. 'Of course, Ross.'

It was not until he had followed the footman into Fal-mouth's study that the faint surprise registered that for once she had not returned some flippant or satirical answer.

III

'I am the unhappiest of men,' Hugh Armitage said.

'Why?' asked Demelza.

'Because the woman I have come to hold dearer than life is married to the man to whom I owe my life itself.'

'Then I think you should not say what you have just said.'

'The condemned man must surely be allowed to speak what is in his heart.'

'Condemned?'

'To separation. To loss. I leave for Portsmouth tomorrow.'

'Lieutenant Armitage, I –'

'Will you please call me Hugh?'

They broke apart but presently came together again.

'Well, then, Hugh, if it must be . . . I don't think you're condemned to loss – for how can you lose what you haven't never had?'

'I have had your company, your conversation, the inspiration of touching your hand, of hearing your voice, of seeing the light in your eyes. Is that not grievous loss enough?'

'You're a poet, Hugh. That's the trouble –'

'Yes, let me explain, as I wished to explain before. You think I set up an ideal which is impossible of attainment. But all poets are not romantic. I have *not* been a romantic, believe me. I've been in the navy since I was fourteen and I've knocked about and seen a lot of life, much of it sordid. I have seen and known a number of women. I have no illusions about them.'

'Then you must have no illusions about me.'

'Nor have I. Nor have I.'

'Oh, yes, you have. That poem . . .'

'I have written others. But I couldn't venture to send them.'

'I think you shouldn't have sent that.'

'Of course I should not. It was wholly improper of me. But if a man sings a love song he hopes that once, just once, the object of his love may hear him.'

Demelza said something under her breath.

'What? What did you say?'

She raised her head. 'You trouble me.'

'Dare I hope that that means – '

'Don't hope anything. Can't we not be happy just in – in being alive? D'you mind what you told me at Tehidy about appreciating everything over afresh?'

'Yes,' he said. 'You turn my own words against me.'

She smiled at him brilliantly. 'No, Hugh, *for* you. In that way – that way we can feel affection, and hurt no one and come to no hurt ourselves.'

He said: 'Is that what you feel for me – affection?'

'I don't think you did ought to ask that.'

'Now,' he said, 'I have cut off the sunshine – all that your smile is. But it was worth it, for I see you're too honest to deceive me. It's *not* affection that you feel.'

'The dance is ended. They're going off the floor.'

'You don't feel for me what you would feel for a brother. That is true, Demelza, isn't it?'

'I have a lot of brothers, and none of them quite like you.' Sisters?'

'No.'

'Ah. Alas. It would be too much to ask. God does not repeat his masterpieces.'

Demelza took a deep breath. 'I'd dearly like some port.'

IV

'This smuggling,' said Viscount Falmouth, 'has reached outrageous proportions. Do you know that last week a schooner, the *Mary Armande*, arrived in Falmouth harbour with a cargo of coal. But someone had told upon her and she was boarded by preventive men while the coal was being unloaded. She was found to have a false bottom, under which was hid 276 tubs of brandy.'

'Indeed,' Ross said. He reflected idly that this at least was something Falmouth, Basset and George Warleggan had in common: a hatred of smuggling. Since he, Ross, had not been above indulging in it himself, and not so very long ago, he felt that the single word was all he could suitably offer. In any case he did not suppose he had been invited to see his lordship to discuss such a matter.

Falmouth was sitting beside a small fire, which was smoking and looked as if it had been recently lighted. He was wearing a green velvet jacket and a small green skullcap to cover his scanty hair. He looked like a well-to-do gentleman farmer, youngish-middle-aged, healthy, putting on weight. Only his eyes were autocratic. A bunch of hot-house grapes was on a plate at his elbow, and occasionally he plucked at one.

Suitably, they talked of the crops. Ross reflected that they might have talked on almost any subject to do with the county: mining, shipping, boat building, quarrying, fishing, smelting, or that new industry of the south-east, digging up clay to make pottery, and Falmouth would be likely to be involved. Not on any such down-to-earth basis as the War-leggans, not a question of becoming *personally* involved; but an interest looked after by managers, by stewards, by lawyers, whose livelihood it was to see their employer's business done and well done; or by possession of the land on which industry or mining stood.

Presently Lord Falmouth said: 'I suspect I am indebted to you, Captain Poldark.'

'Oh? I was unaware of it.'

'Well, yes, doubly so, I think. But for you my sister's son was likely to be still languishing in a foul prison in Brittany. If by now he had not been already dead.'

'I'm happy to seem to possess merit in your eyes. But I must point out that I went to Quimper solely to try to release Dr Enys – who is here tonight – and the rest was accidental.'

'No matter. No matter. It was a brave enterprise. My soldiering days are not so far behind me that I can't appreciate the courage of the conception and the overwhelming risks you ran.'

Ross inclined his head and waited. Falmouth spat some pips into his hand and put three more grapes in his mouth. Having waited long enough, Ross said:

'I'm happy to have given Hugh Armitage the opportunity to escape. But I cannot imagine what second obligation you may feel you have towards me.'

Falmouth disposed of the rest of the pips. 'I gather that you refused the nomination to oppose my candidate at the by-election in Truro.'

'Oh, dear God in Heaven! . . .'

'Why do you say that?'

'I say it because apparently it is impossible to have any conversation, however private, without the substance of it being disseminated throughout the county.'

Falmouth looked down his nose. 'I don't suppose it widely known. But the information reached me. I take it it is true.'

'Oh, true enough. But my reasons, I must tell you again, were wholly selfish and in no way concerned with obliging or disobliging other people.'

'Others, it seems, are not at all unwilling to disoblige me.'

'Some people have one ambition, my Lord, others another.'

'And what may yours be, Captain Poldark?'

Faced with the sudden sharp question, Ross was not sure how to answer.

'To live as I want,' he said eventually; 'to raise a family. To make the people round me happy; to be unencumbered of debt.'

'Admirable objectives but of a limited nature.'

'Whose are less limited?'

'I think those with some ideal of public service – especially when the nation is at war . . . But I suspect from your adventure of last year that you understate your aims – or possibly lack a channel to direct them.'

'At least they don't tend towards parliamentary life.'

'Whereas Mr George Warleggan's did.'

'Presumably.'

Falmouth chewed another grape. 'It would give me pleasure one day to obstruct Mr George Warleggan's parliamentary life.'

'I think there is only one way you may do that.'

'How?'

'By composing your differences with Sir Francis Basset.'

'That will *never* be!'

Ross shrugged and said no more.

Lord Falmouth went on: 'Basset forces himself into *my* boroughs, buys influence and favours, contests rights that have been in my family for generations. He is no more to be commended than his lackey!'

'Is not all borough mongering a matter of buying influence and favours?'

'At its most cynical, yes. But it's a system which works

adequately for the maintenance and transaction of government. It breaks down when brash and thrusting young landowners with too much money interfere in the long-established rights of the older aristocracy.'

'I'm not sure,' Ross said, 'that the maintenance and transaction of government is at all well served by the present system of representation and election. Of course it's better than anything that went before because neither king nor lords nor commoners may rule without consent of the other. It may save us from another 1649, or even, if one looks to France, from a 1789. But since Sir Francis invited me to contest the seat in Truro I have been taking more notice of the system as it exists in England today, and it's – it's like some old ramshackle coach of which the springs and swingle bar are long broke and there are holes in the floor from bumping over rutted roads. It should be thrown away and a new one built.'

Ross did not bother to mince his words, but Falmouth would not be ruffled.

'In what way do you suggest there should be improvement in construction of the new coach?'

'Well . . . first some re-distribution of the seats so that the interests of the country as a whole are more evenly represented. I don't know what the population of Cornwall is – I'll wager less than 200,000 – and it returns forty-four Members. The great new towns of Manchester and Birmingham, whose populations can be little short of 70,000 each, have no parliamentary representation at all!'

'You are an advocate of democracy, Captain Poldark?'

'Basset asked the same question, and the answer's no. But it cannot be healthy that the big new populations of the north have no voice in the nation's affairs.'

'We *all* speak for the nation,' said Falmouth. 'That is one of the purposes of becoming a Member. And one of the privileges.'

Ross did not reply, and his host poked the fire. It burst into a reluctant blaze.

'I suppose you know that there's a rumour that your friend Basset may soon be ennobled.'

'No, I didn't.'

'He may well become one of Pitt's "Money-bag" peers. A

barony or some such in return for money and support from the Members he controls.'

'As I said, it's not a pretty system.'

'You will never eradicate venality and greed and ambition.'

'No, but you may control them.'

There was a pause.'

'And your other reforms?' There was a hint of irony in the voice.

'These may offend you more.'

'I did not say that the other had offended me.'

'Well, clearly some change in the method of election. Seats should not be bought and sold as if they were private property. Electors should not be bribed, either with feasts or direct payments. In many cases the election is a mere sham. Truro, at least, has some able-bodied men who affect to be voters, however they may or may not be influenced. Others in the country are far worse. Many in Cornwall. And they say that in Midhurst in Sussex there is only one effective voter, who elects two Members on the instructions of his patron.'

Falmouth said: 'Oh, true enough. At Old Sarum, near Salisbury, there is nothing but a ruined castle, not a house nor an inhabitant; but it returns two Members.' He chewed reflectively. 'So. How would you build your new coach?'

'With a broadened franchise to begin. There cannot –'

'Franchise?'

'Electorate, if you prefer. Until you broaden that you can get nowhere. And the electorate must be free, even if there were only twenty-five voters to a seat. And the seats must be free – free of patronage, free of influence from outside. That maybe is why franchise is becoming the word used in this respect – for it means freedom. Neither the vote nor the seat must be up for sale.'

'And annual parliaments and pensions at fifty and the rest of that rubbish?'

'I see you're well read, my Lord.'

'It's a mistake not to know what the enemy thinks.'

'Is that why you invited me here tonight?'

For the first time in the interview Falmouth smiled. 'I don't look on you as an enemy, Captain Poldark. I thought I had made it clear that I considered you a man of undirected potential. But in truth, though you disown the worst extremes of the Corresponding Societies, do you believe that seats in parliament can possibly be made free of patronage, that electors can be free of *any* sort of payment?'

'I believe so.'

'You spoke of electors being *bribed*. You spoke contemptuously of them being bribed by money or influence. Is it any worse to pay a reward at the time of voting than to *promise* a reward, a promise which you know you may afterwards easily break? Come, which is the more honest: to pay a man twenty guineas down to vote for your candidate or to promise him the passing of a law which *may* put twenty guineas in his pocket when you have been elected?'

'I don't believe it would have to be like that.'

'You take a kinder view of human nature than I do.'

'Man is never perfectable,' Ross said, 'so he fails always in his ideals. Whichever way he directs his aims Original Sin is there to confound him.'

'Who said that?'

'A friend of mine who is here tonight.'

'A wise man.'

'But not a cynic. I think he would agree with me that it is better to climb three rungs and slip back two than to make no move at all.'

Falmouth rose and stood with his back to the fire warming his hands.

'Well, we are on opposite sides on this, and I imagine will remain so. Of course, you see in me a man in possession of hereditary power, and with no intention at all of giving it up. I buy and sell as I can in the world of government. Soldiers, sailors, parsons, customs officers, mayors, clerks and the like depend upon my word for their appointment or advancement. Nepotism is rife. What would you put in its place? Power is not an endlessly divisible thing. Yet it must exist. Someone must possess it – and since man is not perfectable, as you admit, it must at times be misused. Who is likely to misuse it more: the demagogue who finds it suddenly in his possession, like a man with a heady wine who has never tasted liquor before; or a man who by heredity has learned – and been taught – how to use it, a man who, having known liquor all his life, may taste the heady wine without becoming drunk upon it?'

Ross got up too. 'I believe there may be some between the peer and the demagogue who may do better than either; but no matter. I realize there's always danger in change but would not shun it for that reason . . . I think I should be getting back to the dance.'

'You have a pretty wife and a worthy one,' Falmouth said. 'Appreciate her while you still have her. Life is uncertain.'

At the door Ross said: 'There's one favour you might do me. And it would be by the exercise of that hereditary power which I have – at your invitation – ventured to deplore. Do you know the living of Sawle-with-Grambler?'

'I know it, yes. I have land in the parish.'

'I believe the living is in the gift of the Dean and Chapter in Exeter. The incumbent has died, and the present curate, an overburdened underpaid little man who has struggled to maintain services there for nearly twenty years, would be transported with joy if he were granted it. I do not know if there are other applicants but, while there will be many with better connections, there will be few who would more fully deserve it.'

'What is your curate's name?'

'Odgers. Clarence Odgers.'

'I will make a note of it.'

CHAPTER XIII

As he came down the passage Ross heard laughter, and thought he could detect Demelza's voice. He began to feel irritable. This visit seemed to him to be becoming a peculiar and undesirable repetition of the visit to Tehidy. He had been taken aside and engaged in stiff and sober conversation about the country's and the county's affairs by his stiff and sober host, as befitted his rapidly advancing years and considerable status, while his young wife enjoyed herself with people of her own age and flirted with a naval lieutenant. By rights he should be developing a pot belly and be taking snuff and having twinges of the gout. To hell with that.

He crossed the hall, a man half looking for trouble, but restrained by his inherent good sense. He at once saw that Demelza was not among the group who were laughing: Caroline was the centre of it; and his hostess, Mrs Gower, came across to him.

'Oh, Captain Poldark, your wife has gone upstairs with a group of others to see the view from our cupola while the light lasts. Would you permit me to show you the way?'

They climbed two flights and then a narrow stair which brought them into a glass dome looking over the roofs of the house. Demelza was there with Armitage and Dwight and St John Peter, Ross's cousin. Ross emerged into the small glass room with no pleasure in his soul; but Demelza's welcoming glance salved his annoyance.

He dutifully admired the view, and Mrs Gower pointed out the landmarks. The day had cleared with the sunset, and already a few stars glinted in the nacreous sky. The river, lying among its wooded banks, looked like molten lead. In a 'pool' nearby a half dozen tall ships were anchored and had their sails hung out drying after the rain. In the distance was Falmouth harbour and lights winking. Three herons creaked across the sky.

'We were talking of seals, Ross,' Demelza said, 'and I was speaking of those we have in Great Seal Hole betwixt ourselves and St Ann's. Great families of them. In and out of the caves.'

'D'you know I've been a sailor for ten years,' Hugh Armitage said, 'and have never seen a seal – believe it or not!'

'Nor I, for that matter,' said Dwight.

'Why, God's my life!' said St John Peter, 'you get 'em on *this* coast too. You can see 'em any day round Mevagissey and the mouth of the Helford. Cavortin' on the rocks. But who wants to? I wouldn't walk a yard for the privilege of seeing 'em!'

'I remember when I was a girl,' said Mrs Gower, 'we took an expedition from St Ives. We were staying with the St Aubyns, I and my brother and sister, and we set out one sunny morning but the weather turned stormy and we were near shipwrecked.'

'Wouldn't trust that damn' coast,' said St John Peter, his voice slurring. 'Treacherous! Wouldn't get me in a boat large or small. It is all too much like sailin' in and out of the teeth of an alligator!'

'We go fishing now and again,' Demelza said. 'It is all right so long as you know the looks of the weather. Pilchard men do and they come to no harm. Well, hardly ever.'

'It would be agreeable to have a little adventure tomorrow if the day were fine,' said Mrs Gower. 'It's no great distance to the Helford, and I know my children would love it. You could not delay your departure, Hugh?'

'Alas. I must be in Portsmouth by Thursday.'

'Well . . .' Mrs Gower smiled at Demelza. 'Perhaps we should postpone it and come to the Great Seal Hole some time. I have heard of it. It is quite famous.'

Ross said: 'If the weather ever sets fair in this unaccommodating summer, bring your children to Nampara, Mrs Gower. It's twenty minutes at the most from my cove to the Great Seal Hole, and I think there would be little risk of disappointment.'

Demelza looked at Ross in surprise. For someone who had not wanted to come today this was an unexpectedly friendly move. She was not to know that his change of mood from irritation and jealousy to reassurance at the sight of her had spurred a brief accompanying impulse to set his own conscience to rights.

'And please to spend the night,' she said to Mrs Gower rashly.

'That would be delightful. But . . . perhaps we should wait till Hugh is home again.'

Armitage shook his head. 'Much as it would pleasure me, it may be two years before I am in England again.'

'Damn me,' said St John Peter, 'there are better ways of employing one's time than going out in a pesky boat staring at an aquatic mammal with a set of whiskers. But *chacun à son goût*, I suppose.'

They went down again and drank tea and danced and talked and danced again, and Demelza drank too much port and behaved more freely in the house of a nobleman than she would otherwise ever have dared to. Knowing her own liking for the drink, she had kept off it while Clowance was small, but her indulgence tonight had an emotional, almost a masochistic, motive. Hugh Armitage saw her as an example of flawless womanhood, as a creature of Greek mythology, as his ideal beyond fault; and must be disillusioned for his own good. In spite of his protestations that he had known other women and knew their shortcomings, he refused *obstinately* to recognize hers. So, sad though it was to behave in this way – for she cherished the image even though she knew it to be false – only thus could she show herself to him as undifferent from the rest.

It was particularly necessary before he went away. She really valued his friendship and wanted to keep it by her like a good thought, a warm memory, until such time in two or three years as she met him again and their companionship could resume where it had left off. Warm affection was right. Even admiration if, Heaven help him, he felt that way. But not idealism, not adoration, and not love. It was bad for him to go away in that rapt, deluded frame of mind.

In the bedroom that night she had a sharp reaction from these level-headed instincts and sat on the edge of the bed pulling off her stockings with a sudden feeling of depression. It was rare for her, and Ross soon noticed it.

'Feeling sick, love?' he asked.

'No.'

'You were a thought liberal with your port. It's long since you drank it for Dutch courage.'

'It was not for Dutch courage.'

'No. I think I know.'

'Do you?'

'Well, tell me.'

'I can't.'

He sat on the bed beside her and put his arm round her shoulder. She leaned her head against him.

'Oh, Ross, I'm so sad.'

'For him?'

'Well, I wish I were two people.'

'Tell me.'

'One, your loving wife, that I always wish to be and always

shall be. And mother. Content, content, content . . . But for a day . . .'

There was a long silence.

'For a day you'd like to be his lover.'

'No. Not *that*. But I'd like to be another person, not Demelza Poldark, but someone *new*, who could respond to him and make him happy, just for a day . . . Someone who could laugh with him, talk with him, flirt with him maybe, go off with him, ride, swim, talk, without feeling I was being disloyal to the man I really and truly and absolutely love.'

'And d'you think he'd be satisfied with that?'

She moved her head. 'I don't know. I suppose not.'

'I suppose not neither. Are you sure you would?'

'Oh, yes!'

The candle had a thief in it, and the smoke it was sending up was as dark as from a mine chimney. But neither moved to snuff it.

Ross said: 'It is not a unique occurrence.'

'What's not?'

'What you feel. How you feel. It occurs in life. Especially among those who have loved early and have loved long.'

'Why among those?'

'Because others have supped at different tables first. And some others do not consider that loyalty and love must always go together. And then – '

'But I do not *want* to be disloyal! I do not *want* to love elsewhere! That's not it at all. I want to give another man some sort of happiness – some of *my* happiness perhaps – and I cannot – and it hurts . . .'

'Peace, my love. It hurts me too.'

'Does it, Ross? I'm that sorry.'

'Well, it's the first time I have ever seen you look at another man the way you look at me.'

She burst into tears.

He said no more for a while, content that she was beside him and that he was sharing her mind and emotion.

She had a handkerchief up her sleeve and she waved his away. 'Judas,' she said. 'This is nothing. Just the port coming out.'

He said: 'I've never before heard of a woman who drank so much port that it popped out of her eyes.'

She half giggled, and it ended in a hiccup. 'Don't laugh at me, Ross. It isn't fair to laugh at me when I'm in trouble.'

'No, I won't. I promise. Never again.'

'That's an untruth. You know you will.'

'I promise to laugh at you just half as often as you laugh at me.'

'But this isn't the same.'

'No, love.' He kissed her quietly. 'This isn't the same.'

'And,' she said, 'I promised to get up tomorrow morning to tell him goodbye. At six.'

'So you shall.'

'Ross, you're very good to me and very patient.'

'I know.'

She bit his hand, which happened to be within reach.

He nursed his thumb for a moment. 'Oh, you think I am become self-satisfied in my role as husband and protector. Not so. We both walk on a tightrope. Would you rather I gave you a good beating?'

'Perhaps it is what I need,' she said.

II

Dwight on his visit to St Margaret's vicarage had been able to report an improvement in Morwenna's health. The excitability of the tender tissues of the womb had much abated. She suffered no discharge, and her nervous condition was in a better state of tone. He told her she could now get up at a normal time, rest for a while after dinner, and then come down again in the evening. She might go short walks in the garden with her sister when the weather was suitable, feed the swans, pick flowers, undertake small tasks about the house. She must be careful not to over-tire herself and must continue with the prescribed diet at least until the four weeks were up.

That would be in another week. Dwight said he would call next Thursday, when he expected another unpleasant scene with Mr Whitworth. During his year in the prison camp and his own illness which had followed it, Dwight had had time to observe the effects of elation and depression on the course of his complaint, and that of others, and he had come to

believe that there was a peculiar relationship between what
the mind and the emotions were feeling and the responses of
the body. He was convinced – as Caroline was not convinced –
that his own physical salvation depended on his returning to
full practice at the earliest possible moment. If his mind
animated his body against its will, at the end of the day his
body felt better and *was* better for being so driven. And this
in its turn seemed to reactivate his mind. So with other people.
Of course, you did not cure a broken leg by telling a man he
could walk; but often and often if you put a man's mind to
work for his body's good you were half way to a cure.

And there was no question in his view that, apart from a
mistaken medical diagnosis, Morwenna had been suffering
from acute melancholia. Still was, but less so. And gentle
conversation with her, around the subject and about, left him
with the unmistakable impression that she dreaded her husband's physical attentions and that that at least in part was
the source of her depression.

Her husband was a man of God and Dwight was only a man
of medicine, so it put him in an invidious position to do more
than make a few suggestions on the subject – which he knew
in advance would be deeply resented. In any case he was not
really in a position to assume responsibility for the guide reins
of an unhappy marriage. Last time he had been entirely within
his rights as a medical man to forbid intercourse for a matter
of four weeks. No one could question his entitlement to do
that. But Morwenna was now really well enough in body to
resume a marital relationship. She just was not well enough in
spirit. She simply did not want sexual commerce. Either she
loathed her husband or she was one of those unhappy women
who are incurably frigid.

By what right could he as the doctor intervene? Obviously
the situation put Mr Whitworth under considerable strain. Yet
Morwenna was *his* patient. Whitworth looked strong enough
to lift an ox. Would he, Dwight, now be within his rights
medically to forbid any relationship for, say, another two
weeks? Whitworth as a Christian and a gentleman would
probably obey him. Two weeks more might make a considerable difference to his wife. It might then be more proper if
he dropped a hint or two to Morwenna on the obligations of

marriage. An equally difficult task.

But fortunately that was all yet a week away.

In the household, after he had left, dinner was a quiet meal. The resident vicar of St Margaret's, and the would-be non-resident vicar of Sawle-with-Grambler, sat between the two tall sisters at a table far too long for their needs. Good cutlery shimmered as the footman in white gloves served the boiled knuckle of veal with the rosemary sauce.

'So his Lordship says you're finely, Morwenna,' the vicar remarked, spearing a lump of meat. He thrust it well into his mouth as if afraid of it escaping, and chewed meditatively. He had adopted this sarcastic name for Dwight ever since his first visit. 'The strengthening treatment is a success and the distemper is passing off. Eh?' He glanced at Rowella, and his glance lingered.

'Yes, Ossie,' Morwenna said, 'I'm feeling favourable. But Dr Enys said it would take a time yet to become quite well.'

'I don't know at all what sort of bill he's going to send in, but I expect it will be in keeping with the high pretensions he has assumed since he married the Penvenen girl. Who's to say Behenna's treatment might not have been as good in the end – rest and quiet was what you needed, and that's what you've had.'

'But Dr Behenna's treatment was lowering, Vicar,' Rowella said. 'Dr Enys's has been the reverse. Would you not think that had made a difference?'

'I see it's two to one, so I must give way,' Ossie said amiably. It had been noticeable over the last few weeks that his amiability when in the company of the two girls was greater than when alone with his wife.

'What is the Penvenen – Mrs Enys – like?' asked Rowella. 'I don't remember ever to have seen her.'

'A great thin outspoken red-headed stalk of a girl,' said Ossie. 'She hunts with the Forbra.' Little inflexions of malice moved in his voice, memories perhaps of rebuffs. 'Her uncle would not agree to her marrying a penniless saw-bones, but when he died they were quickly wed. Of course it won't last.'

'Not *last*, Vicar?'

Ossie smiled at his sister-in-law. 'Oh, in the eyes of the world perhaps. But I cannot see the noisy Mrs Enys being content for long with a husband who when not visiting his patients spends all his time in experimentation.'

'It reminds me,' said Rowella; 'd'you remember Dr Tregellas, Wenna?'

'Yes, yes, I do.'

'He was an old man who lived near Bodmin, Vicar,' Rowella explained, her face for once animated. 'They say he was looking for the method to turn copper into gold. When my father called once he found him in his gown and square tasselled cap, stockings fallen round his shoes, reading some Arabic book and sipping out of an empty tea-cup while the water had all boiled away out of the kettle and quenched the fire!'

'Ha! ha!' said Ossie. 'Well told! I must say that's a very good story.'

'But true, Vicar. Honestly true!'

'Oh, I believe you.'

'Once he was ill – Dr Tregellas – and he fell from his chair in a dead faint – and his two daughters lifted him back upon his chair, whereupon he went on reading the book where he had left off, never conscious that he had fainted!'

The veal was finished, and was succeeded by a forequarter of roasted lamb, served with mint and asparagus. Morwenna's eyes had been on her sister once or twice. Now Rowella looked up.

'You're eating nothing, Wenna.'

'No, dear. I have all this to drink.' Morwenna pointed to the tall glass of porter. 'And the eggs in the morning, though they slip down very easy, take an edge from my appetite. But I'm eating *well*. Compared to a few weeks ago I'm a positive gourmande!'

The lamb was followed by two spring chickens, with cauliflower and spinach and cucumber; then plum pudding and a syllabub. Ossie, who always drank well but in moderation for his time, took another half bottle of canary and finished with a substantial glass of cognac.

By this time Morwenna had retired for her afternoon rest. Rowella lingered on at the table as she sometimes did these days, and Ossie talked to her about anything that came into his head: his first wife, his mother, parish matters, his ambition to become vicar of St Sawle, his relationship with

Conan Godolphin, the progress of the Warleggans and the misdeeds of the churchwardens.

Presently Rowella rose, tall and thin and apparently shapeless, her shoulders drooping, her long frock just touching her flat-heeled velvet slippers. Ossie rose with her, following her as if by accident into the gloomy hall. The whole house was dark on this close dank July afternoon. A thin mist rose from the river and made the trees at the end of the garden drift like ghosts.

Rowella picked up her book from the parlour – it was the Iliad – and went upstairs, past the playroom where Anne and Sarah were at their lessons, past Morwenna's room and the nursery where childish sounds suggested that John Conan Whitworth was awake. She went up the next flight to her bedroom, and it was not until she had opened her bedroom door that she allowed herself to become aware that the Reverend Osborne Whitworth had followed her. With her hand on the door she looked up at him enquiringly, her eyes narrowed, inscrutable, conveying nothing in their green depths but a casual fronded curiosity.

'Vicar?'

'Rowella, I have been meaning to speak to you. May I come in a moment?'

She hesitated and then opened the door, waiting for him to pass. But he held the door for her and followed her in.

Although an attic it was a pleasant little room, and she had made it pretty with a few feminine things: flowers, a bright cushion, a coloured rug over the one easy chair, curtains changed from a downstairs room.

He stood there, heavy and tall, and his breathing was noticeable. She inclined her hand towards the one comfortable chair, but he did not move to sit down.

'You wanted to speak to me, Vicar?'

He hesitated. 'Rowella, when we are alone, would you call me Osborne?'

She inclined her head. He looked at her. He looked her over. She turned a page of her book.

He said: 'I envy you being so familiar with Greek.'

'My father taught me young.'

'You are still young. Yet in some ways you do not seem so.'

'In what respects?'

He shied away from answering this question.

'Where are you – in the poem?'

Her eyes flickered. 'Achilles has allowed Patroclus to go and fight.'

He said: 'I learned a little Greek, of course, but regretfully have forgot it. I do not think I even remember the story.'

'Patroclus leads an army against the Trojans. He leads them to victory. But he is possessed by *hybris* –'

'By what?'

'*Hybris. Hubris.* Whichever you wish to call it –'

'Ah, yes.'

' – and so he pushes his triumph too far.'

The day was very still.

He took her hand. 'Go on.'

She withdrew her hand to turn a page, her lip trembling, but not with fear, not with embarrassment.

'You *must* remember, Vicar. Patroclus is slain by Hector. Then a terrible fight ensues around the body, for it is of great importance to the Greeks that the funeral rites shall be performed in full upon the body of their hero . . .'

'Yes, yes . . .'

'Are you sure you are interested in what I am saying?'

'Yes, Rowella, of course I am . . .' he took her hand again, and this time kissed it.

She let him continue to hold it while she went on with the story.

'All this time Achilles is sulking. Folly (they call her *Ate*, the goddess of mischief) has possessed him, so that he has refused to fight because – because Agamemnon has insulted him. Vicar, I think –'

'Pray call me Osborne.'

'Osborne, I think you are not really interested in this story at all.'

'I very much suppose you are right.'

'Then why have you come up here?'

'I wanted to talk to you.'

'About what?'

'Can we not – just sit and talk?'

'If you wish.' She waved him again to the chair and this

time he sat down. Then still holding her hand he pulled her cautiously until she came to be sitting on his knee.

She said: 'I don't think this is proper, Osborne.'

'Why ever not? You are but a child.'

'Girls, you must remember, grow up very young.'

'And you are grown up? Har – hm! – well, I –'

'Yes, Osborne. I am grown up. What did you wish to talk to me about?'

'About – about yourself.'

'Ah, I suspicioned that was it.'

'That was what?'

'That it was not the fight about the body of Patroclus that interested you. That it was not Patroclus's body that interested you at all.'

He stared at her, shocked at her outspokenness – coming so strangely from such young lips – and shocked that she should so clearly have perceived his preoccupation.

'Oh, come now, my dear, you mustn't have thoughts like that! Why I –'

She slipped quietly off his knee and stood there, thin and gawky in the faded afternoon light. 'But *are* you not interested in me? If I am a child – even if I am a woman – should you not tell me the truth? Surely you have been interested in me very much recently.'

He cleared his throat, grunted, sat there awkwardly for a moment. 'I do not see why you should suppose that.'

'Do you not? Do you not, Vicar? Then why have you been staring at me every meal time, every time we meet? You stare at me all the time. And most of the time you stare at me here.' She put her long thin hand to her blouse. 'And now you have followed me upstairs.' Her look slanted at him. 'Is it not true?' she asked.

Looking at her, his eyes suddenly reddened, became heavy and unashamed. The physical contact of her having sat on his knee, and then having moved away from him, was the last straw.

'If you ask me . . .'

'I do ask you.'

'Then yes. I have to tell you. It is true. I have to – to tell you, Rowella, it is true. It is true.'

'Then what is it you want?'

He could not answer, his heavy face taut and strained.

'Is it this you want?' she asked.

He stared the more, blood pounding, licked his lips, nodded without breath.

She glanced out at the lowering day, mouth pouting, eyes hidden under lashes.

'It's a dull afternoon,' she said.

'Rowella, I –'

'Yes?'

'I – I cannot say it.'

'Well, then,' she said, 'perhaps you need not. If you would like it. If this is really what you want.'

She began carefully and slowly to unlace the front of her blouse.

CHAPTER XIV

Drake said: 'Pass me that other hammer, will ee? No, the small one. Else I'll not get the head in.'

'I don't know how you *do* it, Drake,' Geoffrey Charles said. 'I didn't know you were such a craftsman!'

'I was apprenticed four year to Jack Bourne. But he was jealous – I always helped but was never left to do one on my own. So I'm not so good as I did ought to be.'

He was making a new wheel for a wagon belonging to Wheal Kitty mine. The back wheel and the side of the wagon had been crushed by a fall of rock and it was easier to begin again than to try to reconstruct matchwood. Since taking over Pally's Shop he had done little of this work, being regarded mainly as a smith; but gradually people were learning that he could create a good serviceable wheel, and he was cheaper and it saved going farther afield. But this meant the purchase of seasoned wood, which was expensive and hard to obtain, and Drake had been restricted in the amount of such work he could take on.

Geoffrey Charles said: 'Why do you make the face of the

wheel dished like that, sort of hollowed?'

'Well, he has to go over hard and bumpy roads. If you made him flat the jolting would knock all the spokes abroad.'

'Some day you must teach me. I'd far rather be able to make a wheel than worry over stupid Latin declensions.'

Drake paused and looked at the boy, whose pallor in a few weeks had turned to a healthy tan. 'Tedn't only Latin you d'learn, Geoffrey Charles. You're learning to be a gentleman.'

'Oh, yes. Oh, yes, I know. And a gentleman I intend to be. And I intend to inherit Trenwith. But I ask you as a friend, which do you think will be most useful to me when I am a man – to be able to make, or even repair, a wheel or to be able to state the nominative case of a finite verb – or some such nonsense?'

Drake smiled and weighed a strip of ash in his hand, calculating whether it would match the other pieces which were to be pegged together to make the rim.

'When you're a man you'll be able to pay me to make the wheels.'

'When I own Trenwith you shall come and live there as my factor and we'll make wheels together!'

Drake went to the well at the side of the yard and picked up the wooden bucket. 'I'll learn you to make one of these here some time. They're not so hard. But now you've been here more than two hour and your mother will grow angry at us if ye're away too long.'

'Oh, Mother . . . she's no trouble. But Uncle George is expected next week or the week after, and then the sparks may fly.' Geoffrey Charles banged a hammer on the anvil. 'Like that, I shouldn't wonder. But he's not my father and he's not my overlord and I shall suit myself.'

'I think, Geoffrey, that twould be an error to put yourself into more trouble on my part. Coming over here nigh every day . . .'

'I shall suit myself and shall consult neither you nor Uncle George. *Ma foi*, I am not being corrupted!'

'Yet twould be wise in you not to bring another quarrel on. If only for your mother's sake. Isn't it best to meet now and again on the quiet, like, instead of maybe being forbid to come and then coming whether or no?'

Geoffrey Charles went over and looked at the bucket. 'Pooh, I could almost make this now! It's only a few staves and some iron bands.'

'Tis not so easy as you d'think. If *you* made a bucket all the water'd rush out through the staves.'

Geoffrey Charles swung the bucket over the well and lowered it. 'I saw Morwenna last month.'

Drake stopped with his hammer raised and slowly lowered it. 'You never telled me that.'

'I thought first perhaps better not.'

'And now?'

'I thought perhaps you had forgot it or were forgetting it. I thought, why reopen the cut?'

'So?'

'But the cut isn't healed, is it?'

'How is she?'

'All right.' Geoffrey Charles, having brashly broken into this forbidden field, had sense enough not to speak of Morwenna's illness. 'She has a baby, did you know?'

Drake's face flushed scarlet. 'No, I didn't know. What — when were that?'

'In June – early June.'

'. . What is it?'

'A boy.'

'She'll – she'll be happy 'bout that.'

'We-ll . . .'

'What did she say? Did she say aught?'

Geoffrey Charles wound the bucket up, and it reached the surface awash with spring water.

'She – she said I was to say she'd never forget.'

From being flushed Drake's face went very pale. He turned the haft of the hammer in his hand. 'When you go back school . . . be seeing her again, will you?'

'I may. It's quite likely.'

'Will you tell her something from me, Geoffrey? Will you tell her something from me? Will you tell her that I know tis all over betwixt us and there can never be nothing more but, but . . . no, no *don't* say that 'tall. Say *nothing* 'bout that. Just say as – just say that one day I'll hope to bring her some winter primroses . . .'

Geoffrey Charles said: 'That reminds me of when you used to call and see us before Christmas, the year before last. Some-how – somehow life was all dark and secret and beautiful then.'

'Yes,' said Drake, staring blindly. 'Yes. That was how it was.'

II

Sam had just come off core and was digging in his garden. That it was misty-wet made little difference. Shawls of fine rain lay over the countryside. In the distance the sea was sulky and nibbled at the crusts of sand it could reach. Wafting about in the mist, seagulls swooped and cried.

He had finished one row and was wiping the damp earth from his spade. In most parts it would have been difficult to dig in the rain, but here the soil was so light and sandy that it scarcely clogged at all. He was about to start again when a voice spoke:

'What are you doing there, Sam?'

His stomach turned over. She had come across the soft ground behind him unawares.

'Well, Emma . . .'

'Poor lot of taties ye've got,' she said, peering into his bucket.

'Nay, I drew them last month. I'm just digging over the ground a second time t'see if any little small 'uns be left behind.'

She was wearing a red serge cloak and a black shawl over her head; wisps of hair had come loose and hung in half curling dankness on her cheeks.

'Not at church praying, then?'

'Not yet. There's a Bible reading later.'

'Still looking for lost souls just so smart as ever?'

'Yes, Emma. Salvation is the gate of everlasting life.'

She stirred a snail with her foot and it instantly retracted into its shell. 'Not been quite so smart after my soul recent, I notice.'

He leaned on his spade. 'If you'd give but a thought to God, Emma, twould rejoice me more'n anything else on earth.'

'That was my impression until this month. Following me, you was, even into Sally Chill-Off's. Not seen ee now for all of a month. Found another soul to save, have ee?'

He rubbed a wet hand across his mouth. 'There's no soul s'important to me as yours, Emma. Though all may be alike in the sight of our Redeemer, there's none I'd so dearly like to bring into the light!'

She stared across towards the misty sea. Then she laughed, that big hearty laugh, full-throated, unrestrained.

'Tom d'say you're afeared of he. That's why you've left off.'

'Tom Harry?'

'Yes. I d'tell him he's all wrong. Tedn *that* at all. Tedn Tom you're afeared of.'

He stared at her, heart thumping. 'And what d'*you* say I'm afeared of, Emma?'

She met his gaze frankly. 'The Devil.'

'The Devil . . .' He stumbled over the word. 'My dear, we all fight – the Devil. And those of us who have enlisted in the army of King Jesus –'

'The Devil in *me*!' she said. 'Maybe tis best to admit the truth of it, Sam. Isn't that what you're afeared of?'

'No,' he said. 'Never that. I could never fear any ill in you, Emma, unless twas in *me* also. Satan within me I fight every day of my life. There can never be an end to the enemies within. But there are no enemies without. I – want to *help* ee, Emma. I want ee to find eternal Salvation, I want ee to be . . . I want –'

'You mean you want *me*,' Emma said.

Sam looked up at the sky. There was a long silence. 'If I want you, Emma, it is in purity of heart; because tis my earnest belief that your soul if turned to Christ would be a noble one and a beautiful one to offer Him. If I want you in – in another way it is not from carnal lust but from a wish to wed you as my wife, and take you to my bed and to my heart – in – in a true spirit of grace and worship . . .'

He stopped, short of breath. He had hardly intended to say anything like this, but it had come up out of his throat unbidden.

Emma stood there, stirring the retracted snail with her toe. The fine rain continued to fall on her face, washing it clean of expression.

'You know I'm promised to Tom Harry.'

'I didn't know.'

'Well, half promised , , , And you know tis said I'm a whore.'

'I sha'n't believe it till I hear it from your own lips.'

'I been out in the hayfields wi' many a man.'

'Is that the same thing?'

'Folk'll tell you so.'

'But d'you tell me so?'

She said: 'You seen me drunk.'

'I've prayed for ee every night – in great distress of mind. But tis not too late, Emma. Ye know what Ezekiel d'say: "Then will I sprinkle clean water upon you, and ye shall be clean; from all filthiness and from all your idols will I cleanse you."'

She made an impatient movement. 'Oh, Sam, what do *pray= ing* do? You're a *good* man, I know. You're happy in your goodness. Well, I'm happy in my filthiness, as you d'call it. What difference do it make in the long run?'

'Oh, Emma, my dear, my dear, can you not *feel* a conviction of error, of sin? Is not the love of the Redeemer more precious to you than the arms of Satan? Leave me help you to find repentance and faith and salvation and love!'

She looked him up and down with narrowed glinting eyes. 'And you'd wed me, Sam?'

'Yes. Oh, yes. That would make –'

'Even if I didn't repent?'

He stopped and sighed, the wrinkles coming and going on his face. 'I'd wed you in the hope and faith that God's bountiful love would able me to bring you into the light.'

'And what would happen to your flock, Sam?'

'They be all men and women who have received sanctifica- tion, who have been forgive their sins by Him who only *can* forgive. As we forgive them that trespass 'gainst us. They would welcome you among them as a prodigal daughter –'

She shook her head so vigorously that raindrops spattered from it. 'Nay, Sam, tedn true and you d'know it! If I just came as a convert they'd look at me athwart, so much as to say, what be *she* doing here, she that's been flaunting around. What be *Sam* up to? Ar – Sam be tankering after she, like all they others! But if I *wed* ee and wed ee without so much as saying sorry for my sins, what'd they think then? They'd think their glorious Leader had gotten himself into a deep mire of vice and malefaction, and they'd say we don't want nothing more to do with he; wouldn't touch him with a pole, they'd say, can't touch pitch without getting fouled, they'd say. And that'd be the end of your precious Connexion!'

The rain was getting heavier. The turning world had moved into deeper regions of cloud.

He said: 'Come inside, Emma.'

'Nay. It wouldn't do for ee. And I must be off back.'

But she did not move either way. He blinked the rain off his eyelids.

'Emma, dear, I don't know what the truth is of anything you say. I'm all confused. We live in a world where malice and uncharitableness d'constantly rise within the souls of else-wise godly men. I've had reason to know that, and he was a leader 'mong us, and twas because I heeded his thoughts that I've seen little of you these pretty many days. So tis hard for me to deny that good men and women think ill when tis unchristian to think ill . . .'

'So there.'

'But I believe, Emma, I truly believe, Emma, that love will overcome all difficulty. The love of man for his Saviour be the greatest possession we can have in this life. But the love of man for woman, though it be lesser, can be sanctified by the Holy Spirit and, when such do happen, it be above carnal bonds and above the ill thoughts of lesser men, and – and it can *triumph* over all. I do believe it, Emma! Emma, I do believe it!'

His voice was trembling, and he blinked again, but this time it was not to get rid of the rain.

She came a step or two forward, walking awkwardly over the muddy earth. 'You're a rare good man, Sam.' She briefly put her hand on his arm and kissed his cheek. 'But not for the likes of me.' She drew back and pushed the strands of wet hair away and pulled her shawl more closely over her face. ''Tis not in me to be so *good*, Sam. You believe because *you're* good. I'd be much better wed to a hard-swearing, hard-drinking jack like Tom Harry. That's if I wed 'tall. You go on with your classes, your Bible reading, your praying; *that's* your life – not tangling wi' a woman like me. Honest, Sam, dear. Honest love. Honest to God. There, I said it! I said His name, so mebbe there's hope yet. But tis a long way off. Too far for you, Sam. So I'll say goodbye.'

'I'll *never* say goodbye,' Sam muttered indistinctly. 'I love you, Emma. Do *that* mean nothing to ee?'

'It mean I should go away and leave you alone,' said Emma. 'That's what that d'mean. For twould be ill-wished from the start.'

She turned and began to plough her way back to the firmer ground of the moorland. He stood with his head bowed, his hands on the spade, the tears dripping on his hands.

Overhead the seagulls were still swooping, crying and moaning their intermittent litany.

BOOK TWO

CHAPTER I

The summer moved gently towards its close. It had not been much of a summer anyhow, the land having been swept by constant south-westerly breezes – and sometimes gales – which brought with them dark days of cloud and drifting rain. Moulds sprouted, slugs and snails abounded, moths laid their eggs in clothing, toadstools and mushrooms prospered, wood beetle multiplied.

On the Continent the French flag sprouted in as many places as the toadstool. The cost of articles in Parisian shops might have gone up by twelve times in a year, but her armies marched where they would, and plunder of all sorts, including forty million francs in gold, flowed into the capital. Prussia, Sardinia, Holland and Spain had all made or were asking for peace. Austria was tottering. England's grand alliance had finally been holed below the water line. Opposed by his king, Pitt began to consider coming to some accommodation with the enemy across the Channel.

It was after all, as more and more people said to each other, only a war of principle on England's side, of opinion even. She wanted nothing from France, or indeed from anybody, no extra commerce, no new overseas possessions, no naval or military supremacy. She just detested Jacobins and Jacobin propaganda and bloody revolutions. And maybe now the worst of that was over. Revolutionaries who become rich and successful generally tend to care less about revolutions. It might be worth a try. One could even consider bargaining for peace by giving up a few islands or pieces of overseas territory. In the last two years England had lost forty thousand soldiers in the West Indies, almost all from tropical disease. It was a high price to pay for Empire, and no one the better for it.

At home, except for the occasional flash of a small naval victory, life looked as dark as the weather. The closing of more and more Continental ports to English trade set off a succession of bankruptcies, which in turn began to shake the banks and send some of the smaller ones into liquidation. Taxes and the national debt mounted together, and in the defence of freedom, freedom was being put in pawn.

In the middle of it all Pitt introduced some startling new ideas for giving more justice and fairer treatment to the poor. He was trying to counter the grim decisions of Speenhamland, and proposed to introduce insurance on a national basis, old age pensions, loans to buy cattle, training in crafts and trades for both boys and girls, and a family allowance of a shilling a week per child for all who were in distress. The measure delighted some of his supporters but incensed more. Ross read about it in the *Mercury* and thought, in the middle of a war, *this* was the way to fight the Jacobin. If *he* ever got a vote he decided he would vote for Pitt.

It was a thought that for different reasons was also in the mind of Sir Francis Basset, for, as Lord Falmouth had acidly predicted, Sir Francis was just then ennobled and assumed the old family name of de Dunstanville, becoming Baron de Dunstanville of Tehidy, thereby ensuring Pitt of the support of that small group of Members he controlled in the House, and necessitating a further by-election, at Penryn.

At Nampara life continued on its accustomed way. The library and new upper storey were now structurally complete. The lumber room and apple cupboard above Joshua Poldark's old bedroom had become a passage leading into two new bedrooms above the library. Joshua Poldark's old bedroom had been emptied of its oak box bed, the cupboards had been torn out, the heavy chimney piece removed and a lighter one put in its place; the rattling sash window that always gave notice of a rising wind – that window through which Garrick had once wriggled to comfort his mistress on her first night at Nampara – had also been removed; it had been replaced with a wider sash with better glass; cracks in the walls had been filled in and on the walls hung an almost white, figured paper; the ceiling between the beams had been re-plastered and painted: it was the new dining-room, and so light now that they might have knocked out two extra windows, and with a bright turkey rug covering all but the edges of the uneven floorboards. A new pedestal table was being made, with eight chairs to match – of Cuban mahogany and to a new and elegant design. They were vastly expensive.

Yet to be purchased – yet even to be ordered – was new china and plate, silverware, decanters and the rest. It was astonishing, once you had created a pretty room, light and elegant, how shabby all one's old things looked. Ross was for taking Demelza up to London for a few weeks so that they could order all they needed, but Demelza said no, this is handsome, doing it bit by bit. We shall never have this kind of fun again, let's spread it out, what does it matter if it doesn't all match at once?

If the dining-room was nearly finished – they ate in it regularly now – the library furnishings were hardly yet begun. The room was complete; the plasterer – Lord de Dunstanville's plasterer – had been, and Demelza had wanted to drop everything and stand watching him all day, his skill, his speed, his deftness, the way he created decoration, formed it seemed in no time, so that the big room was given a deep fluted cornice and the ceiling two circular Grecian motifs exactly placed and precisely similar. During his work he had lived in the house and he had charged a fortune; but she didn't begrudge a penny. It was wonderful.

The walls below the cornice were panelled in light pine, and some furnishings had been bought: two applewood claw tables, a sofa, a rosewood side-table cross-banded with tulip wood, a good local carpet. But it didn't yet quite amount to a *room*. It was a beginning. Nothing yet clashed or was out of place, but one had to be careful. Conversations about it often went on long into the night. Shelves, for instance, had been fixed at one end to give the room a right to its original title; but most of Ross's books – and they were not extensive – were old and shabby and well-read; they would not look right. Yet he found no attraction in the beautiful books he saw in Trelissick and in Tehidy. Their gold lettering on half-morocco bindings seemed a part of the decoration, not something to be read.

Jeremy passed his fifth birthday and Clowance neared her second. She was quick to walk but slow to talk. Her only recognizable sentence so far was 'Bit-a-more!' and this she regularly uttered when sitting at the table when her plate was empty. Every fine day Demelza took them on the beach where they all paddled and Clowance frequently sat down at the wrong moment. The feel of the cold water round her buttocks, however, only made her crow the more.

Sometimes they would go out in the boat from Sawle Cove fishing. And occasionally they would see seals slipping off the edge of rocks as they approached, and this would temporarily, disconcertingly, jog Demelza's mind back to her visit to Tregothnan and Hugh Armitage's leave-taking.

'Whatever you say, Demelza, whatever you say now, it will not prevent me from having you in my mind wherever I go. You will be by my side, a memory of someone I have once seen – and known a little – and, with your permission, loved.'

'You do not have my permission, Hugh. I'm sorry, but . . . I'm *happy* to be your friend, really I am. But that is all it can be. And it is wrong, I have said it is wrong in you to suppose you have met some perfect creature and hold her up in your mind so that other women don't come to that level.'

'I can do what I please.'

'But it isn't *true*! No one is like that! D'you know I'm a miner's daughter, and never had no education?'

'I did not. But of what importance is that?'

'I would have thought to someone of your breeding twould mean a deal.'

'I do not know if you misjudge my class, but you misjudge me.'

'You have answers to everything I say.'

'And they avail me nothing, without your kindness.'

'How can I be kind?'

'By letting me write to you.'

'May I show your letters to my husband?'

'No.'

'So you see.'

'Can you not stretch this very small point? I'm likely to be away for some years.'

'But Ross is bound to see them when they come,' Demelza had protested, weakening her position.

'I can arrange for them to be delivered.'

'But this makes a wickedness of it!'

'May I, then, send you poetry?'

She had hesitated. 'Oh, Hugh, don't you see how I am set?

I'm happily wed. Two beautiful children. Everything I want
in the world. I *want* to be kind to you. I like you deeply. But
you do see I cannot be more than kind . . .'

'Well,' then, I will write to you by the post and you may
show my letters to Ross and you may read them together and
laugh together in a kindly way about this stupid young lieutenant who is suffering from an affliction of calf love. But –'

'You *know* we would never do that!'

'Let me finish. You may laugh together – kindly I'm sure –
and Ross will perhaps excuse my earnestness on the grounds
that it's a youthful affliction that I will grow out of – but *you*
will know different, Demelza, *you* will know different. *You*
will know that it is not a youthful affliction, that it is not
something I will grow out of at the first port of call. You will
know that I love you and will go on loving you to my life's
end . . .'

Such a declaration is not something a woman may easily
get out of her system, and Demelza particularly was not of
the temperament to do so. She loved Ross no less and was no
less contented with her house and family, no less able to pluck
enjoyment like a wayside flower from simple things as life
passed. But the words remained, often warming her heart, but
sometimes ringing disconcertingly clear, as if they had been
spoken only yesterday and needed an answer.

Hugh Bodrugan, that hairy old baronet, and Connie, his
young stepmother, called a couple of times and Sir Hugh
asked Ross if he might buy a few shares in his mine. Ross
replied politely that at the moment he had no need of further
capital, but he gave a faithful promise that if he disposed of
any holding in the mine Sir Hugh should have the first offer
of it. Bodrugan grunted and went away dissatisfied. At least
Ross thought him so, but he must have continued to have some
hopes in this direction because a couple of days later he sent
over as a present for Demelza a couple of black and white
piglets of a new breed which were claimed to come to a better
weight than any that had gone before.

The two piglets were so small and so engaging that they
immediately made friends with the elderly Garrick and became
pets for the children, who occasionally would allow them to
escape into the house. Ross solemnly warned them that if

they continued to do this there would come a day when the piglets would suddenly swell up and grow so big they would never be able to squeeze out of the doors again. Demelza named them Ebb and Flow.

In the dark days of late summer moths became such a problem in the house, there never being a candle lighted and a window ajar without the room being filled with fluttering wraiths of all shapes and sizes, that a general war was declared on them. To amuse the children Demelza kept them up late one night to go on a moth-sugaring expedition. This was done by mixing sugar and beer in a bowl and stealing out into the dusk and brushing the sugared beer on to tree stumps and fence posts. By the time this was done you could go round with a bucket of water and pick the moths off the sugary surface – where they clung with quivering pleasure feeding on the liquor – and drop them in the water. But Demelza tired of this quicker than the children. The moths were too beautiful to destroy, and about half of them she set free. Then Garrick, having followed them out, spoiled it all by finding the sugared beer to his taste, and began to lick the stumps clean, moths and all, before they could stop him.

Yet in spite of the weather, or perhaps because enough sun got through the clouds at intermittent intervals, and the gales were too early to do the damage, and the rain was slight in September, it was a good harvest. All Cornwall, most of England, had its best corn yield for four years – and never more welcome. And in spite of the lack of prosperity in the land and the depression which had come so suddenly after the expanding and favourable conditions of the first war years, Wheal Grace yielded up her ore and Ross invested more money in Blewett's shipbuilding business in Looe, and talked over seriously with Captain Henshawe the building of a new and more powerful engine for the mine.

Ross engaged the recovered Zacky Martin as underground captain. It was really more than Henshawe could do to keep an eye on everything; and miners, like other people, needed supervision. Some of them were picking out the richest ground and leaving the lower-grade stuff behind. Economics in a copper mine made this an acceptable practice; not in a tin mine, except to the tributers concerned who added to their own earnings this way. Some too, the foxiest ones, brought up indifferent stuff for a month before the next setting day so that they could argue their pitch was yielding less and bargain for a higher share in the profit on the ground they stoped. Once the contract was struck the ground miraculously improved. Zacky also discovered a little syndicate whereby some of the rich ore found its way into the barrows of those contracted to work poorer ground. The extra profit would be shared out later.

It was all part of life, and no one thought too hard of these practices; it was up to the boss to stop them. Considering most of the bargains he struck were pretty generous, Ross thought himself entitled to stop them.

II

When it came to that next weekly visit to Morwenna Whitworth, Dwight had found her still improving, and he had braced himself for the unpleasant interview he had to face with her husband. After he had been upstairs he asked for the vicar and was shown into his study. Without too much preamble, since offence would be taken anyhow, he had stated his medical opinion. But he had misjudged his man. The anger and stilted dignity of last time were absent. Osborne had asked after his wife, brusquely it was true, but seemed no longer put out by this further demand on his continence. He said he supposed women were like that sometimes. Important thing was to get her right. Very inconvenient for everybody this continuing illness; sooner she was wholly recovered the better. A vicar's wife had many duties, and it just wouldn't do, this weakness, sickliness. Why, many women were pregnant again by this time, after a first baby, and taking it all in their stride.

Dwight came away, not really liking the man but realizing that under that rather stupid, brusque exterior, which no doubt in the marital relationship repelled his wife, was a kinder person than he had first supposed.

When he got home he had a bowl of soup and a glass of canary and went to his study, where Caroline found him at five on her return.

'What is it?' she demanded, coming into his study like the wind. 'They tell me you've had no dinner. Are you ill?'

'No. I was not hungry.'

'Then why are you not out succouring your patients as you're accustomed to be at this time of day? What is wrong? Dwight, you *are* ill.'

He closed his book and smiled at her. 'I was tired. I thought I'd change my habit today.'

She sat on the edge of her chair, burnished hair on shoulders, eyes looking into his.

'Take your thumb out of the book,' she said, 'otherwise I'll know you're not attending.'

He laughed and obeyed.

She said: 'Who is the nearest doctor?'

'You see him before you.'

'Don't prevaricate. I shall call in Dr Choake.'

'Heaven forbid! You could as well send for Mr Irby.'

'Him too if you like. Though there are enough drugs and potions in this house to set up a shop of our own, if I knew which to give you.'

'I don't need drugs, Caroline. A good night's rest will work wonders.'

'Wonders . . . I tell you what a good night's rest will do. It will return you a small and limited portion of energy which you will dissipate in half a day seeing to your wretched sick people, and then you will be ill again and exhausted and like to take to your bed. Isn't that so? Tell me if it isn't so.'

Dwight considered. 'Work is good for a man, Caroline. It stimulates his mind, and in the end his mind will re-stimulate his body –'

'And tell me what else is good for a man. Love for his wife?'

He flushed. 'If sometimes I fail in that it is a failure of body, not of loving intent. You have reassured me –'

'If failure of the body is the outcome of the prison sickness you still suffer, then loving intent is all I ask. But if *all* the time, every atom of your regathering strength, you dissipate upon your work – as fast as it is gathered it is given out – then one begins to question the loving intent.'

Horace came waddling through a slit in the door on his fat legs and whined at them, but for once he was ignored. He rolled over on his back and they still took no notice.

'You question that, Caroline?' Dwight asked.

'Tell me,' she said, 'what have you done today?'

'Today? This morning I saw a dozen poor wretches who waited outside the servants' door for advice or attention; then I went to see Mr Trencrom, whose asthma is bad. Then, as it was my day for riding farther afield, I made a half dozen calls on the way and so reached Truro, where I visited Mrs Whitworth and Mr Polwhele. So I rode home. When I reached home I felt disturbed in my breathing and my stomach, so ate lightly. I am recovered now.'

She got up, as taut as whipcord, went to the window, picked up a book and fingered it without looking at it. 'And do you know what I have done today? I have spent an hour perfecting my toilet, then an hour with Myners seeing to matters of the estate, then I picked some flowers for my empty parlour, then I changed my attire and rode two hours with Ruth Treneglos. I dined with her and her sweaty husband and her crew of noisy infants and so came home. Do you observe any point at which our paths crossed?'

'No,' said Dwight after a moment.

Horace jumped on his knee.

Dwight said: 'But we have never pretended that our daily life must go side by side.'

'No, my dear, never side by side. But not the poles apart.'

'And do you think it is now the poles apart?'

She turned, still light in voice; but that did not deceive him. 'When I took a fancy to you, my dear, my uncle disapproved because he said you had no name – which was untrue – and no money – which was. Unwin Trevaunance was to be my mate, and all my upbringing had accustomed me to a life which would have matched with his. But I fancied you; and you fancied me; and nothing else would do for the either of us. But even then we quarrelled, or had a disagreement, as to how we were to live after we were wed. Lacking Uncle Ray's money, I still had enough of my own to set you up in Bath, and so this was agreed. And . . . we were to elope . . . and we did not elope because you preferred – or seemed to my distorted imagination then to prefer – your patients here to marriage and a fashionable practice with me. And we separated – and would have remained separated for good if that interfering fellow Ross Poldark had not forced us to meet again and almost banged our heads together. And . . . so we made it up. But by then you were in the navy, with the results that are still with us . . .'

'Why are you saying all this, Caroline?'

'Because I went through agonies waiting for you – and your return brought me new life. And I don't want it to be said – or rumoured – or even entertained as a passing thought – that all our interests are so different that, in spite of our love, Ross Poldark was wrong.'

He got up, spilling Horace grunting upon the mat.

'My dear, you can't mean that.'

'Of course I mean it, for others will think it if we do not.'

'What matters it what others have to say?'

'It only matters if it is reflected in ourselves.'

He was still unsteady standing and sat on the edge of the table. His narrow, thoughtful face was lined this evening. He looked what he was, a sick man with a strong will.

He said: 'Tell me how I must alter.'

After a moment she shook her hair back and knelt on the rug beside Horace.

In a different voice, but so subtly different that only he could detect the softening, she said: 'I know I am a scatter-brained creature –'

'That is a lie.'

'– frivolous and –'

'Only on the surface.'

'– with no ideas beyond the ideas of a –'

'You have plenty of ideas.'

'Dwight,' she said, 'I was making an effort to be contrite to you; but I cannot even do that if you interrupt me all the time.'

'It is I who should be contrite for having grossly neglected you.'

She sat down with her back against a chair, her legs tucked under her. 'Then I'll not catalogue my faults. Let's just agree that I love the country life and riding and hunting, and I like occasional soirées and parties, which you do not. Nor, though I would like to, can I get myself a true interest in medicine. Unless they are *worthy* people, of whom there are all too few,

I don't see the virtue in curing them. The world is over-populated. People swarm everywhere. It's very sad, but generally speaking I would say, let 'em die.'

'I don't believe that. It's your uncle's old belief and not yours at all—'

'Yes, it is! In this instance it is very *much* my belief, for it concerns my husband. He is neglecting *two* things. He is neglecting his wife—which I very much resent. But still more important, he is neglecting himself. It is only one sin on your part, Dwight, but it has two evil consequences; and the second is even worse than the first.'

'You're wrong, Caroline, I'm sure you are. If I neglect you, then I'm much to blame and it shall—it shall be changed. But the other is not a consequence at all. I am—not very well; but neither am I very ill. It is a state which I believe a year or two will clear up, but I don't suppose it depends on the number of patients I see or the efforts I make to cure them—'

'Well, then,' she said, 'if you will not take heed to the second consequence, take heed to the first.'

'I'll try to spend more time after dinner with you, limit my work to the mornings—'

'Oh, you will *try* . . . You will try to do this and that, but will you succeed? It is—it is like a drug with you, Dwight, like drink with another man. He swears he will give it up, but in a day or two he slides back into his old ways . . .'

He went to kneel beside her on the mat, and she noticed his unsteadiness. He kissed her and squatted beside her. Horace grunted and yapped with a return of his old jealousy. 'Tomorrow I'll turn over a new leaf. You see. The drunkard will reform.'

She said: 'D'you know it's not very long ago that I was in daily attendance at the bed of a man dying of the sugar sickness. My uncle took a long time dying. Almost all the time you were away it took him to die. And I became disgusted at the sight and smell of illness—of pills and potions and night commodes and food untasted and a body shrivelling away, and—and comas and half-recoveries, only to see him sink again. I'm *young*, Dwight. *Young.* And frivolous, though you may pretend not to think so. I *love* you. I want to be young with you and to enjoy my youth! You came back—almost it

seemed from the dead. I don't want you to go back to the
dead. I don't want to attend on *your* bed of sickness. I'm
selfish, you see. Wait, wait, let me finish.' She paused to brush
the tears impatiently from her eyes. 'I know I have married
a surgeon, a doctor. That I knew and that I'm prepared for.
That you should continue to practise was part of the bargain.
It was never so stated in those words but I understood it as
part of the bargain. I do not expect you or wish you to turn
into a country bumpkin squire to please me, nor did you
expect me to become a downtrodden mouse mixing the potions
or writing out the bills for her husband. But you *did* marry me,
and I *am* your wife for better or worse, and you *must* take
account of that fact! As well as being a doctor's wife I am
a young woman with an estate, and as well as being a doctor
you are now a landowner and a man of property. There *has*
to be compromise on both sides, or there will be a risk – there
will be a risk of our waking up one day and finding there is
nothing left between us at all.'

The little pug now climbed pertinaciously on to the twisted
lap she presented to him and tried to lick her hair.

Dwight said: 'Horace is doing exactly what I ought to be
doing.'

'Ought to be or wish to be?'

'Wish to be.'

'But must not, or I shall not want your salute to stay so
chaste.'

'Do you suppose I'd want it so myself?'

'But *I* must. You're unwell, Dwight. You must have felt very
unwell today or I shouldn't have found you in.'

'It will pass. It has passed.'

'Maybe. I have my doubts. Give over, Horace; your tongue
is rough.' She pushed her tawny hair back out of his reach. 'So,
my dear, I am prepared to be a demanding wife in some ways
but not in others. I demand you cut down your work. I
demand that on occasion, just once in a while, you spend a
whole day with me, doing what I want you to do. But for the
moment I demand nothing more, even though the more to
which I refer is what I would wish for most . . .'

'And I.'

'Well, prove it.'

'I will –'

'No.' She put her hand against his lips. 'Not tonight. Fulfil my other demands first. For out of them will come what I believe will be something better for us both.'

They sat there together on the faded Kashan rug. They were holding hands, but somehow Horace had insinuated his obese body between them so that he was wedged into a position where he divided them and could not lightly be moved.

For the moment the tight little storm was over. They were both exhausted by it, Dwight, because it was his nature, much the more so. And because he had so much less nervous energy to begin. Caroline was aware of victory, but of how carefully she must guard it; for she knew the thin streak of determination – or obstinacy – that ran through his character. She was sorry she had not been more downright before. But, because of his narrow return from death and subsequent illness, his preoccupations were hard to combat. It was not going to be an easy marriage. It never had been yet over the few months it had so far run. But she was determined to win it. Her determination – or obstinacy – must be no less than his. Their love was not in question. What was in question was what they would make of it.

CHAPTER II

So Ossie Whitworth received a letter from Dr Enys telling him that for reasons of indifferent health he was compelled to restrict his practice to areas nearer his home, and therefore he would not be available, unless there were some sudden deterioration in Mrs Whitworth's health, to be called in for further attendance. He told Mr Whitworth that in his view Mrs Whitworth was now greatly recovered from the illness following her pregnancy. A strengthening rather than a lowering diet was still to be favoured; and everything should be done to ensure that Mrs Whitworth followed a simple and quiet life and avoid shock to her nervous system. If this course were pursued, he felt, there would be nothing further to fear.

He was, with respect, their humble and obedient servant, etc.

Ossie grunted when he had read the letter and tossed it across the tea table for Morwenna to read. 'So you see, his Lordship has tired of us, so now we must go back to Dr Behenna.'

'Oh, dear!' Morwenna exclaimed, still reading. 'What a shame! He was so kind. Like a kind friend. One felt one could talk to him.'

'As quite obviously you did, my dear. More than would be considered seemly by most women to another man. A man, I mean, other than her husband.'

'He was my doctor, Ossie. I don't think I ever discussed anything with him that was not pertinent to my illness.'

'Opinion will differ on that. Well, now you are well again and putting on weight and looking quite buxom, no doubt you'll be able to resume your full duties as the vicar's wife in this parish.'

'I'm already trying to. I have been busy all day about your affairs. I'm sure you don't wish me to list them, for you listed them yourself this morning. It has been a happy day for me that I've been able to do so much, and although I'm now tired it is a pleasant tiredness, not at all like the old fatigue. I look forward to another such day tomorrow.'

Ossie grunted. 'I'm playing whist tonight at the Carharracks', so I shall be late home. Tell Alfred to wait up for me.' He took his watch out of the pocket of his fancy waistcoat and looked at it. 'That girl's late. What is she doing out so long?'

Morwenna took off her spectacles. 'Rowella? She's been gone barely an hour and it's broad daylight. She could scarce come to any harm.'

'It's not physical harm I mean so much as moral harm,' Ossie said. 'I know she has gone to that library for books. You both spend half your days over them. Too much reading is demoralizing, especially of that kind. It leads to dreams, unworthy dreams. One loses touch with the reality of a godly life. You know I never preach to you, Morwenna. Tain't in me to be Methody or sanctimonious. We should all do our best in the world as we find it. But we cannot continue to do our best if we try, through books, to lead *other* people's lives. It's enervating, unhealthy – for you both.' He finished his tea and rose. 'I'll be in my study for an hour.'

'I wished some time,' Morwenna said, 'to discuss Sarah and Anne's schooling. While I've been ill Rowella has had her hands full and has not been able to devote as much time to them as we wished. I think they've come to no hurt, but Sarah is a trifle saucy. Rowella has been such a help to me, and with the baby, that I would gladly enlist her in those duties only.'

'Another time,' he said restively. 'We'll discuss it some other time.'

When he had left the room Morwenna reflected idly that her sister's name had a peculiar effect on Ossie. Sometimes he seemed actively hostile towards her and referred to her as 'that girl', so that Morwenna feared he might decide she was not fulfilling her duties and send her home. At others he seemed jocular and friendly, and he was polite enough on the rare occasions when he directly addressed her. But they hadn't ever quite settled down together as a brother-in-law and a young sister-in-law should. Morwenna put on her glasses again and read Dwight's letter. His withdrawal was a great loss to her, the loss of a real friend, and somehow there were few enough about.

She wandered out into the garden and down to her favourite place by the river, but the river was out, the mud smelt dank and stale, and Leda and her three friends were not there. Morwenna dropped the pieces of bread and cake on the bank where they could reach them, if the water-hens and the other birds had not grabbed them up before the swans returned. This was where she had once thought to plunge and suffocate in the mud to avoid the obligations of married life. It was still a possibility, but a brief message Geoffrey Charles had recently brought her, though without hope, had given her a new heart.

As for Rowella, Morwenna valued her company and help, but they too hardly ever got to talk in the intimate casual way of sisters in daily contact about a house. Had it been Garlanda, Morwenna knew there would have been constant warm unrestrained chatter to help the day along. Whatever happened, Rowella was always herself, dry and cool of speech, critical of eye, able and willing but never 'warm'. Perhaps it was something lacking in her nature.

As he sat in his study, drafting out yet another letter to Conan Godolphin about the still-vacant living of Sawle-with-Grambler, Ossie Whitworth could have given his wife some interesting sidelights on Rowella Chynoweth's nature. Indeed, at this moment he could not quite bring his whole concentration to the letter because he was waiting to hear Rowella Chynoweth's footstep. Her *footstep*.

It was all very disturbing to him. He was not by choice a praying man – except, that is, for public prayers, a commission for which he had been sensibly ordained. He did not pray a lot in private; but over the matter of his sister-in-law he had once or twice asked for guidance. And noticeably had not received it.

He sometimes thought himself in a very poor way, as for instance now, and as for instance often when he knew the girl was about and listened for her footstep. It was a very peculiar thing. No other woman had affected him so before. Not even his wife when he lusted after her so earnestly before the wedding. When Rowella was in the house it was as if he could hear her breathing. Perhaps it was only that he knew what happened *when* she breathed that so occupied his mind. At times, at the most disconcerting times, his visual memory of her swam before his eyes and made him hesitate and stumble in his thoughts.

In her long slim ill-fitting gowns she padded about the house, and her body, now that he knew what was there, flaunted itself at him through the flimsy disguising material. And of course her feet, which were so marvellously cool and slim in his hands, the skin so fine, the shape and bones so slender, so marvellously, seductively slender. Her manner about the house was impeccable; never by any flicker of her sly, close-set eyes did she betray anything in public of what might have happened the night before when they were alone.

Sometimes he wondered if she were a witch, a witch sent specially into the world fully fledged in all things evil while still a child. For she understood more about captivating a man, of inflaming a man, than either his first or second wife had ever dreamed of. She seemed to know more even than the light women of Oxford or those by the quay of this little town. She was of course so much fresher than they were and so damnably more provocative. The attitudes she took up on the bed when he had clumsily half undressed her were wildly wicked. She would spit at him, contorting her face and arching her body like a cat, she would offer herself and her startling breasts and then refuse him, she would sulk or bite or grin or scowl and, when at last she let him take her, all the elements that preceded the possession became a part of it, so that he discovered sensations he had never known before.

It was bemusing and horrible, and usually he hated her. It was the fact that he had to lower himself so much that he most resented. He was brought to the level of a fifteen-year-old boy, asking, pleading, arguing, cajoling. And then in the middle of some particularly abandoned moment she would call him 'vicar', as if jibing at him, challenging him, daring him to consider his dignity.

Yet sometimes he thought he loved her. In spite of her lack of looks, she had terrible charm, and sometimes after their love she would stroke his brow and seem to be trying to mend his self-esteem. He had never had a woman stroke his brow, and he liked it. Of course his attitude to women before had always been that they were there for a purpose; they existed for his pleasure and not for their own. He had never before seen a woman get pleasure out of it – and it made him all the more suspicious of this tigress he had discovered masquerading as a kitten. She was not *natural*. In his more moral moments he knew that she was evil through and through. There were enough examples of such women in the Book from which he preached every week. There were even more examples of evil men, but he tried not to think of them.

He realized also, even if Rowella did not, the pitfalls that lay ahead if he did not break off the attachment. It had been begun partly because of his deprivation of a normal relationship with his wife. If he had any sense he now knew that he should make some excuse to have Rowella sent home. Now that Morwenna was about so much more there was a greater risk of discovery, and, apart from everything else that would ensue, he much disliked the thought of his wife having any *sort* of moral excuse for her fastidiousness towards him. Even if that did not happen, there always was the risk of a servant suspecting something and starting a rumour in the parish.

While Sawle lay in the balance he particularly wanted to avoid this.

But against all those sensible and cautious thoughts, heavy in the balance, one factor weighted down the other side: Rowella. There was nobody like her. There never had been. There never would be again.

So Rowella perhaps would be sent home next week. Or the week after. She was only fifteen; a child. Although a dean's daughter, she appeared to suffer no qualms of conscience at committing fornication, nor even at the compounded sin of lying with her sister's husband. It was his duty to instruct her in the sin. It was his duty to show her the wrong of what she was doing, apart altogether from his own wrong. Some day soon they would talk together. Soberly and properly, not wildly and improperly, and then she would agree to go home . . .

Outside in the hall Ossie heard the padding footstep that he had been listening for. Rowella was home. She read too many books. Perhaps she had learned something of her total wantonness from the books she read. In the evenings she should play whist or piquet instead of having her head in a book. One day perhaps he could teach her. But no, that was risky. Nothing must be done to suggest he was singling her out for any special attention. If they were careful, very careful, it might be quite a while yet before he had to send her home.

II

Jud Paynter was a man whose grievances against life had become a part of the lore of the parish. Beginning as a miner, he had been befriended by Ross's father, and had come to live at Nampara with his putative wife, Prudie. He had been part of an era when Joshua Poldark was running wild. Joshua's other chief companion had been Tholly Tregirls; but Tholly had always been much more the dare-devil. Even in those days Jud had been the reluctant adventurer, pessimistic of every outcome, sure that the world was against him.

When Ross returned from America after his father's death he had retained the Paynters for a year or two, but had found them too unreliable and they had been ejected and found a broken-down shack at the north end of Grambler village. After that for quite a while Jud had worked for Mr Trencrom and 'the trade', but he was too often in his cups and too often talkative in his cups to please the more cautious members of that profession who remembered the night of February '93 when their landing had been surprised by the preventive men and several of their friends transported or imprisoned as a result.

So one day Mr Trencrom, wheezing, and daily more closely resembling Caroline's pug dog, had called at the little cottage and paid his retainer off. Shortly after this, a fortunate chance had killed the gravedigger at Sawle Church and Jud had been appointed to the vacant see.

It was work that suited his age and his temperament. Now in his middle sixties, labour was something he had tried to avoid all his life, but he did not so much mind a little if he could do it in his own time. When asked to dig a grave he usually had a couple of days' notice and it was in the open air, which he preferred; he could turn a couple of spades and stop for a smoke, and the employment, while earning him a few pence, gave him the excuse to get away from Prudie.

It suited him to bury people. The gloom that had surrounded him all his life was lightened by observing the gloom of other folk. He was interested to watch and comment freely on the relative grief shown by two widows who he happened to know had detested their husbands anyhow. The quality or lack of quality of a coffin was something he was willing to talk of at some length in Sally Tregothnan's kiddley – or even at home unless Prudie shut him up. Paupers' graves and the lack of coffins was another subject that interested him. And, while many of his clients were children and young people carried off by this or that epidemic, he found a special pleasure in burying his contemporaries. He saw each one underground with relish and smacked his lips that he had outlived another of them. In his cups, the evening after the teeling, he would gladly give anyone who would listen a potted biography of the deceased, heavily weighted towards the dead man's or woman's misfortunes and faults. Since he had lived in the village all his life and was now one of its oldest inhabitants, he knew everyone and knew 'about' everyone; and as always liquor would light the fires under the pot of reminiscence so that all the past was boiled up like milk into a dimension larger than life.

It depended on the mood of his listeners whether they appreciated him or not. Sometimes they thought him good entertainment and let him have his head; sometimes they were impatient at the very sound of his voice and shouted him down. Although he bitterly resented this, it helped to confirm his view of the injustice of the world.

One day in September he walked to the graveyard in a special state of pessimism and annoyance because he had been thrown out of the kiddley the night before by Ed Bartle. Old Aunt Mary Rogers, keeper of the one tiny shop in Sawle, had died and Jud had had to see her safely underground. Over his rum he had snorted his disgust at Parson Odgers and what he had said at the graveside: 'Our sister has now departed to the place prepared for innocence and virtue.'

'Innocence? *Er?* Dirty ole malkin! 'Er an' 'er pindy shop! Never a ha'penny would you get from she, never a ha'penny would she let you owe! Never a ha'penny nor the half nor the quarter. Open shop door, you would, and go in – out she'd crawl from inside blinkin' like a want, besting 'ow to cheat you.' Jud took another gulp. 'An' virtue, mind! *Virtue*. That d'make you laff. That made me laff till the water spouted out of me eyes. Why, ole Aunt Mary took in Wallas Bartle when she were fifty-eight and he were twenty-one, and we all d'know what used to 'appen in that there back room . . .'

Jud had not been allowed to finish his rum for he had omitted to think that Ed and Wallas Bartle were cousins and that Ed might take exception to these remarks. Jud arrived home earlier and soberer and sorer than he had done for months.

So the following day he was looking more than ever for reasons to complain about the injustices of the world. He bickered for a time with Prudie, but she gave him no sympathy and no quarter, so he took himself off to his playground. Aunt Mary Rogers still needed two feet of earth on her to bring her up to the common level.

It was a pleasant day, sunny, with wisps of high cloud, and when he got there he settled with his back against a head-stone which ran: '*Penlee. Father and Mother and I, chose to*

*be buried as under. Father and Mother lies here, and I lies
buried yonder.*' This always appealed to his sense of humour;
and it was a comfortable stone with a slight slant that fitted
his back. He smoked a pipe of baccy and then had a snooze;
but about midday he roused himself, picked up his spade and
went to finish off Aunt Mary. And then he saw the lurcher.

Jud had always hated dogs. He hated the noise they made,
the way they walked, their wobbling tails and lolling tongues,
their panting breath, their dirty habits and the places they
sniffed at other dogs. Somewhere hidden in Jud – *deeply* hidden
– was a Puritan. In his own behaviour he had no difficulty in
forgetting this, but it showed in his prejudices. He thought
dogs weren't *decent*. Licking, snuffling, ranting, rutting, four-
legged obscenities.

And of all the dogs he disliked he disliked most the two
lurchers that pestered him in this holy ground. They didn't
belong to anybody, were just running wild, and they were a
proper nuisance, scratching and sniffing around, quarrelling
and yelping, barking at him from a distance and 'turding' – as
he called it – all over the place.

Today there was just one of them – the bigger of the two – a
big brindle-coloured mongrel with something of the collie in
him, and he was scratching away at some soft earth near
James and Daisy Ellery and their six children. And, of all
things, the dog was burying a bone.

This seemed a peculiar insult to Jud, who knew all about
the bones already buried in this place and wanted no additions.
And then he noticed that not only had the lurcher got his
back to him but that the shape of the old gravestones just there
formed a sort of cul-de-sac which might serve as a momentary
prison if he could be surprised. Jud believed that all dogs
should be hanged – which no doubt would be the fate of these
two if they were ever caught; but catching was the difficulty.
He picked up his long-handled spade – the lazy-back, as it was
called – and began to creep nearer.

The grass between the graves was rank and soft, and the
breeze was blowing away from him. Almost to his own surprise
he came within striking distance. As he raised his shovel high
above his head the lurcher heard him. All the pent-up grievances of weeks went into Jud's blow, but the dog had leapt up

and away; he let out a pained yelp as the spade caught his flank and tail; the spade struck a stone and jolted out of Jud's hand, and Jud overbalanced and fell.

As he fell he saw that the bitch was there too, behind a gravestone, and suddenly the two dogs were trapped and snarling at him; then they were up over the top of him and away. Among the flying paws across his back came a nip in the seat of his trousers, and then he was sitting up dusting the earth off his bald head and shouting and cursing to high heaven.

One of the Ellerys who were still alive, little Nigel, was the next moment startled to see emerge from the churchyard on to the track in front of him an angry and alarmed Mr Paynter who clutched the seat of his trousers and said: 'I've been bit! Bit by a danged blathering whelp of a mad cur!'

He set off towards his home – no distance – and little Nigel followed him, passing on the message in a fluting treble as he went, so that by the time the last shack was reached a dozen or so people had been gathered to escort him.

Prudie was making tea for her cousin Tina from Marasanvose when the cavalcade arrived. Prudie made tea as often as she could afford to; the big teapot Demelza had given her was only emptied once a week, boiling water and another pinch of tea being added from time to time.

'I been bit!' Jud shouted as he entered 'Bit by a mad dog. Tedn right, tedn proper! Ravin' mad twas – tongue 'anging out like twas falling off. A lurcher near so big as a pony. Knocked me down, it done, savaged me; I 'ad to fight'n off wi' me bare 'ands!'

'My ivers!' Prudie started up, teapot in hand, put it down, glowered at Jud suspiciously, caring that he should continue to live and be a nuisance to her but knowing his capacity to make mountains. 'What d'ye mean – bit by a mad dog? Where ee been bit? I don't see no bites!' She stared over his shoulder at the group who crowded in after him. 'What mad dog? Seen a mad dog, 'ave ee?'

They all started talking at once, explaining to her what they hadn't seen, repeating Jud's own words. Jud shouted them down, his two teeth showing in a snarl. 'I been bit 'ere. Maybe other places too if the truth be known. Send for surgeon!

I been bit by a mad cur! Tedn *safe*!'

'Naow,' said Prudie, 'out you go, all of ee. Out you go while I see what the 'urt is. Go on. Go on. You too, Tina.'

'Ais,' said Tina.

'Send for surgeon!' shouted Jud, clutching his seat.

'Now wait. 'Old yer sweat. Where you bin bit? On yer bum? Well, take yer britches down and leave me see. Bend over. Bend over this chair.'

Grumbling, Jud did as he was told. Prudie knitted her heavy brows as she surveyed the very substantial area exposed. 'That it?' She prodded.

'Aye! Rabies ye get, mad rabies, and *phit*! – yer dead. Mad curs . . .'

The mark was a tiny nip, a little reddened rim, about an inch long, no skin broken.

'Giss along, tis naught, you old dooda. Bleating like a lammy . . .'

'Twas a mad cur, I tell ee! Send for surgeon!'

Jud was straightening up but Prudie impatiently shoved his head down again.

'Wait, I'll deal wi' ye,' she said.

A bundle of sticks in the grate had been lit to boil the kettle. The kettle had boiled but the sticks were still burning. She bent to the grate and took out a stick with a blazing end. With a great puff she blew out the flame and then pressed the end to Jud's bottom.

III

It was the following day that Demelza walked to Sawle Church. She started off with both Jeremy and Garrick; but Garrick as usual nowadays would not venture beyond the clump of pine trees surrounding the mine of Wheal Maiden and the new meeting house. He knew the limitations of his energy, and a brief rest at the top, head on paws, would revive him sufficiently for the gentle trot down the valley home. Demelza suspected that he put on this pose as an elderly gentleman especially for their benefit, but as he was now thirteen he was entitled to his foibles.

This time Jeremy decided to return with him, so she went on alone. It was another fine day; the miserable summer was

turning into a sunny autumn, and Ross had asked her to see
if Boase, the stonemason from St Ann's, had begun to put up
the granite for Agatha's grave. She took with her a small posy
of flowers to put on the grave and a half guinea for Prudie
Paynter.

When she got there she found no work had yet been begun
on Agatha and no sign of Jud; but she stopped a while looking
at the inscriptions in the churchyard. Ross's father and mother
and brother were there.

'Sacred to the memory of Grace Mary, beloved wife of
Joshua Poldark, who departed this life on the ninth day of
May, 1770; aged 30 years. Quidquid Amor Jussit, Non Est
Contemnere Tutum.

Also of Joshua Poldark, of Nampara, in the County of
Cornwall, Esqr., who died on the eleventh day of March,
1783, aged 59.' And on a small headstone beside: 'Claude
Anthony Poldark, died 9th January, 1771, in the sixth year
of his age.'

Demelza took a piece of paper and a crayon she had brought
in the pocket of her skirt and copied down the Latin tag. She
had asked Ross what it meant but he said he had long since
forgotten what little Latin he had ever learned. She felt she
would like to know. All she knew of his parents was Joshua's
reputation as a young man, of his brief but happy marriage
and of his returning to his old ways when his wife died. All
she had ever seen of Ross's mother was a damp-spotted minia-
ture; of Ross's father nothing at all; there was not even a
portrait of him among the stacked pictures at Trenwith.

This morning a letter from Hugh Armitage. Fortunately
Ross had been out with Jack Cobbledick looking to a sick calf,
so she had been able to slip the separate piece into her pocket
before he came in. It was on the back of this that she now
copied the Latin inscription.

Hugh's letter was on board HMS Arethusa. Although it was
addressed to her it was couched in general and unexception-
able terms. 'Dear Mistress Poldark,' and 'pray convey to your
husband and my liberator my warmest greetings and friendship,' and signed 'believe me, Mistress Poldark, your humble
and obedient servant.' Between the lines Demelza fancied she
detected a note of melancholy. It seemed a sadness more for

life than for her. Perhaps most poets felt this, a grieving for
the timeless tragedy of all love. Unrequited it pined away.
Requited it still pined away, either from staling or when one
or the other ceased to live and was thrust into the cold
ground. As now. As here. Sacred to the memory of Grace
Mary who died in May 1770, aged 30 years. *Quidquid amor
jussit* . . . How did it go?

And Hugh, it seemed, loved and must write now from sea
where the harsh winds blew and England was at war. Yet his
pity, one felt, was not for himself but for human kind. And his
poems, whatever the distance from which he wrote them, were
becoming more direct and more amatory. She took the piece
of paper out and glanced around before she read it, as if the
people quietly sleeping here might look over her shoulder and
disapprove.

It was quite short. The wind rustled the paper in her hand.

> *If she whom I desire would stoop to love me*
> *I would come heart in hand*
> *And kneeling ask that kindly she receive me*
> *And deign to understand,*
> *That all I have is hers and hers for ever,*
> *For ever and a day.*
> *Press but her lips to mine and never*
> *Let love decay.*

IV

By the second of the two great chimneys belonging to the
derelict Grambler Mine, with the pigeons flapping and fluttering in the sun about the fallen roof of the changing shed, she
met Will Nanfan, who told her with great chuckles of Jud's
mishap yesterday. She went along, therefore, knowing the tale
of woe that would greet her. What she did not expect when
the door was creaked open for her was to see Prudie with a
perfect shiner of a black eye. Jud was lying on his face on
the bed trying to smoke, but every now and then the smoke
got in his eyes and he coughed and swore feebly, like someone
who has but a short time to live.

'Oh, tis you,' he said. In spite of frequent proddings from
Prudie, Jud could never forget that Demelza had first arrived

in Nampara as a miserable little scut of a scullery wench, pinched and starving and illiterate and hardly fit to be let in the house – *far* inferior to him and Prudie, who were the senior servants. She might have changed and grown out of recognition and become mistress of the house all because Cap'n Poldark took pity on her, but that didn't alter how and where she had begun.

Then he added: 'Come thee wayst in, mistress,' remembering just in time not Prudie's proddings but that Demelza sometimes brought money. 'Yur I lie creening all day. No doubt ye've heard?'

'Yes,' said Demelza. 'I'm sad for you.'

'There's naught amiss wi' him,' said Prudie. 'Lazy old gale. Sit down, my dear, an' I'll fit a cup o' tay for ee.'

Demelza perched on a shaky chair. She noticed that the mirror she had given them last year had a crack in it and that one chair lay drunkenly against a wall with two of its legs broken. It looked as if there had been an argument.

'Curs!' said Jud, levering himself on to one elbow. 'I'd 'ang the whole danged blatherin' boiling lot. Tedn right! With mad curs roaming over my yard, twas a mercy I weren't ravaged to death!'

'One nick!' came Prudie's booming voice from the other room. In honour of her guest she was trying to find a clean cup. 'One nick like you might've pinched yer bum wi' a pair of tweezers. Scarce that! Scarce that!'

'And what did ee do, eh?' Jud in his annoyance sat up further, and then subsided with a groan. 'Casterized me wi' a burning brand! Casterized the wound and made it twice as deep! Grafty old roach!'

The conversation continued on the same lofty plane while Prudie prepared the cup of tea. Demelza would willingly have escaped it, but she had slipped the half guinea to Prudie as soon as she entered, and Prudie would be hurt if she didn't stay and take a cup. It was a way of saying thank you, and she knew Jud would not hear of the gift today.

'I've been to the church,' she said, taking a tentative sip at the hot black liquid, 'to see if Boase had begun his work on Miss Agatha's grave, but I see he has not. Has he been to take measurements, d'you know?'

'I not seen sight nor sound of him,' said Jud. 'I seen Cap'n Ross once or twiced. Boase – he not been nigh the yard, no, not since he set up that gashly morial to old man Penvenen. Oft I wished twould fall down and crust him when he'm building of 'n. Great gawk of a thing . . . Cap'n Poldark, now, I seen he one even in J'ly – '

'Jud, ye black worm!' said Prudie. 'Yur's yur tay. Gulge it down and I 'ope it chokes yer!'

Jud accepted the cup and slopped some of it on to his wrist. He cursed weakly and sipped the drink.

'Cap'n Poldark I seen one eve in J'ly. There was I, been filling in after Betsy Caudle. When I seen Cap'n Poldark waiting neath a tree – '

'Jud, ye louse-hound!' said Prudie. 'Hold yer clack!'

'What for? What's amiss? What's awry? What's toward? I seen Cap'n Poldark – dedn I say so? What's amiss wi' saying that? And I seen this woman quaddling towards he and I thinks twas you, mistress. I thinks, ah, they've come to meet each other like two little birds on a tree, and dang me if when she come up if tesn't Mistress Elizabeth Warleggan – Poldark that was – and they greet each other, and he raises his 'at and they d'walk off towards Trenwith arm in arm!'

'More tay?' said Prudie to Demelza, breathing over her. 'Dear life, you've scarce touched'n yet and I'm through with mine. Leave me put a drop more.'

'Thank you,' Demelza said. 'No. It's real nice but a small matter hot. I mustn't stay for there's much to do home. We got all our corn cut but there's still some to fetch in.'

Prudie smoothed her black frock, which looked as if it had been used for covering potatoes in an outhouse. 'There, my dear, tis brave of ee to come and see after we, edn it, Jud?'

Jud glanced up sidelong with his bloodshot eyes and received a look from Prudie that seemed to suggest that as soon as their guest had gone she would dash his brains out. Any treatment he had received yesterday would be the balm of angels compared to this. He sat up sharply and winced at his sore seat.

'I – what've I – ' He stopped. 'When this Boase d'come along I'll tell him as you've been around and you d'want to 'ear sharp when 'e be going to begin, eh? That right, mistress?

That what ee d'want?'

'That's what I want,' said Demelza. She sipped the tea again, feeling it hot in her throat. She stood up.

Jud blinked again uneasily at Prudie, and tried to think of something agreeable to say to their guest.

''Ow's your two little grufflers?' he asked as Demelza got to the door.

'Brave,' she said. 'Clowance is cutting teeth and is a thought fretful in the morning, but most of the time she's happy and contented.'

'Like 'er mam,' Jud said, showing his gums in a weak smile. 'Like 'er mam.'

'Not always,' said Demelza. 'Not always.'

They went out into the sunlight. Prudie smoothed her dress again and coughed. But she said nothing; for her none too agile mind had come to the conclusion it would be an error to apologize for Jud because it would emphasize the need for apology.

'I think Jud be going down'ill,' said Prudie, scowling in the sunshine. 'Rapid down'ill. Can't rely on him 'tall. 'Alf the time 'e don't know where he's to, and the other 'alf he's worse. I'll keep that gold away from 'im else he'll slop it down 'is throat. Thank you, mistress, for coming to our aid.'

Demelza gazed towards Trenwith. 'Are the Warleggans at home now? We see nothing of them.'

'Yes, I b'lave them still there. Seen young Master Geoffrey Charles out on 'is pony last month. But I reckon he'm off back school by now.'

'I expect he's grown.'

'Oh, yes, grown like a beanstalk. Be taller'n ever 'is father was, I suspicion.'

'Well, I must get home. Goodbye, Prudie.'

'Goodbye, mistress.'

Prudie stood in the doorway watching Demelza walking off back to Nampara. Then with an apocalyptic face she turned in to the cottage.

George had returned from London in early August but it was not until mid-August that he came to Trenwith. He had been annoyed to learn by letter that Elizabeth had moved to the sea, and his continued absence when he returned to Cornwall was intended to indicate that fact.

Yet when he finally joined her he was a prey to conflicting feelings. His experiences in London had been impressive and exciting. He had met many notable and titled people who apparently took him at his face value; he had seen the Prince Regent and Lady Holland together at a theatre; he had shared a box at Ranelagh, where some of the men still wore swords; he had been introduced to the Mother of Parliaments whose occupants one day behaved with the solemnity of a Star Chamber and another with the levity of a bear pit; and he had missed Elizabeth to be by his side, for her inborn knowledge of the proper thing to do on any occasion would have been invaluable.

He realized that this life as a Member of Parliament was one he wanted more than any other. He had not known before he experienced it, but now he knew. Yet on his return home his natural pride and tight-held self-possession had prevented him from satisfying the curiosity and answering all the questions of his mother and father. The only person with whom he could converse at all freely was Elizabeth, and she was ten miles away and she had gone there in despite of him.

Combating the worm within himself, the worm of suspicion, hatred and jealousy, was the awareness that he wanted to see her again. If the evil suspicion was wholly without foundation, then he was ruining his life – and hers and the child's – for nothing, at this time in his affairs when all else was prospering. On the other hand, if the evil suspicion were wholly true, what had he left? A child that was not his and a woman whom he still consummately desired. If there had been a betrayal it had been before their marriage – she had postponed the marriage by a month: did that signify guilt or innocence? Either might be the case, but surely a scheming woman would not have delayed. The betrayal, if it had happened, had been before their marriage, and if he had known of it before their marriage it would not have altered by a degree his need to possess her. The prize was too great. The prize he had always wanted and never really believed possible of attainment was within his grasp – whatever his anger and bitterness then he would still have grasped it.

And that had not altered. The familiarity of marriage and the satisfaction of possession lessened his sensations when they were together; when they had been apart for several weeks he knew he was still their captive.

It was the two levels which made her irresistible. The poised wife, bred of countless generations of gentlefolk, always perfectly if quietly dressed, equable, kind, dignified, beautiful, young, thoughtful, at ease. But the other level was the unpoised wife, whom he might create whenever she chose to let him. The wife become a woman, bereft of her clothes, her long fair hair falling across naked shoulders and breasts, his, *his* and no other's. Of whom, in these moments, he was the complete master and possessor. George was not a carnal man; his needs seemed so often to sublimate themselves in the conflicts of commerce, in the pursuit of power. During his weeks in London he had found no difficulty at all in remaining faithful to his wife. Two women of rank had made suggestions to him and he had chosen to ignore them without a pang of regret.

But his wife he sometimes did need, and he needed her now.

So the coldness of his departure in June was not matched by a similar coldness of return, much as one side of his nature would have liked it to be so. Amid the scurrying servants he kissed Elizabeth on the mouth and shook Geoffrey Charles by the hand (carefully overlooking the stiff formality of the boy's manner) and actually lifted Valentine from his chair and kissed him and remarked on how heavy he had become, and even had a good word for Elizabeth's father and mother (who by an unfortunate coincidence were both suffering from summer colds) and opened some French champagne for supper.

And so presently at the end of the evening when the long

twilight had faded and the candles were lit, he claimed his rights as a husband and she did not deny him. Afterwards they talked for a while, and in his new relaxed mood he told her much of his time in London and of his intention to take a house up there next year and have her with him.

During the next weeks things altogether went pretty well. Elizabeth had lectured Geoffrey Charles as to his behaviour.

'Remember, my dearest, that Uncle George is a kind generous man who only wishes to be a good father to you. You may greatly have resented what he did last year, but do not forget that you are still young and sometimes you must allow your elders to be the judge. Don't look like that, or I shall become angry . . . Of course it was Morwenna's failure of duty that brought it all to pass; had she not been so careless and forgetful it would never have been necessary to do what we did. And if you think we were angry at your part you are mistaken. Our annoyance was directed entirely at her, and, as you observe, I have raised no objections to your meeting Drake Carne again – though I still think you spend too long with him. Wait! Let that pass. You have been always, as you know, my dearest child, and I think, I believe, you are fond of me. If that is so, then let your love for me govern your behaviour in this house. Uncle George, as you still may call him, is nevertheless your stepfather and my husband. If you and he quarrel, if I find your manner to him hostile and disobedient, it will not only grieve him, it will hurt me. It will damage my happiness. It will ruin a part of my life that I hold most dear.'

So Geoffrey Charles behaved. On the third day of his stay George came to her with a cold face and said Tom Harry had told him that Geoffrey Charles spent every spare moment of his holidays with that insolent young puppy who had forced his way into this house last year in pursuit of Morwenna. So Elizabeth had to reverse her persuasions.

George said: 'Oh, there may be no harm in it, except for this young oaf's connections. I am surprised that you of all people should encourage a friendship with one of Demelza Poldark's brothers.'

'I do *not* encourage it, George. Far from it. But Geoffrey Charles is at a difficult age. You may crush him now, quite easily, but if you do he'll remember it against you – against us – and in a few years he'll not be so easy to control. And the surest way of encouraging this friendship is to forbid it. *You* know that. If you leave it alone, if we don't interfere, it will likely burn itself out in the course of another holiday or two. Don't forget that Geoffrey Charles is very impressionable, and the strongest impression he is receiving now is from his schoolfriends at Harrow. The contrast between their conversation, their view of life, and this young blacksmith's will soon make itself felt. If Geoffrey Charles finds there's nothing to defy he will soon find there's nothing to attract him.'

George turned the money in his fob. 'Yours may be the greater wisdom, Elizabeth; but it angers me afresh that the Poldarks should have seen fit to set this fellow up, as if in defiance of us, practically on our doorstep! There could be – '

'Oh, George, our doorstep! . . . it is two miles if it's an inch.'

'Well, near our mines. I'll see he gets none of our custom . . . And two miles is nothing. It's as if they were deliberately taunting us with this young man. I regret now I did not send him to prison when I had the chance.'

'It would only have made matters worse.'

'Have you seen anything of them since you came here?'

'Nothing,' said Elizabeth; her first lie. 'They never come to church.'

George went off to his study and said no more. So Geoffrey Charles, while limiting his visits to Drake, found no obstacles put in his way. George did not, however, forget the matter. The conviction had grown on him that Drake Carne had been responsible for the episodes of the toads. No one else, so far as he could see, could have had the necessary knowledge of his own movements, no one else would have wished to make him look a fool. Since then little bits of evidence had dropped into place.

So one day when Tankard was there he said to him: 'Pally's Shop. This property now belonging to young Carne. Do we own the adjacent land?'

'No, sir. I think not, sir. It belongs to farmers. Trevethan, I believe. And Hancock. I can find out for sure if you want me to.'

'Do. Find out anything you can about the place. See if Carne owns the mineral rights. Check wells and streams. Find out who Carne mainly does work for. Apart from our mines there is only Wheal Kitty and Wheal Dream within easy distance. And the odd job for the farmers or the gentry . . . See what we can do to discourage him.'

'Yes, sir.'

'But nothing without my prior permission. Suggestions may come from you but decisions from me.'

'Yes, sir.'

'There's no hurry, but report to me by the end of the month.'

II

George went over to see Basset three or four times, and they all dined together at Tehidy, with Geoffrey Charles at his liveliest and best with little Miss Frances Basset. Then the Bassets came to dine at Trenwith. For this George asked Sir John Trevaunance and his brother Unwin, John and Ruth Treneglos and Dwight and Caroline Enys. Taking no great part in the conversation at the dinner table, Dwight thought that once or twice George slightly irritated the new Baron de Dunstanville. It was far from being a difference of opinion; rather that George sometimes seemed to take up Basset's views and carry them to ends more forthright than their originator cared. Knowing George to be a man whose principles were often shaped by self-interest, Dwight thought he detected occasional false notes, and wondered if Basset did the same.

The following day the Warleggans were dining with the Tranegloses, and this meant a detour round the property of that other and unmentionable Poldark. Tankard went with them, for George wanted to look at Wheal Leisure, the mine he had recently closed, and decide whether any more use could be made of it. He had had full reports, but, like all good men of business, he made a point of seeing things for himself.

On high ground near the now empty Gatehouse where Dwight had once lived he reined in his horse and peered down at the straggle of Wheal Grace mine and Nampara House lying at the end of the narrow valley with its feet almost in the sea. He studied it for a few minutes.

Wheal Grace looked busy. Although it was not time for the changing of the cores, the engine had just been coaled and thick smoke issued from the chimney. The great arm of the pump moved up and down, the tin stamps turned and rattled, bonneted women worked on the washing floors, a train of mules with panniers filled was about to move off, carrying their ore to be stamped in Sawle Combe.

George said: 'I see the addition is complete.'

Elizabeth moved her horse nearer to him. 'What is that?'

'The addition to the house. You knew about it, of course.'

'Not until this moment . . . It looks the same to me. Oh, you mean this end.'

'They've added a storey and rebuilt the library. Basset was telling me last night – they had his plasterer from Bath.'

'Has he been over?'

'Basset? I don't think so. I don't think he has been invited.'

The wind was fresh, and Elizabeth put up a hand to steady her green tricorn hat.

'I was seldom over even when I was married to Francis. And after Francis died Ross used to come to see me once a week, but I did not ride this way.'

'That was when he cheated Geoffrey Charles out of his rights in this prosperous mine.'

Elizabeth shrugged. 'The mine, he thought, was foundering and he bought the share thinking he was helping us by doing so. It was half a year after that that they found tin.'

George smiled. 'At last I have provoked you into defending him.'

Elizabeth looked round, but Geoffrey Charles had moved on with the groom. She was not smiling.

'Your suspicions don't do you credit, George. Not these nor any others.'

'What others?'

'Whatever others you may entertain. As a distinguished man, as a Member of Parliament, as a magistrate – also as my husband . . . and as Valentine's father . . . I think you are too big a man now for such small matters.'

The wind thrust at them, and their horses were restless. A bell rang in the mine, sounding far distant because of the gusty wind.

She had trailed her coat: it was up to him whether he said more; but she had chosen her moment well; one could not fling black accusations at a woman on horseback on a windy moor while her son and their groom were only twenty yards away and had reined in waiting for them.

Yet it was a sort of challenge. It was spoken with more firmness than she had ever used before. It alerted him to her awareness of his moods, and possibly the reason for them. And it alerted him to her willingness to fight. It meant that he must take greater care of his moods or that some time in the future it must indeed come to that fight.

He said: 'What's that building among the trees on the rise going towards Choake's?'

'I believe it's the new chapel.'

'On Poldark land?'

'I think so. Didn't they build it out of the stones of the old mine?'

'It looks like a cattle shed.'

'It was all done by the Methodists in their spare time.'

'No doubt initiated by the two Carne brothers.'

'No doubt. I'm sorry we moved them from the meeting house near Trenwith. It can do no good to become unpopular in so small a cause.'

'We do not need to curry favour with such.'

'I never have – curried favour. But we have to spend our lives among these people.'

'Less and less,' said George.

'Well,' Elizabeth said. 'That will please me. I shall look forward to London.'

George glanced at her. 'Trevaunance was asking me last night about my position on the bench. I have only made one appearance this year. But I don't intend to leave this district altogether. After all, it is Geoffrey Charles's inheritance.'

Elizabeth nodded but did not speak.

George said: 'The last time I met Ross he asked me if I had ever thought of selling Trenwith.'

'He did?' She was surprised into a flush.

'Perhaps, now that his little mine is prospering, he has the illusion that he could find enough money to buy Trenwith for himself.'

'That could never be! As you say, it belongs to Geoffrey Charles.'

'Well,' George looked down at Nampara and gathered his reins more tightly, 'I can understand his ambition. Whatever he may do to that place he can achieve nothing in the end. As well try to make a good shaft out of a pig's tail.'

III

Since the day she had left in Sam's company Drake had seen nothing of Emma Tregirls. He himself seldom went away from his forge and anvil. This was his work; the craft fascinated him; it was what he had been brought up to do; it was what he could do best; and he owed Ross and Demelza a duty to succeed. In spite of his grief he sometimes looked round his property and found it good. Every hour he worked on it made it better and every hour away from it was a wasted hour because there was nothing outside his work that interested him.

And if he needed company the company was here. His social life was his customers. A farmer would bring his horse to be shod and would gossip away while the work was being done, or a plough would need a new handle, or the wall of a cottage would need an iron cross for support, or a miner would bring a shovel in need of a new haft. Caroline Enys had taken a fancy to the tall pale youth and sent over any work she could. Sometimes she came herself and strolled about the yard talking to him and tapping her skirt with her riding crop.

But not Emma Tregirls. Then one Wednesday afternoon in early October, her half day off, she arrived with a kitchen hook used for suspending a kettle over a fire. It was badly bent and needed re-shaping, but Drake wondered that a handyman at Fernmore could not have done the job himself.

'Will ye wait?' he asked.

'I'll wait,' she said, and took a seat on an upturned box and watched him.

There was silence while the hook was heated to a proper temperature. She was dressed in her usual scarlet cloak, scarf, blue dress – her Wednesday best – sturdy boots, knees crossed, one ankle, surprisingly slim, swinging free. Drake decided he didn't dislike her face. Its boldness had a freshness about it, a frankness, unaware or careless of prohibitions. You could see how the men would be attracted to a girl who made no pretence of shyness or dissimulation. Yet in the end they would come to accept the general verdict of other women, or the community in general, and despise her.

'Got a nice place here,' Emma said.

'Yes, tis looking better now.'

'All tidied up. Cleaned up proper. Done it all yourself, have you?'

'Yes.'

'Don't Brother never come over t'elp?'

'Once in a while. But he's got his own living to make.'

'And all that praying. Was you ever a praying man yourself, Drake?'

'Yes. Still am betimes.'

'But you keep it in its place, eh? Not like Brother who can scarce open his mouth wi'out calling on God.'

'That's as maybe. We're all made different.'

'Yes,' said Emma, and the conversation lapsed.

The hook was red hot, and he picked it from the fire, put it on the anvil, and began to tap it back to shape. She watched his long slim arms, sleeves rolled above elbow, his intent face.

She said: 'Drake.'

He looked up.

'Drake, d'you ever laugh, play, enjoy yourself? Specially d'you ever laugh?'

He thought. 'I used to – a lot.'

'Before you became a Methody?'

'Oh, after that.'

'And Sam? Do he ever laugh?'

'Yes, sometimes. For joy.'

'But for *fun* – for good earthy fun. Like most young folk.'

'Not much. Life's serious for Sam. Not that he didn't used to.'

'Did he? When?'

Drake examined the hook, turning it this way and that, gave it a few more taps. Then he plunged it into a bucket of water. The steam rose hissing to the sky. 'There you are, mistress. That's done.'

She did not speak and he considered a moment whether he wanted to say any more to her about Sam. He met her eyes.

He said: 'When Father was converted we all had to be converted along of him. I was a little tacker but Sam were fourteen. It never took with him. Always he'd be off away somewhere when twas time for chapel. Many's the rowings he got. But when Father was converted he gave up the strap so twas all moral suasion. Right till he was nigh twenty Sam were the black sheep. Not real black, mind. Lighthearted, as you say. Always joking. Always up to pranks. A tankard of ale or a tot of rum. Wrestling. Running races. He were the best wrestler in the family after Father. Used to go round competing at fairs. Sonny Carne, they used to call him.'

'Why Sonny?'

'From Samson, I s'pose. Sam – son.'

The hissing had died away.

She said: 'What spoiled him?'

Drake laughed. 'Sam wouldn't say that. He'd say what saved him.'

'Well?'

'A girl he liked – oh, no more'n liked – and a boy he liked – brother and sister – died of typhus. They'd been converted bare a month and he was there when they died, and he says it all happened from that. Joy was in their faces, he said, 'stead of pain. For weeks after he was in terrible trouble, suffering much and struggling with Satan, until the Evil One was at last vanquished and Sam became a child of God.'

'You're talking like him now,' Emma said.

'Should I not?'

She stood up and went to the tub of water. She took the tongs from him and lifted out the hook and put it on the bench.

'That'll do well and fine. How much do I pay you?'

They were standing close together. He had not been so close to a young woman for a long time.

'Why d'you ask 'bout Sam?'

'He troubles me.'

'How? Why?'

'He's in love with me, Drake.'

'And you?'

'Oh,' she shrugged. 'Tis no matter what I d'feel. I've told him no.'

'He wanted to wed you?'

'Yes. That's comic, isn't it? Him and me. Oil and water. He think to reform me. I'd poison his godly life. Honest I would. Can you see me among the Methodies? That'd duff you, wouldn't it?'

Drake looked away. She spoke lightly and there was no hint of trouble in her eyes.

'Why d'you come to me, Emma?'

'To get the hook fixed, what else?'

'Well . . .'

'But I just thought to mention Sam.'

Drake touched the hook experimentally. It had cooled. 'That'll be twopence.'

She gave him two pennies.

Drake said: 'He have asked to wed you and you've told him no. Isn't that an end on it?'

She picked up the hook and banged it hard on the bench. 'Yes!'

'You'll do it hurt that way and be coming for another straightening.'

She said: 'I come to you because there's no one other to talk to, and I like your looks. Fact when I come that day with the lifting bar twas out of curiosity to see you and I was vexed to see Preaching Sam here. I still like your looks . . . but Sam d'get into your *bones*. He's got into *my* bones, I tell ee, and tis no pretty way to be!'

'You love him, do you, Emma?'

She shrugged impatiently. 'Love? I don't know what love d'mean. But I can't be free the way I used to be! I can take my two-three pints with the best, laugh and joke; nobody d'see the difference in Emma. People d'say I'm a whore. What is a whore? A woman that d'sell her body. I never sold nothing to no one! I'm not so loose as folk say but . . . What I done I don't regret. But since I seen Sam, since we talked, I've lost the pleasure of it! I wish to God I never met him!'

After a moment, Drake said: 'Is it the conviction of sin

that's growing in you, Emma?'

Bang went the hook again. 'No! And to Hell wi' your damnation preaching! No, I don't know what tis but I feel no *sin*. Sin? Sin is doing ill to other folk, not enjoying what you've got in the world! Sometimes I think Sam's not a good man but a rare wicked one. What d'ye think *I* got to be happy 'bout? Brought up in the poor's house, lent out, worked to death, never a moment free to call me own, half starved, no chance of betterment, men prying, pawing. Now I'm with the Choakes – tis betterer'n most. Bit of time to meself now and then and a half day a fortnight. So I want to be *happy*, to enjoy what I got, a tot of rum, flirting wi' a man, running races at Sawle feast, a bed to sleep in, nigh enough to eat. What for should *I* feel sin? What sin ever have I done in the world 'cept to try to make a few folk happy! You and your damned brother! I wisht you'd both go jump down a bal!'

She had worked herself up into a rare anger. Her whole body was trembling with annoyance and she held the hook as if she would swing it at Drake and slay him.

Drake said: 'Emma, I cann't answer all for Sam. But truly if you come to God in the way he has come, you have *first* to feel the conviction of sin, *then* you feel the forgiveness, the deliverance, *then* the joy of Salvation. The joy you d'feel at the end is far in excess of any joy you may have felt afore. That is what he preaches. That is what he tries to bring folk to understand! He wants you to *be* happy, but happy in the right way, happier than ever you have been in the past!'

Emma put the hook under her arm. 'Well, tis all *lost* on me, I tell ee. Look at 'em, look at the Methodies crawling about, pinched mouths, frowning brows, afraid to say boo to a goose, case the goose is Satan in disguise – *are* they happy? Cursed if I can see it!'

Drake sighed. 'We must do what we think best, sister. The world have gone sour on me, as doubtless you will have heard. It is not in me to give you any answer. I'm that sorry you've become taken up with Sam. I'm sorry for your sake and I'm sorry for his. But if you can find nothing in his promises then I b'lieve there's nothing that'll help you with him at all.'

Emma stood there retying the knot in her scarf. 'Down a mine,' she said. 'That's what did ought to happen to the both of you. Cast down a mine with a lot of water in it so's you'd both drown.'

She went off, leaving Drake staring after her. He did not go in until her figure had dwindled away in the distance of the hill.

CHAPTER IV

Except for a short spell around Christmas, it was a beautiful winter. Compared to that of two years ago England was a different island set in a friendlier sea. All through the worst months frosty nights were followed by days of hazy sunshine; and in Cornwall there was not even frost. Primroses bloomed all winter, birds sang, winds were mainly easterly and light.

Ross and Demelza and both children bathed on the 21st December. The water was icy to get in but the air delicious to come out into, and while they rubbed themselves with towels the low sun peered over the sea, casting long cadaverous shadows of themselves across the silent beach. Then indoors, giggling and still damp, to stand before the fire and sup bowls of steaming soup and sip toddy. It was Jeremy's first taste of spirituous liquor and it went to his head and he lay on the settle shrieking with laughter while Clowance gazed gravely at her brother thinking he had gone off his head.

The one break in the good weather came at Christmas with snowflakes and a howling easterly gale, and Ross had visions of another such year's beginning as January '95, but in less than a week the storm was over and the sun came out again.

Save for the mildness of the weather there was little to rejoice in. Lord Malmesbury, sent to Paris to discuss French terms for a European peace settlement, was kept on a string until mid-December and then summarily dismissed. The Directory did not want peace. Spain had at last declared war on their side. Corsica had been taken, the French landing at one end of the island as the British left it at the other. Catherine of Russia was dead and her successor, Tsar Paul, a neurotic and a tyrant, had no interest in pulling English irons out of the fire. The day before Malmesbury was sent home a French fleet of forty-three ships, with sixteen thousand troops aboard under the redoubtable young Hoche, slipped out of Brest, dodged the British fleet and sailed to invade an Ireland waiting to be liberated.

Only Captain Sir Edward Pellew, the hero of the fight in which Dwight was captured, was once again in the right place at the right time and drove his solitary frigate into the heart of the French fleet during the night, blazing off with everything he'd got and causing confusion, panic, and three enemy ships to run on the rocks. But most of the invading armada reached Bantry Bay and while Ross and Demelza were enjoying their bathe were assembling to proceed up the bay to land their troops. Thereupon came the Christmas gale, more valuable to England than all her blockading squadrons; and blew for a week, making any sort of landing impossible; and in disappointment the French fleet turned for home.

Yet when the escape became known, there was despondency in England, not relief. If such an occurrence could happen once, when might it not happen again? Belief in the blockade was shaken. Belief in the omniscience of the British navy was lost. More banks suspended payment and Consols fell to 53.

Nothing more was heard at Nampara of Hugh Armitage, and his name seldom came up in conversation. But Ross wondered if his shadow had come between them. It never *had*, while he was here; they had talked once or twice about him, about his infatuation for Demelza, about her feeling of vulnerability, like true lovers discussing something which had arisen and needed to be considered, yet without any feeling of there being a real menace in it towards their own love. That was while he was here. After he was gone it had at first been just the same; but it seemed to Ross that something in that last letter of Hugh's in September had unsettled Demelza and she had slightly withdrawn from the frank companionship of most times.

He had asked her twice if anything was amiss, not of course mentioning Hugh's name, and each time she had said no. The change in her indeed was so slight that someone less close to her would have noticed nothing. She went about in the same way as ever, cheerful, lively, talkative, witty, enjoying life and enjoying her children. The furnishings for the new library were coming on well, and she took interest in seeing everything was right. Twice she rode to Truro with him about the chairs. Other times they shopped together in Padstow and Penryn. They had the Enyses to dinner. She was always busy. Twice in love-making she turned her mouth away from him.

In January to his very considerable annoyance Ross learned that the Reverend Osborne Whitworth had been appointed to the living of Sawle-with-Grambler. The following week, the weather being so open, Mr Whitworth rode over with his wife and sister-in-law, slept with the elderly Chynoweths at Trenwith, and duly read himself in. It was learned that he had decided to increase the Odgers's stipend to £45 a year.

'It shows,' Ross said, 'what value can be placed on Lord Falmouth's promise of assistance.'

'Why? Did you ask him?'

'Yes. When we were there in July. He said he would make a note of it.'

'I expect he forgot, Ross. I expect he's too big a man to ask for things like that.'

'Not, I would imagine, if they were of any advantage to himself.'

'How do you suppose Ossie has got it, then?'

'He may have influence with the Dean and Chapter – his mother was a Godolphin. And of course George, occupying the largest house in the parish and being a Member of Parliament . . .'

'Well, I suppose Elizabeth will be pleased, since it will be preferment for her cousin's husband.'

'Odgers will not be pleased. It was his one hope of a comfortable genteel life. Now he knows he must slave and scrape for the rest of his days.'

'Would you be able to have more influence, Ross, if you were a Member of Parliament?'

'Who knows? God knows. I am not and shall never be.'

'Never is a long time.'

'Anyway, you consider me unsuited to hold such an office.'

'Twas *you* refused, Ross, not me. I know you asked me before you said no, and we talked of it; but you'd really decided to say no before ever you spoke to me, hadn't you?

I thought – what it was in me to think – and I said to you that you had chosen right if you go on all the time being judge and jury to condemn yourself.'

'Yes, yes, I remember; the coat of armour. Well, my dear, perhaps one of these days I shall grow one and become a borough monger and conspire with the best. Perhaps I shall be able to regulate, order and arrange my prickly conscience if I contrive benefits only for my friends and not for myself, and refuse any payment for them. That way my nobility of soul will shine through.'

'It is not so much that I care vastly for Mr Odgers,' Demelza said. 'He's a teasey little man. But Mrs Odgers is so hard worked, and the children so down-at-heel. And also Ossie Whitworth thinks so highly of himself already that it seem a pity he will have reason to be still more satisfied.'

II

Ossie was indeed satisfied. As soon as he was summoned to Exeter to be collated he wrote assiduous letters of thanks to Conan Godolphin, George Warleggan, and all others who had assisted him in the struggle; for he was nothing if not punctilious about his own affairs, and one never knew when one might need one's friends again. It was a very pleasant weekend, the last in January, that he spent at Trenwith, and with his two women and a groom beside him he knew it made a distinguished cavalcade.

It was Morwenna's first long trip since her illness but she stood the ride well. Her health had improved steadily from the time of Dwight's ministrations. True in September there had been a relapse that had lasted two weeks; she had retired to bed and had refused to speak to anyone in the house – not even Rowella, certainly not Ossie. Dr Behenna had declared it a light paludal fever caught from the river, and had given her purges and Peruvian bark. This treatment had had a good effect and had restored the family's faith in their medical man.

And from then on, although quiet and sad, she had gained strength, and this visit to Trenwith showed her to be in perfect good health again. The return to this house was a test of another sort; every room had some memory in it of the tragedy of her young love. Knowing of Drake's nearness, she almost yielded to the temptation to rise very early on the Sunday morning and walk to see him, but at the last her nerve failed. Ossie might wake before she returned and then there would be great trouble. And, in any event, what could it profit either Drake or herself to rub their wounds raw again? She knew of his enduring love; he knew of hers; it must be enough.

It was a full church, with the Reverend Clarence Odgers fussing about his new vicar and assisting in the service. Ossie preached 1 Tim. 6 (UCP). 'Perverse disputings of men of corrupt minds, and destitute of the truth, suppose that gain is godliness: from such withdraw thyself. But godliness with contentment is great gain. For we brought nothing into this world and it is certain we can carry nothing out. And having food and raiment let us be therewith content.' He thought it went well. It was a timely sermon at this period of unrest. (There had been another food riot at St Just last week.) He had thought of collecting perhaps fifty of his sermons and having them published. There was a handy little printer he had met in Exeter who would keep the costs down, and it did a man's name good to have some published work on sale. He fancied he had made a good impression on the new Archdeacon and had invited him to stay with them at St Margaret's when he came round on his next visitation.

After church he met the rest of the Odgers family, and they all trooped back to Trenwith for dinner. Elizabeth had sent written instructions to the servants to prepare a meal for twenty, but, the Chynoweths being incapable of overseeing anything, it was all badly arranged. Ossie determined to have a word with George about it when next they met.

They went home on the Monday morning, Ossie having left a list of matters which Odgers was at once to see to: overgrown churchyard, ill-fitting door, cracked window, mice in vestry, fabric over altar, holes in curate's cassock, inattention of choir during sermon, omitting words from service and use of erroneous doctrine. There were other things Ossie had noticed but he thought that would do to begin.

As soon as they reached home Morwenna ran upstairs to see how John Conan had fared in her absence, and Ossie, who had been unable to keep his eyes off Rowella's thin back all the way home, beckoned her into his study.

She came demurely, stood just inside the door, eyes glinting out at the trees and the river.

'Shut the door,' he said with a hint of impatience.

'Yes, Vicar.'

He said: 'It may be late tonight. It is becoming more and more difficult . . .'

'Whenever you say.'

'It is not whenever I say, as you well know. Else it would be now!'

'Yes, it would be nice now,' she said.

His look was half lust and half anger. 'Do not . . . you must not . . .'

'What, Vicar?'

He brushed some dust from his coat, put his hands in their favourite position behind his back and stared at her.

'Go, now. Go and help your sister. It is improper that we should be much alone. But I thought I must tell you about tonight. It must be tonight, you understand?'

'Yes,' she said, nodding. 'Tonight.'

And it was that night, after he had had his way with her, that she told him she was going to have a baby.

III

She wept in his arms, while he wished he had the strength to throw her in the river.

It seemed sometimes to him that God was trying him too highly. True his call had not been great – his mother, finding him unable to pass the sort of examinations that the law entailed, had chosen the ministry as a suitable alternative for the son of a judge – but, once so chosen, he had pursued a highly successful career in it; he had read a good deal of ecclesiastical law and, among the natural frivolities of a moderately well-to-do young gentleman, he had sought and obtained preferment which did not at all seem undeserved.

But nature had endowed him with powerful appetites, and marriage had been a necessity if he were to obey the relevant doctrines of the church. The death of his first wife had been followed by marriage to a second who, after the birth of their child, had been forbidden him on the strictest medical advice. Then and there present, occupying a seat at his dining table, and presently coming wholly to occupy his thoughts, was this thin rake of a girl with the most astonishing figure and appetites of her own, who had lured him with her mock-modest wiles, enticed him upstairs with learned talk of Greek heroes and had then unclothed herself and thrown herself at him as if, instead of being a dean's daughter, she had been the vilest wanton off the streets.

So he had become wrapped in her toils, bound hand and foot by her lures and his own deprivations. So he had allowed himself to become seduced by a wanton child. So he had broken the seventh commandment and offended against all the laws of the society of which he conceived himself to be a leader.

This far it had happened, but this far it had happened in secret. Now, *now*, this Medusa weeping on his shoulder would shortly begin to bear within her body, in such a way as could not be disguised, the evidence of her shame. *And* the evidence of his guilt. *His* guilt. For all to see. His very special guilt in having contracted a liaison with a woman, scarcely more than a child, who was his own wife's sister. It was intolerable, impossible. The church, the Archdeacon, the churchwardens . . . What would happen to his preferment, even to his position in the church at all?

'Come, come,' he said, 'I do not believe it can be so.'

'Oh, it is so,' she sobbed. 'Oh, it is so! Last month I have missed what I should have had, and this week should have been the second. And I have been quite venomous sick as if I had been given a poison! All these last weeks I have hoped and prayed that it should not be so!'

They lay there for a long time saying nothing. Although she continued to weep, he felt that he could not be absolutely sure that her tears were not exaggerated to exact from him the maximum of pity. For a time his mind was drugged, as if unable to bestir itself from the morass into which her words had plunged it; but gradually it began to work. All the choices were nasty. If she were to commit suicide . . . If she could be persuaded to visit one of the old women of the town . . . If she could be sent away somewhere to stay with some crone who would 'adopt' the child after it was born . . . If she could be sent home to her mother in disgrace . . . If some other man could be blamed . . .

Of course he would deny any responsibility. It was only her word against his, and who would not take the word of a respected clergyman against that of a hysterical half-demented girl? Send her home in disgrace, let her mother make what she could of it. Scarcely anyone in the parish need ever know. Morwenna, perhaps, but it would be in her own interest to keep it secret, whatever her private thoughts.

Rowella moved away from him and tried to dry her eyes on the sheet. A worm of doubt moved in Ossie. In spite of her extreme youth Rowella was not to be trifled with. If she chose to keep quiet about him, she would keep quiet; but if she chose not to, her accusations would not, he suspected, be barely audible between heart-rendering sobs. She would make her points, whether overshadowed by age and position or not. It was a horrible situation and one about which he ventured to feel a grievance against God.

'We will have to think gravely about this,' he said, as if he had not already been thinking gravely.

'Yes, Ossie.'

'I must go now. We will consider it again tomorrow in the light of day.'

'Do not tell Morwenna.'

'No, no. I shall not do that!'

'It is a terrible thing to have happened.'

'Yes, Rowella, it is.'

'I do not know what anyone will think of me.'

'Perhaps they will not know.'

'It will be very hard to hide.'

'Yes, that too I know,' he said in intense irritation.

'Perhaps you will think of something, Vicar.'

'There, there. We shall have to think and pray.'

'I could kill myself for this.'

'Yes, yes, my dear.' Was there hope?

'But will not,' said Rowella, wiping her eyes.

In early February the de Dunstanvilles dined with the Poldarks at Nampara. It was something Demelza had set her face against ever since Ross first mentioned the possibility. Dining out with the nobility was one thing, entertaining them in this small house, and with untrained servants, was another. And of all the nobility, these were the two she feared most. She would rather have welcomed three Lord Falmouths and a couple of Valletorts thrown in; the simple reason being that she could not detach the Bassets from memories of her childhood – or indeed from the knowledge that three of her brothers and a stepmother and stepsister still lived in a wretched cottage half a mile from the gates of Tehidy. Since she married Ross she had never found much difficulty in dealing with the lesser fry of the social scene: the Bodrugans, the Trevaunances, the Trenegloses and so on, and even with Lord Falmouth she had established a very slight rapport (in that on the rare occasions when he had spoken to her she thought she detected a gleam of approval in his eye), but the new Baron and his lady, though always gracious to her, suffered her, she thought, entirely on account of Ross.

Also poverty, until the last two years, had virtually cut off any formal entertaining at all; so she had had no practice. It was totally and impossibly unfair to begin by entertaining the two richest and most sophisticated people in Cornwall, who anyway must by now know exactly who she was and where she came from.

For a while Ross allowed himself to be put off by these objections; but eventually, as he told her, it became impossibly ill-mannered not to invite them, since Basset had several times expressed a wish to see the work that his recommended plasterer had done for them.

'I have said this too often to you already,' Ross added; 'in England we are not near so rigid in our class structures as you still appear to suppose. Thomas Coutts, the banker, married a maid in his brother's employ, and she now entertains princes. Besides, in all countries, England as elsewhere, a woman at marriage takes her husband's position and rank. Why do you think Frances Hippesley-Cox became first Lady Basset and then Lady de Dunstanville? Because of her marriage to Francis Basset.'

'Ah, but you can tell, she was gentlefolk to begin.'

'No matter. Just as she is now Lady de Dunstanville, you are Mrs Ross Poldark, and if any person ever treated you different from that I would turn him out of the house, even if it were the King himself. After all these years you must understand that.'

'Yes, Ross.'

He did not like her in one of her meek moods. They usually boded no good.

'Oh, I appreciate all about the Bassets and Tehidy and the rest. Try to forget it. You only have to be your natural self. Pretend nothing, for you have nothing to hide. Rather you have everything to be proud of.'

'And who shall do the cooking, Ross?'

'Jane knows many of the dishes you serve. Perhaps you will have to oversee it in its early stages . . .'

'And in its late stages too. If Jane knows we have the Baron de Dunstanville at our table she'll tremble so much she'll drop the goose in the fire and pour mustard sauce on the apple tarts.'

'Mrs Zacky would come in, I'm sure. If she can deliver a baby she should be able to put the dishes into and out of an oven.'

'And who will wait at table in white gloves? Jack Cobbledick?'

'Nobody will wear white gloves. Ena can wait very well now and Betsy Maria can help . . . It has to be, love. I'm sorry, but there is no way out short of a discourtesy I cannot possibly show. If they do not like our country cooking they can go back to their palace and rot.'

'I believe they're much more likely to go back to their palace and laugh.'

'There you do them an injustice. If they hadn't wanted to come he would not have almost reached the point of suggesting it. And gentlefolk never laugh at simplicity; they only laugh at pretence.'

'And where can I show her upstairs? Downstairs may be lovely – if we keep the pigs out and Garrick in the scullery – but we have no new furniture for our bedroom and still only an outside closet.'

'Much healthier. For the rest, show her into Jeremy's room. It is simple, but all new and fresh, and there's a good mirror.'

Demelza considered the gloomy prospect ahead. Ross put his arm round her shoulders. 'I rely on you.'

'Perhaps you should not always.'

'Whether I should or should not, I always will.'

'Well, if I have to I have to; but on one condition: we must invite Dwight and Caroline too to water them down.'

'I was going to suggest it.'

So the dinner came off on a fine Tuesday in mid-February. Demelza had given great thought to the menu for she knew, whatever Ross might think, that she would have to oversee the meal until the last second. She did pease soup, which could be got ready beforehand, then a boiled tongue, similarly easy, followed by a fat little turkey hen roasted, with chopped bacon, then her special raspberry jam puffs, and ended with a syllabub and mince pies. The day before, Ross had been over to Mr Trencrom and cajoled him into selling him a half dozen bottles of his finest claret, which Mr Trencrom always had run over specially from France. With Geneva, brandy, and Demelza's favourite port, there was plenty to drink, and good drink at that. Basset, in spite of his wealth, was no toper, and everyone ended the meal pleasantly full, pleasantly relaxed and pleasantly talkative.

There was much to talk about: Mantua had fallen and resistance in Italy was at an end; the last Italian ports were being closed to English shipping; and Austria, the only bastion remaining, was tottering to a fall. The last attempt to invade Ireland had been foiled by the weather, but any day another might begin, especially as the Spanish and Dutch fleets were now available to combine with the French. As troops were freed from their other conquests in Europe they were being drafted to the Channel coast. Next time it might not be Ireland that was attempted. More volunteers were being recruited throughout the land, and at every tiny port men were being pressed for the navy. Miners were exempt from impressment but here and there were forming patriotic groups for resistance against the French.

They later moved into the new library, whose plaster-work was much admired, and then, the day being so fine, it was suggested they should all go for a walk as far as Damsel Point, and Demelza, to her horror, found herself partnered by Lord de Dunstanville. The way lay along the narrow path skirting the Long Field, so there was no hope of breaking this order until they reached the rocks. Ross led the way with Lady de Dunstanville, and Dwight and Caroline had meanly contrived to stick together and bring up the rear.

Conversation between the lady of the house and her guest centred chiefly on crops. This was easy enough, and a polite question now and then kept him going. Demelza had long since realized that most men liked the sound of their own voices, and the new baron was no exception. Not that what he said was boring or in any way dull; he was incisive, to the point, and full of ideas that were new to her. After a while she began to relax, reasoning that the more he dominated the conversation the less time he was likely to have to think about her social deficiencies.

They reached the end of the field, where the end of the cultivable land was and rock and gorse began. He stopped and looked across at Hendrawna Beach. Ross and Lady de Dunstanville were on ahead, Dwight was picking a thorn out of Caroline's shoe.

Basset said: 'Where I live, as you know, we are well guarded by cliffs. But long stretches of sand such as this and at Gwithian offer easy landings for the invader if he chooses his weather right. It makes one apprehensive for the safety of our shores.'

'If he came,' Demelza said, 'I do not believe he would be graciously received.'

He glanced at her. 'Of that I'm sure. But our casual forces against the war-hardened veterans of Europe . . . Now as to the navies, that is another matter.'

She gazed over the sea. This morning had come another

letter from Hugh and another poem. Again she had succeeded in slipping the poem away without Ross noticing it. The letter had been bare, a catalogue of events, and those but few, seeing that they covered four months. The navy's duties were monotonous and hard, a fight far more often against wind and tide than an enemy ship. Endless patrol, endless vigilance, and then the French navy slipped out unawares. Demelza hoped – or part of her hoped – that the tone of his letter showed he was losing interest. Unfortunately the poem did not confirm this idea. It was longer than the others and less direct, but one could be left in no doubt as to the sentiments. And the last line of his letter said that there might be a chance of his being in Cawsand next month with leave to visit his parents, and possibly his uncle.

'. . . so possibly his choice was the right one,' Basset ended. In panic Demelza licked her lips. 'Please?'

'I was saying it is a difficult age for a man in time of war. I think it was that that mainly caused him to refuse. At twenty-seven he would naturally join his regiment. At forty-seven he might more readily have accepted the seat.'

'Yes, I suspicion he might,' she said, groping cautiously.

'His brilliant exploit in France two years ago shows that his preferences are still towards a more active participation in war; yet I think he might have done well in the Commons. But it was not to be.'

'Our neighbour took his place,' she said.

'Indeed. And a very . . . diligent Member he is proving himself.'

Ross and his partner were at the edge of the rock-strewn moorland sloping down into Hendrawna Cove. Frances de Dunstanville looked very small beside him.

Basset stopped again. 'There is bad blood between your houses. What is the cause of it, Mrs Poldark?'

Demelza put her foot on a stone and looked across the beach. 'Over there are the Dark Cliffs,' my Lord, those you were asking me about.'

'Yes, I see.'

'The bad blood lies too far back for me to explain. And even if I could, tis not for me to do it. You must ask Ross.'

'I do not like it shown in public. One should not wear soiled linen where it may be seen.'

'One should not wear soiled linen at all, my Lord.'

He smiled. 'Nor wash it in public, eh? In any event such ill-will between cousins and neighbours is uncalled-for. It should be buried, where all old rivalries belong, especially in time of war when we have a common enemy to fight. Tell Captain Poldark from me, will you?'

'If you will tell Mr Warleggan . . .'

He looked at her sidelong. 'I am informed that the fault lies mainly on the Poldark side.'

Demelza's heart began to thump. Then she met his glance and let out a slow breath. 'My Lord, I b'lieve you are teasing me.'

'I would not venture to do that, madam, on so short an acquaintance. What is that mine on the cliffs?'

'Wheal Leisure. Closed by Mr Warleggan two years ago.'

'On Poldark land?'

'Treneglos land. But Ross began it ten years ago.'

'Old feuds and old rivalries no doubt die hard.'

'So do old mines.'

'I conceit that Captain Poldark has a stout defender in you, ma'am.'

'Would you not have it so?'

'Indeed. Indeed. I tremble to say more.'

'My Lord, I do not believe you would tremble at anything. But talking of feuds . . .'

'Yes?'

'No, it was not a proper thought.'

'Please go on.'

'Well . . . talking of feuds . . . do you not have one yourself with Lord Falmouth?'

He looked at her in surprise and then laughed. '*Touché*. But it would be more proper to say that he has a feud with me. I feel nothing in the matter at all.'

'The fault lying mainly on the Boscawen side?'

'Now, madam, I believe you are teasing *me*.'

She was not sure whether his smile had a little ice in it now, as if she had gone far enough in reply. But after a moment his face cleared and he put his hand out to help her over a boulder.

'Doubtless you know, Mrs Poldark, that Lord Falmouth mislikes the way in which I captured the seat from him at Truro; and no doubt when a general election comes he will lose the other one there too. We have, after all, been rivals in this way for years. But for my part I would not object if some sort of an accommodation were now proposed. Now that I have moved to the Upper House the situation has a little changed. I control Penryn. I control or contest several others. But I am beginning to lose a little of the zest for constant battle.'

'Indeed, sir, I didn't know.' She hesitated. 'So my reply was unseemly after all.'

'Not at all: you responded very properly with a woman's wit.'

Where in Heaven Ross was taking Lady de Dunstanville Demelza could only guess. They had disappeared from sight and she could only suppose they were climbing down the rocks to Nampara Cove. Dwight and Caroline had lagged still farther behind, and Caroline now had her shoe off.

'My Lord,' Demelza said, fumbling in her pocket, 'I wonder if I could perhaps ask you over another matter? Ross tells me you are a Latin scholar.'

'Hardly that. I read Latin and Greek at Cambridge and have pursued some study since . . .'

Demelza took out her piece of paper. ''Twould oblige me if you could tell me what this means. It is from Sawle churchyard, but for a special reason I would like to know . . .'

He took the paper and frowned at it. The breeze stirred the sharp grasses under their feet.

'*Quidquid* . . . oh, it means – er – Whatever – no – it means Whatsoever Love hath ordained it is not fit to despise.'

'Thank you, my Lord. Whatsoever . . . yes, I will remember that.'

'What is this on the back?'

'Nothing, nothing at all.' Demelza hastily retrieved the piece of paper.

'I think it is a quotation, that Latin. Where did you see it?'

'On a gravestone.'

'A strange thing to put. But a good one.'

'Yes, a good one,' Demelza said.

II

They climbed right down into Nampara Cove and then up the valley beside the red-stained stream, across the creaking bridge and back home. By now the afternoon was far advanced, and the de Dunstanvilles took tea and left with their two grooms as dark fell. The Enyses stayed a while longer, and then they too left. The Poldarks returned to their own parlour, where a bright fire was burning and the candles had just been lit. Demelza went into the kitchen to see that everything was well, and all was clamour for a while as Jeremy and Clowance, like water let out of a dam, followed her back into the parlour and took over their role as entertainers and conversationalists.

At last they went to bed, and Demelza stretched her feet towards the fire and put up two hands to thrust through her over-tidy hair. 'Coh, I'm as tired as if I'd been loustering in the fields all day. Ross, you try me hard.'

'But it was a great success. No one can deny that.'

'Did you see Betsy Maria put her thumb in Lord de Dunstanville's soup? And then she licked her thumb!'

'Worse things than that will happen in his own kitchen every day of his life but he won't see it.'

'I hope he didn't see this!'

Ross took out his pipe and began to fill it.

Demelza said: 'And Ena dropped a mince tart and it rolled right across under Dwight's chair. And you should have seen the kitchen ten minutes before they came! Twas like a battlefield; everyone falling over everyone else! And I thought the turkey was going to come out half cooked! Mrs Zacky had forgotten the stuffing until –'

'It was all splendid. A lavish meal would have been pretentious. They could not find better food in the county nor better cooked, and that was what mattered. How did you get on with Francis Basset on our walk?'

'Well enough, I fancy. He provoked me, and then I provoked him, but I believe it was all in very good part. If I did not fear him I think I should like him.'

'What was all this provoking about?'

'Well, he told me you ought to heal your break with George Warleggan.'

Ross lit a spill from the fire and put it to his pipe. Brown and blue smoke began to go up towards the ceiling together.

'At least he has now condescended to notice it. I hope you reminded him that it takes two to make peace, as well as war.'

'I reminded him of his own feud with Lord Falmouth.'

Ross stared. 'The devil you did! That was very brave of you.'

'I had taken three glasses of port.'

'Four. I saw you sneak another as we were leaving. And how did he answer that?'

'Very polite. I do not think he took any offence. But he said a strange thing, Ross. He said he would be willing to make it up with Lord Falmouth.'

There was a long silence. A cow was lowing in the yard at the back.

Ross said: 'From what Falmouth said to me I do not think he is in a mood for making up anything. But it is an interesting thought. I wonder on what terms? As for George and myself, it would be good to have less ill feeling so close at hand; but such attempts as I made to ease things between us, three or four years ago, met with no response; and the trouble over Drake in '95 started it all off again. Besides . . .'

'Besides?'

He hesitated, wondering again whether to mention his meeting with Elizabeth, but decided not. 'Besides, something else rather nasty is occurring. Drake is meeting with little unpleasantnesses at Pally's Shop.'

Demelza looked up quickly. 'Drake? He never told me.'

'Nor me. He is not the sort. But rumours reach me. His new fences have been broken down. Someone has diverted the stream so that he depends for all his water on the well, and that in so dry a winter is running him short. One or two people who have had things repaired by him have had them broken again overnight.'

'And you think? . . .'

'Who else?'

'But *why*? It is so – *petty*! Even George, I would have thought! . . .'

'Even George. Yes.'

'Having killed Drake's romance, what more can he want?'

'I think Geoffrey Charles may have been seeing a lot of Drake again.'

'Does Drake have the cholera?'

'No . . . just a blood relationship with you – and therefore at another remove with me.'

'What can we do about it?'

'Nothing – yet. It may pass. It is so petty that I feel it must pass. But clearly one cannot see a new accord growing between George and me just yet.'

It was in Demelza's mind then to ask Ross why he had been seeing Elizabeth and what further horrible enmity and jealousy would result from it among all four of them. Were all the very darkest seeds of hatred to be sown over again? Yet she could not speak of it. She could not force herself to lower herself to ask . . .

Later that evening when she was alone in her bedroom before Ross came up she looked at the Latin inscription with the translation that she had written in crayon underneath. 'Whatsoever Love hath ordained it is not fit to despise.'

The few words brought Ross's parents more fully to life than anything Ross had ever said or anything remaining of them in this house. Grace Mary, aged only thirty years, tall and slim and dark, with long dark hair, dying in great pain in this house, with the shadowy figure of Ross's father sitting beside her. Then, when she had gone, when she could no longer speak to him, touch his hand, smile or be smiled upon, when she was buried deep in the sandy clay and Joshua Poldark was utterly alone, then he had had a stone raised over her grave and those lines inscribed on it. 'Whatsoever Love hath ordained it is not fit to despise.' To Demelza they seemed to say more, to express more truly the depth of love of one human being for another than all Hugh Armitage's poems.

It was not fair to compare them, for Hugh was young and could suffer in a different way. Joshua, or the unknown Latin poet, had expressed a deeper suffering.

CHAPTER VI

'May I talk to you?' Rowella said, insinuating herself through a nick in his study door and closing it behind her.

'What is it? What is it?' Osborne demanded angrily.

For two weeks he had not visited her room, had not spoken to her during the day except when compelled for form's sake. Twice during that period he had intruded upon Morwenna's blessed privacy, claiming the rights he had for a time seemed ready to abandon. For the rest he had been irritable with everyone; his servants had scattered like surprised insects at the sound of his step; his two little daughters wept at his reprimands; his churchwardens were offended by his brusqueness; Mr Odgers had received a stinging letter because he had not written to say what he was doing to rectify the complaints already laid before him.

The Reverend Mr Whitworth was in a cleft stick, and he was never one to hide any vexation he might be feeling, however much on this occasion he must conceal the cause. Now he stared coldly at this creature disfiguring his vision. Far from showing any evidences of her condition, she looked thinner than ever, her face pinched and wan, her long loose frock hanging from her narrow shoulders as from a clothes horse. He could not imagine what lure she could ever have had for him: an over-grown child with a surly face; pallid, featureless, standing there like a discarded doll. Had it ever happened? Had they ever indulged in such wicked, wanton behaviour: he a young-middle-aged parson of unimpeachable character and she a ridiculous undignified chit of a girl? Or had it all been a strange carnal dream? Seeing her now, he could almost persuade himself of it.

'What do you want?' he said.

'I wanted,' she said, 'just a word . . . May I sit down? Sometimes I feel faint.'

He waved her to a chair with a gesture of dismissal rather than invitation. He had stayed awake of nights – an unheard-of occurrence – weighing up the choices before him. He had thought longingly of the nostrums on sale which it was claimed would get rid of an unwanted child. (If sometimes they got rid of the mother as well, this must be for her a happy release from the humiliation and the shame.) But it was difficult to go into one of the hovels and *buy* such a potion – especially for a clergyman. And it might also be difficult to persuade Rowella herself to go to such a place.

The other choice was to do nothing, say nothing, ignore the girl until she was forced to tell someone else, then, with great dignity, and pity for such a sad little sinner, to deny any involvement or responsibility whatsoever. After all Rowella went out every day. Who was to say what she got up to? Or he might put the blame on Alfred. Though it would be a pity to lose a good manservant.

'I think,' Rowella said, 'I think, Vicar, that there may be – that I may have found a way out.'

He flipped and flapped the pages of his accounts book. 'What *do* you mean?'

'Well . . . if I were to marry someone else . . .'

His heart leapt, but he was careful to show no change of expression. 'How could that be?'

'I think there is a young man who would marry me. At least, he has shown a definite interest. Of course I don't know. It is only a thought, a hope . . .'

'Who is it?'

'Of course he knows nothing about *us*, about my condition. Perhaps he would utterly spurn me and refuse. As most men would . . . I do not know if he would be willing to give his name to – to . . .' She stopped and took out a handkerchief and dabbed her long nose.

'*Well*. Who is it?'

'Arthur Solway.'

'Who the devil? . . . Oh, you mean that young fellow – that librarian fellow . . .'

'Yes.'

Ossie's mind began to work more quickly than usual. 'Why? Why should he marry you? Have you been – *going* with him?'

She looked up at him tearfully. 'Oh, Vicar, how could you say that?'

'But I *do* say it!' He rose and straightened to his full height, confidence flooding back. 'This – this child that you are going to have is probably his! Now, tell me! Tell me the truth, Rowella, as your brother-in-law and your friend – '

'The truth,' said Rowella, 'is that I never was with him after dark, nor in any private place where such a thing could have happened. *You* saw to that! *You* made sure I was never out alone for long.'

He blustered and they wrangled for a space. He could not help but notice that under her meakness and distress ran a note of determination. The argument ended when she said quietly: 'I was never with no other man but you, Vicar, and the child I am carrying is your child, and I am prepared to declare that before all the world.'

Silence fell. After pacing the study he thumped down into his chair.

'How do you know he will marry you?'

'He asked me last week.'

'By the living God! . . . And what did you say?'

'I said I could not answer without your consent – and my mother's. And – and I said I did not think it would be forthcoming.'

'Why not?'

'He is socially of a lower status, Vicar. His father is a carpenter.'

'Does he – is he quite unaware of your condition?'

'*Quite* unaware!' She raised her head. 'As you instructed me, I have told nobody. If you – '

'Yes – er – yes. And you think if you married him he would never know?'

'Of course he must *know*! I could not be so dishonest! I'm surprised that you could even suggest to me that I might cheat him!'

Ossie glowered at her. 'Then what are you suggesting?'

'If I had your permission to marry him, then I would go to him and tell him the truth. Oh,' said Rowella, as Osborne started a protest, 'not whose baby it was; but just that I was in this dire trouble and that marriage to him would save me from disgrace. If he – if he would give this child a name and a father's love, then I would be a good wife to him and he would gain the advantages of marrying into a genteel family.'

The more he heard of it the more this seemed to him truly a way out, a better way out than he had ever dared to imagine. But it looked too easy. There were risks.

'Do you love him?'

'Of *course* not. But – but beggars can't be choosers. If it saves me from disgrace – and you also . . .'

He winced. For a moment as they spoke a little twinge of jealousy had moved in him, to think of another man enjoying the voluptuous delights of her enticement; but the last three words brought him to his senses – his other senses.

'What of your mother and Morwenna? They would have to be told – and persuaded.'

'I think they could be persuaded if they knew my condition – and I told them that Arthur Solway was the father.'

'By God, child, you seem to have this well worked out!'

'For weeks I have thought of nothing else. How could I? My mind has been going round and round and round.'

He nodded. That made sense. He began to feel a little warmer towards her. If it all could be arranged in this manner the horrors that had haunted his bedside would begin to melt away.

'You would keep everything else secret?'

'Of course . . . It would be greatly to my advantage to say nothing of what has happened here.'

'So . . . if this much you have planned in your little head, Rowella, have you also planned the rest?'

'The rest? What do you mean?'

'Well, how you would go about it?'

'I could do nothing, make no real plan until I had your approval. But – but if I have that – if I have that I shall see Mr Solway in the library tomorrow and – and tell him everything.'

'In the library, with others moving about?'

'He has a desk which is quite separate. In a sense I shall – shall find it easier speaking to him in this way.'

'And then?'

'If he consents – *if* he consents I shall ask him to come and see you.'

'Why?'

'To ask for my hand. It will have to seem formal, in order to deceive Morwenna. There will be matters to discuss.'

'What matters?'

'He is very poor, Ossie. *Very* poor. As librarian he is paid £15 a year. He works hard in the evenings copying letters for Mr Notary Pearce. By that means he earns another £3 a year. His lodgings, I believe, are miserable and he studies half the night. It is going to be a hard life for me, but I do not complain: it is what I deserve . . .'

'Yes. Well . . .'

'But for the child, which will be yours . . .'

'Yes? What is it you want?'

'Perhaps some small present would help us to start in life together. It could be looked on as a wedding present to – to your sister-in-law. Morwenna would be pleased . . .'

'How much are you suggesting?'

Rowella looked startled. 'I had not gone so far as that. I was only – hoping perhaps that you might see your way . . .' She began to sniff again. 'If – if I could say to him that I would not come penniless it might make him look more favourably on – on what is proposed.'

Ossie rubbed his nose. The girl was a schemer; but if he could get out of it all this way it would be the most outstanding relief. With the new income from Sawle he could afford to be generous; it would be a pleasant enough attitude to take up: the benign and forgiving brother-in-law; it would make him popular with Morwenna and with Mrs Chynoweth. A woman caught in adultery. Cast not the first stone. He as a vicar would practise what he preached. Twenty-five guineas he could well afford – it would be more than an extra year's salary for the miserable fellow – it would help to set them up. God be praised for such a happy outcome.

For effect he still hesitated. Then he said: 'Very well, my dear. If your young man agrees to your proposition, send him up to see me. I will see that he gets a little present to encourage him and to start you off in life together.'

II

Arthur Solway did not come up the following day but the day after that. He came by arrangement when Morwenna was out taking tea with the Polwheles. Rowella had thought it better that Morwenna should not be in when Solway came the first time. It proved a fortunate decision.

Solway was tall and thin and spectacled. His shoulders were narrow, rather like Rowella's, and he had a scholar's stoop. His face was young and kindly and anxious and he was sweating with nerves. Not the sort of young man, one would have thought, to stand up to the vicar, who not only had his office but also his breeding and his class to support him; but stand up the young man apparently did. A low murmur within the room grew perceptibly to angry voices, chiefly Ossie's. In the end it became very noisy indeed, and presently Solway half issued, was half ejected from the room and ran hurriedly from the house. Mr Whitworth slammed the front door behind him and returned into his study, which door was also shut with sufficient vehemence to shake the house.

Ten minutes later Rowella ventured into the room. Ossie was standing by the window clenching and unclenching his hands. His coat tails shook with every movement, and his face was grim and red.

'Vicar? . . .'

He turned. 'Did you set him up to this, woman?'

'Up to *what*? What is the trouble? Oh, God, has it all gone wrong?'

'Well might you call on your God! Yes, it has gone wrong and will stay wrong! That insolent lickspittle! Had he stayed a moment longer I should have laid hands on him and given him the thrashing of his life!'

Rowella wrung her hands. 'Oh, Ossie, what has gone amiss? Just when I was hoping . . . Just when I thought we had found a way out of this terrible dilemma . . .'

'Amiss? Tell that jackanapes if he comes near this house again I'll have him arrested for trespass and consigned to jail!'

She came up to his desk. 'Tell me. It is only fair to tell me.'

He turned and glared at her. 'This little present. In order to marry you – you, a fallen girl of fifteen, penniless, pregnant, without looks or family, he expects, nay demands, the ignorant donkey, a wedding present of a thousand pounds!'

She stood there with her hands to her face while he ranted on. The words 'insolent', 'disgraceful' and 'impertinent' repeated themselves at intervals. In a brief lull in the storm Rowella said: 'I do not know what can have got into him.'

'Nor do I! Nor do I! The impudence and effrontery of this cheap little upstart! Well, Rowella, you may dismiss him entirely from your mind. He is not for you, and you do not marry him with any blessing or small present from me! That I can tell you.'

'I had thought,' said Rowella, 'I had thought at the very most that you would give us a hundred pound.'

Ossie suddenly went silent. 'Oh, so you thought a hundred pound, did you? Are you sure it is not you who put a thousand into his head? Are you sure you did not say ten thousand?'

She gave a wail. 'No, Vicar, no, I swear! I swear it on oath! How could I ever have thought such a thing?'

He stared at her. 'I sometimes believe you are capable of *anything*! I wonder sometimes what evil genie presided at your birth. It cannot have been a man of God who fathered you. A dean. A dignitary of the church. A man given grace by the laying on of hands!'

Rowella burst into noisy tears.

Mr Whitworth abruptly sat down and put his elbows heavily on the desk. Anger might still be boiling in him, but the old anxiety was beginning to rear its head. 'So what is to be done with you now?'

Rowella went on crying. Eventually through her tears she gulped: 'Perhaps if I saw him again I might bring him to see reason.'

'He must have known, he must have suspected that I had some other motive than to see you settled! Did you *tell* him, did you give him reason to suspect?'

'No, no! Never! Never! I would not do that to you, Vicar, unless driven to it.'

'And what will drive you to it?'

'Perhaps if I see him again,' she sobbed. 'Perhaps I can bring him to see reason.'

III

She saw him again, and with infinite patience paved the way for another meeting between the two. Sweating, knees shaking, hands trembling, privately stiffened by a Rowella not present but always in the background, Arthur Solway stuck to his guns. Ossie went to a hundred, and then, as a last resort, to two hundred – more than his total additional stipend in a year from Sawle. Solway came down from a thousand pounds to seven hundred, but the gap was unbridgeable. Osborne might have been reminded, but was not, of the bargaining he had undertaken with George Warleggan when a suitor for Morwenna's hand.

At last, as a last resort, Rowella began to show her teeth.

'You don't realize,' she said to Ossie one day, 'what poverty Mr Solway has endured. If you think him greedy, then think of what his family is and has seen. His father lives in Quay Street in a cottage belonging to the corporation. There are nine children, of whom only Arthur has been able to make a way for himself. The eldest girl has fits, the next boy is in service at the Cardews', then there are three more girls; then a boy of three, another of eighteen months, and the mother is with child again.'

'Breeding like rats,' said Ossie.

'*Living* like rats,' said Rowella. 'Oh, Vicar, please have some understanding of his position. Out of the money he earns he is trying to help his family. They pay two guineas a year rent for their cottage, and his father, who was ill last year, has fallen behind in the payment, so the corporation have seized all his tools and some of his furniture. So the father *cannot* earn the money to pay! He has applied for parish relief which has been offered him if he would go into the Poor House with his family. But you can see that that would mean separation from his wife and children and would destroy what little he has left. He is honest and industrious – like Arthur – but he is at present staying in the cottage in defiance of the corporation. The children are without shoes – they eat nothing but bread and potatoes – their clothes, which are given them by charitable neighbours, are in rags . . .'

'You know a great deal about them,' Osborne said suspiciously.

'I went to see them for the first time yesterday in the forenoon. It makes your heart to ache!'

'So now you can afford to be generous with them, eh? On *my* money! On two hundred pounds! That is what I have offered you! It is four times what you deserve –'

'Sh! Sh! Morwenna will hear.'

He swallowed. 'Merciful God, you have the impudence of a guttersnipe! I will listen to no more! D'you not suppose that if I went round to those creatures and offered them *twenty* pounds they would not be in a transport of delight? That you can give them with my blessing and one hundred and eighty will be left over to set you up after your marriage. That is my final word. Now please go about your duties. Return me the answer tomorrow at the latest or the offer will be withdrawn.'

'Yes, Vicar,' said Rowella. 'Thank you, Vicar.' And left him. She was back the next day in the evening.

'I could scarce get a word today, for Morwenna was in the room and everything had to be done with him very quick; but I gave him your message, Ossie, and he said no.'

'No!'

'Wait, please. I argued with him and pled with him but he said he would come no lower. He said – I do not understand these things, Ossie, but he said that it would cost us high to get a cottage and furnish it, and seven hundred pounds, he said, however wisely invested, and however hard he worked himself, would bring him in scarce enough to support me and bring up a family. That is what he said. I am very sorry. He is very determined.'

'Then he may go to the devil!' said Ossie explosively. 'And you with him. This is extortion of the most flagrant kind! Damn you both! I say it deliberately. Damn you both! Get out of my room! And do not cry. That is a device you have tried too often. Get out, I say!'

'In the end,' wept Rowella, 'I *made* him come down to six hundred. But I do not believe he will budge an inch below that, and if he will not, then I have lost a husband!'

'I can only say,' Ossie said, 'that such a one as he would be well worthy of you!'

IV

Through it all and around it the household went on much the same as ever. John Conan Osborne Whitworth flourished and was noisy and aggressive, and everyone said he was just like his father; Sarah and Anne continued to learn a little French and Latin from Rowella, and could be surprisingly noisy and aggressive themselves when Papa was not about; Morwenna lived the busy life of a vicar's wife but continued within herself to be profoundly reticent; the Reverend Mr Whitworth sounded out one or two of his friends on the prospect of getting himself elected a Capital Burgess of the town, but decided that any definite move in that direction must wait until George Warleggan returned at Easter; and the servants dusted and cooked and swept and whispered among themselves. Mr Whitworth continued to hold his twice-weekly whist parties, and when they were in progress Morwenna and Rowella sewed and embroidered together in the upstairs parlour, and conversation between them, never fluent, now seemed to have dried up altogether.

The following week Rowella brought a sheet of paper in to Ossie. She said: 'When my papa was first taken ill of an apoplexy his right hand was frozen and so he could not write to the clergy in his charge. I was then but eleven years old but I wrote the best hand of the family, and he used to ask me to set down what he told me to write. Then I used to make a fair copy for his files. After he died I kept some of these for a keepsake and last month I asked Mama to send them to me. I have been reading through them. Here is one writ to a vicar in South Petherwin for getting a young girl with child. I believe – I believe he was suspended for three years . . .'

Ossie glared at her as if Satan had just entered his room. She put the piece of paper on his desk and slid furtively out. Ossie's eyes flitted over the page, jumping sentences and then coming back to them.

'Dear Mr Borlase,' it said,

'Aggravated as your guilt appears to be by many circumstances, I own I think little can be said in extenuation of it. For God's sake, sir, how could you so entirely lose sight of the Clergyman, the Christian, the Gentleman, and violate at once the Rules of Religion, Morality, Hospitality, and even of Humanity itself? Look on the complicated miseries to which the woman, who has been unfortunately-induced to make a sacrifice of her honour and her virtue, is on every side exposed, and consider whether there can be a more infamous, a more detestable practice than seduction. The Murderer, the Ravisher, whose violence affects the body only, are in many respects venial characters compar'd with the seducer.

'But supposing this not to be the case, and that the accomplice of your crime was in every way a partner of your Guilt, was it for you to take advantage of a thoughtless inconsiderate girl? Had it not better become you to have used your utmost endeavour to preserve her from the misery and infamy she might have been afterwards wise enough to have avoided? Do not a thousand considerations suggest to you how much it was your duty to have tried by every argument to reclaim her to a sense of Religion and Honour? Where, then, was the friend, the father, the brother? — such might you to have been to her: where was the disciple, the minister, the missionary of the Holy Jesus? . . .

'With what face can you recommend and enjoin to the flock of Christ committed to your charge virtues which your practice and example declare to be unnecessary? How can you propose to awaken the hopes or alarm the fears of others by considerations by which you thus openly and palpably avow yourself to be uninfluenced? . . . But I despair of saying anything on this dreadful subject which you have not already heard or which your own heart has not already suggested to you . . .'

Mr Whitworth stared at the sheet of paper much as he had a moment before stared at Rowella, as if the serpent were before him. Just after Easter the Archdeacon would be in Truro on his annual visitation, and Ossie had invited him to stay here . . .

He got up and tore the sheet of paper furiously into little pieces and flung it into the fire.

V

He said: 'I have called you in here to tell you of my decision. I am paying you the courtesy of acquainting you with my decision before I inform your sister. You will be returned to your mother. You have proved unsuitable to teach my daughters or to companion my wife. Ever since you arrived, but more particularly since Christmas, you have been over-presumptuous and malapert, given to brazenness of conversation and insolence of manner. In your behaviour you have become uncontrollable, have flouted my advice and have made yourself free and wanton in the neighbourhood. I can do no more with you and leave it to your poor mother to try to effect a change. I shall make arrangements for you to be sent home early next week.'

She stood there in her brown frock. It was a garment which was slimmer fitting than usual, and it just hinted at some of the curves which had enticed him. He hated her now — unto death.

She said: 'And the baby?'

'What baby? I know nothing of any baby. What unfortunate brat you may have conceived as a result of your flaunting yourself about the town is entirely your own affair.'

She thought about it.

'I shall accuse you, Vicar.'

'No one will believe you. It is my word against yours.'

'Five hundred and fifty pounds is the lowest I could get Mr Solway to accept.'

'You shall have nothing now!'

'I am a dean's daughter. People will listen to me. I will even write to the Bishop.'

'The wild accusations of a hysterical child.'

'You have a scar on your belly, Vicar. It was made by a boy you were tormenting at school. He took a knife to you. You were lucky not to be more serious hurt.'

Ossie licked his lips. 'I spoke of it once to you in jest. Anyone could know.'

'And a mole on your left buttock. Of a peculiar shape. I will draw it for the Bishop.'

Mr Whitworth did not reply.

Rowella said: 'If you will give me a pen I will draw it for you. It must be difficult for you to see. It is black and slightly raised from the skin. If you will give me a pen . . .'

'I will see you dead first,' Osborne whispered. 'I will see you dead before I pay a penny to you or to that snivelling yard of pump-water you hoped to marry! That I should have been brought to the pass where an insolent slut of fifteen presumes

– *presumes* to dictate to me what I shall and shall not do! Where you came from, how your father bred you, it is beyond my capacity to imagine. Get out of my life! Once and for all, get out of my life!'

They settled for five hundred pounds.

CHAPTER VII

A week after these events a French raiding force of four vessels, manned by the riff-raff of their armies and under American command, landed by surprise at Ilfracombe and Fishguard and made a brief nuisance of itself before retiring and sailing hurriedly back to France. But the rumour spread that Bristol and the west had been invaded and that large areas of territory were in enemy hands. Many country people had already withdrawn their money from banks and hoarded their gold where they felt it safer against invasion. Now a run began throughout the country, and every bank was besieged with customers trying to get their money out before it was too late. The country, they thought, was going bankrupt, and to justify all these fears the Bank of England suspended payments.

The situation was very tense in Truro, where all three banks were under pressure, the question being whether they could all weather the storm or whether one, or even two, must close their doors. In the end it became clear that the two larger and newer banks were coming through best, chiefly because of the known wealth and industrial strength of the Warleggans and because of the great wealth and prestige of Lord de Dunstanville. The third, and oldest and smallest, still known as Pascoe's Bank in spite of its enlarged name, teetered on the brink of disaster. It seemed, Harris Pascoe said, as if, far from aiding him, or even standing neutral, the other two banks were using their strength to assail his credit in order to ensure their own salvation. But after several days of mounting tension Lord de Dunstanville arrived post from London, there was a switch of policy, and new credits became available to Pascoe's Bank which just saved the day.

Ross was in Truro the day after the worst was over. He found Harris Pascoe looking thinner and greyer, as if two years rather than two months had passed since their last meeting.

For a time Pascoe seemed to want to talk not about his personal peril but about the more general one, as if it eased his mind to see it all in perspective, helped him to defuse his own emotions.

'Pitt has been walking a tightrope for years. The strain of the war upon the whole economy . . . A crisis was bound to come.'

'Which has been set off by a handful of Frenchmen who landed and burned a farm house and ran away or surrendered at the first sign of resistance! It wouldn't have happened in Elizabeth's time!'

'That was the spark. Another might have done as well. It's a crisis of nerves, Ross. Except for the last one, a succession of bad harvests . . . we've had to buy overseas. Two and a half million pounds spent on foreign grain last year alone. Then the cost of maintaining our forces and bolstering up our allies – s-six million pounds lent to Austria in one year – and of supporting Ireland too. All this has been financed by borrowing; and rising prices and falling output have gone hand in hand. Everything is more expensive to buy and there are fewer people with the money to buy it. Even relief to the poor has become vastly more expensive because there are more poor to be cared for. Also – and this is a wry reflection – while French currency ran riot foreign investment in England rose. Now, with the new type of government there and with the success of their arms, the franc is at last beginning to look more stable and the flow of gold into England is drying up.'

'So what is to happen?'

'Now? We shall struggle along as we are for a while. The Bank of England has been empowered to issue £1 and £2 paper notes as legal tender. They have also stated that they have more than enough assets to meet all claims on them. It will steady the country. But will people in general be c-content with paper when they have been used to gold? Certainly not in the provinces. Certainly not here.'

'The worst is over in Truro?'

'So far as one can reasonably s-see. It was fortunate that we had been so cautious in our extension of credit and in our discounting of bills, for, as you know, no bank can hope to meet its liabilities if called upon to do so at short notice. It will, of course, mean a heavy loss for us, for we have been compelled to sell valuable stock at much below its true worth in order to remain solvent.'

'A year or two ago everyone was expanding, money was easy, interest rates low . . .'

'Conditions change, the grey-heads weigh up the situation and reach quiet conclusions of their own. And then who is it, who among them first begins to narrow his commitments, to shorten the credit he gives, to draw in his resources, to call in money already owing – and finally to turn his paper wealth back into gold? No one knows, but it happens, and one affects another, and another another; and then the slide begins. And once it has begun no one knows where it will stop.'

'George Warleggan is in Truro?'

'He arrived back a week or so before the panic began. He returned to London by this morning's coach.'

'And – Elizabeth?'

'I believe she remained in London.'

'Basset's bank was helpful to you?'

'Right at the end. Else we might have gone, for a mere five thousand pound.'

'So he clearly owes you no ill-will for your voting defection.'

Pascoe met Ross's look.

'I had thought the opposite until near the very end.'

II

The rest of the spring slid by against a background of crisis and counter-crisis. The gloom of a nation bankrupt of money and ideas was lit briefly by news of a great sea victory won against the Spanish by Admiral Jervis, who destroyed an enemy fleet twice his own size and ended, for a sensible time, the awful danger of a union between the Spanish and French navies. Aside from Jervis and the other admirals a new name was being talked of. It seemed that Commodore Nelson's actions had been conspicuous for the most brilliant and unorthodox sea tactics and the most daredevil personal bravery. His name was emerging from among a group of brilliant naval officers, just as Buonaparte's had from among the French generals.

But relief at news of this battle was soon tempered by terrible tidings of some sort of a mutiny in the British fleet at Portsmouth. True it was a rather respectful rebellion against unbearable conditions; and some of the demands were met and the meeting collapsed without much hurt; but there were mutterings in other ports, and the confidence of the nation took another knock.

Ross grew more and more restless, as if he felt that living a comfortable squireen's life in a west-country backwater was no place for a man who could bear arms. Training with the Volunteers was no real substitute, for this force seemed more and more to him a refuge for the inefficient and the half-hearted. Demelza would have been glad to keep the weekly newspaper away from him had she known how. He spent ever more time meeting with his fellow landowners to concert means of area defence. Yet they seemed often to be more concerned with taking measures to guard against subversion from within.

In late February Miss Rowella Chynoweth was wed to Mr Arthur Solway at the Church of St Margaret, Truro. The vicar of St Mary's performed the ceremony. The vicar of St Margaret's gave the bride away. He had never in his life been so glad to give anything away as his sister-in-law. The ceremony was a nightmare to him, especially that question put by his colleague to the small congregation: 'Therefore if any man can show any just cause why they may not be lawfully joined together in Matrimony ye are to confess it . . .' It deeply angered him to go through this farce in his own church when the girl should by rights have been hounded out of the town in disgrace as a fallen woman.

Mrs Chynoweth did not attend. She had been profoundly shocked by the letter Rowella had sent her, and almost more offended by the social status of the man named as father of the coming child. She had never been able to understand her youngest daughter. Rowella was the nearest in character to Amelia Chynoweth's own father, the notorious Trelawny Tre-

gellas who had spent all his life floating companies which never
survived the first wave. Yet little Rowella, one suspected, had
survival qualities unknown to her grandfather.

Garlanda travelled down and partnered Morwenna who,
after her own interview with Rowella, had been taken ill again
with shock. It was a drab little wedding. The carpenter came
with his eldest daughter, the one who had fits; but fortunately
she avoided one for the duration of the ceremony. His wife
did not accompany him as she was expecting her tenth child
any day. The carpenter was not as obsequious as Ossie thought
he ought to be. He was quiet and polite but he did not touch
his forelock, and he had a certain rough dignity which amply
explained his saucy refusal to go into the Poor House and
accept the right and proper charity that the guardians offered.
It equally explained his impudent refusal to vacate the council
cottage just because he was behind with the rent. Arthur
Solway, the thin, reedy, narrow-shouldered, presumptuous,
greedy Arthur, was a chip off the old block.

Arthur Solway appeared, in fact, much less at ease than his
young bride, who contrived to look dowdy in her best frock
but not at all downcast. Osborne had refused to offer them
any hospitality in his house after the wedding; but two of his
servants brought tea and cakes into the church, and people
stayed talking for the best part of an hour before the party
broke up. The young couple had found lodgings in River
Street, and there they would stay until they could buy a suitable cottage.

They were modestly comfortable now. Arthur Solway had
been in to see Mr Harris Pascoe at the bank and explained
that he had a legacy to invest, and Mr Pascoe had advised
him to take a risk on the continued solvency of the country
and buy Consols which, at their present depressed price,
would yield him an income of about £30 per annum. This,
with his wage at the library and the little bits of work he
could pick up elsewhere, would enable them to make do. All
the same, between the date of the agreement and the wedding,
Rowella had often wondered if she might not have stuck out
for more. Sometimes she thought she might have squeezed
another hundred; sometimes she thought from the look in
Ossie's eye at that last bitter round of bargaining that he

might have killed her first.

Once they had all gone, the two sisters returned to the vicarage and Ossie grumpily went up to his room to change for cards. He had announced, when husband and wife first spoke together of Rowella's disgrace, that because she was Morwenna's sister he intended to give the unhappy girl fifty pounds in order that she should not sink into ultimate squalor with her vile seducer. Though she might not deserve it he would be generous. Nor, though temptation here sided with duty, would he follow the rightful course of denouncing the wretched young man to his employers. By doing that, richly though he deserved it, not only would he lose his employment but Rowella's disgrace would become public. As it was, the fiction of respectability might just be preserved, and feeling for the vicarage would be limited to sympathy that Mrs Whitworth's sister had made so unacceptable a marriage. It was a great pity, he observed, with his hands under his coat-tails, a very great pity, that the newly-weds should have to continue to live in Truro. He very much hoped that Morwenna would not visit her sister socially. Morwenna said: 'It is very probable I shall not.' Knowing the closeness of the Chynoweth family, Ossie was pleasantly surprised by this reply. He realized that Morwenna had no more patience with immorality than he had.

When he had gone to his whist the two sisters ate a quiet supper together and talked in a desultory way before going to bed. Garlanda was returning to Bodmin tomorrow. There was no question of another sister coming to live at the vicarage. Ossie said he had suffered substantial losses in the recent bank crisis, and they could afford no further help with the children or in the house. The two little girls would be sent off to school and Morwenna would be freed to spend more time with her own baby.

It had altogether been a trying visit for Garlanda and she was not going to be sorry when it was over. Pursued by her mother's laments – muffled, since no one must know the truth in Bodmin – she had arrived at a vicarage where the three principal occupants each seemed ranged against the other. Mr Whitworth, it was understandable, was completely offended and alienated by his sister-in-law's utter disgrace. Morwenna, though hiding it better and treating the unhappy girl with *some* degree of consideration, yet clearly felt the slur on her family and the slur upon herself that it could have happened while her youngest sister was in her charge.

While Rowella, though occasionally tearful and downcast, as if that were the demeanour family and society expected of her, was yet subtly unchanged; one even dared to suspect in the dark of the night not utterly repentant. Until the actual morning of the wedding she continued as before, reading, ever reading, teaching and talking to the little girls, sitting silent at meals, the centre, the quiet centre of the thundercloud that overhung the vicarage.

Garlanda had fitted in as best she was able, talking brightly of Bodmin affairs when the chance arose, otherwise limiting her observations to the trivia of everyday life. Clearly anything about the wedding beyond the merest arrangements was taboo, unless one of the other girls mentioned it first, and they did not. So had come the wedding, and the thin nervous bridegroom and the few ill-at-ease guests and the tea and cake and then the little gig to take the happy pair to their new lodgings. Rowella had kissed her sister with the casual ease of someone going out for the afternoon. Arthur took Garlanda's hand and smiled into her eyes but made no attempt to kiss her, as if taking liberties with a young lady were the last thing likely *ever* to occur to him.

And then they were gone and now with Ossie out at whist the two remaining sisters sat before the parlour fire for the last time.

Garlanda noticed a big change in her elder sister. Her reticence before had come from shyness; her dealing with anyone with whom she was intimate had always been completely frank and unguarded. Not so now. And while Morwenna occupied herself wholly with her duties as a vicar's wife, she no longer managed the house so well. Nor was she as careful about her own appearance. In the family of girls she had always been the precise one, taking care of her neatness and cleanliness after even the noisiest romp. Often when her mother was not around she had taken over and seen that her younger sisters, though by so little younger, were up to the mark with their hair and their frocks. Now she was untidy in dress and casual about order in the house.

Yet she had regained her figure and seemed in good health, and Garlanda found it difficult to reconcile her present looks with the picture of the emaciated and ailing creature her mother had drawn when describing a visit to Truro last July to see her grandchild. If appearances were all, there would be little cause for concern.

But Garlanda saw the changes in her sister's manner as symptomatic of some deeper malaise. If she couldn't care for her husband it was proper enough to treat him with a polite but shallow courtesy which neither he nor anyone else could take exception to. But need this attitude apply to everyone, even her sisters? And in so far as one could relate such an attitude to a child, she appeared to carry it into her dealings with her own son. She was much more like a *nurse* to the baby than its mother.

Knowing that in Bodmin there would be a desire to know all there was to know, Garlanda forced herself this last evening to discuss not merely the trivialities of the wedding but to bring up twice the not so trivial matter of Rowella's downfall. The second time Morwenna put down her work, smiled short-sightedly and said:

'My dear, I simply cannot talk of it. Not yet. It is all too raw and too sore. Forgive me, my dear. You have been very patient.'

'No, no. I understand how you must feel, Wenna.'

'Tell Mama I will write. It will be better that way.'

'Elizabeth was not at the wedding. Nor Mr Warleggan. Did you invite them?'

'They are still in London – fortunately. I believe they will be back next week.'

'Shall you tell Elizabeth the truth?'

'The truth?' Morwenna looked up. 'The truth – oh, no. What would be the purpose? The truth should be hushed up. It will be sufficient if I tell Elizabeth that Rowella has made an unfortunate marriage.'

Shortly after, the two girls went to bed. The coach would be passing at seven so they had to be astir early. When Garlanda had climbed the second flight Morwenna went in to see if John Conan were asleep, found him so, tucked him in, and then retired to bed herself. She had a book which she hoped would take her mind off the tensions of the day; but even this, as it came from the library, was not without its tormenting links.

Presently she gave up, set the book down and leaned over to put out the candle. On this came Ossie, still in his elegant evening suit, frilled shirt, striped canary waistcoat, tight trousers showing his thick sturdy legs.

Morwenna drew her hand back from the candle. 'Why are you back so soon?'

Ossie grunted. 'Pearce had an attack of his old cholicky gout, played only six hands. Said then he was in too much pain to continue. If it were not for those I meet there I'd drop him completely. The fellow's never well these days!'

'Well, he *is* old, isn't he?'

'Then he should give us due warning! By the time he gave up it was too late to find a fourth.'

Mr Whitworth went across to a mirror and patted at his cravat, stared at himself. His eye caught Morwenna's looking at him through the mirror. He had not been in this room much recently, for during her illness they had slept separately and he had not rejoined her since, except occasionally to claim his rights. Of course the awful regularity of the early days had never been resumed; but Morwenna knew instantly that that was what he had come in for tonight. After all, his whist game had gone wrong.

For a moment or two as he stood there, still looking at himself, he attempted to make conversation about the wedding, but it remained a monologue. After replying, yes, once or twice, his wife said nothing more, but just let him go on. And so presently his voice stopped.

There was silence. The pendulum of the French ormolu clock on the mantelshelf wagged a small admonitory shadow on the wall.

He said: 'Morwenna. No doubt you have rested this evening after the events of the day –'

'No, Ossie,' she said.

He still did not turn. 'No? You have not rested? But all this evening you –'

'I mean no to the question that you were about to ask.

I hope – I hope now that you will not have to ask it.'

'I was going to say – '

'Please do not say it, and then – and then this conversation can end before it has begun.'

'My dear,' he said. 'I think you forget yourself.'

'I think – I think perhaps, Osborne, it is you who forget yourself by coming in here tonight!'

Her face was almost grey when he turned. She had never spoken out so freely against him before, and his body seemed to swell, as it often did when anger gripped it.

'Morwenna! What an outburst! I have come in here in all friendliness to see you before I retire. Certainly I had in mind, and still *have* in mind, the natural attention that a husband properly owes his wife, and I expect you as my wife to consider her duty under the terms of our holy marriage bond – '

'That I have done. But will no longer – '

He was not listening. 'To – to attempt, even to attempt to rebuff me shows a wilful and contrary spirit which I had never thought to find in you. Nor shall I take any notice of it, for it deserves only to be ignored. But I would warn you that I – '

'No, Ossie,' she said, sitting up in bed.

'What do you mean, *no*!' he half shouted. 'Merciful heaven, what fancy has got into your brain that you think yourself able to refuse the love and affection that it is a husband's pleasure and duty to bestow? What – '

'I ask you, Ossie, please to leave this room and do not come near me tonight – or any other night!'

'Any *other* night? Have you taken leave of your senses, woman?' He began to unpin his cravat. 'Certainly I shall not go. And certainly I will have my way.'

She drew a deep breath. 'Is it – was it with such brutal words that you took Rowella?'

His hands stopped. They were not quite steady. He put down the cravat. 'What lewd and indecent thoughts can be passing through your mind?'

'None except such as have been put there by your behaviour.'

He looked as if he might strike her. 'Are you meaning to imply that I laid so much as a hand on that brazen, wanton child who has just left this house for ever?'

She put her hands to her face. 'Oh, Osborne, do you think I have been blind?'

There was a pause. Then he said: 'I believe your sister has some evil within her which only some special rites of the church could exorcise. But I did not think she would ever try to poison my name to you by uttering such slander – '

'I said *blind*, Osborne. *Blind!* Do you know what that means? Do you think I have never seen you creeping up the stairs to her room? Do you think I did not once, just once, pluck up the courage to follow?'

The solitary candle flickered with some gesture she had made, and the shadows grimaced as if shrinking from the words she had spoken. Nothing now could ever be the same again.

Osborne took off his coat and hung it on a chair. He rubbed a hand across his eyes and then took off his waistcoat and folded it beside the coat. Whether it was the anger that was going out of him or just the divestment of clothes, he looked a smaller man.

He said: 'What I have just told you about your sister is still true. She has some evil within her which – which drives one out of one's *mind*. I had never thought – never dreamed that anything could ever happen between us. She is – possessed. For a while I became possessed. There is nothing more to say.'

'*Nothing?*'

'Well, little. Except that your illness deprived me of the natural outlet for my feelings. She – she preyed on that.'

'And now she is married off in shame to a man she hardly knows – to hide your shame?'

'I do not think you have the right to say that!'

'And do you have the right to – to return to me now that she has left us?'

'What happened was nothing, meant nothing; a temporary aberration on my part.'

'Which she has connived at helping you to cover up?'

'At a price.'

'Ah . . . so I suspected . . .'

His face flushed again. 'I do not like your tone. Not at all, Morwenna, not at all.'

'I have not liked your behaviour.'

He went across to the window and parted the curtains, looked out. He had never known his gentle, submissive wife so fierce, so cutting, or known her answer him back in this way. Normally a raised voice, a stern word was enough. Of course he was at a disadvantage, a grave disadvantage, because he had erred in his own conduct and she had found him out. He was shocked that she had known, and wondered how long she had known, and was angry and fretful that she should seek to censure him for what in essence had been caused by a failure on her part. And surely the very fact that she *had* known implied a degree of complicity. If she had known she should have instantly sent her sister off back to Bodmin – as any decent wife would. Perhaps the two sisters had conspired together against him! He felt he would never be free of their toils and heartily wished he had never married this useless creature who, it was true, had borne him a son but who otherwise had been a passive thorn in his flesh ever since he married her.

He turned and stared at her, sitting up in the bed in her fine woollen nightdress, ashen-faced, dark-eyed, tragic. Her long white hands were gripping the sheet, her black hair hanging lank upon her shoulders. For three weeks now he had been deprived of any woman. It was grossly unfair. He licked his lips.

'Morwenna . . . your sister is gone. She will never return. What has happened between us – little enough as it was – is over, finished. Perhaps there were faults on both sides – on all sides. I have suffered much, I assure you. Only God can determine where blame may rest. Not us. Not mortals. Therefore I suggest that we close a page and begin again. We have been joined together as man and wife, and no man shall put us asunder. Indeed, our union has been blessed by the gift of a son. I suggest that we say a little prayer together and ask God's blessing on our future union and the fruit that may spring from it.'

Morwenna shook her head. 'I cannot pray with you, Ossie.'

'Then I shall pray alone – and aloud – beside this bed.'

'You may pray – I cannot stop you. But I must ask you to look elsewhere for the – the satisfaction of your desires.'

'That I cannot do. I am bound to you by the sacrament of the church.'

'It has not prevented you from disgracing my sister.'

'Then you must help me to try to avoid such error in the future. It is your *duty*. Your bounden duty.'

'It is a duty I cannot fulfil.'

'You must. You swore it.'

'Then I must break my oath.'

He began to breathe more deeply, as anger and frustration grew in him again. 'You must help me, Morwenna. I need your help. I will just – say a little prayer.'

He came to the foot of the bed and knelt down in his tight nankeen trousers. She stared at him with horror.

'Lord God,' he began. 'Creator and protector of all mankind, giver of all spiritual grace, and Author of everlasting life, send Thy blessing upon us, man and wife, that we may cleave again and be of one flesh. We beseech Thee –'

'Ossie!' she screamed. '*Ossie!* You shall not *touch* me!'

' – and look mercifully upon Thy servants, that with meek and quiet spirit we may enter –' He broke off his prayer and looked at his wife. 'You cannot deny me, Morwenna. It is against the teachings of the church. It is even against the explicit law of the land. No man in law can commit rape upon his own wife. The definition of marriage renders this impossible –'

'If you touch me I shall fight you!'

'Almighty and ever-living Father, who by Thy ordinance did institute the holy state of matrimony in the time of man's innocence so that –'

'Ossie!' she whispered vehemently. 'Ossie! And I shall do something else. *Listen* to me. If you force yourself upon me – tonight or any night in the future – the next day – some time during tomorrow or the next day – I will *kill your son*.'

The praying stopped. Mr Whitworth unparted his hands and looked across the length of the bed at the anguished woman pushing herself away from him towards the curtains of the bed canopy.

'You will – what?'

'You think I love our son? Well, yes, I do. Partly I do. But not so much as I hate what you have done. We are bound

together by the vows of matrimony, and so I cannot leave you.
And so – and so, if you agree *never* to touch me, never even
to *touch* me again, I shall continue as your wife, shall be it in
name, shall look after our son, shall be a good mother to your
daughters, shall tend the house and help you in parish matters.
No one shall say I ever fail in my duty to you or to them!
But – come near me, *touch* me, force your body upon me, and
next day or the day after I will *kill your son!* I promise it,
Osborne, I promise it before God! And nothing, nothing you
can do or say will alter me!'

He got up. 'You're *mad*! You're insane! Merciful heaven,
you are utterly out of your senses! You should be locked away
in Bedlam!'

'Perhaps. Perhaps that is what will happen to me after John
Conan is dead. But you cannot have me locked away before,
for I have done nothing and would deny that I had ever
threatened you – or him. But I'll do it, Osborne. I swear it to
you! I swear it to you! Before God I *swear* it to you!'

He was on his feet, licking his lips, staring at the fury he
had aroused. Could this be the demure girl he had married?
This drawn-up, convulsed, tear-stained shrew who was prepared
to spit at him like a cat if he made another movement towards
her? And threatened such a thing! And threatened his son!
John Conan Osborne Whitworth, his first male heir! And
her son too! Could she possibly mean a word of it? Nonsense! It was just the hysteria of an over-wrought woman
working herself into a frenzy over some real or fancied wrong
she had suffered! He remembered the convulsions she had had
during childbirth. It was clearly all part of the same nervous
malfunction. Tomorrow she would altogether have forgotten
what she had said tonight. Yes . . . was it not best to leave
her just this once? Was it not better, a little bit safer this once
not to bring the situation to a head, especially with the other
beastly sister in the house?

What a day! A dreary wedding, offensive to his very soul;
a frustrated whist evening thanks to that old crock Pearce;
and now this! He stared at Morwenna again to see if by any
chance her mood were changing, if perchance, having made
her vehement protest, she was likely any moment to dissolve
into tears, whereupon he might comfort her and then a little

later come almost casually to share her bed.

But the tears on her face were tears of determination not of near-collapse. The dementia was still upon her. He knew it was dangerous to give her best even once, lest she should think herself able to dictate to him in the future. Yet the alternative was to assert himself now, to crush her physical resistance and to claim his marital rights. It would not be difficult and it was not an unattractive prospect; but the threat, the spoken threat, echoed uneasily through his mind. If he took her now he would be worried tomorrow, worried for the health of his baby son. It was outrageous but it was a fact. Tomorrow would be another day. Everything would seem different once Rowella had been out of the house and out of sight for a while.

He said: 'You are grossly over-wrought, Morwenna. You have been ill and I do not wish to upset you again. I will leave you now. Leave you to think over your position in this household and your duties to me. But *never* again let me hear you say what you have said tonight! Never! It is the greatest blasphemy that can be conceived of, even to utter it as an empty threat. Drive such evil from your mind, or you will indeed become deranged and have to be put away. As your father's daughter pray for forgiveness that such thoughts have ever been allowed to enter your head. I too will pray for you. If you are not better in a day or so I will send for Dr Behenna.'

He turned and left her, shutting the door behind him with unnecessary force. It was a fair exit, covering up what he believed to be a temporary set-back. But that he forgot to take his coat and waistcoat with him was a measure of the defeat he had suffered.

CHAPTER VIII

Just before Easter Drake learned that the Warleggans were back at Trenwith House, so he decided to call on Mrs Warleggan.

Geoffrey Charles had not come home at Christmas because

his parents were in London, and Drake knew that the Easter
holiday at Harrow was of only two weeks' duration, so there
was no prospect of *his* being at Trenwith too.

He did not intend his call as in any way a presumption, and
he would certainly try to make that clear at the outset; he
just wanted a few minutes to speak respectfully to Mrs Warleggan about Geoffrey Charles and about the increasing
persecutions to which he himself was being subjected. Having
seen Mrs Warleggan in the distance more than once, and
knowing the respect in which she was held in the surrounding
villages, he could not believe she could be privy to what was
going on.

He wanted to point out first that, though his liking and
esteem for Geoffrey Charles was great, his continuing friendship with him was not of his special seeking. But living where
he now did, he could hardly rebuff the boy or refuse to speak
to him when he called. He valued his friendship and hoped
it would continue all through their lives; but if, as seemed to
be the case, Mr and Mrs Warleggan disapproved wholly of
the association, then please would they put a stop to it from
their end. If they wanted this, and then forbade Geoffrey
Charles to come to Pally's Shop, that would finish it. By no
act on his part would he attempt to revive the friendship. But
did Mrs Warleggan know that the farm immediately above his
shop had been bought by a Mr Coke, who everybody said was
a nominee of the Warleggans, and that as a result of this the
stream running through his shop had been diverted so that in
dry weather he hadn't enough water to ply his trade? Did she
know that attempts, partly successful, had been made to poison
his well-water by dropping dead rats into it? Did she know
that often carts and other articles he repaired for people one
day were found broken again the next? Did she know that
some folk were no longer coming to him because they feared
the consequences?

All this he was hoping to say, quietly and respectfully, and
then he hoped to ask her if she could do anything to bring
these occurrences to a stop. And supposing she were to tell
him that these were all imaginary persecutions on his part, he
had some small pieces of evidence to produce to prove his
points.

He knew there was a risk that he might be refused admittance at Trenwith House. He knew he was only a humble tradesman and he knew his unpopularity with Mr Warleggan. So he had hoped for a day or two that he might be lucky enough to catch Mrs Warleggan when she was out in the village. But he did not see her.

So on Maundy Thursday he set out to make his call. It was a brilliant day but with a fierce east wind which made one walk brisk in the sun and shiver out of it. A heavy swell had developed overnight and the rollers kept over-balancing and sending up siphons of spray as the wind caught the cracking tips. The sky was gun blue and the landscape without colour.

Since his business was formal he did not take the forbidden short cut but went up to the gates and along the main drive. It was a way he had taken many times to see Morwenna and Geoffrey Charles two years ago. Whenever he passed the gates the pain-pleasure of that time returned; walking up the drive made it all more poignant.

As the house came in sight a solitary man crossed his path coming from the direction of the wood where he had picked the bluebells. Drake recognized Tom Harry, and he very slightly quickened his pace to avoid him.

'Hey!' shouted Harry.

Drake had almost reached the second gate, which led into the garden.

'Hey, you! Where d'ye think *you're* a-going?'

He could only stop then. Harry was carrying a stick and he hastened up, his face sourly swelling.

'*Well?*'

Drake said: 'I come to ask if Mrs Warleggan'd kindly see me for favour of maybe five minutes.'

'See *you*? What for?'

'I come to ask a kindness of her. Just to see her on a matter as concerns me close. I just want to go to the back door and ask. If she says no, I'll come away again.'

'You'll come away again afore ever you get there!' said Harry. His dislike for the Carne brothers had grown over the last year. First, Sam the Bible-preaching one, had tried to worm his greasy way round *his* girl, trying to turn her into a praying Methody; and although he'd failed and although she laughed at Sam every time they passed each other by, he, Tom, was not quite convinced that there hadn't been some ill-wishing along the way, some stinking, crapulous Bible-spell that had been put on Emma – for though she was still his girl she still wouldn't marry him, and upon times she was moody and discontented and her big handsome laugh disturbed the crows less often than it had been wont to.

And second, and *second*, whisperings had been begun more than a year gone, and had eventually reached Tom Harry's waxy ears, that all that there trouble with the toads, all the trouble that had come to Harry following from that, had been the work of Drake Carne, the younger brother, the one that was standing in front of him now, claiming with his arrogant, insolent, damn-cursing gall the right, the actual right to force his way into Trenwith House and talk with Mistress Warleggan. It was more than a decent man could stand. It was certainly more than Tom Harry was prepared to stand. He put his fingers in his mouth and blew a piercing whistle.

Drake stared at him. This was the encounter he would have done anything to avoid. He was not afraid of Tom Harry, stick or no, but the very last outcome he desired of this visit was that there should be fighting. He could hardly go on with this big gamekeeper barring his way; and a sure prejudice to the attempt to convince Mrs Warleggan as to the fairness of his complaint would be to leave one of her servants behind him with split lips and a bloodier nose and present himself to her in a likely similar state.

'Well,' he said, 'if you'll not leave me through I must call 'gain. Tis a peaceful request I came to make and tis no part of my wish to force myself anywhere. So I'll bid ee good-day.'

'Oh, no ye'll not,' said Tom Harry with a tight grin. 'Not yet just awhile. Overbrangled up-jumps like you did ought to be taught a lesson for trespassing on private property. Ye could be jailed for less!'

Drake heard footsteps behind him and turned to see two other gamekeepers coming up. Theye were of Harry's type and he had seen them about together in Grambler and Sawle.

'We caught a trespasser, lads,' Harry said. 'Like as not a poacher. Reckon he's been setten his snares in our woods. Got to be dealt wi', lads. What do ee say?'

One of the others had a stick, the third a dog's lead. They came to within about six feet of Drake and surrounded him. They stared at him, then at their leader, not quite used to being asked for advice, not quite aware that they were not being so asked.

One said: 'Reckon he'd best be took up to 'ouse. Mr Warleggan'll deal wi' 'im.'

'Nay,' said Harry. 'Nay. We don't wish to be hard on him, lads, do we? Tis more a lesson he d'need. Just so's he'll mind not to come this way 'gain. Just a bit of a cootin' – *Catch 'im.*'

Drake had made a sudden feint towards Harry and then darted with that exceptional speed of his between the two other gamekeepers. A hand clutched his coat, held, tore, held and then the coat was from his back and he was running. A stick had come across his legs making them numb, but he only stumbled and did not fall. He made for the wood.

He was much faster than any of the three men and would have reached it well ahead of them but for one thing. Across the first field was plain running, then over a Cornish wall into a ploughed strip before the wood. Normally he could have jumped the wall with one hand on it, but he had not realized that some muscles were still numbed by the blow from the stick and his foot caught the stone at the top. Instead of landing lightly he fell over with a crash, all his weight awkwardly on one ankle and a pain shot up his right leg.

He got to his knees, put his foot down and it gave way and he fell over. He tried again, hopping on one foot. But by that time they were on him like a load of bricks, fists and sticks flying. They beat him down on the ground and then, mad at his near escape, took turns to kick him into insensibility.

II

They stood round him in a group, breath coming fast, heavy faces flushed with the zest of it. Only one of the three, a man called Kent, was a thought troubled by their enthusiasms.

'Reckon that's 'nough, Tom. Reckon he won't come this way 'gain in haste. Leave'n be now.'

'Leave'n *be*? Not on our land! Twould be a failure o'duty.'

'Reckon he'll take some mending.'

'Nay. Rats; ye can't hurt rats. Crush all their bones; they'll crawl into their 'oles and be out sniffing around next day as if naught had 'appened!'

'Take'n up to 'ouse now then, shall us?' the other one asked.

Tom Harry shook his head. It was conceivable that Mr Warleggan might think they had exceeded their duty. If by any chance they should be confronted by Mrs Warleggan they might even lose their jobs.

'Nay. Heave'n in pool. Twill cool him off, sure 'nough.'

The pool was the other side of the wood and adjoined the main cart track between Sawle and St Ann's. It was used by anyone rich enough to own a sheep or a goat, for watering them, and Trenwith cattle were driven down to drink there. Across the other side of the track was the big piece of common land which was used for any assembly or feast day and for grazing whenever on its barren surface grazing was possible. The common land drained across the track into the pool, which in wet weather stretched a hundred yards either way and was four feet or more deep. In dry weather, after a specially dry spell such as this, it shrank to a quarter its size and half its depth and was unsavoury with trailings of green slime and the droppings of the animals that drank there.

'Heave 'n up, lads,' said Tom Harry.

They frogmarched Drake between them round the wood, came to the edge of the pond, and, swinging a couple of times to gain momentum, flung him in.

The shock of the water revived him and he rolled over and sat up, gasping and choking and spitting, head and shoulders above the muddy pool.

'Aunt Sally!' shouted Tom. 'Aunt Sally! Ten shies a penny! Eh, lads? Ten shies a penny!'

He encouraged the other two but Kent would not take part. Tom and the second gamekeeper picked up stones and mud and began to pelt them at Drake. Some missed, some hit him, and he tried to get up, could not, floundered, sat up again, and began slowly to edge his way painfully to the other side of the pool. They pursued him, giggling with laughter, challenging each other to better aim, arguing about the prizes they had won. As the pool narrowed towards its end so the distance narrowed, and one sizeable stone from Tom hit Drake in the

temple and he slowly sank into the water. It was not more
than a few inches deep, but first he went down face first and
then seemed to turn over and came up with his face up, part
above water, part submerged. Bubbles formed on the surface.

'God dam' ee, ye'll kill the lad!' muttered Kent, and came
round the side of the pool, waded in and caught Drake by
the front of his blood-stained shirt and dragged him to the
edge of the pool, where he dropped him in the soft slime.
A pink stain coloured the water where he had been.

Kent wiped his fingers and straightened up and looked at
the other two as they approached. They stared down at the
unconscious figure, from whose lips a faint bloody froth was
issuing.

Tom Harry spat on Drake and said: 'That's for the toads,
cookie. Next time think again.' Then as he turned away and
the others lingered: 'Leave'n be! He'll be all right. Leave'n
be! Leave'n for 'is Bible-thumping brother to pick up.'

III

Surprisingly in that area where the movement of a human
being – any movement – scarcely ever passed unnoticed, no
one had seen the incident by the pool. One of Will Nanfan's
boys first saw the figure, went up cautiously to stare at it, then
ran and told his mother. Char Nanfan, that strong comely
woman with the handsome golden hair – now tarnished with
the years – came out of her cottage with two of her little girls,
exclaimed: 'My dear life and heart!' and rolled Drake over
on his back, cleaned the mud and blood from his mouth and
nostrils and got the sturdy ten-year-old to help carry him
back to their cottage. There they laid him on the earth floor
of their kitchen, splashed his face with cold well-water, slapped
his hands and presently brought him back to choking consciousness. Will Nanfan was summoned from tending his
sheep and looked the boy over, feeling for broken bones, and
then said he would send for Dr Choake.

Drake would have none of it, nor would he satisfy them
as to the identity of his attackers. He just said it was three
vagrants who had set on him and tried to rob him. He didn't
know them and he'd scarce recognize them if he saw them
again; they had their faces muffled up. He choked again on

the Geneva he was given, and looked as if he was going to
throw it up, and said give him ten minutes and he'd be on
his way. Will Nanfan said, best to send for Brother, but
Drake said Sam'd be down mine till six and not to trouble
or tell him, he'd be right as a trivet give him ten minutes.

Char said it was all a wicked, wicked shame, having more
than once had a woman's eye for this handsome young man
and wondering now if his looks were spoiled permanent. He
looked disfigured for life with a gash in his cheek, his lips
swelled up, one eye blackening and an eyebrow split. She put
a rough bandage over his cheek to try to stop the bleeding
and a cold compress on his swollen ankle and said he must
lie quiet for an hour or two before thinking of moving a
yard. Drake said ten minutes was all he needed, but having
said it twice more at intervals he finally gave up and fell into
a half-drunken coma from which he was roused by Sam.

'Did they send for you?' said Drake, 'they should never've
sent for you,' but Sam said twas after six o'clock and he had
come straight from core, and Drake said, 'All Saints, have I
been here that long? My fire'll be out!'

So in half an hour they set off home, with the sun like a
red-hot coin smoking into the misty sea.

On the way Sam got the story out of him. With a borrowed
coat, and hobbling and making such slow progress that dark
overtook them, Drake swore Sam to secrecy. 'Tis not for
myself as I care, but d'ye see, there must be no bad blood
twixt them and we. Mebbe I was wrong to suppose I should – '

'Mortal foolish,' said Sam gently. 'Mortal foolish. I should
have comed with ee. That Tom Harry's a sad man, a sad man
asleep in his sins. The pains of hell have gat hold upon him.
But bad blood we cann't prevent – '

'We cann't prevent it, but tis some important that Cap'n
Ross shall not get to know.'

'Yes . . . Yes . . . Tis hard to keep a secret in this village.
Did no one see ee?'

'I reckon not. It seems not. You see, I've sown trouble
'nough twixt the Poldarks and the Warleggans. If this be
known, who can say what more trouble will follow? We owe
too much to Cap'n Ross as tis. If he heard tell of this,
gracious knows what he might do. And he mustn't, Sam. For

Demelza's sake and for his own.'

'It is a Christian duty t'eat the bread of forgiveness. But Drake – '

'Hold hard, I'll go on in a few minutes. What was you going to say?'

'It is our duty also to follow in the path that the all-seeing God has chosen for us. To rise early, to wreak late, to practise industry and carefulness, is what our heavenly Father enjoins 'pon us, following the cleansing of our souls. But . . . Tis hard to see how ye can continue as a smith in this neighbourhood, Drake, wi' this persecution. All that you work for, fast as tis wrought, so tis destroyed. Now . . .'

Drake got up and they lurched on again. Drake said: 'Well, I tell ee one thing. I aren't giving up.'

'No . . .' Sam peered at his brother's sorely damaged face. 'But I have fears for ee.'

'Fears for my soul?'

'That too, as you well d'know. But fears for your earthly survival and well-being. Twould've taken little extra to've drowned ee today. Or broken your cage of ribs. I ask God's pardon if I hold the carnal welfare of my own brother too dear in this mortal life; but twould try me hard if aught happened to ee and I can see no comfort to the either of us if you go all your days in fear of your life and safety . . . Mebbe if you sold shop, twould not be hard to take similar employment in Redruth or Camborne – nearer home. Then you'd be – '

'I aren't giving up,' said Drake.

No more talk passed then until they reached the smithy. Sam would not help his brother up the stairs in case by tomorrow he had so stiffened that he could not get down. He brought a rug and a blanket. There was a piece of a boiled rabbit in the kitchen and he hotted this and served it with potatoes and barley bread. To his satisfaction Drake ate a few mouthfuls.

After it was over Sam cleared away and then said a prayer. He would stay the night, but before he settled down to sleep he wanted to know what was in Drake's mind. A blind determination just to stick it out no longer seemed feasible. Besides, the persecutions might increase. He said this.

Drake nodded: 'Yes, that's true.'

'And Ross and Demelza . . . I see that,' said Sam. 'But if ye will not bring them into this trouble . . .'

'I'll do what I set out to do today. See Mrs Warleggan.'

'I'll come with ee, then. Alone, twould be asking for the same only worser. Together – '

'Nay . . . You keep out of this too, Sam. I'll get to see she another way.'

'What other way? She may be out riding, but I'd not reckon she'd welcome – '

'When she's gone back I'll go Truro – see her there. She cann't háve gamekeepers in a town house.'

'There'll be footmen. They might be nigh as far gone in their wickedness.'

'They won't know me. I reckon she'll see me. I'll tell her and ask her for her help.'

Sam pondered this for some moments. 'You've never spoke?'

'No, never.'

'She was agin ye over Geoffrey Charles.'

'Yes, but she left him come see me all last summer.'

'Why d'ye reckon she'd help?'

Drake turned himself over, with great pain and with infinite patience.

'I got a feeling she'd want fair play.'

CHAPTER IX

The Warleggans stayed at Trenwith until the third week in April. In the meantime Drake's multiple bruises mended. The gash in his face became a scab, the blues and reds of his body faded, he came to walk without a limp. But it seemed improbable that his face would ever be quite the same again. There was a swelling in his jaw that would not go down, and there was going to be a permanent division of his left eyebrow.

Demelza did not hear until the second week, and then she was furiously angry that it could have happened, upset at the sight of him, grieved that her youngest brother seemed never able to shake free from the bad luck that had dogged him ever since he met Morwenna. She taxed him on his statement that he did not know the three men who had attacked him and would not know them again. She presently said she did not believe it, and had he come in contact with some of the Warleggan gamekeepers? 'I had a nasty experience once,' she said, 'with Garrick, and when Ross got home he went over to Trenwith and warned George that any repetition would have ill results for him. I tried to stop Ross going,' she added. 'I didn't want any more trouble between the families, but he took no notice and went just the same.'

'*I* don't want any more trouble neither,' said Drake.

'So it *was* them.'

'I'm not saying.'

'That makes it worse.'

'What I *am* saying is, don't tell Cap'n Ross. Whether twas gamekeepers or vagrants makes no matter; it *will* matter if you tell him I got hurt, for he'll leap to his suspicions just so quick as you.'

'He's like to hear you got hurt whether or no. But he's been away with the Volunteers and will not be home till Friday.'

'Then if he hears, tell him twas nothing. Tell him I had one or two bumps and twas nothing serious.'

'But if it is gamekeepers and not vagrants it may well happen again.'

'Not if I'm careful. And I'll be careful, Demelza.'

The continuing easterly wind was blowing through the yard, creating tight little whirlwinds of dust and ash and making the forge glow without the use of bellows. She drew her cloak round her and pulled a wisp of hair from her mouth.

'These – persecutions . . .'

'Will stop, I b'lieve.'

'How? What is to stop them?'

He smiled at her, though lopsidedly. 'With patience, sister. You mind what Sam is always saying: "Through hidden dangers, toils and death, Thou, Lord, hast gently cleared my way." '

'Oh, *Sam* . . . I dearly love Sam – who can help it? – but he's not fitted to deal with wicked men. Besides, it is only of the spirit that he is thinking.'

'Maybe. But I hope I mayn't need his help, spiritual or other. I've a sort of plan.'

'What plan?'

'Tis not for me to say, sister. If it d'fail I'm no worser off.'

Demelza stared at her brother. He had matured very much of late. She was sad that so much of that ineffable youthful charm had gone.

'Have care for yourself,' she said. 'For if more hurt comes to you I shall tell Ross whether you wish him to know or not.'

'I'll have a care.'

II

It was easy for Drake to learn the day the Warleggans left for Truro. As soon as he heard he packed some bread and cheese and walked after them. Now that Mr Warleggan had a seat in parliament one could never be sure how long they would remain in Cornwall, but it was reasonable to suppose they must spend at least a couple of days in their town house before setting out for London.

He was right. He called at the house the following morning and found Elizabeth in. He gave his name to the scullery maid at the back door and then to the footman who presently appeared with a stony, hostile face and tried to stare him down. Drake simply asked if he might see Mrs Warleggan, and would not state his business. He guessed that they could hardly turn him away without reference to her, and that she, knowing instantly who he was, would hardly refuse to see him, thinking that his business might in some way involve Geoffrey Charles.

She saw him in the large drawing-room on the first floor. She was in white, in the style she often favoured: a simple bodice and a straight full skirt, tight at the waist, and lace at throat and wrists; she looked cool and unspotted by life; although he had often seen her before, in church and riding by, he was impressed, as most men were, by her beauty and apparent youth. She, on the other hand, had not seen him except at a distance. She too was a little impressed: this tall, pale, dark-eyed boy, face scarred, the soft Cornish accent, his modest but un-nervous demeanour; there were resemblances to the woman she disliked, yet in a young man it was different.

While he spoke she remembered his outrageous presumptions towards her cousin, Morwenna, and all the trouble he had caused between her husband and her son. And she realized the unbearable presumption of his appearance here today.

So she scarcely listened to what he said; she closed her ears and prepared to pull the bell to have him turned out. Then a sentence here and there began to impinge. She held up a hand.

'Are you suggesting – are you daring to suggest that this – this persecution you speak of is the work of our servants?'

'Well, yes, ma'am. I'm that sorry to bother you, but I firmly believe that it must be quite unbeknown to you. If – '

'Unbeknown to *me*? And are you then saying that these things occur on the instigation of Mr Warleggan?'

'I cann't say that, ma'am. Maybe someone else have instructed Mr Coke to buy the farm above me and cut off my water supply. And Tom Harry, and Michael Kent and Sid Rowe, those that beat me and kicked me so that I quammed off into a faint. And this eyebrow, ma'am. And this side of my nose I can't breathe through now – '

'And what were you doing when you say they caught you?'

'Walking up the drive, ma'am, hoping to see you and offer never to see Master Geoffrey Charles again, if so be as I could be left to live my life in peace and quiet.'

Elizabeth went stormily to the window. She still wanted to have this young man turned out; she badly wanted to deny his every word and have him branded as a liar. But her difficulty lay in her not being certain that he was. She knew of George's resentment at this boy being given the black-smith's shop, and his resentment, almost jealousy, at Geoffrey Charles's continuing passionate friendship. George thought, or affected to think, that Drake had been deliberately installed where he was as an irritant and a challenge. She also knew that the gamekeepers had been instructed to be hard on anyone they found trespassing.

But not walking innocently up the main drive to see her! She wondered how far she could trust Drake Carne's account. He might be here as a mischief-maker. After all, he had had the effrontery to call regularly at their house two winters ago when only Morwenna and Geoffrey Charles were at home.

Impertinence must not be encouraged. She turned and looked at him, met his eyes. How far was her own son a judge of character? This was the young man Geoffrey Charles found more desirable company than any boy in the county of his own class. Carne did not look an arrogant liar. How could one judge?

'Tell me again,' she said. 'Everything from the beginning. When do you pretend that these persecutions started?'

So he told her all again.

'And what proof have you?'

'Aunt Molly Vage – up the hill from me – she say she saw men scat my fence abroad when I was from home – Trenwith men, she say; she know by their clothes. Jack Mullet say tis common knowledge, what I repair Trenwith men'll break again. No one seen – no one saw Tom Harry and Sid Rowe and Michael Kent that day, but I've got marks that's proof of a sort, ma'am. If you'd excuse me, ma'am, tis near on three weeks since it was done but you'll see from my face and if you'll excuse me, ma'am . . .'

He opened his jacket and pulled at his shirt, showing the fading black of heavy bruises about his ribs.

'Enough,' Elizabeth said, short of breath. 'That is enough. I think you presume –'

'What is this man doing here?' George Warleggan demanded from the door.

Drake flushed and drew his jacket across his dishevelled shirt.

George came a step or two farther into the room and then stood with his hands behind his back.

Elizabeth said: 'This is Drake Carne. He asked to see –'

'I know who he is. By what right was he admitted to this house?'

'I was about to tell you. He asked to see me and I thought it proper to discover what he wanted.' She nodded to Drake. 'I think you should go.'

'Most certainly he will go,' George said, 'and I shall leave instructions that if he sets foot in this house again he is to be thrown out.'

'Go now,' said Elizabeth.

Drake licked his lips. 'Thank you, ma'am. I meant no disrespect . . . I'm sorry, sir. I never meant to upset or distress no one.' He walked slowly to the door, passing close by George. He looked tall and strong and thin and, even in this situation, not without dignity.

'Wait,' George said.

Drake waited. George pulled the bell. After a few moments a servant came.

'Put this man out,' George said.

III

After he had gone George followed him from the room without saying another word to Elizabeth. They did not see each other again until supper time. George's face was stony, but by the time the meal was half through he observed that Elizabeth's face was stonier. George had ordered a post-chaise for eight a.m., so final packing had to be done today. Eventually, when the servants were temporarily out of the room, he asked his wife if all her arrangements were complete.

Elizabeth said: 'Since this forenoon I have done nothing at all.'

'Why is that?'

'Because I will not be spoken to in front of anyone the way you spoke to me before Drake Carne.'

'I scarcely spoke to you at all! But Carne should never have been admitted.'

'Allow me to be the judge of that.'

George raised his eyebrows. He perceived now the extent of Elizabeth's anger.

'What had the young upstart to say?'

'That you had been attempting to drive him out of his shop.'

'Do you believe that?'

'Not if you tell me it is untrue.'

'It is not altogether untrue. His presence there is a deliberate affront. And, as you see, it has enabled him to maintain his friendship with Geoffrey Charles.'

'Must you then resort to – to pressures, such as cutting off his water supply – damaging the fences he had put up, threatening the village people who patronize him?'

'Good God, I know no *details*! I leave the details to others.

They may well have exceeded the verbal limits I gave them.'

She dabbed her mouth with her napkin, considering her own pent-up resentment, only partly trying to contain it. 'If you are too big for details, George, are you not also too big a person to descend to petty devices to intimidate a young man who has happened to cross you?'

He said: 'I see Demelza's brother has a persuasive tongue.'

His use of the name was deliberate, challenging her old dislikes, reminding her of so much.

'And must you also,' Elizabeth said, 'must you also have hired bullies on our estate who will beat a young man senseless and disfigure him, perhaps for life?'

He took a short-cake, broke it and put a corner in his mouth. 'Of that I know nothing. As you must be aware, I am not a believer in brutality. What is the story you have been told?'

She repeated it, watching him.

He said: 'Of course he was up to no good. That's the truth of it. It was he who brought the toads back to our pond, you know.'

'Has he said so?'

'Is it likely? But there's evidence enough. I have no doubt he was bent on some illicit matter when Tom Harry caught him. He's a plausible young upstart and no doubt made out a good case for himself to you.'

'But even if he were *poaching*, Harry has no right to treat him in that way.'

'If it's true, he'll be reproved.'

'Is that all?'

'What else would you have?'

'He should be dismissed.'

'On that fellow's evidence?'

'It should all be enquired into. I think you are making a terrible mistake, George.'

'In what?'

'I . . . I have lived at Trenwith for nearly half my life. I was not happy with Francis, as you know; but the Poldarks had been there for two hundred years; they maintained a reputation for – for having a care for the village folk. Your way is different. I don't quarrel with your wish for greater privacy, for better-defined boundaries, for putting a greater distance between us and the village people. That is your way. I am your wife, and so that is my way too. But . . . you cannot wish surely to inspire dislike, to inspire hate – and this is what Tom Harry and his bullies will do for you if you don't get rid of them. You only see them when we spend holidays there. How do they behave when we're not there? How have they behaved to Geoffrey Charles's friend? Can you imagine what Geoffrey Charles will feel if he hears of this? What sort of a friendship can you and he build up, how can I hope to *restore* a friendship between my son and my husband if this can happen – if not on your instructions, at least with only mild expressions of disapproval from you afterward? Tell me that, George. Tell me that!'

He was prevented from telling her that by the arrival of a servant to snuff the candles and another to serve the brandy. They sat in tense angry stillness opposite each other, their gaze bisected and made tangential by the flickering lights. The servants seemed to be in the room in endless progression, one coming in as another went out. Elizabeth refused brandy and rose. George rose with her, politely standing until she left the room. Then he reseated himself and put his hands about the glass, warming the brandy and allowing it to move around so that the aroma of it was released. He was aware that a crisis in his relationship with Elizabeth threatened.

IV

It was resolved in her bedroom. He came in and found her brushing her hair. It was a nightly routine which she would leave to no maid. She brushed it gently, rhythmically; it had some soporific effect on her, preparing her for sleep. She always complained that her hair came out; every night fine strands of it clung to her brush when she had finished; but such was the new growth that the thickness of her hair was never less. Nor yet had it lost much of its colour.

He said with controlled politeness: 'Your cases are still incomplete. Polly says you have not given her enough instructions to finish it for you.'

'No. No, I haven't.'

'May I ask why?'

'Because I doubt the wisdom of coming with you tomorrow.'

He closed the door and took a seat in a chair, crossed his legs, slightly hunched his shoulders in that formidable manner he had when there was a conflict on his hands. From this position she had her back to him but they could each see the other's face through the mirror.

'What virtue would there be in your staying behind?'

'Only that we seem to be drifting farther apart – in behaviour, in sympathy, in understanding – so perhaps it is more suitable that we should stay apart in fact.'

'Does this all – all this state you find yourself in – does it all derive from the visit of a vindictive boy?'

'No,' she said slowly. 'But one straw – do you know – one straw, the last one.'

'You find his view of things more acceptable than mine?'

'Not at all. But his coming, what he has to say, points the – the differences, the divisions that have grown between us.'

'Explain to me a little more. You are suggesting that our life is foundering on the type of servants I employ, the disciplines I set them, the restrictions I impose upon the free and unbridled access for all and sundry to my – to your – property. That is the present cause of your offence. Now tell me the rest.'

She stopped brushing, lowered her eyes to the dressing table, then raised them to meet his through the glass.

'I believe our married life is foundering on suspicion and jealousy.'

'Now it is an attack on me, not on my servants.'

'Oh, *George*! . . . your servants are but a *symptom*. Are they not? You must admit that or we have no common ground even for *argument*. This dislike of Drake Carne . . . I know all there is to say against him. I do not like the young man and want nothing better than to be rid of him. But this – this petty persecution – and worse – does it not really stem in your heart from the fact that he is Demelza's brother – and so Ross's brother-in-law?'

'Ah,' said George, and uncrossed his legs. 'I wondered when we were coming to that.'

'To what?'

'You say that my dislike of young Carne stems from the fact

that he is Ross's brother-in-law. Doesn't your belief in what he has told you, your championing him against my servants, spring from the same source?'

Elizabeth put down her brush. Her heart was beating as if it had to pump some more viscid fluid than blood.

'I said our life together was foundering on suspicion and jealousy. Have you not this very moment confirmed it?'

'You think I'm suspicious of Ross, jealous of him?'

'Of course. Of *course*. Aren't you? Isn't it eating you up, corroding all your success, poisoning your family life, turning everything you achieve to gall?'

'And are all my suspicions unfounded?'

She turned to face him, her hair about her shoulders.

'Tell me what they are and I will answer.'

His whole body gave a shiver of anger. 'I believe you still love Ross.'

'That's not all! That's not all you think.'

'Isn't it enough?'

'It's *more* than enough! That I suppose is why you have me followed when I'm in Truro, spied on by your creatures as if I were some criminal suspected of a grievous crime but the evidence as yet insufficient! Lest I should meet Ross in some dark corner! Lest I should be plotting some love tryst with him! That's certainly enough.' She got up; her voice had a break in it; she held her throat as if seeking some extra control. 'But it's *not* all! Do you wish me to – to prompt you to say the rest?'

At this last moment his native caution, his mercantile common sense prompted him to hold his ground but to go no farther. He was not prepared to voice his worst suspicions at the cost of losing her. The situation was slipping out of control. He was not used to emotions having their way. One knew instinctively how to deal with an ordinary crisis of affairs, but not this. Not this crisis with a woman. It was like being in a tide race.

He got up. 'Enough.' He spoke with command in his voice. 'We've said enough. We can talk again in the morning when we are more ourselves.'

'No,' she said, with equal decision. 'If there is anything to be said it must be said tonight.'

'Well, I'll make a bargain with you,' he said. 'Come with me tomorrow as arranged, and I'll write to Tankard before I leave instructing him that any and all harassments of Carne must stop forthwith. Other problems, other contentions, can be dealt with later.'

'No,' she said again. 'There is no later, George. This is the latest it can ever be.'

He walked towards the door but she stood in his way. Her lips were blotchy with lack of colour. His good intentions sliding down to hell, he raised his hand as if to strike her. She did not flinch.

She said: 'Why do you treat your son as if he were not your son?'

'Valentine?'

'Valentine.'

He licked his lips. 'Is he?'

'How could he be any other man's?'

'You have to answer me that.'

'And if I do?'

'If you do?'

'Will you *believe* me? Will you for one single solitary second think that what I've told you is the truth from my heart? Not at all! That's why I say jealousy is eating you up! That's why I say our life together has become *impossible*! It must end! It is going to end tonight!'

He dropped his hand, stared at her with all the lowering intent of a goaded bull.

'You must tell me, Elizabeth. You must tell me! You *must* tell me!'

She hesitated, swung on her heel and went into her dressing room, hair floating in the wind of her own movement. For a moment he thought she was ending the scene, had done with him and was going to leave him, his most prized possession lost for ever. But she came back as quickly as she had gone. In her hand was a bible. She came up to him, set the bible on a table.

'Now,' she said. 'Listen to this, George. *Listen* to it, I say! I swear on this bible, as a believing Christian and in the hope of my ultimate salvation, that I have never, *never* given my body to any man except to my first husband, Francis, and to you, George. Is *that* enough? Or do you consider even my sworn oath insufficient to convince you?'

There was a long moment of silence.

'Now,' she said, tears beginning at last to stream. 'I have done. I know already that even *that* is no use, a waste of time! I will leave for Trenwith in the morning. We can come to some arrangement – some separation. I can live with my parents. You can do what you please. This is the end . . .'

He said thickly: 'We mustn't let this get out of hand. Elizabeth, listen to me.' Quicksands moved in him. 'If I have been in error – '

'*If!* . . .'

'Well, yes. Well, yes. If what you say . . . You must give me time to think . . .' He coughed, trying to clear the phlegm that had gathered.

'To think what?'

'Of course . . . I accept what you say – naturally I accept that. I suppose I have been a little misguided – perhaps a little crazed. Suspicion and jealousy, as you say, have been at the bottom of it . . .'

She waited.

He said: 'But you know . . .'

'*What* do I know?'

'Suspicion and jealousy – you may condemn them – and rightly – but they indicate, in however distorted a way, a measure of my regard. It's true. You may not think so but it is *true*. Love – love can be very possessive when it thinks itself threatened. Especially when what is threatened is – is dearer than life itself. Oh, yes,' he hastened on as she was about to speak, 'it's simple to argue that one does not show love by lack of trust. But human nature is not so uncomplex . . .'

She half turned away. He followed her.

'*Look*,' he said. 'The very intensity of feeling I have for you breeds a contrary fever that no assurances – no ordinary assurances, that is – can bring to intermittence. Do not cry . . .'

'How can I *help* it!' she flared at him. 'For months – and more months – your bitter, vile unkindness – your coldness towards me and towards your son – '

'Will cease,' he said, deep emotion still gripping him, swamping his natural caution. 'From now. From tonight. It's not too late. After this we can begin again.'

'Tonight,' she said scornfully, 'perhaps you feel this tonight! But what of – of tomorrow and the next day? It will start over afresh. I cannot – I will not go on! . . .'

'Nor I. It shall be. I promise, Elizabeth, listen to me. Do not cry –'

She waved away his handkerchief and wiped her streaming eyes on the sleeve of her nightgown. She went back to the dressing table, picked up the brush in her agitation, set it down.

'I do not *want* to leave you,' she said. 'Truly I do not. Everything I said when we were married holds good today. More so. But I *will* leave you, George. I *swear* I will, if this ever –'

'You shall not. Because I shall not be like this again.' Again he had followed her and, taking a risk, he kissed her head; but she did not shrink away.

'Well,' she said. 'I have sworn on oath! One can go no further than that. So *you* swear on oath! Not ever to *mention*, to bring up, to harbour thoughts, evil wicked suspicions –'

'I swear it,' George said, taking the bible from her. The emotion was still carrying him along. He had never before in his life been so stirred. Tomorrow, in spite of the oath he was about to take, and true to her predictions, he would think again. But never perhaps quite in the same way. He must not, could not, for it had been a near thing. So Valentine, after all . . . He was convinced by her oath. With her quiet but steady religious beliefs, it was inconceivable that even to save her marriage she should imperil her soul by lying on the bible. So emotion caught him both ways. The nearness of the loss and the enormity of the gain. His own eyes were moist and he tried to speak but his throat closed up and he could not.

She leaned against him and he put his arms round her and kissed her.

As the shadows of doom lengthened round England, so the shadows of the early summer shortened and the sun climbed high. New fleet mutinies had broken out, far worse than the first, many ships imprisoned their officers and most flew the red flag; an English revolution similar to the French was beginning, while a Dutch fleet with 30,000 troops gathered in the Texel preparing to invade; even the Guards were thought to be on the brink of seizing the Tower and the Mint.

And the weather set fair – perfect invasion weather. And everyday life went on as usual: farmers tended their animals and their crops; miners dug their ore; people clattered over the cobbles to do their shopping, buying ever less for ever more; ladies complained of the unwonted heat; there was a shortage of water in country districts; the sea lapped at the iron coast, docile and scarcely raising a shiver of spray; fishermen barked their nets and prepared for the pilchard season. Sawle feast would soon be due, and in spite of war threats there was to be the usual procession, the races, the athletic contests; Tholly Tregirls was organizing some wrestling matches. Jeremy Poldark caught the measles at last and gave it to his sister, but they both suffered mild attacks and there were no complications. Dwight Enys was looking recovered in health, but, just to make a change, Caroline was not well. Demelza hoped it was not frustration.

Ross's frustrations, though of a different kind, continued. It was no pleasure, he said to Demelza, to command a company of slackers. Yet if he left the Volunteers and joined the Fencibles he could be moved anywhere in England at a moment's notice, leaving not only his mine and his business concerns but his wife and children unguarded. If the French or the Dutch or the Spanish arrived they would be as likely to choose this coast as any other, and he would prefer to be on hand to receive them.

If he *had* to leave Cornwall, then better return to the army proper. At the moment, with half the navy in revolt, the army was suddenly finding itself popular.

'It would not be popular with me,' was all Demelza said. 'You have not yet been back two years safe from your last adventure.'

So summer. The Cornish sea settles into an egg-shell blue when the weather is warm and fair and likely to remain so. None of that brilliant cobalt which comes when the north-west wind is picking up, nor the transparent lacy green of the easterly breezes. Now there was no breeze, for several days no breeze at all, as if the peninsula were a three-decker, becalmed, the air become warm as well as the sun. The bent trees crouched in their accustomed postures, flinching from a task-master who had suddenly gone. Grasses were still, smells grew stronger, smoke rose in complacent spirals.

A day in June after Ross had left for Falmouth – he was seeing military leaders and spending the night with Verity – Demelza took the children to a pool on the edge of the sea near Damsel Point, and they all bathed in its cool bottle-green depths and then fished for shrimps and other exciting creatures that darted in and out among the seaweed and the sea anemones.

Depths, of course, was hardly the word. As a child Demelza had seen nothing of the sea except at a distance, and so had never learned to swim. Ross would have taught her long before this except that the constant surf on Hendrawna Beach made it almost impossible to try. So her pool was shallow, yet deep enough for Jeremy to swim in and shallow enough for Clowance to avoid total submersion. And she went briefly into a deeper pool herself near-by and managed to her satis-faction to make the other side without drowning.

It was still early, scarcely ten o'clock, when they returned to the house glowing and laughing. A few wanton clouds with vaporous edges had formed about the sky but one knew better than to take them seriously; they would soon be sucked up into the general heat. The two children had run shouting indoors; not content with a morning dip they were now going with two of the Martin children and two Scobles, in the charge of Ena Daniel, down to the beach to built a great sand wall against the incoming tide. Demelza had carried a basket chair into the shade of the old lilac tree beside the front door and was combing out the tangles in her damp hair when she saw two horsemen riding down the valley.

With instant recognition, which seemed to come as much from instinct as from eyesight, she got up, flew indoors and changed into a casual but seemly green linen frock from the loose twill dressing-gown she had been in, and she was down in the parlour rapidly straightening and tidying when Jane came in to say a gentleman had called.

Hugh Armitage with a groom. Hugh in a light grey long-tailed riding coat and black breeches and riding boots. His stock was loose-tied and he wore no waistcoat. He seemed older and less good-looking. But then he smiled and bent to kiss her hand, and she knew his attraction was unchanged.

'Demelza! How fortunate to find you at home. And what joy to see you again! Ross is here?'

'Not – just at the moment. Tis a surprise to have you call! I didn't know . . .'

'I've been at Tregothnan only since Monday. I came over at the first opportunity.'

'You are on leave?'

'Well – in a manner, yes . . . How are you? How have you been keeping?'

'We're all brave, thank you . . .' They looked at each other uncertainly. 'Please sit down. You'll take something?'

'Not at the moment, thank you. I am – at this moment I need no sort of refreshment.'

'Then – then your man? Perhaps some beer or lemonade?'

'I'm sure he'll like that; but there's no hurry.' He waited until she had seated herself and then took a seat on the edge of a chair. Although he was bronzed, she thought he did not look well. Or perhaps it was just that his eyes were troubled when they looked at her.

'How are your uncle and aunt?'

'Forgive me,' he said, 'I forget my manners. Indeed when I see you I forget everything. They send their warmest good thoughts. My aunt was coming with me today, with both children, intent on asking you to fulfil your undertaking; but John-Evelyn – that's the younger – has a touch of summer fever and Mrs Gower did not feel she could safely bring him out.

I should, I know, myself have delayed a day or two, but the weather at the moment is so fair and one fears to lose it.'

'Ross has only been gone a couple of hours; he'll be sorry to have missed you . . . Our undertaking? What is that?'

'He invited us – you both invited us – to ride over one day this summer and see the seals.'

'Oh?' Demelza smiled. 'Dear life, I *thought* you meant that. What a pity!'

'When will he be back?'

'He is – perhaps not until nightfall. I'm not sure.' She did not want Ross to be thought of as too far away.

'Perhaps another time then. But it's such a refreshment to see you – all my most vivid memories revived and renewed. It's like visiting a green oasis in a barren desert.'

'In deserts do they not have things called – what is it – mirages?'

'Do not poke fun at me,' he said. 'Not just at first. Not until I have got used to looking at you again.'

His reply affected her. She wrinkled an eyebrow and said ruefully: 'Is not fun like a curtain one draws over other feelings? Of course I'm glad to see you too, Hugh. But it's a summer day and more fitting to be gay than romantic. Shouldn't we sit outside and talk in the cool for a while? Then you can send your poor groom round to the stables and he can unsaddle and rest and be fresher for the return.'

So they went out, he a trifle clumsily as if striving with a stiffness of the body; and they fetched another chair and she a fan and Jane brought them cool orangeade from the still-room; and pleasant conversation continued for a while.

His leave from the navy was indefinite, he said, and one did not know quite how long it would extend. He told her of his service, and the one brief but bloody fight he had been engaged in, lasting a solitary hour out of all his nine months at sea. Thank God, it looked as if the mutinies at the Nore and Plymouth and elsewhere were over. After days when the fate of the country hung in the balance, one ship after another had lowered the red flag and allowed its officers to take command again. The ringleaders were arrested and would be duly tried. Many of the grievances would be met.

'I wholly agree with the complaints that were made,' said

Armitage; 'the navy is *grossly* neglected and *disgracefully* treated at all times; many of its enactions are centuries out of date. But as for these Nore scoundrels, I'd gladly string them up from my own yard-arm.'

'You sound very severe,' Demelza said.

'War is a severe thing, if I may so put it. We're fighting for our very lives, and I do not know how we may prevail. The country seems to have lost faith in itself, to be no longer willing to fight for the principles in which it used to believe. As a nation we are slothful or altogether asleep.' He paused and his face relaxed. 'But why do I trouble you with such thoughts? Only because I believe you to be too intelligent to be content with idle chatter. Tell me more of your own doings since last we met.'

'That would be idle chatter.'

'Well, I am happy to listen to anything you have to say. Sitting here I am happy anyhow.'

She began to speak of one or two things, but not in her usual fluent style. Usually talk at any level came easy to her, but not now, and she was glad to break off at the sound of screams of laughter and childish voices behind the house.

'It's my children and some of their friends,' she explained, 'they're going off to build a great wall of sand against the tide.'

'You were going with them?'

'No, no. They have someone to look for them. I took them down to a pool for a swim earlier.'

He had risen and was screwing up his eyes, peering towards the beach. 'The tide is flowing then?'

'Yes. It will be full soon after midday. But it's not a high tide. The highest tides here are always about five in the afternoon.'

There was silence for a while. She watched a bee feeding iself on a lilac flower. It crawled on heavy drunken legs from one stamen to another like a fat soldier burdened with too much loot. The flowers were just past their best but the scent was heavy on the air.

He said: 'Could we not go today?'

II

Looking back, she remembered quite well the somewhat dis-
organized defences she put up against his request. Because her
brain was impeded by unexpected emotion it was not quick
enough to know that no defence at all was needed to such
a suggestion – a plain polite refusal would do. Instead she
made a number of excuses, each of which sounded lamer than
the last in her own ears, and in the end, confronted with his
tentative solutions to her excuses, she found herself saying:
'Well, I suppose we could.'

On their way down Nampara Cove, with the emaciated
stream whispering a thin treble tune beside them, and the tall
groom solemnly carrying oars and rowlocks, she wondered
whether it was indeed unseemly of her to have agreed to his
suggestion. The behaviour of the aristocracy was something
she was still not wholly familiar with. Ross might not like it
when he knew. Nobody else mattered. But what harm could
there be? Even without the big servant, the seals would be
chaperone enough.

'Why is the water in the stream so red?' Hugh asked.

'It's the tin washings from the mine.'

But when they got to the little shingly beach and pulled the
dinghy out of the cave and dragged it down to the sea she saw
that at least the groom was not to be a chaperone.

'We shall be some time?'

'Oh – perhaps an hour. One cannot always be sure. There
may be none about.'

'Well, stay here, Mason. I shall need your help to pull the
boat up again.'

'Yes, sir.'

'Oh, I can do that,' Demelza said. 'I have pulled this up
myself before now.'

Hugh said: 'Mason might just as well stay here as at the
house.'

'Should he not come with us and row?'

'No – if you'll permit it, I'll row myself.'

She hesitated.

He said: 'It's such a rare pleasure to talk to you that I
should like the privilege of privacy.'

'Oh, very well.'

Used to clambering into a boat with bare feet and wet to the knees, she found a mild amusement in being handed into the dinghy by the two men as if she were porcelain. She sat in the stern and tied a green silk scarf about her hair as they were pushed off.

The sea danced little measures around them in the sunshine. Hugh had taken off his long coat and rowed in his shirt-sleeves, his forearms pale with a freckling of dark hair along the bone. She had thought when she saw him first at Tehidy that he was a hawk-faced man, but the sharpness of his features resembled something less predatory; the fine bones were too fine, the shape of the face aristocratic rather than aggressive. He wore no hat in the boat and his hair was tied with a ribbon at the back.

The dinghy had a mast and a small sail which could be hoisted, but the only air today was that created by their passage through the water. Hugh was soon sweating, and even Demelza, though so scantily clad, was hot.

She said: 'Let me row a while.'

'What?' He smiled. 'I couldn't permit it.'

'I can row very well.'

'It would be unseemly to try.'

'Then row easy. It is no more than a mile.'

He slowed and allowed his oars to keep way on the boat without putting much effort into it. They made progression westwards in the direction of Sawle, keeping not more than a hundred yards from the towering cliffs. Here and there little beaches showed sandy lips in coves unreachable except by sea. There were no boats about. Sawle fishermen, amateur and professional, always tended to find more profit in the waters beyond Trevaunance.

Hugh stopped and put an arm across his brow. 'I am happy that you've come with me. Wasn't it Dryden who said: "Tomorrow do thy worst, for I have lived today." '

'Well, the weather may not last.'

'It's not the weather, my dear Demelza. There are other things I have to say to you.'

'I hope they are not things you should not say.'

'They are things I do not *wish* to say. Believe me.'

She looked her surprise, and he smiled again, then twisted the oars in his hands, looking down at his palms. 'Surprising what small practice one gets at rowing when one is an officer. I was a horny-handed boy, but it has worn off.'

'What is it you are going to say to me?'

'Sadly, I have to tell you that my leave from the navy is not indefinite. It is permanent. I have been discharged. Otherwise, of course, I should not be here. Shore leave in time of war is scanty indeed.'

'Discharged?'

'Well, not altogether as a mutineer. Ours was a happy ship. Captain Grant is of the mould of Collingwood and Nelson. But it's mutiny of a sort . . . Or, at least, inefficiency.'

'*Inefficiency?* You? How could that be?'

'Your incredulity warms my heart. Well, no, but it's, as I say, a form of insubordination. My eyes will not behave. Once they refused to recognize a flag at two hundred yards – now they'll not do it at fifty. Like any rebellious *matelot*, they will not respond to discipline.'

She stared at him. 'Hugh, I'm that sorry . . . But what are you trying to say?'

He began to row again. 'I'm saying I can see the land from here – just. Tell me how we go.'

Demelza continued to stare at him in silence. Her hand had been over the side, and she drew it in and let the drops fall on the seat beside her.

'But it was to be better! You said that when we first met.'

'It was to be better but instead it is to be worse. I have seen two special doctors in London, one a naval surgeon, the other private. They agree that nothing can be done.'

For Demelza the heat had gone out of the day. 'But even if you are short sighted, there must be naval work ashore, or . . .'

'Not with this verdict over me. They think I have a short time.'

'A short time? –'

'Oh, it is all dressed up in the Latin tongue like ribbons on a maypole, but what emerges is their opinion that there is something amiss behind the eyes and that in six months or so I shall be following in Milton's footsteps, though without a suitable share of his talent.'

III

Hugh said: 'Is this the season for the young to be born?'

'Not usually for this kind. Most seals have the young now, yes, but these – these are usually born later – September or October. Or that's what I've noticed. I don't really belong to know much about them.'

'And the breeding season?'

'Much the same. You should hear them then – they go on and make such a noise.'

'Demelza, do not look so sad, or I shall regret having told you.'

'How can I be anything else?'

'Perhaps they'll be wrong. Doctors know very little even these times. And today is fine; remember what Dryden said.'

'Why did you tell me, then? *Why?*'

'Because no one else yet knows – I have kept it from my family – and I had to tell someone – and you are my closest friend.'

She studied and perceived the tensions and the bitterness under his bantering tone. 'That makes it worse.'

'Explain to me more about this cave.'

'It's just over there. No more'n a quarter of a mile. If you use your left oar. It's – a big cave. There used to be a mine that drained into it in the olden days but it's been dead for half a century or more. Later in the year tis crowded – the rocks are crowded with seals. Now – I'd expect some – it is just luck.'

'Please. I am sorry I said anything now.'

'Would you expect me to be joyful and act as if nothing had happened?'

'No . . . I'm sorry. I was selfish in not realizing what it would mean to you. I am – very flattered.'

'Don't be. It is not to flatter you that I am upset.'

He shipped his oars and took a deep breath. 'So . . . but it must not spoil today. Of course I should have written, told you. But look – look at me, listen to me . . .'

'Well . . .' She raised her eyes.

'We live in an uncertain world,' he said gently. 'At its best life is short. Tomorrow the French or the Dutch may land, and ravage and kill and burn. Next week the cholera may come in in a ship at Padstow or Falmouth. Or the smallpox rage. Six months! Even if they're not wrong there's still six months. What would those naval mutineers now waiting trial give for six months of life and laughter? "Tomorrow do thy worst, for I have lived today." Can't I persuade you to forget what I've told you – or at least to ignore it?'

'Well, it's easier said than done.'

'Smile at me, please. When I saw you first you didn't smile all through dinner, and it was not until we went down to the lake afterwards . . . It was like someone spilling diamonds.'

'Oh, *nonsense*, Hugh.'

'Come, please. Just a little one. I'll not row you till you do.'

'I can row myself,' said Demelza.

'That would be mutiny on the high seas and I have no convenient yard-arm.'

Demelza smiled uncertainly and he gave a little whoop of joy.

'Quiet!' she said. 'You'll scare them. They scare easy and then you'll never see one for all your trouble.'

'Seals?' said Hugh. 'Ah, yes, was that what we came out to see?'

He unshipped his oars, and, obeying her instructions, began to paddle towards the cliffs.

The sun was overhead and shadows were at their shortest. Because of the angle of the coast to the sun the face of the cliff was sunlit, and even when they were ten feet from the rocks they were still in full light. Demelza again wanted to take the oars, for she knew they had to approach the cave from an angle so as not to disturb their quarry. But he still rowed. Already ten or a dozen great cow seals had slithered off the rocks as they approached.

On the rocks near the mouth of the cave was the wreck of a ship. Most of it had been pounded to pieces long ago, but a few spars and the bow had become wedged where they were protected from the weight of the waves, and seaweed hung from them like shrouds from a corpse. Opposite it was a strip of fine sand no more than thirty feet across with sharply shelving sides.

They could hear the hooting coughs of the seals, and now and then a strange moaning wail which might have come from a human throat in distress, as if long-drowned mariners were hiding in the cave. Here, in spite of the calmness of the weather, one was conscious of a rise and fall of the sea, not so much a wave as the breath of an ocean.

'I don't think we've disturbed them,' Demelza said, as they came round the corner.

At the entrance of the cave, sunning themselves on the rocks, were a score or more of grey seals, some large, some half grown. Hugh stopped rowing and the boat drifted slowly towards them. At first it seemed that the mammals did not notice the intruders, then that they were merely curious and not at all alarmed. The eyes of one after another settled on the dinghy. Their faces were human, or half human, and old-young, childish and whiskered, innocent yet worldly wise. One of them gave a curious hooting sound, and a small one, its calf, responded with a whiskery bleat. Another yawned. Mixed noises came from inside the cave.

Demelza said in a low voice: 'I hear tell they're awful fond of music. Sometimes, they say, Pally Rogers comes out here with his flute and they all gather round his boat.'

They had drifted a little too near one cow, and she rose, curving her back upwards, and threw herself farther up the rocks with a series of convulsive jerks. The sun was too warm for her to want to take to the sea.

'I wish my aunt were here,' said Hugh. 'And the children. Yet I would be a little concerned lest, if this group took suddenly to the water, they might upset the boat.'

'It's possible.'

'You can swim?'

'. . . I could keep afloat, I b'lieve.'

After a few moments he said: 'I'm sorry they're not here for they'd be enchanted. But I'm happy they're not here because I am enchanted.'

'I'm glad.'

'Oh, not with the seals, though I never thought I should see them so well, and thank you for bringing me. My enchantment is in spending the morning with you.'

'Well,' said Demelza uncertainly. 'The morning is half gone, so I think we should just go into the cave a little and then start home.'

The dinghy had come to a stop and was grating against a seaweedy rock. Just then the ocean breathed again and Hugh had to make a sudden movement with an oar to prevent danger. This was enough for the seals. One after another they dragged their fat sleek bodies laboriously across the rocks with their forepaws and slid and dived and belly-flopped into the sea. For a few moments all was commotion; heads and bodies swirled and snorted close beside the boat; it rocked and lurched, and the quiet rock-strewn sea was a-boil with little waves. Then as quickly as it had begun the storm died, the boat settled and they were left gazing at the empty rocks, in silence except for a disturbed seagull crying.

Demelza laughed and wiped the splashes of sea water from her face and frock.

Hugh said: 'You had the worst of that!'

'Twill help cool me. I don't think we have scared the grey-beards in the cave. But go cautiously and not too far in.'

Around them the sea was an iridescent blue pierced by the black shadows of the rocks, but at the mouth of the cavern where the sun was not falling it turned to a limpid jade green which lit up the roof of the big cave with a dim reflected light. As they went into this world the light faded, and, peering after the bright sun, they could just see that the cave went far back into the distant darkness. But not far to their left was a branch cave with a pebbly beach littered with drift-wood, seaweed and cuttle-fish bones. On this beach great dark shapes lay. Hugh put his oars down to slow their movement as twenty or more grey faces peered at them, older than those they had seen outside, fiercer, more burdened down with the knowledge of good and evil, of the search for life and inevitable death.

One of them set up a terrible low moaning in the dark. It was a cry out of the wind and the waves, yet it seemed to have humanity in it as well as the sea. It was a cry without enmity but without hope. Then suddenly they moved: an avalanche of flapping forms seemed to launch itself in an attack on the boat. The dinghy lurched wildly, was half swamped in foamy water, was bumped and pitched and tossed

amid a frenzy of magnified bellows and grunts; and it crashed
hard against the rock wall of the cave. Then once again it
began to settle and they stared at the great shiny grey creatures
swivelling and turning in the water as they rushed out to sea.

IV

The show was over. Hugh paddled back into the sunshine.
There was six inches of water in the dinghy, but he peered
over the side where they had struck the rock and there was
no damage except a few dents in the stout planking. They
were both wet and they were both laughing. Not a seal was
in sight.

'More than ever,' he said, 'I'm relieved we did not bring
Mrs Gower. Do you invite all your friends to this delightful
experience?'

'I've never been in the cave myself before!' she said.

He laughed again. 'Well, I'm glad we ventured. But I suppose if we had lost the boat there was no way back?'

'I b'lieve we could have climbed.'

He frowned as he peered up at the cliffs. 'I'm used to
climbing to the trees, but I shouldn't have fancied that. I am
sorry you're so wet.'

'I am sorry *you* are so wet.'

He peered around. 'That strip of sand. We can get the water
out of the boat. Otherwise you would have wet feet all the
way home.'

'It's not important. I shall catch no chill.'

But he rowed towards the beach and jumped ashore. As
she followed him the ocean breathed again and lifted the
dinghy with ironical gentleness so that it was aground with
no effort at all. Forgetting his views on her frailty, he allowed
her to help him turn the boat until the water was drained out.
Then they both sat on the sand looking at their clothes and
allowing them to dry off in the sun.

He said: 'Demelza.'

'Yes.'

'I wish you'd let me make love to you.'

'Jesus God,' she said.

'Oh, I know it is – ill of me to say such a thing. I know it
is both unfair and indiscreet of me even to utter such a

thought. I know it looks as if I am trading on this kindness you are doing to me in an unforgivable way. I know it seems – must seem – utterly despicable of me to attempt, or even to think of attempting, the virtue of a woman married to the man who saved me from prison. I know all that.'

She said, stumbling over the words: 'We had better start for home now.'

'Give me five minutes – if only sitting here with you.'

'To say what more?'

'Perhaps to explain a little of what I feel – so that you shall not think too harshly of me.'

She crumbled the fine sand in her hand. Her head was down and her hair fell forward over most of her face. She had kicked off her shoes, and her feet were sunk in the sand.

'I cannot think *harshly* of you, Hugh, even though I cannot understand how you can say it, especially today.'

He brushed the water off his shirt. 'Let me explain about one thing first. You think this is a terrible thing, asking you to be disloyal to Ross. And on the narrowest terms it is. But – how can I try to make it more clear? By giving love you do not diminish it. By loving me you would not destroy your love for Ross. Love only creates and adds to itself, it never destroys. You do not betray your love for Ross by offering some of your love to me. You add to it. Tenderness is not like money: the more you give to one, the more you have for others. You feel something for me, don't you?'

'Yes.'

'Then tell me – could you have felt as much for me, as much warmth and understanding, if you had not loved Ross?'

'Maybe not. I don't know.'

'Love is not a possession to hoard. You give it away. It's a blessing and a balm. You know the parable of the loaves and the fishes? It is always misunderstood. Christ was distributing *spiritual* bread. That was why there was enough for five thousand. It's the miracle that is occurring all the time.'

'Five loaves of love,' Demelza said; 'what were the two small fishes?'

'You're very hard, Demelza.'

'No, I am not very hard.'

One of the greater black-backed gulls swept quite low over-

head, his wings temporarily flicking across the sun. Two more
screamed high in the cliffs above. The heat of the day had
drained the sky of colour. There seemed to be no air at all
in the cove.

Hugh said: 'You said that you could not understand me
asking this, especially today. I ask it today only because there
is no other day, and never will be another day. Not because
of any frailties I am likely to succumb to but because of plain
circumstance. There will *never* be another such day. You may
think I am – unfairly – asking you to do this out of pity. You
are right. But *not* – not at all out of pity for a man who may
be losing his sight. Out of pity for someone who loves you as
he loves Heaven and thinks to be kept for ever outside the
gates of paradise.'

Demelza stirred almost irritably. 'That's not *true*, Hugh!
There's no paradise in love! It's – you're thinking in the wrong
way. Love – the sort you're asking me for – is of the earth,
earthy. Beautiful, maybe – sometimes it be like a gold mine
that one digs into. But of the earth – earthy. Tis all wrong to
speak of paradise. Love may be the nearest human beings can
get – but it is still outside the gates – for it is *human* – easily
lost – animal in the way it work, though more, much more than
animal. Oftentimes it – uplifts, transports . . . but – but it
should not be mistaken. It is a – a terrible mistake to pretend
it is something quite different.'

There was silence. He looked at her with his dark sensitive
eyes.

'So you think I have been using the wrong arguments. You
think my reasoning is specious?'

She looked back at him through her hair and smiled. 'I
don't know what that means. But I think so.'

'How then – if you wished to be persuaded; how would you
advise me to set about it?'

'But I don't wish to be persuaded.'

'Is there any risk?'

'Not risk. Risk is the wrong word.'

'Hope, then.'

'Not hope, neither. But, Hugh, you must know that I am
troubled by you, moved – and it is not pity. I wish – I only
wish it was.'

'I am glad it is not.'

'All those pretty words you spoke about love being – what is the word? – divisible. Can I ask you if you think other things are divisible too – such as loyalty – such as trust?'

He knelt up, sat back on his heels. The great damp splashes on his cambric shirt were drying.

'No,' he said humbly. 'There you have me beat.' He shook his head. 'There you have me beat.'

She began to trace figures in the sand. Her heart was beating as if there was a drum inside her. Her mouth was so dry she could not swallow. The nakedness of her body inside her frock seemed to have suddenly become more apparent to her, seemed to flower. She gave a slight groan which she tried to suppress altogether but could not quite.

He sat back looking at her, a foot away from touching her. 'What is it?'

'Please let us go.'

'May I just then kiss you?'

She raised her head and pushed her hair back. 'It would be quite wrong.'

'But you will permit it?'

'Perhaps I cannot stop you.'

He moved towards her, and knew the moment he touched her that something had won his battle for him. He took her face in his hands, held it like a cup to be drunk from, and then kissed her. With a serious unsmiling mouth he touched her eyelids, her cheeks, her hair, and sighed, as if for the moment her acceptance were all and there was no further desire in him.

'Hugh – '

'Don't speak, my love, don't speak.'

He put his left hand to the nape of her neck, supporting it, until slowly she leaned against it and so lay back in the sand. Then, fumbling, with his right hand, he began to undo the buttons of her frock.

BOOK THREE

CHAPTER I

Ross was away three nights, not one. He stayed the first with Verity, as arranged; the second, defence meetings with various gentlemen having left many matters unresolved, he spent at Pendennis Castle on the rocky promontory overlooking Falmouth harbour as the guest of its governor, John Melville. Governor Melville came barely to the top button of Ross's waistcoat and dressed in a scarlet uniform and a square cocked hat, which he wore even at meals. The stump of his left arm hung in a black silk sling, so that an orderly had to cut up his food, and the socket of his right eye was covered with a black silk patch and satin ribbon. He strutted as if he were on parade and barked his orders like a little terrier. Not quite Ross's type, but it made a pleasant change from the lackadaisical attitude of most of the amateur officers whose business it was to organize the defence of the country. The following day he took Ross to see the ever-growing French prisoner-of-war camp at Kergillack, near Penryn. This now held upwards of a thousand men, a great many of them sailors; and Ross was interested to see how it compared with the horrors of Quimper. Many of the men were under canvas, and in this fine hot weather were looking sunburnt and healthy enough, and the food was just adequate; but it would be a bleak spot on the top of the hill in the winter when the gales were roaring.

They rode on then to see Mr Rogers at Penrose and supped there. With the long evening fading and a four-hour ride as the alternative, Ross was about to accept the invitation to sleep there, when a messenger came on a lathery horse with a request from Lord de Dunstanville that they should all proceed at once to Tehidy on a matter of vital national emergency. It was in the minds of all sitting at the table that the French had landed somewhere and they must raise the countryside; but the messenger explained it concerned grievous riots which were taking place in Camborne, and Lord de Dunstan-ville needed all aid to contain them.

Of the male diners all but three were elderly, and Governor Melville was of the opinion that it would be improper of him as a military man to take any part in suppressing a civil disturbance unless civilian authority failed; so Ross and Rogers himself and two others accompanied the groom to Tehidy.

There, though the countryside through which they passed was peaceful enough, they found great activity. The rioting had in fact taken place the day before. A crowd of angry miners, estimated at five or six thousand, many accompanied by their wives, had assembled and descended on the village of Camborne, in the neighbourhood of which a number of millers had their mills, and had demanded corn at a price decided on by themselves. The millers had appealed for help to the local gentry, but such as there were had been afraid to stir. So, to the accompaniment of rebellious songs, the corn had been seized and distributed and the miners paid the arbitrarily low price. What was worse, some houses and barns were broken into and the goods in them stolen and various persons who tried to impede the rioters were roughly dealt with.

About thirty men were assembled in the big hall of Tehidy and were being sworn in as constables. This number was ever growing as de Dunstanville's messengers brought in fresh recruits from outlying districts: farmers, factors, farriers, clerks, anyone who could be relied upon to do his civic duty in an emergency. Ross went into the drawing-room where the depositions of the millers were still being taken, and was greeted in a most friendly but grim manner by Basset, who clearly took the gravest view of the disturbance. Possibly, Ross thought, it was not so much the gravity of the acts committed, for it seemed, listening to the depositions, that the violence had been small and the thefts petty; it was the failure of his fellow magistrates to act which caught Basset on the raw. Let it be once seen and widely known that magistrates were afraid or powerless before a rioting crowd and all authority would be at an end. Basset himself had only arrived from London that day – last night he had been at Ashburton – and he was resolved that lawlessness and anarchy must not be tolerated in the district in which he was the principal landowner and held the King's authority to maintain the peace.

Once apprised of the facts, Mr Rogers was of the same mind, and an air of general resolve and determination ran through the assembled men, some of whom were the men who had not stirred yesterday. They had lacked a leader of sufficient energy and courage; now they had one.

Ross, with his usual split sympathies, would have been glad to have excused himself and ridden off home. The millers and merchants were a well-fed lot and not people for whom he had any tender feeling. But to have gone off now would have been to take sides against his own class in a situation where the issues were no longer clear cut. It was not in fact so very long since he had led a riot himself; but the mutinies in the navy – particularly the later ones where men such as Parker had set themselves up as little dictators hardly distinguishable in manner from their French counterparts – had hardened his feeling against mass lawlessness; and to refuse to help now that he was here would have aligned him with ideas that he had come to detest.

So he went along, though finding the action when it took place hourly more distasteful. This being a country district, the names of most of the ringleaders were known and had been attested by the millers in their depositions, so identity was not a problem. Eighty constables in all were sworn in, and Basset divided them into ten groups, each of whom had the allotted task of arresting five of the rioters. If by morning fifty of the leaders were under lock and key there would be no risk of further disturbances. Basset took one group, Rogers another, Mr Stackhouse of Pendarves a third, Ross a fourth, and so on.

In the event nothing could have been more peacefully effected. By the time all arrangements had been made it was one o'clock in the morning and nearly two when most of the arrests were complete. The miners were in bed and asleep, except for one or two who were in work and happened to be on night cores; they were knocked up, taken by surprise, and arrested without resistance and mainly without protest. For an extempore operation Ross had to admit it was well done, and he could acknowledge Basset's ability as an organizer. By the time the men were lodged in lock-ups under guard day was beginning to break. Ross declined the offer of a bed at Tehidy but sat and dozed in a chair for an hour until he could set off home.

On the way he called at Killewarren and found Dwight up, though Caroline still abed, and learned to his further discomfort that Dwight had been sent for on the previous night and had refused to go. After Ross had sourly recounted the events of the night, Dwight said:

'Oh, well, our situations were quite different. You were there, I was not. I had an excuse, you had not. You are a landowner of the district, I am only recently such by marriage. I think you did right to help.'

Ross grunted. 'Well, I did not at all like knocking up those half-starved devils and turning them out shivering in the dark. It is not a picture I shall live with very comfortably for some time to come.'

'What is the plan to deal with them?'

'Well, thank God I am not a Justice. Oh, I expect it will all be sensibly tidied up. Basset was talking of dealing summarily with about thirty-five of them and then sending the other dozen-odd to Bodmin on the more serious charges. He's not at all a vindictive man and now that he has exerted his authority I think he will be satisfied with light sentences.'

Dwight pursed his lips. 'Let's hope so. It's a bad time for those who get at cross with the law.'

Ross rose to go. 'My respects to Caroline. I trust she's over her indisposition.'

'Not altogether. I believe her to be anaemic, but she's a hard woman to doctor. Most of my potions, I suspect, are secretly tipped into the flower bed.'

'Why d'you not take her away? You've had no proper honeymoon, and you're much recovered yourself.'

'Perhaps next year.'

'That's a long time away. D'you know, while you were in prison Caroline drooped and faded like a cut flower that's been left out of water. When you returned she blossomed over again. I think – you'll consider all this an impertinence, no doubt.'

'Not yet.'

Ross contemplated his friend before going on. He felt in a

mood for plain speaking. It was the shortness and discomfort
of his own night . . . 'Well, I believe she is a young woman
whose looks and health are peculiarly susceptible of her good
or bad spirits. You suffered greatly at Quimper – but not so
much spiritually, I venture to think, as she did here. You
were – you have the nature and the mind to be always busy.
What she had here was the waiting and the anxiety and a dying
man to care for who for months would do everything but die.
I would guess she still suffers from that in her own way as
much as you have suffered physically from the hardships of
the prison camp. She needs a change, Dwight, a stimulus.'

Dwight had coloured. 'Dr Poldark.'

'Yes . . . I'm fond of Caroline. Through the years I've seen
a good deal of her and conceit that I know her next best only
to you. Perhaps in one way better, because I am more
detached.'

Dwight said: 'We have discussed this together, Caroline and
I, not so long ago, the difficulty of our adjusting our way of
living, each to the other. I have attempted to – to meet her
ideas in a number of ways.'

Ross grunted, as if unconvinced.

Dwight said rather sharply: 'If you attribute her health to
her mood then you point the obvious cause of her lowered
spirits. Namely that our marriage is not the success it should
be. Who am I to say you are not right?'

Ross picked up his crop. 'If it is not the success it should
be, then I would add the word, yet. The fact that you're
opposites in many things is not the end of the world, nor even
the end of a marriage. You know it, you both knew it long
ago. So far you have had less than two years to make the
appropriate adjustments. It's only time and patience that are
needed. Caroline, I know, is not notable for her *patience*, but
you both have *time*. And I think you must go along with her
more, Dwight. All right, all right, *still* more, then. You must
count your blessings and take the consequences . . . This
lecture, I know, is the height of interference and you would
do right to call for pistols; but remember I have a vested
concern for her happiness and yours.'

'Since without you,' Dwight said, 'there would have been
no marriage. Doubly so.'

'Doubly so,' Ross agreed. 'It's a chastening thought.'

'So I'll not call for pistols,' said Dwight, 'but only for your horse. And send you on your way, with no chastening thoughts, happily, about your own marriage.'

'It has had its storms,' Ross said. 'Make no mistake. We none of us come to port without risk of shipwreck.'

II

Demelza was giving Jeremy his early lessons when Ross arrived. That was, she had the boy on her knee with a horn book teaching him his letters while Clowance, not at all co-operative, beat out a regular rhythm on the floor with an old tin cup she had found. Demelza had got into this routine during the fine summer so that Jeremy was obliged to do a little learning before being allowed his first bathe.

Ross's arrival broke up this scene, and Demelza kissed him warmly while Jeremy embraced his leg and Clowance increased the rate of her drum beat and crowed in tune. If he had noticed, Ross might have been aware of some extra warmth in Demelza's kiss and that her hands, holding his coat by each upper arm, retained their grip longer than usual. But, knowing of nothing at home to disturb his peace of mind, and much outside, he was preoccupied with the events of last night and anxious to tell her about them.

So he broke his fast while he talked, and then they went to sit in the garden, and Ross pulled off his coat and Demelza took out a parasol, and they spoke of this and that, and in the course of the conversation she mentioned that Hugh Armitage had been over on Tuesday.

Ross raised an eyebrow and said: 'Oh? How is he?' the question being a rhetorical one.

'Very unwell,' Demelza said. 'Leastwise, not in ordinary health, but he has had to leave the navy.'

'I'm sorry. What's amiss?'

'Who was Milton?'

'Milton? A poet. There was one such anyway.'

'Did he go blind?'

'Yes . . . Yes, I believe he did.'

'They tell Hugh that this is what will happen to him.'

'Good God!' Ross frowned at her. 'I *am* sorry! When did he learn that?'

'I don't rightly know. He came over with a groom, who I think was with him because of his sight. He would not stay for dinner, but before that I took him to Seal Hole Cave. He seemed to want to go and I couldn't properly refuse.'

'. . . In the row-boat, you mean?'

'Yes. He said Mrs Gower was to have come with the children but one of the children was ill and so she could not.'

'The seals were there?'

'Oh, yes . . . More'n I've ever seen before.'

Ross's frown deepened, and there was a heavy ominous silence.

'I wonder if he has seen Dwight?'

'Dwight?' said Demelza with relief.

'Well, I know Dwight has no special eye knowledge but he has such intuition, such insight on physical matters, that Hugh might do worse than see him . . . Good God, what an ill thing! Has it been brought on by his imprisonment, do they say?'

'They think so.'

Ross leaned down and patted Garrick, who was crouched in the shade of his chair. 'An ill thing indeed. At times the world seems very senseless and cruel. Cruel enough to man without man himself inflicting further cruelties . . .'

Demelza picked up a blue satin petticoat that needed a repair to the hem. She began to stitch. A bee, she wondered if it was the same bee, was working in and out of the lilac flowers.

'What is he going to do?' Ross asked.

'Hugh? I – don't know. I think he will go home to his parents in Dorset.'

'Is he still as much in love with you?'

She glanced up briefly, shyly. 'I don't know – now.'

'And you?'

'I'm very grieved for him, as you'd naturally expect.'

'Have a care. Pity, they say, is akin to love.'

'I do not think he would ever want pity.'

'No. That was not what I was supposing.'

Garrick heaved himself up from beside the chair on his

bony black woolly legs and ambled off into the house.

'He does not like the heat,' Demelza said.

'Who? Hugh?'

'No, no, no, no.'

'I'm sorry; it was not meant as a joke.'

Demelza sighed. 'Maybe it would be better if we did joke about it all. Maybe we all take life too serious . . . I'm that *glad* you're back, Ross. I wish you wouldn't go away so much. I *wish* you would not!'

'It would be as well. I achieve little but frustration.'

That evening while the last light was still luminous over the sea they made love, and he was aware, though he did not remark it, of a return of some warmth and richness in her that had been lacking these last months in however barely perceptible a degree. Not for the first time he was conscious of emotional lights and shades in his wife that could not be categorized, could not be named as sensuous or emotional as such, perhaps derived from each and gave to each but in essence grew out of a deeper fund of temperament that he still could not altogether apprehend. The simple miner's daughter was not simple in character at all.

They talked in a quiet, contented, desultory way for a while, and then he went to sleep. After lying there staring at the dying twilight on the ceiling she slipped from under his protecting arm, slid out of bed, put on her nightdress and went to the window. The stars were out in a wide gloom of sky, with the beach and the cliffs rock-dark and empty. A scar of surf divided sea from sand. Some night birds were winging their way home.

She shivered a little, though it was warm in the room, as she considered the enormities of Tuesday.

To her Ross had always been one step more than just a husband. He had, as it were, almost created her out of the nothing that she had once been, a starving brat barely able to see or think beyond the horizons of her immediate needs, illiterate, uncouth, lice-ridden. In thirteen odd years she had grown, with his encouragement, into a woman of some modest attainments, someone who could read and write and talk a fair English and play the piano and sing and mix and not merely in the company of gentlefolk but, recently, in the company of the great. More than that, he had married her, given her his love – most of the time – his loving care – all the time – his trust, his confidence, a fine home, servants to do any work she did not want to do, and three beautiful children, two of whom survived. And she had betrayed all that in a sudden unexpected quirk of pity and love and passion for a man she scarcely knew who happened to call and ask.

It was not quite credible. Some years ago when Ross had gone to Elizabeth, had *left* her, *deserted* her, and gone off to Elizabeth, she had herself ridden alone to a ball at the Bodrugans' determined to revenge herself in the only way open to her, and had thrown herself at a Scottish army officer called Malcolm McNeil. But when it came to the point, when she found herself alone in her room with a strange man who was trying affectionately to undress her, she had repelled him, actually with force, had bitten him like the brat she was and had made her escape. *Whatever* Ross did, she had found, almost to her own fury, that she was Ross's woman and wanted – indeed could accept – no other man. *Then* when the motive was there, goading her on, with the absolute certain knowledge of Ross's unfaithfulness burning into her soul, she had been unable to be unfaithful in return.

Now, with no more than a suspicion that Ross was again meeting Elizabeth on the quiet, she had allowed herself to slip gently into the infidelity she had thought impossible in herself.

She peered out at the night. It was going no darker; behind the house a moon was rising.

But to be honest she could not allow herself even the luxury of blaming her lapse on Jud's tale-telling, on Ross's secret meetings. It had of course been in the back of her mind all these months, a little corrosive eating away at her normal contentment; and on the soft sand beside the Seal Hole Cave with the cliffs towering and a man kneeling in the sand watching her, the knowledge had come suddenly to the forefront and on the instant eroded her will. But it could only have done that if the impulses were already so strong within her that they seized on any excuse to have their way. It was an *excuse*, she knew that with certainty. A good one or a bad one, who knew? But an excuse for what was inexcusable.

Nor could she really pretend to herself that she had been

swept away by Hugh's romantic approach. Of course it was delightful to be someone's chivalrous ideal. But she was altogether of the wrong temperament to be much affected by it. She knew well enough that such a poetic view of love was impossible to sustain, and she had made this clear to him all through their friendship. Indeed his extravagances, charming though they were, would have tended to defeat their own object. (Was it unfair to him to suppose that he had *tried* to charm her, to weave a spell around her, to hypnotize her with idealistic attitudes and beautiful words? Perhaps it *was* unfair, for his sincerity could hardly be doubted.) Anyway, she had refused to be so hypnotized. Yet in the end she had not refused *him*. She had given herself to him with warmth and sensuous ease. There had been little or no embarrassment. It had happened, cut off from the rest of the world, under the hot sun.

So what was the reason? Attraction, sheer physical attraction, which she had felt from the moment they had first met last year; sadness, for the news he brought of himself; opportunity, which had settled on them like a strange bird, making unreality out of isolation and giving her the feeling that she was no one, except a nameless woman to be taken by a nameless man.

Were these reasons, except the first, any better than more excuses? From the moment he set eyes on her he had wanted her, and now he had had her. Perhaps it would cure him. Perhaps now that he had brought her down to the level of other women he would be able to go away and forget. There was an old saying that all women were the same when the candle was blown out. He had had many other women, he had implied; now she was one of them. Now he could turn his idealism on some other girl. Perhaps her giving herself to him would in the end be a good thing, clearing his mind of his desire, enabling him to come to terms with himself, and to forget.

She wished she could believe this. Or she almost wished it. No woman really wants to feel that by giving herself to a man she has expended her attraction in his eyes. But that likelihood now seemed less probable than it had done yesterday. While Ross was asleep this afternoon, sleeping off some of the

frustrations and unease of the sinister night, the same tall
groom had arrived again, clattering over the cobbles at the
front door – alone, thank God, but all the same openly deliver-
ing a message to her that Ross might well have asked to see.
Admittedly the covering note was formal enough, a polite
letter thanking her for her hospitality of Tuesday and expressing a hope that she and Ross would dine again at Tregothnan
before he returned home. But folded inside it was another
poem, and who knew whether she would have had the sleight
of hand to get it into her pocket without its being seen?

The metre had changed, but not the style.

> Hallowed by sea and sand
> Beauty was in my hand.
> In taking her I came
> Moth to the whitest flame,
> Body caressed and turned
> Wings of desire unburned.
> Lips to my lips unfold
> Tale of our love is told.
> Yet there can be no end,
> In love our lives extend,
> And if this day be all
> Proud is my heart's recall
> Proud is my funeral pall.

It didn't seem to have altered his attitude as yet, or to have
'cured' him of anything at all. Then had it cured *her*? But
cured her of what? A compulsive sensuous impulse to lie with
another man for once in her life? A perverse desire to be
unfaithful to the man she loved? A wish to give happiness,
if it was in her power, to someone sorely threatened? A sudden
moral lapse, lying in the warm sand with the salt water drying
on her body?

The odd and slightly disconcerting thing was that she was
not quite sure that she had anything to be cured of. She felt
no less in love with Ross than before – perhaps, perversely, a
little more so. She felt no different – or very little different –
towards Hugh Armitage. She was taken with him, warmed by
his love and returning some of it. The experience, the physical

experience, if one could separate it even in one's thoughts
from the heart-stopping tension and sweet excitement of the
day, had not in essence varied from what she had known
before. She did not feel that she was becoming in any real
way a light woman. She did not see it as a happening that was
likely to recur. It was just a trifle disconcerting that she did
not feel very much changed in any way as a result of it.

That was not to say that she had spent a happy two days
since. At times the discomfort and apprehension she felt
might well have been mistaken for bitter remorse for wrong-
doing. Unfortunately the remorse was something of which
she had to remind herself rather than a sensation welling up
naturally from her conscience. The true discomfort grew out
of something different. At the moment, what had happened on
Tuesday was an event in isolation, unconnected with the past,
unattached to the future. But if Ross knew of it, even got
to suspect it, then the anonymity of the experience would be
shattered, the isolation broken into, and her life with him
might be laid waste.

It was not an agreeable thought, and, standing at the
window with little shivers going through her body in the
warm night, she did not much like herself. It seemed to her
that if she had committed adultery it was for the wrong
reasons, and if she was sorry she had committed it, it was
again for the wrong reasons.

On the Tuesday it had been after one when they left the
beach. They had rowed straight back.

He had said in the boat: 'You have not asked me to dinner
but I'll not stay. If Ross should return I should feel embarrassed, and in truth all I want now for a long time is to be
alone.'

'Your groom will be tired of waiting.'

'*I* have been tired of waiting . . . When can I see you again?'

'Not, I believe, for a long time.'

'A long time will be too long for me.'

'When are you going home?'

'To Dorset? I don't know. My uncle believes there is an
election coming shortly and thinks to invite me to stand for
Truro.'

'But your – oh, I suppose he doesn't know?'

'Not yet. In any event, if the election occurred this summer I could still no doubt deceive the electors. And I suspect there have been blind Members of Parliament before this.'

'Do not say that.'

'Well, it will have to be said sooner or later.'

'Are spectacles no use to you? I'm still not sure how much you can see?'

'Today I have seen enough.'

'Hugh, please, we should talk no more like this . . . I need not ask you when we get ashore to talk no more like this.'

'You need not ask me, Demelza. My lovely one, no hurt shall come to you from anything I say. I assure you.'

So they had landed, and the impassive groom, who had been sitting in the shade of the rocks, came to help them gravely in, and, the boat stowed in the cave, they had walked up the narrow valley to the house talking of seals and other casual things, and he had refused to come in but had stood chatting in the doorway until the two horses were led round, and they had mounted and clattered off up the valley. Hugh had not waved as he left, but he had turned and stared at her for a long moment, as if trying to memorize what he might not see again.

She turned from the bedroom window and looked about her at the familiar room. The teak beams running lengthwise of the ceiling, the new green velvet curtain over the door, the window seat with its pink grogram hanging; the wardrobe door ajar and a corner of the frock, the green frock, peering out like a guilty secret; Ross's dark head and regular breathing. My lovely one, no hurt shall come to you from anything I say. But what of the things you write? In the sort of company in which Hugh was brought up, possibly letters were brought on a platter to the breakfast table by a manservant and everyone was too well bred to ask even whom a communication was from, let alone expect to see its contents. In Nampara household, on the other hand, such was the amity and friendship between them, that Ross always tossed any letters he received across to her to read after, and she, on the rare occasions when she had one, automatically did the same. However folded within another letter, the last poem was dangerous indeed. Body caressed and turned, Wings of desire unburned.

Lips to my lips unfold. Judas! No wonder she shivered in the warm night!

The bit of paper should have been torn up at once. It was like a little heap of gunpowder waiting for a chance spark. But sometimes caution can go too far, and she couldn't quite force herself to destroy it. However little or much the *incident* might come to mean in future years, the *poem* meant something. It meant something to her and she could not lose it. So instead she had slipped it with the other poems she had received into a little wash-leather bag that she had found in the old library long years ago. It was safe enough there, she felt, for no one touched the drawer it was in except herself.

She came back to the bed. She wondered for a moment if perhaps she had been dismissing Hugh's romantic persuasions too lightly. What had he said? By giving love you do not diminish it. Love only adds to itself, it never destroys. Tenderness is not like money; the more you give to one the more you have for others. Perhaps there was hard common sense in this as well as poetry. Certainly there was, if one could overcome loyalty and possessiveness and jealousy and trust. But how could one? What if Ross had been sleeping with Elizabeth? What if his story about aiding in the arrest of the miners were an untruth and he had spent the night in Elizabeth's arms? How would she feel then? That Ross's love had grown for her because he had been intimate with another woman's body? Love only adds to itself, it never destroys. Tenderness is not like money. But neither is trust, Hugh, neither is trust. Neither is loyalty. You can give *those* away and they are gone for ever, Hugh. Though only a part of love, they are a vital part, gathered, stored, built up over the years, like something growing *round* love, protecting it, warming it, adding another strength to it and another savour. Give *those* away and they are gone for ever . . .

She drew back the thin sheet and slid in beside Ross, very cautiously so as not to wake him. She lay on her back for a moment, wide eyed, silent breathed, staring at the half-dark ceiling. Then Ross moved, as if conscious that she had been away and had come back. He did not put his arm around her but his hand came to rest on hers while he slept.

The thirty-five rioters tried locally were let off lightly; it was widely known that the magistrates were concerned more with the ringleaders than with those who had been misled. The fifteen others were due to appear in court at Bodmin. Among the fifteen were several who were friends of Sam's and Drake's from the Illuggan area. They dicussed this one evening as they walked down to Sawle together to inspect the first pilchard catch.

The pilchard season had been poor for five years or more, and this early catch raised everyone's hopes that the hot summer and the warmer water would bring a bounty to the coast. The nets had been hauled in early that morning, but work was still going on sorting and packing, and the brothers, like most of the people around, were hoping to pick up some cheap fish. It was an hour yet from sunset. Crowds filled the beach, watching, helping, gossiping.

It was the custom when the catch was hauled ashore in baskets which had been filled from the nets, to tip the fish into wheelbarrows and run them up the slope to the cellar, which was in fact a large shed, not a cellar at all, and there women picked the fish over, sorting them and sizing them. Broken or damaged fish were thrown to one side to be sold cheap to those who wanted to buy, and any surplus was dumped and mixed with refuse salt and sold to the farmers for seven or eight shillings the cartload to be used as manure on the fields.

The good fish were arranged in layers on the floor of the cellar by other women, working quickly but with exactness, each fish being laid head to head and each layer being sprinkled with salt before the next layer was begun. Three people worked as a team – one woman to sort and carry the fish and one to pack them, with a young girl or boy to fetch the salt and make himself generally useful. Such a team working together could sort and stack seven or eight thousand fish in a day's daylight.

By the time the Carnes arrived much of this had been done, and the heads of the fish presented a regular serried barrier five feet high across the length of the cellar. So carefully were they arranged, in spite of obvious variations in size, that it would have been possible to count them. This of course was the beginning of the work. The fish would stay here a month while the oil drained out of them and was caught and preserved. Then the fish would be taken up and washed and pressed into hogsheads, about 2500 to a barrel, and allowed another eight days for the last of the oil to drain away through a bung before being headed up. Apart from the labour, the cost for salt and other materials ran to about thirteen or fourteen shillings a hogshead, and in mid-September such a hogshead, weighing nearly five hundredweight, would sell for upwards of forty shillings. That was in normal times. In normal times a quarter of the total catch was exported to the Mediterranean. Now with the Mediterranean closed to English ships no one quite knew what would happen.

But it was a profit of a sort and food in plenty off the fish that did not reach the standard requirements. Among the crowd were many destitute people who waited for the end of the day. At dusk, when all was finished, the fishermen would give the last few hundred damaged fish away.

Sam noticed with satisfaction that Mary Tregirls and one of her children were working on stacking the pilchards. She would have money in her pocket now and would be able to lift the whole family, including the resentful Lobb, a little farther up from the pit of poverty in which he had last seen them.

Drake had gone over and was buying a sack of broken fish from one of the fishermen. With the bargaining went a great deal of banter, and Sam was pleased to see Drake laughing and joking as he had not done for a long time. Since his visit to Mrs Warleggan in Truro the persecutions had altogether ceased. No one disturbed him at his work, no one harried his customers, no one broke his fences down. It was a blessed relief. Against all Sam's expectations, the visit had served its purpose. Only the stream remained diverted by the farmer above him, and in this dry weather he was very short of water. But Sam had advised Drake to do nothing more. By careful husbanding of the well water, by the use and re-use of it, he could make do. A man was entitled to divert a stream.

With the last sun firing lances over the edge of the cliffs, the brothers turned up the valley for home, each carrying a sack. All around them people were murmuring and chatting, laughing and talking. Others were coming up and down the lane, most of them burdened in some way. Then Sam saw four people clattering down past the last of the better cottages, and the way was so narrow that it was impossible to avoid them. Tholly Tregirls, Emma Tregirls, Sally Tregothnan – or 'Chill-Off' – and Tom Harry. Tom Harry and Tholly carried jars of rum.

When they saw Sam and Drake Tom Harry said something that made them all laugh. The brothers would have passed on but Tholly stopped them with his hook held out.

'Ah, Peter, now, just the man I want. Just the man I need. Reckon ye're a fine upstanding lad, and would do well for what I have in mind.'

'Sam,' said Sam.

'Sam. There now, I've a memory like an addle-pipe. Put it in one end it comes out the other – '

'Drake Carne,' said Tom Harry, lurching up to Drake. 'What's gone amiss wi' your face, eh? Something scat your eyebrow, 'as it?' He looked at Emma for her approval, and she laughed, but it was not a free laugh. The sun scorched her hair with copper lights.

Behind the four were a half dozen other men, including Jack a Hoblyn, Paul Daniel and his cousin Ned Bottrell and one of the Curnow brothers. They had all been at Sally's and had decided to come and look at the pilchard scene before dark fell.

'Closed up!' shouted Widow Tregothnan to a woman looking out of a window. 'Shut up, see! Taking an hour off, see. Turned all these lob-lollies out afore they fell out!' She laughed heartily.

'Peter, now,' said Tholly. 'Sam, curse it. Sam, me boy. I'm in charge of the games at Sawle Feast, come Thursday week. You done some wrestling. Reckon ye could be a useful 'traction. Prize money! I'm organizing prize money 'n all. We got six lads taking part, and some from over St Ann's and the Breague brothers from Marasanvose. Does your baby brother wrastle, eh?'

'If so be as you mean me,' Drake said. 'The answer's no.'

'Only good at running away, aren't ee, boy?' Tom Harry said. 'Only sometimes you get catched and then ye get a cooting!'

'Leave off,' said Emma. 'Leave off, you stupid great lootal!' And she gave Tom a shove. 'How's my old preacher?' she said to Sam. 'Been prayin' much of late?'

'Every day,' said Sam. 'For you. And for all men. But specially for you.'

Sally Chill-Off laughed loudly again at this. She was a buxom, good-tempered woman of forty-five, and she had struck up a friendship with Emma. They were the same type. This had led to Emma being more in the company of her father, and she had learned to tolerate him.

''Ere, what d'ye mean?' Tom Harry said, pushing his face forward at Sam. 'Prayin' for she? I'll 'ave no snivelling prating Methody mooling away at his prayin' for no girl of mine! Look see here —'

'Give *over*!' said Emma again, pulling at him this time. She had had a drink or two and was as boisterous as Sally. 'I'm no girl of no one's — yet — and ye'd best mind it. Don't be so piffy, Tom. Tis a fine eve and we're going down see pilchards. Got a fine sackful, 'ave ee, Sam? Let's see.'

Sam opened his sack and various people peered in, laughing and jostling each other.

Ned Bottrell said: 'Char Nanfan got some this noon, but I b'lieve they're not so good as they. *Do* ee wrestle, Sam?'

Ned was the soberest and the steadiest of the group. He was a newly-saved member of Sam's flock and Sam had been much gratified by his conversion.

'Nay, not for these pretty many years,' Sam said. 'Scarce ever since —'

'Go on,' said Paul Daniel. 'I reckon I seen you once when I was over Blackwater. I mind that tow head of yourn. Brave ye were too. He wrestle, don't 'e, Drake?'

'Wager he've forgotten how,' said Emma, her eyes catching the light. 'All this praying for lost souls like me. Make a man tired, don't it, Sam?'

'What I had in mind,' shouted Tholly over the general noise. 'What I had in mind—' He was seized with a fit of coughing, during which he hunched his square shoulders and hawked horribly.

'There, there, my dear,' Sally Tregothnan said, slapping him cheerfully. 'There, there, my old lover-cock, spit'n out. You gulge your drink too fast, that's all that's wrong—'

'We put Tholly to organize the games,' Ned Bottrell said to Sam. 'He were champion wrestler once, afore he lost his arm. We reckon t'ave a fine spread. Tis for church, ye know. There's nought to say we should not rejoice, is there?'

'Nothing,' said Sam. 'So long as ye rejoice in the Lord, through work or through play. But the greatest joy of all, Ned, be in the salvation of the spirit through cleansing repentance—'

'Aye,' said Paul Daniel, a fallen convert, 'I seen you over to Blackwater. Twas four or five year agone. How old are ee, Sam?'

'Twenty-five—'

'Then ye'd be scarce more'n twenty when I seen ee. I reckon—'

'What I had in mind,' shouted Tholly between gasps, 'was t'ave a real 'nation feast day like there's never been not before. How 'bout you wrastling, Sam? And you, Drake. More the merrier. And you, Tom; and you, Ned. The more the—'

'I'm wrastling any'ow,' said Tom Harry, with a grim smirk. 'Wrastling wi' you too, aren't I, Emma?'

'Go on with you! That'll be the day—'

'We'd best be off,' said Sam to Drake. 'I have a class at sundown—'

' 'Ere,' said Tom, thrusting past Emma. ' 'Ow 'bout you, baby brother? You never learned to wrastle, eh? Scared to get yer breeches ploshy, eh? Scared you might get yer muggets pulled out, eh?'

'I'm scared of fighting you,' said Drake, 'when it's three to one.'

Tom, empurpled, made a sharp rush at Drake, but both Sam and Ned got in his way, and for a few seconds there was a lot of confusion and noise. As the entangled figures separated Tom could be heard shouting that he'd fight either of the

Carne meaders with one hand tied behind his back, and break them across his knee. The two women had become equally involved in the struggle, the only one taking absolutely no part being Drake, who stood exactly where he was in the centre of it all, his face composed and set.

After a while he found Tholly Tregirls peering into his face, the flattened nose and puckered scar making Tholly look like some masked performer representing evil at a Miracle play.

'No offence meant, young Carne. Our Tom's a bit hot, like, hot off the mark, like, but no offence. You like to wrastle on Thursday sennight, eh? Or race? You looks as if ye could race.'

'No,' said Drake. 'I'm not in a feasting mood.'

Tom Harry and Sam were staring at each other, Emma holding on to Harry's arm, though it was hard to tell if this were to restrain him or support herself.

Harry said: 'How 'bout you'n me fighting, eh? Wrastling. Fair and proper. If your baby brother don't like to wrastle, how 'bout you'n me. If you're so careful to keep me off baby brother.'

Drake said: 'If I fight you, jack, it won't be wrestling.'

'Nay, brother,' Sam said. 'Leave off this useless quarrelling. Twill do no good at all. But I shall hope even so that –'

'I'll fight any way you say!' Harry roared at Drake, baring his teeth. 'Fists, sticks, knives –'

'Hush, hush –' Emma had her fingers over his mouth. She squealed as he gave a playful bite at them. 'Why don't ee fight 'im, Sam, show who's master! Great lerrup! You nipped my fingers! Fight him, Sam! Wrestling, I mean, with a stickler 'n all. Fair and proper and on top of the board.'

'Come away, Drake,' said Sam, making a move up the hill.

Tom Harry was trying to wind his arms round Emma, but she gave him a hearty thrust to free herself, and he staggered back into Daniel, who cursed him for stepping on his foot.

'Right!' said Tholly. 'That's of it! Special match, eh? All on top of the board. A guinea for the winner. How's that, Sam? Guinea for your preaching house if ye win? See the –'

'I'll lay a shillun on Sam!' shouted Ned Bottrell, who before now had fallen foul of both Harry brothers. 'Even money.

Come on, Sam. We'd all be there to see he fought fair!'

'Yes, come on, Sam,' said Daniel. 'Make a change now, wouldn't it? Wrestling preacher!'

'Guinea the winner!' shouted Sally. 'Nay, I'll make it two guineas!'

The way being narrow and the movement up and down considerable, a crowd of about thirty had now gathered, and others began to press the match. Two motives combined in the enthusiasm: the first, a special challenge wrestling match with a bit of spite in it had a great appeal; the second, Tom Harry, for all his attempts to mix in village life, was second only to his brother in unpopularity, and *any* attempt to take him down a peg would be universally welcomed.

Sam, however, was having nothing of it. Smiling his grave thin smile, he told them that his way was no longer the way of violence, even if it was only the violence of sport. Let others have their games; the Lord had chosen him, however unworthy, to witness as in a glass the glory of God and to work early and late for the liberation of souls –

He was interrupted in this impromptu sermon by Emma, who had freed herself from Tom Harry's clutches and now stood right in front of Sam, her hair flowing loose, and shouted at him: 'What about *my* soul!'

Sam smiled at her, though his eyes were suddenly dark. '*Yours*, Emma? I just said I pray each night of my life for that.'

'A lot of good it do me,' said Emma, and there was a general laugh. 'I feel no betterer. Honest, Sam. What's wrong? Polish my soul every night, I do, shine it up bright as a door knob. Don't do no good at all.'

Everybody laughed again.

Sam said: 'Sister, you should come meetings. Then we would all pray together.'

'Mebbe I would,' she said, 'if you beat *him*!' She gestured at Harry with a thumb. Harry grimaced in the background.

'Sister,' Sam said. 'I'm sorry but tis no jesting matter. If my words could but reach your heart, twould be a different concern – '

'Oh,' said Emma. 'I thought you was serious. I thought you

wanted to save me.'

'I do. You know I do. Tis one of the dearest wishes –'

'All right,' she said, hands on hips. 'Fight this lerrup and beat him fair Thursday sennight and I'll *come* your meetings!'

There was a gust of laughter all round and a few cheers. Drake now took Sam's arm and tried to edge him away.

But in the midst of all the laughter two people were now on the edge of a deeper challenge.

'Serious?' said Sam.

Emma nodded. 'Serious.'

He said: 'The wine is speaking.'

'*I'm* speaking!' said Emma. 'Damme.'

''Ere,' said Tom Harry, coming into it. 'What do I get if *I* win? Marry me, will ee?'

'Maybe,' said Emma. 'Maybe not. That's your worry.'

'Come along, Sam,' said Drake. 'Come along.'

'Special match, eh?' shouted Tholly. 'Winner gets me daughter!'

There was another roar of laughter.

'How long?' said Sam.

'How long what?' asked Emma.

'How long will you attend meetings?'

'If you *win*. Think you'll *win*, do ee?'

'Maybe.'

'He 'asn't got a smell of a hope,' said Tom Harry. 'I'll break him in twain.'

'Not if I'm stickler ye won't,' said Tholly. 'If I'm stickler twill all be fair on top of the board. Fair wrastling or nothing.'

'Three months,' said Sam.

'Hey, come along!' said Emma. 'Three *months*! Tis a life sentence!'

'Not less,' said Sam. 'I could do no good for ee in less. Ye'd have to learn to pray.'

Emma laughed. 'Good cripes! I reckon I bit off more'n I can chew!'

'Chew away, maid!' shouted someone.

'Well,' said Sam. 'Twas your idea. If tis your wish now to withdraw, then I'll withdraw too.'

'No!' said Emma, temper flashing. 'Three months it be. But don't ee forget – you've got to *win* first, mind!'

'Hooray!' shouted Tholly. 'Now don't ee go away, Sam.
Don't ee go away, Tom. We got a match but we got to get the
details worked out!'

II

Fifteen rioters appeared in court at Bodmin. Five were found
not guilty of the charges brought against them and were discharged. Ten were found guilty and sentenced, three to terms
of imprisonment, four to be transported, and three to be
hanged. The news startled the villages; but presently it was
known that after the trial Lord de Dunstanville had had
private word with the judges and they had together agreed
that the execution of one only of the three might have
sufficient deterrent effect, so two had had their sentences
reduced to transportation — which in these days of war meant
impressment in the navy.

The two reprieved were William 'Rosie' Sampson and
William Barnes. The one left to die was John Hoskin of
Camborne, nicknamed Wildcat, for 'violently assaulting one,
Samuel Phillips, miller, and for stealing goods above the value
of 40s. In an outhouse belonging to a Dwelling House'. Hoskin
was the elder brother of Peter Hoskin, Sam's partner at Wheal
Grace, and Sam remembered the last time he had visited the
Hoskin family with messages for Peter, and John Hoskin and
'Rosie' Sampson had come in flushed and excited from a
protest meeting. So now it had brought them to this.

That week Ross rode over to see Baron de Dunstanville.
There were two or three things on his mind, and he arranged
to arrive about five when he knew Basset was often in his
study seeing to estate business. But today he was shown into
a dining-room where dinner was not quite over, although the
ladies had left. Six men were there, two strangers, two he knew
slightly, and Basset himself and George Warleggan. They had
all drunk well, and Ross reluctantly allowed himself to be
persuaded into one of the seats vacated by the ladies and to
accept a glass of brandy, and was introduced to the rest of
the company. They were men from up-country, and it took
a few minutes for him to realize that this was a meeting of
the Members of Parliament whom Basset effectively controlled: Thomas Wallace and William Meeks, Members for

Penryn, Matthew Montagu and the Hon. Robert Stewart for Tregony, and George for Truro. It fell into place when Basset told him that Pitt had dissolved Parliament and that there was to be an election in September.

George had not looked at Ross after the first cold bow, nor Ross at George, but conversation continued on a parliamentary level undeterred by Ross's presence. It seemed that great efforts were being made to bring Pitt down, and after years in office he wanted his majority and policy confirmed by a vote of confidence from the country. Although many of the Whig nobles had repudiated Fox and supported the government – as did Basset – there was sufficient opposition and war fatigue to make Pitt's position difficult to sustain. Indeed, there was strong feeling within the nation that the war now never *could* be won, what with the armed forces still on the edge of mutiny, parts of the country near starvation, the exchequer bankrupt and the whole of Europe ranged against them. To all this Pitt had answered: 'I am not afraid for England. We shall stand till the Day of Judgement.' But he looked a grey, tired man.

Presently Ross said: 'What of his Bill to relieve and help the poor? How has that fared?'

Basset looked puzzled, as if for a moment he could not recall the measure, and George secretly smiled. 'You mean . . .'

'A fund for pensions for old people, parish loans to enable poor people to buy a cow. Schools of Industry . . .'

'Oh . . . It is finished. It was withdrawn for amendment and is never likely to be re-introduced. It met with great opposition.'

'From whom?'

'Oh, most people in authority, I believe. Particularly the magistrates. It was a well-meant but ill-conceived Bill which would have ruined public morals. Mr Jeremy Bentham argued cogently against it, as did most men experienced in law.'

'Perhaps they were not sufficiently experienced in compassion.'

Basset raised his eyebrows. 'I do not think compassion or lack of it was the essence of the objection. But in any event the financial crisis of this year rendered it impractical. Taxes and rates are already a sufficiently alarming burden. The prime objective now is to win the war.'

Ross put his empty glass back on the littered table. 'I should have thought that measure one of the most positive in helping to win the war – by preventing disaffection at home.'

'We have our ways of preventing disaffection at home,' George commented.

Shortly afterwards the dinner broke up and they walked out on the terrace. Lady Basset and whatever other ladies had been present did not reappear. Ross would have made his excuses and left if it had not been apparent that the other guests were about to do the same. George began to talk, rather expansively for him, of plays he had seen in London, of Mr Kemble and Mrs Jordan, of the private theatres of Westminster and of the amateur theatricals that took place there. It was all, Ross suspected, largely for his benefit. Then, as they were leaving, George said to him:

'Oh, Ross, I learn that your brother-in-law is taking part in a wrestling contest with one of my gamekeepers.'

Ross's eyes were not raised from their gaze over the greenery of the park. 'I believe so.'

'Incautious of him, to say the least. Tom Harry is a champion and has taken many prizes.'

'I should have thought from his stomach he was past his best.'

'I do not suspect your brother-in-law will find him so.'

'It remains to be seen.'

The others looked mildly enquiring at this, so Ross explained that the local feast day was next week, and, some challenge having been issued, Sam Carne, a miner and his brother-in-law (as Mr Warleggan had pointed out), and Tom Harry, a gamekeeper, had agreed to a match, the winner to be for the best of three falls. The four other Members of Parliament, being none of them Cornish, had to have something of the method of the wrestling explained to them, and the general procedure that surrounded it. Wallace fancied he had seen something like it in London and had to be persuaded otherwise.

In the middle of this George said to Ross: 'So you think your Methody brother-in-law has a chance of victory?'

Ross at last looked at him. 'I hope so. It is time your gamekeeper was taught to behave.'

'Perhaps you would like to lay some money on the contest.'

'One which you consider so unequal?'

'If you think different, back your opinion with a few guineas.'

The others were all listening, half amused, half serious, conscious of the bite in the conversation. De Dunstanville was taking snuff and frowning.

'What do you suggest?'

'A hundred?'

For a moment Ross looked over the gardens again. 'I accept – on one condition.'

'Ah! . . .'

'That whoever loses shall pay the money to my Lord, here, to dispose of in some charitable way for the benefit of the miners.'

'Pray let us settle on that,' Basset said quickly, dusting his nose with his handkerchief. 'It shall be given towards the new hospital.' He sneezed. 'A first contribution!'

Neither man could openly quarrel with Basset's quick solution, so the bargain was made. General conversation went on for ten minutes or so, George and Ross exchanging no further words, and then one by one the others took their leave until only the local trio were left. Then reluctantly George asked for his horse and galloped away.

Basset watched him go and said: 'My displeasure at your neighbourly spite has no effect in lessening it; but on this occasion it seems that I shall be the benefactor.'

'To the satisfaction of neither party to the wager,' Ross said. 'Why not?'

'George, if he won, would not want his winnings to go to *any* charity. I, if I won, had looked for some more direct and immediate aid for the miners than a hospital not yet built.'

Basset smiled. 'A mercy that I out-generaled you both.'

'I suspect that the guineas will come from me, but, who knows, the unexpected may happen.'

'If it is to be an unequal contest it were a sharp practice on his part to force you into this wager.'

'Happily, as you say, the miners will benefit, though at a far remove. It's a better outcome than our labours of three weeks ago.'

De Dunstanville's lips tightened. 'They are both aspects of the same objective. To reward and help the deserving, to curb and quell those who take the law into their own hands.'

A few rare clouds were obscuring the sun but it was still warm, and the gentle breeze wafted the scent of roses from the garden below the terrace.

'In principle,' Ross said, 'I agree that that is the desirable aim. In practice – in this particular case – I wonder if any real purpose will be served by the death of one man?'

'Hoskin? Oh, it has all been decided. As you will know, we considered the matter most carefully after the trial, and two men were reprieved. This decision was only arrived at as a result of the most careful weighing of the facts, and it was concluded that justice could be tempered with mercy and that an example need only be made of the most vicious and the most profligate of the three.'

'Yes . . .' said Ross. 'Yes . . .'

Basset said : 'It is a misfortune for the good name of British justice that the crime for which a man is actually sentenced is often only an insignificant part of his misdemeanours. Officially Hoskin goes to his death for entering a dwelling house and stealing corn to a value in excess of 40s. But in fact he has been known for years as a malcontent and has been in and out of trouble all his life. His nickname of Wildcat is not unmerited.'

'Perhaps I should indicate my interest,' Ross said. 'John Hoskin has a brother Peter who works in my mine. Peter says that his brother, though a little hot-tempered and by no means of a blameless disposition, has yet never had any great malefaction in him. It may be that a brother's estimate is not unbiased, but I think it's often true in these cases of riot and commotion that the noisiest is not the worst. However – ' He paused as Basset seemed about to interrupt him.

'Go on.'

'I was about to say that I have a more selfish interest in his fate than that – namely a wish to sleep easy in my bed of nights.'

'How does it affect you?'

'It happened that I was in charge of the constables who went to the Hoskin cottage.'

Lady de Dunstanville came out on the terrace, but her husband waved her away.

'My dear Poldark, it is gratuitous of you to take this personally! How do you think *I* feel? The matter of sentence or pardon was laid quite unfairly on my shoulders at Bodmin. It was a most disagreeable decision I had to come to! Indeed, the whole affair has been a worry and concern to me that has done *my* sleep no good, I assure you! If –'

'Why not, then, let us both command an easier conscience?'

'How?'

'By initiating a petition for Hoskin's reprieve. We still have five days. A movement begun from the top is the only one which could have due effect. There is ample time. Many a man has been reprieved at the foot of the scaffold.'

They continued to stare at each other. Basset's lips tightened again but he did not speak.

Ross said: 'It's a difficult time to be merciful, I know. Men have recently been hanged for mutiny in the navy – and rightly so. Men like their ringleader Parker, while prating of freedom, would be the first to impose a rigid rule more onerous than the one they seek to overthrow. But the earlier mutinies were mutinies against unbearable conditions, and the Admiralty, who have been so stupid over so many things, had the wisdom to treat the early mutineers lightly. This riot – these riots in Cornwall, I believe, have nothing of the later type of mutiny in them and everything of the earlier. Empty bellies and dead fires and sick wives and wasting children are powerful advocates of unlawful riot. I do not believe Sampson or Barnes or Hoskin are anything but willing to abide by the law of the land. Their grievance is not against you or against me or against such others as are put in authority. Their grievance is against merchants and millers who grow fat in trade while the majority starve. To reprieve the one condemned man now would be no sign of weakness but would convince everyone that justice had been better served.'

Basset had turned away, and it was as if he had turned not merely his face but his mind away from the arguments that had been put to him.

He said: 'You talk of these men being patriotic, Poldark. Did you know that last month a Patriotick Club was formed in Camborne? Its members are all young men, I understand, and all wear buttons they have obtained directly from France engraved with the words *Liberty* and *Equality*. They have a song which they sing which praises the Revolution and all that it stands for. Mind that, *all* that it stands for, in perfidy and tyranny and bloodshed. Moreover, any French victory on land or sea is hailed with acclaim, any English one with disgust. Nor are they content to keep their views to themselves! They go out among the miners, among the poor, spreading their gospel of sedition and unrest. I happen to know that they were in touch with the leaders of this riot. Were no such clubs, no such people in existence, who knows what might be done . . . Not now.'

The sky was darkening. Instead of dispersing as they had often done this summer, the clouds were gathering and looked like rain.

Ross said: 'I respect your view, my Lord. Things have come to such a pretty pass that no one can say with any certainty which is the right or the wrong attitude to take. But what – surely what created the revolution in France was the degrading poverty of ordinary people compared with a licentious court and a weak government which was also a cruelly severe one. Here we now have conditions of poverty and distress scarcely more favourable than in the France of 1789. This is why Pitt's Bill looked such a beacon of hope, and why it is, in my view, such a tragedy that it should have been withdrawn. But in any event our government is not weak. Need it – is it even politic – that it should seem severe?'

'We have not been severe in condemning one man. We have been merciful in reprieving two.'

'It's a way of looking at it.'

Basset was becoming nettled. 'Do you consider yourself in a position to pass judgement on the judges?'

'The last thing I feel entitled to do is pass judgement on anyone. That is what would have made me such a poor magistrate. But it is not judgement as such I am thinking of. It is clemency – in the narrowest sense – and wisdom – in a wider.'

Basset pursed his lips. 'Who was it said – some great justiciar, I believe – that all men who are engaged in judgement upon others should be devoid of anger, of friendship, of hatred, and of soft-heartedness. That is what, in my way, I try to be. I am sorry you find me lacking.'

'I did not say that—'

Basset said: 'I'm sure you speak from conviction. You know I do. We must differ . . . Ah, my dear, come and join us. Captain Poldark is just leaving.'

CHAPTER III

On his way home Ross caught sight of Sam Carne doing something in the cramped little chapel near Wheal Maiden, so he got off his horse and went in. Sam was alone, and Ross was able to tell him that any reprieve for John Hoskin was now unlikely.

Sam said: 'Thank ee, brother. Twas very brave of ee to try. I did not know you was going to try. I'll tell Peter tomorrow. But I think he know tes likely that his brother will hang.'

Ross glanced at Sam, a little surprised at his resigned tone. Life and death were cheap in the mining districts, and especially so to Sam who spent so much of his spare time helping the sick.

Sam said: 'Peter wish to go, and I shall go along of him.'

'With him? Where? To Bodmin?'

'Yes. At first I tried to tell him no, but really tis right that John's family should be there.'

'But why you? You're not of the family.'

'Peter is my partner, and I shouldn't wish for him to walk all that way there and back alone.'

'What of his parents?'

'Peter's mother and father will be there day before, hoping see him. The others will make their way separate.'

Ross glanced round the bare little meeting house with its forms and primitive chairs, and its bible on the table by the window.

'It's to be Tuesday. Do not forget you have a wrestling

match on Thursday.'

'No,' said Sam. 'I haven't forgot.'

'D'you think you will win?'

'I don't rightly know. I'm more used to wrestling with the spirit within us.'

'How much did you ever do?'

'A fair lot. But I haven't been in a ring, not since I were reconciled with God.'

'Would you not be well advised to get some practice?'

Sam smiled. 'Thank ee, brother, but where would I get it?'

'I could try you with a few falls.'

'You used to wrestle?'

'Oh, yes.'

Sam considered their respective situations. 'I do not believe twould be seemly.'

'Let me be the judge of that.'

'Well, thank ee, brother, maybe twould be of assistance to me. I'll think on it.'

'Think on it soon. You have a few days only.'

When Ross got home he told Demelza the result of his visit to Tehidy.

'It's not to be wondered at,' she said. 'And he won't thank you for going, Ross. He thought he was being generous pardoning two, and it will not please him to be thought harsh after all.'

'Everyone,' Ross said, 'seems a little less concerned than I do. Am I more tender-hearted for others or only tender because of my own conscience?'

'We are not – untender,' she said. 'Not so. But maybe we are more – resigned. When a man is condemned to death we accept it, though it's sad to do so. We know we cannot change it. You hoped to change it – so it's more of a – a disappointment. You feel you have failed. We don't feel *that* because we never hoped to succeed.'

Ross poured himself a stiff brandy. 'I am less and less enamoured of my own part in the affair. It was ill done. And less and less happy at thinking I am fighting the French by commanding a troop of Volunteers. If the French come, well and fine, we may make some good use of ourselves. But if the French do not come we are more likely to be used to put down insurrection here!'

'Are you in favour of insurrection, then?'

He made an impatient gesture. 'How can I expect you to understand when I cannot clearly explain it to myself? My loyalties are hopelessly at cross-purposes one with another.'

'Sometimes mine are too,' said Demelza from the heart.

'And George becomes more impossible every time I meet him! A year or so ago I felt that our enmity was on the wane. Each year we got older and a little more tolerant, and it seemed to me that, so long as we avoided each other, our indifference would gradually improve.'

'Isn't that the trouble?'

'What?'

'Well, since you started knowing Lord de Dunstanville better it hasn't been quite so easy to avoid each other.'

Ross finished his brandy and poured another one. 'It is possible I shall be seeing less of de Dunstanville in the future. That certainly would be my choice.'

'Can I have one?'

He looked up. 'I'm sorry, my dear. I thought you preferred port.'

'Port is for parties,' said Demelza. 'And when I've had one I badly want more. I don't very much favour the taste of brandy, so it does no harm.'

He got her a glass and poured some for her. 'It's odd that by refusing Basset's offer to fight Truro I have seen more of George – and a very bumptious George – than I would otherwise ever have done. Perhaps,' he added satirically, 'I should have become a Member of Parliament just to have seen less of him!'

Demelza made a face over the brandy. 'Would not your loyalties have been even more at cross-purposes then?'

He looked at her, a little nettled that she had taken his sarcasm seriously. 'You told me before that you think I would make a bad Member.'

'I didn't say *bad*,' she said. 'Uneasy.'

'Well, I am uneasy now and have to live with it. You have

to live with it too.'

'Do not tear yourself apart, Ross. You can't re-make the world.'

'You should say that to your brother, who thinks to redeem us all.'

She sipped again, thoughtful, herself on edge. 'Yet *he* isn't uneasy. It's a difference in a person. He seem to have few doubts.'

'I wish he had not chosen to try to redeem George's game-keeper by wrestling with him. I'm committed to a hundred guineas on the result.'

'Judas! How did that happen?'

Ross told her.

'It's not of course Tom Harry that Sam is trying to redeem,' said Demelza.

'No, so I gather. Did you ever see Sam wrestle?'

'No, he was too young when I left home. Eleven or twelve. But I hope now he win, if only to save our money!'

'I hope he wins to spite George. And in any event Tom Harry is a loustering oaf. Sam seems to have no idea that he should make any sort of preparation for this event, so I have told him to take a few falls with me over the next days.'

'Ross! You cannot!'

'Why not?'

'When was the last time you wrestled?'

'You should know. When I threw your father through that window some while ago.'

'Some *while* ago! Thirteen years! It's impossible, my love, you would injure yourself!'

Ross came as near as he could to a sneer. 'You don't think of injuries to Sam.'

'Well, he's almost a boy! And he don't matter so much to me. No, you must *not*. Promise me you will not!'

'I cannot for I have promised him.'

Demelza went across and helped herself to a second tot of the drink she didn't like. 'Dear life, I don't know what to do with you: you're *always* in trouble. Ross, don't think I'm trying to coddle you, it is not that at all, you are fit and strong and have put on no weight, but have a thought, please, for the knowledge that you were about Sam's age when you fought Father, and now are no longer so young.'

'I am about your father's age when he fought me, and he was not easy to overcome. I am just the right sort of opposition for Sam.'

'I wish you would go and fight Tom Harry yourself!' Demelza exclaimed in vexation. 'Then you'd be happy, and I could nurse your broken bones in a better cause!'

'Perhaps,' said Ross, 'we could have a father's contest to follow between George and myself. That really would be worth a few broken bones.'

Demelza gulped her drink. 'Well, look, now we have another small problem. Today Caroline called.'

'Is that a problem? How is she?'

'Better. It was some stomach ailment. She stayed about an hour.'

Ross waited. He was aware now that something of importance to Demelza was afoot and that she had been wanting to speak of it ever since he came home and that she was nervous about it.

'So?'

'Hugh Armitage is sick, and Lord Falmouth has written to Dwight asking him to make an examination. So he is going tomorrow and Caroline is going with him and they are dining there.'

'I'm sorry to hear it, but how does it immediately affect us?'

'Well, Hugh enclosed a note to Caroline asking if she could persuade us – that is you and me – to accompany them. He says he has a special wish to see us both again if – if we're not circumstanced with prior engagements – that's how he put it. He says, can we not ride with the Enyses?'

'I see.'

'Caroline and Dwight are leaving at ten tomorrow so that he can make his examination before dinner, and they should be back by six.'

A page of the *Sherborne Mercury* crackled as Ross turned it over.

'And what did you say?'

'I said I would ask you and leave her know.'

'What is wrong with Hugh? Is it his eyes?'

'Not that altogether. But he's much troubled with headaches and a low fever.'

Ross stared at the close-printed newspaper. 'I'm afraid we cannot go. I've meetings with Henshawe; and Bull is coming over. In any event I don't want to go. My last meeting with George Falmouth was not of the easiest, and he expressly disobliged me by ignoring my request to put in a good word for Odgers.'

Demelza set down her glass and sucked one of her fingers. 'Very well then. But I think I should send word to Caroline tonight. It would be more – polite.'

'*How* have you left it?'

'I said I would send a note if we were not going. Perhaps it doesn't matter.'

Ross hesitated, struggled with himself. 'I suppose you could go.'

She looked at him and blinked. 'How could I go without you? It would hardly be seemly.'

'There'd be nothing unseemly if you went with Dwight and Caroline. I suspect it is you that Armitage really wants to see again.'

Demelza shook her head. 'I don't know. I don't know that I could go just with them.'

'Well, I see no reason, but it's for you to decide.'

'No, Ross . . . really it's for you to decide, not me. I don't – I don't know what to say.'

'Well,' he made an impatient gesture. 'If I tell you to go it may be incautious on my part. If I tell you not to go it will be unfeeling.'

'It need not be. I can well make some excuse. They would understand. But why would it be incautious of you to tell me to go?'

'I do not know how far your feelings have become involved.'

Demelza stared soberly out of the window. The summer sunburn had tinted her pale skin. 'I don't know myself, Ross, and that is the honest truth. I only know . . .'

'Yes?'

'His feelings for me.'

'And that matters?'

'It *matters*. How can it help but? . . . If he's *really* ill, then it seems – perhaps there is reason to go. But I am your wife, Ross, to the – the last day. No other.'

After a moment Ross said: 'There's not really room for two men in a woman's heart, is there? Not in the way that counts.'

Demelza said: 'Or room for two women in a man's?'

'What makes you say that?'

'Isn't it reasonable to ask?'

They were on the brink then of much more; but Jeremy's arrival, flinging back the door and rushing into the room with some plan he had for Sawle Feast day, cut it off short. Nor was anything more said until they were in bed that night, and by then the tension between them, while not disappearing, had eased.

Ross said: 'You haven't sent word to Caroline?'

'No. I didn't know what to say.'

'I think you should go. Why ever not? If I cannot trust you now, when could I ever?'

Demelza winced. 'Thank you, Ross. I shall be – be well chaperoned. Caroline is not of a mind to let me stray.'

'Be not of a mind yourself. As you know, I think well of Hugh, and can hardly dislike him for admiring you – as long as that is all. No man wants his wife to be a woman that other men don't desire.'

'No, Ross.'

'But every man wants his wife to be a woman that other men don't get. Remember that, will you?'

'Yes, Ross.'

'I trust Dwight will be of aid to him. I shall hope for good news.'

'Jane can see for your dinner, I suppose,' Demelza said, still doubtful, though not altogether for the right reasons.

'She has before. Bull will share it with me, by the way.'

'There is that special pie I made. Don't forget that.'

Silence fell. The evenings had drawn in and the luminous lights of June had left the sky.

'On that question that you put to me before Jeremy exploded on us,' he said suddenly.

'Which one?'

'Is there room for two women in a man's heart? The answer is no – not in the exclusive way I meant it. I never told you . . . a year or so ago I was up at Sawle Church about Agatha's stone and I met Elizabeth returning from the Odgers'. I walked as far as Trenwith with her and we talked of things.'

'What things?'

'No matter. What we talked of doesn't affect what I have to say now. It was the first time I'd seen her alone since – well, for years. I think at the end of the meeting we had come a little nearer accord than since – since she married George. She's still a beautiful creature, a woman of a sweet nature, kind and honest and far too good for that fellow she has married. I say all this to you deliberately for it is my view of her.'

'I'm pleased to hear it.'

'No, you are not; but no matter. What I want to say is I came away from that meeting with the renewed conviction that she no longer meant anything to me – that is, in the way you do. I loved her once – as you know too well – and idealized her. I shall always think of her with admiration and affection. But . . . she won't ever be central to me as you are – preoccupying, all-important, indispensable, both as a person and a woman . . .'

He was aware as he spoke that he had hesitated too long to say this and now had chosen the worst possible moment, when there was a half-animosity stirring between them. The circumstances of her affection for Hugh Armitage left him off balance, and his suppressed resentment had made him say the true, the reassuring things in a stiff manner that made them sound pompous and without warmth. It seemed like the beginning of a repeat of that Christmas Eve when, in trying to tell her much the same thing, he had touched off such a spring of perversity in her that she had turned all his reasonings upside down and inside out, every kindness into a condescension, every compliment into an insult, every proof a disproof and every assertion an assertion of its opposite. He had never known such gifted malevolence. Now he waited angrily for its return.

But instead she sighed and said in a muffled voice: 'Oh, Ross, it is a strange world.'

'I'd not argue with that.'

'Words never say quite what we want them to say, do they?'

'Mine certainly never do. I'm glad you appreciate it.'

'No, I didn't mean that. Not *you* – not just what you say – but all. Everyone. And even where there is love there is misunderstanding. We try to speak to each other like through a glass, all of us. But think you, Ross . . . How can I answer what you've just said?'

'Can you not?'

'Not quite. I think to speak now wouldn't help – it would – it might create more misdeeming than it cleared away.'

'On whose side?'

'Maybe on both . . . My dear, I have no reply just at present. D'you mind?'

'Should I?'

'I think I must lie quiet,' she said. 'I feel rather alone.'

He put his hand on her hair and felt it between his fingers. So the battle was not to be. His explanation of his own feelings was to be accepted without question. Even his meeting with Elizabeth. It was good that she took this attitude. But how good? And for what reason? He felt, perhaps illogically, no happier for her quiet reply. It seemed to him that it boded less well for their marriage than an outburst would have done.

II

They were at Tregothnan at twelve, and were greeted at the door by Lieutenant Armitage looking no different at all. He kissed Demelza's hand and stared searchingly and lovingly into her face with eyes that seemed to have no shadow on them. He dismissed his recent illness lightly and said he was quite better and that it had all been a ruse on his part to entice them over to relieve the monotony of civilian life. Lord Falmouth did not appear, and while Dwight and Hugh went upstairs to his bedroom the girls were left to be entertained by Mrs Gower and her own three children, who showed them a walk down to the river and a view of the tall ships anchored in the pool.

At dinner Lord Falmouth joined them, accompanied by

Frances Gower's husband, Captain the Hon. John Leveson Gower, who was the other Member for Truro and who, because of the electoral upset of last year, had been the uneasy yoke-fellow of George Warleggan since. Not that they had apparently seen much of each other except in the House, and that little had been unfavourable. Anything else was hardly to be expected, though the policies of the two gentlemen had seldom been greatly at odds. No mention was made for a while about the medical enquiry which had been going on upstairs until Lord Falmouth said:

'I trust you're going to have my nephew back in perfect health by the time of the election, Dr Enys. I need a young and vigorous candidate to support my brother-in-law and bring the constituency back to its proper interest.'

Dwight's thin face showed no positive expression. 'Perfect health, my Lord, is hard for any of us to attain and I don't think Hugh is likely to achieve it. We must make do with second best, which I hope will be good enough for the electors of Truro.'

'I am not sure whether anything will be good enough for the electors of Truro,' said Captain Gower. 'With de Dunstanville drawing so much water I'm more likely to lose my seat than Hugh gain his. Have you heard yet who they are putting up to link with Warleggan?'

'Henry Thomas Trengrouse, I believe.'

'He'll be a popular candidate and has the advantage of being well known in the town.'

Caroline said: 'To think that I near wed a Member of Parliament once. If I have to belong to a two-Member constituency I believe I prefer my partner to be a doctor.'

There was a laugh.

'I do not know how Hugh will take to a parliamentary life after a life at sea,' said Mrs Gower, 'even if he's lucky enough to attain it.'

'I'm lucky enough to have attained a lot,' said Hugh, glancing at Demelza. 'I shall make the best now of whatever is in store.'

Demelza said, cutting across any possible implications in the remark: 'Why do you not make it up with Lord de Dunstanville, Lord Falmouth? Could not a – a friendship be come to instead of all this rivalry?'

Falmouth looked at her in some surprise, not altogether pleased, as if politics were not for serious discussion with women.

Gower said: 'It would be a good thing if it were possible, ma'am. Unfortunately the thrusting new peer is bent on his own arrogant schemes and has the money to indulge them.'

'Nor would I compromise with such as he,' said Falmouth shortly.

'Well, he said to me only this spring,' said Demelza, a little short of breath. 'Lord de Dunstanville said to me only this spring that he would be quite willing, he said, to come to an accommodation with your – your Lordship over control of the Cornish seats.'

'The devil he did?' said Hugh. 'When was this?'

'They came to dinner with us. Walking on the cliff after, he said that his – that the situation had changed since he became a peer and that he had no wish to – continue the battle, he said.'

There was silence while the company digested more than their meal.

Falmouth said impatiently: 'Oh, the man was talking! He was always a big talker. We meet – or pass each other by – now and again in London. My cousin serves with him in the Fencibles. If he wished to make any move towards compromise he has ample opportunity of doing so, without . . .'

'Without passing on his opinions through a lady,' Caroline said. 'That was what you meant, wasn't it? But it's precisely because he did not suppose his opinions would ever be passed on that he was so frank with Mrs Poldark. With all your prejudice against women you have to see that!'

Good-humouredly, since it was difficult to be anything but good-humoured with Caroline, Lord Falmouth began to protest the complete absence in him of any such prejudice; but conversation at the table did not end there. After all, the feud, the contest over this seat and that, had been going on for years; it had cost a great deal of money and had consumed time and labour. Gower summed it up by saying:

'Well, George, for my part I would be glad to see some sort of an electoral agreement. It is essential for my career in the

Admiralty that I should not be unseated now, and although no doubt another seat could be found it would be deuced difficult to go looking for one. Why do you not let it be known that you too would be willing to come to some sort of accommodation?'

'And what sort do you imagine he would propose?' Falmouth said. 'Not even a *quid pro quo* would satisfy him! He would want two seats for one!'

'It might be worth discovering what his exact thoughts were.'

'And risk a rebuff? Besides, there is no one who would act as a mediator.'

'I would do so,' said Hugh.

'How could you? As a prospective candidate your position would be at once suspect.'

'Hugh is not fit to go out yet,' said Dwight. 'Nor is likely to be for another two weeks.'

'Oh, rubbish, I'm not going to fight a dragon –'

'Who knows? – '

'Wait,' said Caroline, and because she said so they did wait. The sunflower was blooming again today. 'I am much against mediators – they misunderstand inflections of the voice and garble messages – besides the time is short. My Lord, are you too proud to dine with Dwight and me?'

'Proud?' said Falmouth stiffly.

'Well, our acreage is extensive but our house is in disrepair. Since I married I have been so concerned with looking after a husband who was in some disrepair himself that the house has hardly been touched yet. But we eat normal food and our cook is modestly competent. Come to dinner one day next week.'

'With what purpose?'

'Do not ask the purpose and then you will not need to refuse.'

'You are too kind, ma'am. But it would be – '

'Uncle,' said Hugh, 'I think you should go. What is there to lose? Not even face, for if the meeting fails no one else would know.'

'Everyone would know,' said Falmouth. 'No secrets of any sort are possible in this county!'

'I think, my Lord,' said Caroline, showing rare tact for her, 'that we are pressing you unduly. Let us say no more now. But towards the end of the week I will send my man to you with an invitation, and it shall be left entirely open to you at the time whether you accept or not.'

'An excellent idea,' said Mrs Gower. 'Now, ladies, perhaps we should leave the gentlemen to their port . . .'

III

'Well?' said Demelza, as they left the house behind.

'The fever has not been severe,' said Dwight, 'and if that were all I should say there was small cause for concern. But the fever is symptomatic of some other condition, as is the pain, the headache. I have given him a paregoric to take sparingly and some salt of wormwood and Peruvian bark. It should help to prevent a nightly return of the fever, but, if there is some other underlying cause, it will not cure. We may know more in two or three weeks.'

'And his eyes?'

Dwight held his reins carefully while they went over a rough piece of track. 'No cataract. Or none that I can see. I think there is something behind the eye but it's impossible to say what. A blood vessel damaged, a nerve losing its optic power.'

'You think then – you agree with the London doctors?'

'I cannot disagree with them. But in such matters we're still so ignorant. I think they were at fault in telling him.'

'Why? Why should they not?'

'Because in Quimper I so often saw men triumph over disease by the sheer determination to live. I believe the mind governs the health more than we know, and it helps no one to be told an absolute when the absolute is never true until it happens.'

Caroline edged up to them. 'Did Lord Falmouth ask you about Hugh?'

'Of course. I could tell him little for I know little. I did not discourage him in the belief that Hugh would be fit to enter parliament. He may still be. He's young. One eye is better than the other. If it doesn't deteriorate further he will be able to manage well enough with a glass.'

Demelza shivered. 'As yet – as yet you can't tell.'

'We must get him into parliament,' said Caroline. 'It will give him more to think of and more to do.'

They rode on towards the ferry.

CHAPTER IV

Sam Carne and Peter Hoskin left Reath Cottage soon after dusk on the Monday. They had packed bread and cheese and each took a skin of water. They cut across country through Marasanvose and Treledra to St Michael, and joined the coach road from Truro to Bodmin. Sam had never been this way before and Peter but once, so it was easy enough to lose your way in the starlight. They both carried strong sticks, but there was little enough about them to tempt the footpad or the roving cutpurse. They skirted St Enoder, and a single candle in a window in Indian Queen Inn winked and shone and appeared and disappeared like Eddystone miles before they reached it. Here they sat for half an hour, eating some of their bread and cheese, not talking much.

Sam had little sympathy with the riots for which John Hoskin was to be executed. The law to him was the law, and one worked within it for the betterment of mankind and for the souls of all men. However cold and desolate for lack of work, however empty one's belly, one did not assemble and use threatening behaviour, still less seize the smallest piece of property belonging to someone else. If one assembled it was to transmit from one to another the priceless cleansing gift of the Holy Spirit. But, though he could not condone the offence, he felt deep pity for the offender, especially that he should be going to die without any light in his soul. And he felt more pity for the wife and children, and his warming if silent sympathy went out to his partner with whom he was altogether willing to keep company on this twenty-four-mile trek.

They set off again across the moors, and by the time they reached the wooded valley of Lanivet there was a lightening of the sky ahead of them, and a faint drizzle was falling.

'I 'ope twill be fine,' said Peter Hoskin. 'Brother 'as a rare misliking for the rain.'

After a day's work and a night's walk they were tired, and the climb up the hill to Bodmin was a long pull. It was full day before they came to the first street, which was a rutted way between a few huts with dogs rooting in the dust and some offal hanging from a butcher's hook and already beginning to stink. They found an alehouse and ate the rest of the food they had brought, Peter drinking a mug of burnt ale and Sam finishing his water. Then they went to find John's wife and two children and a half dozen others who were waiting outside the jail. John's mother had come, and his next nearest relatives were allowed into the prison to see him.

Sam wandered off up the hill towards the common where the execution was to take place.

A crowd had already gathered, some three or four hundred, drawn from the town and the villages round. The gibbet had been erected and the platform, and one workman was still lazily knocking nails into a supporting prop, pausing for a chat with his neighbours between each nail. Opposite the gibbet was a small stand where the gentry could pay for admission and sit in comfort to watch the ceremony. This was almost empty, but while Sam waited a number of carriages arrived and well-dressed people were escorted through the crowd to take their seats. About half of them were women. In favoured positions near the gallows were two parties of school children who had been brought by their masters and mistresses for the salutary effect the ceremony would have on their minds. To gain a good position they had been assembled before dawn.

Many of those who waited, squatted or sat or lay upon the black heather of the common; vendors moved among them selling pies and cakes and lemonade. Some diced to pass the time. Two groups sang; one lot drunken and bawdy, the other sober and religious. Here and there men and women lay together too close to be respectable, the women with coarse laughs and painted faces. Dogs barked and horses neighed and children shrieked and men shouted. More people drifted up. The sun was shining brilliantly now, but over towards the sea a great cloud lay, as black as the wrath of God.

Some way away in the distance the prison clock began to
strike nine. By the time it had finished an expectant silence
had fallen on the crowd. For a few moments after it had
stopped the only sound was the stirring of the wind. Then the
prison bell began to toll, and people got up from where they
had been sitting and pushed forward into a tight mass around
the gibbet.

For a while nothing happened; people breathed and elbowed
against each other.

'False alarm,' said one woman to Sam, with a giggle.

'Giss along,' said another. 'Great fradge.'

'Mebbe tes a reprieve,' a man near said. 'My uncle d'say a
man 'e knew were cut daown just after he bin strung up.
Reprieve come . . .'

'Nay . . . not wi' the bell tolling . . .'

Although the day was cool, it was hot and smelly in the
crowd. Sam thought: all these souls unsaved, all deep in the
carnal pit of unholiness. So many to care for, so many to lead
to penitence and redemption. If the Spirit would but move
among them as it had done at Gwennap two years ago . . .

'Yur they be!'

A procession was winding its way up the slope. The chief
jailer was in the lead followed by four others. Then came the
cart bearing the chaplain, the condemned man, the executioner
and two other guards. After that six more guards on foot
preceded the governor's coach, in which sat the governor and
the sheriff. Following the coach on foot were the wand bearers,
the gaol surgeon and his assistant; then the six chief mourners,
with a motley crowd trailing behind of some fifty-odd sight-
seers who had waited at the jail. The prisoner, short and
stocky and in his mid-twenties, looked very little changed from
when Sam had last seen him at the Hoskin cottage, hot from
the success of his protest meeting.

The guards cleared a way for the procession, and the cart,
an old one with rasping wooden wheels, creaked to a stop
before the platform, and its occupants climbed off. John
Hoskin had his hands tied in front of him, but he responded
with a half grin to cries of encouragement from friends in
the crowd. He might have been coming to take part in a prize
fight.

Sam felt breath on his neck, and elbows and knees in his ribs and calves, as he was pressed on from all sides. The guards, armed with staves, kept the crowd back from the small arena which had been formed. The governor was making a short proclamation, declaring the nature of the crime and the decreed punishment. Most of it was drowned in the cries of the crowd who were now being pushed back. Sam had his feet trodden on, and a woman half collapsed against him, having been winded by someone in the front.

Presently there were shouts of 'Quiet, quiet!' and it was seen that John Hoskin, alias Wildcat, was kneeling with the chaplain and saying a prayer. His face had paled and he was sweating, but he still looked composed. After the prayer was done the executioner took out the rope and coiled it on the end of the platform; and Hoskin took a step forward to the edge of the planking and began to address the crowd.

'My friends,' he said, 'comrades and companions all. All you 'oove come today see me step off into a betterer world, know ye that I've made my peace with th'Almighty an' go to this betterer world, askin' mercy and forgiveness of all I've wronged in this yur life, and may the Lord 'ave mercy on my soul. But know ye, friends and comrades and companions all, that purty many as my sins may be, never, never, never did I lay 'ands on this yur Samuel Phillips, nor steal 'is wheat, nor nothin' like un! I never seed 'im, not then nor any time before nor after, an' – '

His voice was drowned in a roar from the crowd, who seemed half to sympathize with him, half to be amused. Clearly what he was saying was to the displeasure of the governor and of the chaplain – first because it claimed a miscarriage of justice, which was an extremely bad thought to implant in the minds of his listeners, and second because it implied that the chaplain had failed in his mission to get him to repent. Most prisoners at the last admitted their fault.

But any attempt to stop him now would have produced a riot, so he was allowed his say. And he had it for nearly fifteen minutes, sometimes haranguing the crowd, sometimes turning to his mother and his wife. But half of what he said was lost as the crowd grew tired and inattentive. Some of the young children in the front were screaming, not out of fear

or pity but as if they had caught some infection from the
crowd about them. Sam wished he could get to the man, pray
with and for him properly for a few quiet moments, for his
manner of speaking suggested he had not really understood
the nature of sin or *how* he must repent.

But now it was too late. Too late. The speech was over and
the purpose of the gathering had to begin. Hoskin stepped on
to that centre piece of the platform, which had been carpen-
tered so that it could be rapidly withdrawn. The hangman
had thrown the rope over the gibbet and secured it, and he
came to place the noose about the condemned man's neck.
Hoskin bent his head to take the noose and adjusted the knot
under his ear where it would tighten more quickly. Then he
looked up at the sky a moment before the hangman slipped
the white cap over his head.

Hoskin raised his hand for silence, and now the crowd fell
instantly silent. He began to sing: 'Jesus shall reign where e'er
the sun', in a voice that was noticeably unmusical but did not
tremble or quaver. He sang three verses but that was as far
as his memory went. He lowered his hand. The hangman
pulled away the platform, and Hoskin jerked down a few
inches and hung at the end of the rope.

A great roar went up from the crowd and the children
screamed louder than ever. Then the body began to twitch,
the bound hands clenched and unclenched and went up to the
face as if to tear off the mask. The kicking became violent,
and two friends of his who had broken through the cordon
to 'pull his leg', as it was called, were unable to grasp them.
Blood and froth stained the mask. Then as the struggling
lessened, urine and black wet faeces began to drip from the
figure on to the ground.

Then the figure was still, like a doll on the end of a rope,
like a bundle of dirty wet rags hung out to dry. The sun had
gone behind a cloud but now it came out again, lighting up
the scene. Some crows circled overhead.

The crowd began to move, to stretch, to ease off their
pressure to see what was no longer worth looking at. A few
were quieted and upset, a few excited and talkative, a few
jovial, but most were phlegmatic, and moved away having
seen the spectacle they had come to see, their minds already

turning to the business of the day. The children formed into lines to go to school. The pie-men began re-crying their wares.

The body was lowered to the ground and the prison surgeon pronounced that life was extinct. The governor and the sheriff got into their coach, and four guards lifted the corpse on to the cart that had brought him. The well-dressed people began to move out of their stand chatting together. The hangman yawned and put on his coat and buttoned it. Half a dozen people inched forward to steal the rope, which was supposed to have magical properties, but they were driven off.

Sam spat on the ground among the litter and the trampled heather, then drifted over to join the little group of family mourners who he knew were hoping to be allowed to take the body home for Christian burial.

II

Sawle Feast day dawned in thick fog, a not uncommon occurrence for the time of year when the weather was fine and warm. This was known as pilchard weather, but it would have been more welcome on another day. At nine in the morning you could not see half-way across the field where the games and tea and other festivities were to be held. At ten it lightened and seemed likely to clear. A mile inland, Jud Paynter said, the sun was as hot as dung. But by eleven, when the service at Sawle Church was due to begin, the fog was back worse than ever, clammy, drifting and chill. People moved through the churchyard like spectres.

The church was full, and a few folk standing. It was always the busiest day of the year, and Ross had been persuaded to go, much against his will. Jeremy wanted to be there, as various of his young companions, such as Benjy Carter, were to be there, and Demelza thought she should go with him. Ross thought it particularly undesirable that he should encounter George again so soon, but Demelza, who knew they would both be watching the games this afternoon, said you could as easily avoid a man in a church as out of it.

As soon as he sat down in his pew Ross regretted he had come, for he observed that the Reverend Clarence Odgers was to be assisted in the service by the Reverend Osborne Whitworth. His instinctive dislike of the heavy-legged young man was constantly aggravated when they met by Whitworth's arrogant manners, and the further fact that George had twice outwitted him, Ross, by promoting Whitworth's interests against, as it were, Ross's own candidate. First, he had smartly married off this over-dressed and loud-mouthed cleric to Morwenna Chynoweth when Ross was just waking up to the fact that he might have brought her and Drake together. And second, he had contrived to have him presented with this living instead of the poverty-stricken but deserving Odgers.

It was all provoking, made more provoking by a sense of shortcoming on Ross's own part. In each case, had he been quicker to appreciate the situation and more active, he might, he felt, have gained the day. In each case the ungodly had flourished. And when the ungodly happened to be officiating in a Christian church in the habiliments of the godly it made him an offensive sight.

They were all here, Ross thought sourly, as the service began, the tall dark-haired Morwenna beside the slighter blondeness of Elizabeth; George bull-necked and elegant in a brown spotted silk coat and breeches. Drake here too, at the back of the church, but no sign yet of Sam. Perhaps the young fool would miss his match and then the wager would be void. Ross felt his shoulder reminiscently. They had had a few falls together and, even though rusty, Sam was no novice at the game. A lot would depend on whether he kept his wits about him. Tom Harry was a bull of a man, very little going on behind the thick freckled bone of his forehead. But if Sam took time off to think about his next prayer meeting he would be finished. Perhaps he would remember to concentrate if he thought of the soul he had to gain . . .

Mr Odgers was nervous about his prayers. The previous vicar had never been near, and it was a new and trying experience to have his superior sitting opposite him, listening to all that was being offered up, with a censorious expression on his well-fed face. Odgers knew already from short experience that *some* aspect of his conduct would be criticized; and today it was as if an extra sourness was fermenting in the vicar's mind. Already there had been hard words spoken, about the bell-ringers, about the musical instruments in the choir, about the condition of the churchyard and about the cleanliness of the church. There was more to come. Mr Osborne Whitworth had only been interrupted in his string of angry comments by the arrival of the Warleggans and the need to begin.

So the service was gone through, and Mr Whitworth rose to give the sermon. He climbed into the pulpit and cleared his throat and shook out his sheaf of notes.

He chose as his text Job 26:5-6 (UCP): 'Dead things are formed from under the waters and the inhabitants thereof, Hell is naked before him, and destruction hath no covering.'

It was as good as any for the sermon he was about to preach, but it hardly seemed suited to a saint's day when the parish celebrated its conversion to Christianity by the Irish monk who had founded an oratory here eleven hundred years before. But Mr Odgers in his distress had not been mistaken in supposing that some special sourness was fermenting in Ossie's nature. No hair shirt that St Sawle wore could have been more galling to the new incumbent than the discovery he had made a week ago.

Rowella was not going to have a baby.

Since she left the house there had been no communication whatsoever between the vicarage and the cottage where Rowella and Arthur were making their life. Even Morwenna had made no move to establish contact with her erring sister. Whatever love she might have borne Rowella had been blighted by the events of last winter. It did not matter that she herself had no desire at all to resume a wifely relationship with her husband. It did not even seem to matter that Rowella's – and his – misbehaviour had given her the armour she needed to protect herself against his rightful claims. The whole episode of their affair together so revolted her that she felt ill every time she thought of it. Knowing Ossie, it made her feel sick that a sister of hers should not have found his attentions offensive.

So nothing whatever had passed between the two houses – if the Solways' cottage could be dignified with the name – nothing had passed for five months, until Ossie, about his business at Kenwyn, had one day last week chanced to encounter Rowella, who had herself been on a visit to a new friend, and found her looking as unattractive, as enigmatic, as intellectually nervous, and as *thin* as ever; and when, fighting his way through a mass of restrictive prohibitions, he had made some stiff comment on her condition, she had looked very upset, her lower lip had trembled, and she had said: 'Oh, Vicar, I am so *very* grieved about this! But it does not appear that I was with child after all. I was – was very young and I made a *terrible* mistake . . .'

When she said this her eyes had filled with tears, but as he turned brusquely away his soul was blackened, scorched, charred with unholy fires; and with the conviction that he had been deliberately cheated, deliberately blackmailed by this chit of a girl for reasons of her own. Perhaps all the time she had been in love with Arthur Solway and had chosen this means of setting him up for life. Perhaps she had been in league with Morwenna to humiliate and frustrate him. Perhaps she had been sent by the Devil – indeed was a handmaiden of the Evil One himself – and her purpose had been to tempt and betray and destroy one of God's ordained ministers.

Whatever the truth, Ossie did not, would not, believe in her *innocence*. He had been deceived, lured, tricked, cheated, and finally bilked of nearly three years' stipend from his recently acquired living of Sawle-with-Grambler; and his wife was permanently estranged and untouchable because of it. (He had tried twice more but to his indignation she had remained utterly contumelious and defiant and had repeated her threat to the safety of his son.)

So it was against this background, with this poisoned thorn festering in his heart and in his pocket, that Mr Whitworth preached his sermon straight out of the darkest depths of the souls of the writers of the Old Testament, a sermon full of the wrath of God, of material punishment for spiritual misdeed, of thunderbolts and fiery furnaces, of the end of the house of Jeroboam, of the slaughter of the kings of Midian, of Rechabites, of Amalekites, of the destruction of Sodom and Gomorrah.

This went on for forty minutes, by which time the congregation was getting restive and a little noisy. But this only caused Ossie to raise his resonant voice to a higher level as he returned to his original theme and launched into the sorrows of Job: 'Let the day perish wherein I was born, and the night which said, A man-child is conceived.' This continued for another fifteen minutes and then the speaker reached a splendid peroration and finished his address abruptly, like someone closing a shop. 'Now to God the Father, God the Son and . . .' Ross raised his chin from his chest and woke Clowance.

George also stirred, glancing first at Morwenna, who did not look up, and then at Elizabeth, who smiled at him. He shrugged and half smiled back. Since their reconciliation at Easter the relationship had not always been an easy one. Since the emotional elation of that night when Elizabeth picked up the bible, his careful, business-like brain had gone over and over the words she had spoken, the words she had sworn, and, while his sense of fairness admitted that she had said all that was necessary, his sense of the appropriate suggested that she might have chosen better words. No doubt she had spoken in the heat and anguish of the moment, the first sentences that came to her mind. It was reasonable enough. But suspicion, once implanted in George's heart by Aunt Agatha's barb, died hard. Logically he was convinced that Elizabeth spoke the truth. Logically he was convinced that Valentine was his child. So it was all right. But every now and then the worm twisted to overturn logic.

There was nothing more to be done; he realized that himself. To ask her to add some additional sentences, like a lawyer drawing up a contract for the formation of a joint stock company, would be inviting what it would certainly receive – the angriest of refusals and a final disintegration of their married life. He could expect – and would expect – no other.

Sometimes he felt like a man with a pain whose cause could be either a trivial indisposition or a dread disease. His imagination, working and active on it, could equally convince himself that he was about to die or that he had nothing at all wrong with him. In this case, for the most part, it was the latter. Elizabeth was a pure woman and Valentine his only son. If only that niggling pain would altogether go away . . .

Before he married Elizabeth he had always wanted to possess her, and the wedding ceremony of Thursday 20 June 1793 had given him that absolute possession. But the quarrel of April 1797 had loosened those bonds. He had the good sense now to realize that Elizabeth would never desert him. She would be loyal and faithful to him and his interests, would keep his home and his family and be his companion and his wife in all good things. But she had stated her terms.

At the back of the church Drake had been sitting with an absorbed air which disguised the fact that he had not been listening to the sermon at all. He had heard nothing or thought of nothing since Morwenna came in. As she passed him on her way to the front pew they had seen each other for the first time for more than two years. After the one startled glance of recognition she had lowered her gaze, but he had looked at her and continued to look at her as if mesmerized. He saw that she was terribly changed. She looked older, thinner, harder – there were lines round her mouth that he had never seen before. Her skin, which was always a little dark, had become sallow, her eyes narrowed; her fine carriage was not so fine, in a year or two she would stoop. Whatever the two years had brought to Drake, they had brought no less distress to her. More, thought Drake. More. He felt sick to look at her and at that loud-mouthed cleric standing in the pulpit describing the hosts of Midian.

He would have left the church at some time during the service, glad to get away, glad to sick up his disappointment and distress against some slanting gravestone outside. It was *really* all over now, he told himself; he no longer cared for her, even; she was a vicar's wife, a matron, a tired, experienced, commonplace young woman with lank dark hair and brown myopic eyes and a baby and a husband and a parish to look after; and the dream was gone. It had been there, existed between them for no longer than a rainbow arching between cloud and cloud; the sky pattern had moved and it was lost for ever.

He would have left the church, but some need to stare at her kept him there. From where he was he could see her brown hat and one shoulder. She was of course sitting in the Poldark pew – that is to say the Trenwith pew – next to Mr Warleggan, with Mrs Warleggan on his other side. Ross and his family sat on the opposite side of the church and several rows back. Only three sat in the Trenwith pew. Geoffrey Charles was not there. It seemed likely that he had not come home. Perhaps they were not having him home this summer.

After Mr Odgers had intoned the final prayer the congregation began to file out. It was of course the custom to let the gentry leave first, so Drake was now trapped into remaining. As soon as the Warleggans began to move he lowered his eyes so that he need not embarrass Morwenna any more. Let her look at him if she wanted; he was too miserable to stare her out.

But sometimes the best intentions give way before impulse, and just as he saw Elizabeth's white skirt sweep past the end of the pew he raised his eyes again.

She was looking at him. Morwenna was looking at him. It lasted about seven seconds, and in that time she just had time to smile. It began in her eyes, crinkling them up a little more; it spread to her lips; and then it seemed to break in an irradiation over her whole face. The lines disappeared, the colour of her face changed, the tightness of lips relaxed, the eyes were warm again. For a few heart-beats he was embraced by it; the sun came out, the rainbow shone again; then she was past.

Sam Greet elbowed him to step into the aisle and follow the others into the fog outside.

'Come 'long, my son,' he said. 'Reckon we've had 'nough of praying for one day.'

CHAPTER V

Sawle Feast did not begin properly until two o'clock. It was a holiday at Wheal Grace – the only mine working in the parish – but the custom of the day was that the miners spent the morning cleaning up, brushing out the sheds, whitewashing the inside of the changing-house, sweeping the dressing floors and making everything look its best. And anyway, farmers or those with animals to tend were never ready and free for anything much before noon.

Two o'clock was the children's games; three-thirty was tea; each child received a tin mug of steaming black tea and a

huge saffron bun which it was almost impossible to eat at one
sitting. Adults had had a bite of something, if they were lucky,
before the feast began, but there was any amount of ale to be
had. Each miner was given a shilling by the mine on the day
and this usually went in drink, with money of their own to
follow. At four o'clock there were games and races for the
young grown-ups. At five the wrestling began. Sam and Tom
Harry were due to meet at six in the challenge match, but the
ordinary wrestling was a knock-out competition open to anyone who threw in his cap, with the prize of a guinea and a hat
for the outright winner. A player who brought his opponent
to an approval fall stayed in for the second round, and if he
won the second round he became a 'standard'. The play-off
among the standards was when the real wrestling began.

Drake walked back to his shop after church and made himself a frugal dinner. He had just finished it when Sam turned
up.

'Well, brother,' Drake said. 'Tis good to see ee. I thought
maybe you'd not turn up for your match in time.'

Sam took a seat and began to munch the bread and cheese
that Drake brought him. 'Oh, aye, I'd not forgot.'

'Maybe twould've been better if ee had. I've no liking for
a brother to be fighting my battles.'

'Not yours, boy. My own.'

Drake put down the stave he had been straightening and sat
on a box opposite Sam. 'Ye went then? Did it all happen?'

Sam told him.

At the end Drake said: 'Twas a kind thing to do, brother,
but a sad one. D'you – d'you see God's hand in all this?'

'We cann't measure and guess all that the Divine Spirit
intends. Tis for we to bow our heads and accept chastisement
where it d'fall. It seemed me that twas only one sinner suffering 'mong many who went scatheless. But it grieved me that
he went dead without the chance of laying hold of the true
blessing.'

'I'll pour you some tea,' Drake said. From the scullery he
called: 'Went all the way back Camborne with them, did ee?'

'For the funeral, aye. They left us bring the body away.
We was lended an old cart. Six of us drawed'n, turn and turn
about. I pulled with Peter Hoskin . . . 'Fore ever we reached

Camborne we was met by others. Hundreds of folk downed work and walked on behind. Great procession. Hundreds. Sang hymns while they walked. Many b'longed to the Connexion, ye could tell.'

Drake brought a mug of tea but said nothing.

'Thank ee, boy . . .'

'A stranger thing never I seen,' Sam went on, sipping. 'You mind Sir Basset? Sir Francis Basset? Lord Dunster – Dunstanville as he now is?'

'Oh, yes, I mind him well.'

'Ye know twas he who was at the arresting of Hoskin and Sampson and Barnes and the others, and twas he who was at the trying of them. And twas he they d'say who had to choose whether to sign a reprieve for John, like was done for the others. Well, this procession – nigh on a thousand folk now, I warrant – was passing by this house by the church, and we was a mile maybe from the burying ground, when who should come out of this house but Basset himself, all by his self save for one servant; and sure 'nough all these folk he come up against, most of them miners, many I reckon as took part in the riot with Hoskin and the rest, they all knew who twas. And the man at the door of the house where Lord Basset had been calling tried to draw him back within the house; but Sir Francis wouldn't be sheltered and says as he is in no danger from these men, he says, but let these men make one move against him and they'll surely suffer the fate of the corpse they're drawing home . . . So he comes to his horse and mounts it, and his servant mount his, and quiet as you please he rides slow through the procession, passen near by the corpse – and quiet and peaceable the folk part and separate like the waters of the Red Sea . . .'

Drake nodded slowly.

'Did ye stop by and see William, John and Robert?'

'Yes. But there was only Robert home. And the widow and Flotina, and John's new wife and cheeil. They were all bravish.'

'Bobbie's come well again?'

'Clever. They all asked for you.'

'That Basset be a brave man,' Drake said. 'I'll give him that. Twas more than many a man would've dared to do.'

'For a while I veared for 'n,' Sam said. 'But I reckon he was upheld by his conviction of right. Twas a strange sight to see . . . And a lesson to us all . . .'

'Even when we be in the wrong?' Drake asked with a glimmer of his old mischief.

Sam smiled and shook his head. 'That's what we must try and take care and pray not to be.'

'Where's Peter? He's not back wi' you?'

'He's resting with the family and will come home tonight.'

'You missed two days at the mine? You got leave to go?'

'Oh, yes. There's no pressure t'our work. I come home now for the – for the challenge.'

'Ye'll be weary with the walking.'

Sam put a finger round the top of one of his boots. 'I got sore feet. The rest is naught.'

'I wish ee well, brother. I reckon we've got an hour afore we need stir. I'll get a bucket and you can soak your feet. I hope ye beat him, Sam. But he's as bulk-headed as a mule. You want to watch how he takes his hitch.'

'God will decide it,' said Sam.

II

The Enyses were not in church, but they rode over for dinner with the Poldarks. They were not churchgoing people even on special feast days and holidays. This was a disadvantage to Dwight, for it was an ill thing for a doctor to be thought an atheist. In fact Dwight was not that, and would have made token appearances had Caroline so desired it, but Caroline had an active prejudice against all forms of organized religion and only entered places of worship on such unavoidable occasions as weddings, christenings and funerals.

She was again looking in much better health and chatted amiably through the early part of the meal. Then as the main course came on – it was a leg of mutton boiled with capers and served with walnuts and melted butter – she said she had some ill news to impart, namely that she was with child.

Demelza dropped the serving spoon and jumped up and hugged her and kissed her and then went to kiss Dwight.

'I'm that glad. I'm that glad. Judas, that's happy news! Caroline, Dwight, it is wonderful! Wonderful!'

'It was what was wrong with me all the time,' Caroline said, 'and my husband never diagnosed it!'

'Because she lied to me,' said Dwight, 'and anyway would scarcely let me get near her!'

When Ross bent to kiss Caroline, her lips sought his. 'You see,' she said, 'what you're responsible for – even if at one remove. You *would* bring him home.'

Ross said: 'If it is a boy we'll marry him to Clowance, and if a girl to Jeremy.'

'I'll drink to that,' said Dwight.

'We'll all drink to that.'

After they were again seated at the table and the meal had begun and everyone was silent because they were eating, Caroline said:

'Of course I don't *want* the brat.'

'Caroline!' said Demelza.

'No, in truth, are they not revolting little specimens when they come? Really I can't bear babies! Wrinkled, red-faced little tyrants, greedy, selfish, demanding, incontinent, full of crudities and wind, claiming the whole attention of an adult person night and day and never saying thank you for it. They're warm and moist and clinging, and they smell of urine and sour milk, and there are far too many of 'em in the world already!'

Everyone laughed at her but she grimaced and said: 'No, I mean it! Dwight knows. I have warned him.'

'You have warned us all,' said Demelza, 'and we don't believe it.'

'You have to think of succession,' Ross said ironically. 'After all, the world is not a bad place, and it would be a crying pity to leave it altogether to other people's children.'

'Succession?' said Caroline. 'I would not mind so much if I could breed a little Dwight – or even, God help me, a little Caroline. But one's own child, it always seems to me, turns out to be the living image of one's least favourite cousin!'

'Or parent,' said Demelza. 'Jeremy has my father's feet but I dearly hope there's no other likeness.'

Everybody laughed again.

'I think,' said Dwight, 'as the father of *this* particular embryo I might be allowed to deplore Caroline's remarks.

For my part, if it's a girl, I don't mind what it looks like so long as it is tall and thin with auburn hair and freckles on its nose.'

'You describe a monster,' said Caroline. 'Was that some great-aunt of yours?'

'Seriously,' said Demelza.

They all stopped and waited then.

She thought a moment, crumbling her bread. Then she smiled.

'Will it not be lovely for us all?'

III

By five forty-five all the main wrestling was over. The hat and the guinea had been won by Paul Daniel who, in spite of his age (he was forty) and his liking for strong drink, was yet too fly and too cunning for any of the others. The assembly straggled round a ringed-off circle of the common which adjoined the main track from Sawle to St Ann's and which was the other side of the road from the stagnant pond where Drake had been half drowned. Altogether a couple of hundred people spread about the common land, of whom two-thirds were near the wrestling ring. The rest sprawled or played games or drank beer and talked, dotted haphazard over the rest of the field. Many of them were merry with drink, most of it having come from Sally Chill-Off's just down the lane. This was how she could afford to give prizes for the wrestling.

By now the fog had lifted – or rather it had drifted a few hundred yards farther out to sea, so that the common was just on the edge of it. Most of the time it was in hazy sunlight but sometimes in hot sun, sometimes in dank grey fog. Overhead, but always in the misty part of the sky, the seagulls were being tortured, and constantly screamed *please ... please ... please ...*

Sam and Drake had arrived at five-thirty, tramping up from Pally's Shop. They were now sitting on a bench surrounded by their well-wishers, while Tholly Tregirls lurched like a self-important scarecrow between them and a similar if smaller group surrounding Tom Harry. Emma Tregirls was not to be seen, nor Sally yet. After the giving of the prize to Paul Daniel she had hastened back to open her kiddley again so that she should not lose custom to any of her rivals. Tholly had a small boy posted ready to dart off to warn her when the contest was about to begin. But it could not begin yet. It was said that some of the gentry were coming down from Trenwith to watch the match – there were rumours of wagers having been laid – and, like Mr Odgers at the church, nothing could proceed until the gentry arrived.

The Poldarks and the Enyses strolled up about six. Ross had not wanted to come, nor had Demelza; yet it had been difficult to stay away. Sam was Demelza's brother. It was neither easy to patronize nor to ignore. But as Demelza said, this was not a bare-fist fight, it was a proper wrestling match and there'd be sticklers to see fair play. And there was no need for the gentry to mix with other gentry.

Yet when the time came it was not possible for them to sit far apart. There were only four benches, and these were in a line by the entry to the ring. At fifteen minutes after six George Warleggan and Osborne Whitworth emerged from the gates of Trenwith and sauntered towards the common. Osborne had changed out of his clerical clothes and wore a handsome coat of mulberry-coloured silk with white breeches. The ladies were not with them. The two gentlemen sat at the end of the benches farthest from the Poldark party.

Tholly Tregirls was now in his element. Shoulders hunched in his long coat like a vulture in a tree, scarred and one-armed and asthmatic, he stood in the centre of the ring and announced the contest . . . 'Wrestling challenge contest, best of three falls, three three-point falls, for the prize of two guineas, awarded by Mrs Sally Tregothnan of Sally's Kiddley, contestants to be . . . on my left Tom Harry . . . and on my right Sam Carne . . .'

There were cheers and counter cheers as the two men stepped forward. They were dressed in the prescribed costume for the bout, naked to the waist except for short loose jackets made of untearable linen cloth, with loose sleeves, and secured round the neck by tough cord. They wore breeches to the knees, thick stockings but no shoes. Kicking might be allowed east of the Tamar but it was considered unfair in Cornwall, where all the power and skill had to be in the shoulders and arms. In addition to Tholly two others, Paul Daniel and Will

Nanfan, were in the ring to adjudicate and see fair play.

As the contenders came to shake hands it could be seen that Sam was a good three inches the taller of the two, but Harry was massively broad across the shoulders with matching legs and buttocks. It was not necessarily an advantage to be tall in such a contest.

Tholly blew his whistle; it was one he had had for years, given him, he always said, by a dying bo'sun on one of the frigates on which he had first sailed, as a measure of the bo'sun's esteem. In fact he had stolen it from a Spanish beggar in Gibraltar. As Sam circled round his man he saw Emma Tregirls come to the ringside along with Sally. They stood among the group supporting Tom Harry. Emma was not even looking at the wrestlers as she talked and laughed with Sally. Her laugh floated across the field.

There were a lot of cries and shouts as the two men manœuvred for the first hitch. Sam had most of the support, and he noticed with embarrassment the voices of many of his own flock. It was not that he did not *want* them to support him but that he felt the falseness and wrongness of his own position. On that long dragging walk back from Bodmin, with the mourners and the corpse, he had thought a lot about life and death and his own position in the world, his own privileges and his own duties. And it did not seem that one of his privileges or duties was to spread the Word of God by returning to the old habits of his youth and entering into a public contest of psysical skill and strength with a brute of a man who had assaulted and beaten his brother and threatened to marry the girl who for some reason had engaged his own worldly heart.

Harry made a sudden sharp lunge for Sam's coat as it swung, but Sam, crouching as low as the other man, dodged him and tried to grab his own hitch as they slid past each other. But Harry tore himself away and the circling and feinting began again. This was part of the technique of the play and with champions could sometimes go on for half an hour. But it could not this evening; there was too much feeling in the game.

It might be, thought Sam, that he had persuaded himself into such a contest to try to save a precious soul for Jesus, but

surely in the final searching of one's own soul two other and
very un-Christian motives came in. Revenge and lust. Revenge
and lust. How could you deny it? And if you could not deny
it, how could you justify it? After seeing a man hanged and
the grief and horror of knowing that he had died unsaved,
how could a man indulge in this sort of trumpery violence for
the entertainment of folk on holiday?

Suddenly they were joined and Sam's thoughts went no
farther than self-preservation from being thrown through the
air. Tom Harry had gained the grip he wanted: they struggled
for position; twisting, Harry had his head under Sam's armpit,
was trying the back crook, swung with arms pinioning a
counter move – Sam's feet were off the floor, he was going up
and over; to struggle now was fatal; he went, but dead weight
all to one side so that instead of landing heavily on his back
he landed on elbow and buttock, fell and rolled over – Harry
was on him as he was half up, was now attempting the fore
heave. Sam broke the grip on his collar, fell again to his knees
and suddenly collapsed head down. Harry went over the top
in his turn.

They separated and began to spar again. Harry rushed –
more like a bull than a wrestler – his shoulder caught Sam in
the ribs, seeming to bend them, gripped both Sam's shoulders
till the cord cut at his neck. Sam broke the hold by working
his elbow into Harry's face; hooked his leg behind the other's
leg, and they fell and rolled over on the hard ground together,
first one uppermost and then the other. Tholly had to leap out
of the way as they convulsively jerked towards him: he blew
his whistle, for fighting on the ground was not permitted.

He had to haul Harry away, and the two men got to their
feet to the sound of cheers and hisses and shouts from the
crowd.

It's wrong, thought Sam, it's wrong that I should be here.
Hands gripped his coat and a bull head grated hard against his
chin. A hand was round his waist, the other clutching his
breeches. He fell like a tree with sixteen stone of bone and
muscle on top of him.

In a daze of pain and lack of air he heard the whistle and
felt hands pulling Harry off him. He had lost the first fall.

IV

'I believe,' said Demelza, 'I do not like this.'

'Nor I,' said Ross, 'but we must see it out.'

'That man is not wrestling proper: he's wrestling to do hurt! Why don't they stop it?'

'In honesty they can't without giving the match to Harry. He's not quite breaking the rules; he's just playing rough. The sticklers can interfere, as Tholly did then, but he can't stop the match. Ah . . .'

Anger and spite are not necessarily the best fuelling ingredients for a contest of physical skill, but a measure of combativeness is vital, and until now Sam had lacked it. He knew nothing of Ross's wager but he knew too well the promise that Emma had made, and today more than ever it looked like a joke on her part, unworthy and unmeant. He felt defensive and ashamed.

But in spite of the saintliness that had come upon him with conversion to Christ, and in spite of his present shame, there was enough old Adam in him to dislike the pain of badly bruised ribs, the bleeding from the tooth that had been loosened by Harry's bullet head, the sweaty smell of a brute body forcing him into humiliating and painful postures, the gasps and grunts of triumph coming from his opponent. And Harry, bent on quick success and now sure of it, had begun to relax his guard.

It was more as if Sam's body rather than his conscious brain reacted to a situation it found itself in and took sharp and appropriate action that it had learned in these contests years ago. A sudden change of position under the grasping hands, a twist of body, two arms behind Harry's neck, one clasping the other wrist for strength, and down he went, Sam on top, just avoiding the deliberately upturned knee as they fell. A flurry of dust and heather, and Harry was pinned as neatly as if someone had run him through with a sword.

Roars of delight from the crowd. As the whistle blew Sam rose quickly and stepped back while Tom Harry spat blood that had come from somewhere and got to his feet too. The second fall, Tholly announced, had been gained by Sam Carne. The final and deciding one would now begin.

As he spoke the fog drifted back over the sun and all the shadows evaporated. The ground was chill and grey, and it seemed likely that as the sun was sinking it would not be seen again.

Both men were badly bruised, for it was not at all a gentlemanly contest and both had taken heavy falls on ground which had been baked by the long dry summer. Sam had twice only just avoided serious injury by protecting himself against Harry's knee. (If by 'accident' you fell on your opponent with your knee up you probably put him out of the wrestling ring for life. Of course you would be disqualified if the sticklers saw.) Because both men wanted to avoid another such fall the next catch was a long time in coming, and when it came it was a body-to-body hug rather than an attempt to throw. It was a not unusual end to a match in which skills were nearly equal, and one much to the crowd's liking. Cornish wrestling was sometimes known as Hug-wrestling.

Ross, watching from under scowling brows, saw the two men straining against each other and had a sudden memory of that fight he had had with Demelza's father so many years ago. Thus after some preliminary fighting they had so locked in much the same hold; he, the taller and younger, being bent back from the waist, his hands on the other's chin, almost kneeling on the other's thighs on tip-toes, bending and resisting with all the strength of his back muscles and backbone. Now he felt a sudden identification with old Carne's son, who was fighting, as he had fought, against the same shape and build of man, and almost it seemed for the same things – found himself muttering aloud, half-shouting useless advice. For if Tom Harry won this trial of strength and Sam did not accept defeat he might neither wrestle nor dig again.

Will Nanfan shouted at Tholly and Tholly caught Harry by the shoulder. But neither wrestler took any notice. Tholly blew the whistle. But the crowd was shouting to him to get out of their sights and to let the fight go on. For now it was a fight and the rules of pure wrestling could go hang. Sam's back, having bent so far, was bending no farther, and instead Harry's neck was moving back in its turn. George put away his snuff-box. Ossie dusted some pollen off his coat and day-dreamed of beating Rowella with a stick. Emma took off her hat and plucked out pieces of straw. Demelza sat like a stone.

Then like two old elms crashing they went to the ground, struggled for mastery, and Sam came up on top. Everybody was screaming. Harry was done and it looked like a 'back'. The extra weight only had to be applied to push his other shoulder down to achieve the three-pin fall necessary for victory. Tholly raised his hand and put his whistle to his mouth; and then Sam seemed to relax at the wrong moment. Tom Harry, within an inch of defeat, forced himself a fraction upwards; with a last effort jack-knifed himself away from the compelling hold Sam had had, and in three seconds had somehow come out on top. Then it was Sam who was underneath, who was almost but not completely down, who was struggling to avoid the pressures he had himself just been applying; Sam who was now crushed beneath the weight of the heavier man and in three seconds more finally succumbed.

Tholly blew the whistle. Tom Harry had won.

CHAPTER VI

Tom Harry had won, but it was a cause for instant dispute and constant discussion and argument in every home and kiddley in the days to come. Even the sticklers disagreed. Tholly and Will Nanfan gave the victory to Tom Harry, though in Nanfan's view Harry had lost points earlier in the contest for foul play. Paul Daniel said the contest should be declared void because the rules of wrestling had been totally abandoned in the last round and they had rolled over fighting on the ground like two drunken tinkers. But in the general view, there had been two fair 'backs', one each way, and in the third round both men had fought the same sort of fight and who was on top at the end? It was not a popular view, not one the majority *wanted* to take, but that they took it was the more significant.

Fortunately there was no need for Ross to see George. He sent his draft to Basset and asked Basset if he would be so kind as to let George know he had paid. Crossing with this was a letter from Tankard, 'on behalf of Mr Warleggan', reminding Ross of his debt. Ross mixed this with the pig feed.

After his defeat Sam was off work for more than a week and frequently brought up blood, but this condition mended. He did not see Emma after the contest and she made no attempt to see him. He went about the duties of his Connexion with quiet obedience to the word of God. He would discuss the fight with no one. He prayed a lot, noticing some falling off in the enthusiasm of his flock. It was as if their understanding of the Bible derived more from the Old Testament, where virtue had its material reward, than from the New, where the rewards of virtue were solely spiritual and material things went down to defeat. Sam often thought of what he would have gained by winning – and what he would have lost.

He also read a lot, and he received another visit from Mr Champion, in the course of which Mr Champion expressed his pleasure at the general reports he had had from the parish. It seemed that the unfortunate association with the light woman had been dutifully broken and all was well. He still however had criticism to offer of the way in which Sam tended to keep all the affairs of the Connexion in his own hands, especially the monetary side. Sam said he would mend his ways.

Dwight went to see Hugh Armitage twice more but said his condition was no worse. Hugh wrote to Demelza once, but kept to the polite generalities of correspondence. It was so suitable for Ross to see that Demelza showed it him. Ross said:

'I suppose he'll stay in Cornwall until the election is over and then hope to go to Westminster. It should occupy him.'

'Yes, Ross. If he gets in.'

'I hope he does, not merely for his own sake but because it would unseat George.'

'Would it? I hadn't quite thought of that.'

'Well, the corporation *could* put in one Basset and one Boscawen candidate, but it's improbable. Normally two MPs are elected of the came complexion, since a voter who votes for one of them is like to choose the other also. If George remains it is probable Gower will lose his seat and Trengrouse will be returned. If Hugh gets in Gower will remain with him.'

Demelza said: 'If George was to lose his seat there, Lord de Dunstanville would find him another.'

'He could not do so immediately, for the elections would be over.'

'D'you think that would upset him?'

'Who? George? Yes, very much so.'

'Hm,' said Demelza. 'Yes, I had not thought of that.'

Germane to this conversation was a note Caroline sent over to Demelza a few days later.

'My dear,

We had our dinner party yesterday! Both the lions and myself and Dwight, who, angel though he is, was *quite* out of his element in such a matter. Just the four of us! Odds heart, imagine it! Men are very deceitful, for do you know they each pretended that they did not know the other was to be there! And tried to take offence at it, and had to be cozened into staying! Half through the dinner I thought, what a fool I am to be acting in such a way, for, God help me, who am I assisting? Not myself, not Dwight, not the brat that I carry. Possibly it may help Hugh a little, but that is the most of it.

'And what a pair of little lions they are, the Viscount and the Baron! Neither of 'em above sixty-four inches high and both of them carrying enough self-importance to sink a three-decker! Mind, I have not seen it in such evidence before. George Boscawen in ordinary conversation is an agreeable fellow, short on wit perhaps but amiable and of a good nature. My uncle liked him well. Indeed I perceive similarities of temperament between them! And Francis Basset – how pleasant he can be and simple and easy in the cosy bosom of his family. But put them together, bring 'em into the same house together and set 'em down at either end of a not very long table, and Lud's my life, they bristle and ruffle up, not so much like lions as little bantams preparing to dispute over a hen.

'At the end of our dinner they both were waiting for me to depart but, taking pity on Dwight who so detested the whole thing, and brazen as the fattest whore in Houndsditch, I informed them that as the party was so small and as I was the only woman, I did not purpose to split it further, nor did I intend to take myself off into solitary confinement while they drank all the brandy.

'They did not like it – they did not at all like it – indeed only the exquisite manners to which they had been born prevented them from ringing for one of my own servants to have me escorted out! *But* – I had been saving a rare bottle of Uncle Ray's brandy, of which only three bottles are left. He did not buy it through the Trade but brought it with him from London when he first carried me to Cornwall as a brat of eight. I and the brandy arrived together, and unlike me, the latter has been improving every year. So I thought this an occasion on which one of the last three bottles should be broached, and believe me, my dear friend, it worked wonders.

'Not of course that either gentleman got tipsy the way real gentlemen do. It is against their strict upbringing – or their dislike of ever feeling not totally in command of their judgement lest they should be cheated by someone else. But they were *softened* by it. It acted like the sun upon reluctant dandelions. They slowly settled deeper into their chairs. They stretched their little legs out. They spoke in more expansive tones. And presently someone – I cannot imagine who – happened to mention the dispute, the rivalry that had existed between them for so many years. And Francis spoke first, in a very conciliatory manner. And George spoke second, responding to the opening remarks by equally emollient answers.

'Of course it was not all as easy as that in the end. Two horse dealers at a fair were not more cautious, more argumentative, more anxious that the deal should not fail to favour themselves, than these two distinguished peers of the realm, one tracing his ancestry back to an Irish gentleman who settled in St Buryan in the eleventh century, the other quartering his arms with the Plantagenets (yes, my dear, both claims were made at my dinner table!). But in the end I believe that something of a bargain was struck. And the outcome of it is that rivalry at election time between the two shall cease. The descendant of the Irish gentleman has agreed to withdraw his claims upon the borough of Tregony if the Plantagenet gentleman will withdraw from Truro.

There are other agreements over a number of other con-
stituencies, but so far as we are concerned these are the
important ones. So hurrah for the hustings and may our sick
cavalier win the seat he so deserves!

'I, personally, am in very rude health and have vomited
not at all for the last week. Dwight continues fair but not-
ably thoughtful about the plight of England. I believe I did
not marry the most sanguine of men.

'Warmest love to Ross and a kiss for the children. (I must
say if anything would convert me to the idea of raising a
family it is the sight of those two.)

Caroline.'

II

On the last day of August the Reverend Mr Orborne Whitworth, walking down Princes Street, chanced to see Mrs
Rowella Solway coming out of the library with a bundle of
books under her arm. Her brown shabby frock hung about her
like a cassock as she walked. Her white straw hat shaded her
face from the sun. Her shoes made a scuffing sound on the
cobbles. She looked pale and thoughtful and unkempt. She
raised her eyes briefly to her brother-in-law in startled fashion
and hurried on.

Mr Whitworth had been to take a number of letters in for
collection by Lobb the Sherborner, who would pick them
up and deliver them in the parish of Sawle-with-Grambler
when he took the weekly newspaper round. They were letters
addressed to such people as Sir John Trevaunance, Captain
Ross Poldark, Dr Dwight Enys, Horace Treneglos Esquire,
and they pointed out the defects the new vicar had found in
the church and in the churchyard, defects which should be
made good but which would cost a considerable outlay of
money. The letters set forth, in what Mr Whitworth flattered
himself was a fair but forthright way, that it was the duty of
wealthy parishioners to play their part in maintaining the
fabric of this ancient and beautiful church in a manner which
would reflect credit upon the generosity and Christian responsibility of the persons involved. It was not so being maintained
at the moment, and a total reassessment was necessary.

Sight of Mrs Solway angered and upset the vicar afresh.

Last evening he had had a most distressing experience. Coming away from one of the tumbledown cottages by the quay – whither he had been driven by his physical needs and his wife's criminal obduracy – after dark had long fallen but when a full moon rode over the stinking mud of the river, a man had thrust a lantern in his face. He was not certain but he thought the man was a pot-boy from the Seven Stars Tavern, a man who lived in his parish and whose second child he had buried a few weeks ago. If so, there was a danger of his having been recognized, and if he had been so recognized, the man might drop a word to the churchwardens. Of course nothing could be proven, but respectable men did not usually venture upon the quay after dark, and it might take some explaining away.

It was abominable that he should be placed in such a position and the fault – the fault that he had to go to the quay at all – rested upon that thin shapeless streak of a girl picking her way among the broken cobbles to the other side of the street, on her way home, to her home that *his* money, through *her* trickery, had bought. To her home and her thin snivelling husband. The thought was an abomination to Osborne and he felt sick at the sight of her.

For some reason he felt sick on seeing her anyway. He frequently had fantasies now at the thought of beating her with a hard stick.

On the same day Demelza went blackberrying in the Long Field with Jeremy and Clowance. On the side of the Long Field dividing it from the broken outcroppings of rock and moorland turf sloping down to Nampara Cove was a thick Cornish wall much overgrown with gorse and brambles, and this was an area tacitly reserved for the Poldark family. Anywhere else on their land the village people were welcome to their pickings.

It was going to be a good year – unlike last, when the moisture in the air had turned the blackberries mildewed as they ripened – and they had already picked one crop. They went up with three baskets, one each for Demelza and Jeremy, and a smaller one for Clowance who anyhow had a wayward fancy and was likely to mix her blackberries with daisies and dandelions.

By the sea it was a sullen afternoon; not fog but a lofty

corrugated cloud which Truro, a few miles away, was escaping, and they had been there picking peacefully for ten minutes or so – a peace only punctuated by a cry from Jeremy now and then as he found a good cluster or scratched his finger – when Demelza heard a cough behind her. She turned and saw the tall girl wearing her usual long red cloak over what looked like a uniform, black stockings, black boots, light summer hat put on anyhow over gleaming hair.

'Beg pardon, mistress. Excuse me for coming 'pon you like this. You – you know me?'

Demelza straightened, pushed her hair back from her face with a forearm, lowered her basket.

'Yes . . . of course, Emma.'

'Yes, ma'am. I thought to call 'pon ee but did not have the brock. Then when I seen ee up here I thought t'ask for a word. I hope tis not presuming.' She was a little out of breath.

'I don't know, Emma. It depend what you want to say.'

Emma made a gesture. 'Well . . . I expect you know what tis. Everyone must know what tis. I come out this af'noon – tis not my day and I risk a shine, but Doctor be visiting and Mistress have gone Mrs Teague's to tea – so I come out, meaning . . . meaning to call 'pon Sam. But then I – from the top of the combe I seen you just leaving the house and I thought to trouble you with my troubles, like, as you – as Sam is your brother, like. D'you follow what I d'mean, ma'am?'

'Oh, yes, I follow what you mean.'

Emma swallowed and stared out over the sea. A swell was coming in, and every now and then the top of a wave would break and the swell would go on its way leaving fantails evaporating below the surface.

'I not seen Sam since the wrestling, ma'am. Not sight nor sound. Has he said ought to ee 'bout that?'

'No, Emma. He will not speak of it. I think he better prefers not to speak of it to anyone.'

'Why did he leave Tom Harry win? He did, didn' he? Deliberate. He left him to roll over 'pon him and win.'

'I don't rightly know. You must ask Sam. Maybe he'll tell you.'

'You d'know I'd promised go with his Connexion for three months if he won? Twas as if he bested to lose!'

Though not small herself, Demelza was still slight, and Emma looked twice her size. The hearty laugh was not in evidence today. Demelza recognized that she had a prejudice against the girl, not because of her behaviour but because she was Tholly Tregirls's daughter – which was manifestly unfair.

'D'you love Sam?' she asked.

The brilliant eyes came up, were sharply lowered again. 'I b'lieve so.'

'And Tom Harry?'

'Oh . . . *nothing*.'

'D'you think Sam loves you?'

'I b'lieve so too . . . But . . .'

'Yes, I know . . .'

Demelza picked a few more blackberries and offered them to Clowance, who clutched them in a chubby fist and threw a handful of daisies away.

'You see, mistress, he say he want to reform me, to change me out of my sin, to – to "make me over again", that's what he call it, "to make me over again". He seem think I shall be – be happier if I'm sad . . .'

'That's not quite what he means.'

'No, but that's what it d'sound like!'

Another silence.

'These blackberries are good,' Demelza said. 'Taste one.'

'Thank ee, ma'am.'

They each ate one. It was a good move for it made the meeting more companionable.

Demelza said: 'I don't know Sam near so well as I do my younger brother, Drake. All I know is that he would not be happy married to anyone if they did not belong to the Connexion. Not *would* not, *could* not. For religion means something to him that it doesn't mean to other folk. And if you – if you were pulling one way and his religion the other, you would not win. It would be far, far better not to see him again than – than pull him apart with that sort of choice.'

'Oh, yes,' said Emma. 'We separated. We agreed twas useless to go on – oh, I don't know when twas – last year some time. Twas my choice then. I said twas betterer all round – for him, for me, for his Connexion. For months we never seen each other; but then chancing to meet, and me being a thought merry with ale, we strikes this bargain. Yet he – when he's winning he makes the choice to lose to Tom Harry. Tis like he *rejected* me!'

'Mummy!' shouted Jeremy. 'You're not picking nothing! I'm beating you!'

'All right, my lover! I'll catch you, never fear!'

'But although twas all of a joke on top, and me laughing like a huer, I knew twas not a joke with him, and I truly believe he knew twas not all a joke wi' me. If he'd won I'd 've kept my side of the bargain!'

'Why not keep it whether or no?' said Demelza.

Emma wiped the tears of annoyance out of her eyes.

'If you love him,' said Demelza.

'Yes,' said Emma. 'That's what's come more clearer to me since last year. I thought I could – throw it all over me shoulder, forget him, like any other man. After all, I've had lots of men.' Her eyes met Demelza's. '*Lots*. I thought I could – it meant nothing much. But I b'lieve it do. He's different from the rest . . . But now he've thrown it back in my face.'

'How? By not winning?'

'Wasn't it plain to be seen? The win was there for the taking, and he turned his back on it. I don't want *she*, he seemed to say!'

'Perhaps,' Demelza said, 'he didn't think it was proper to win you that way.'

'But he wasn't winning *me*, ma'am, only me promising to come to his chapel!'

'Even so.'

There was a longer silence. Emma scuffed the dusty grass with her foot.

'So what you d'say – I should join the Connexion whether or no?'

'If you feel the way you say you do – about Sam, I mean.'

'. . . I'm scared to do it.'

'Why?'

'I'd be scared I'd feel naught and then *think* I felt something and then be led into *pretending*. Tis easy to roll your eyes and bow your head and say, "forgive me, miserable sinner", and all of a sudden leap up and screech, "I'm saved! I'm saved!" and mean nothing 'tall. And I couldn't be a cheat, not to Sam!'

'If you know that risk, could you not try and see, and guard against it?'

'I'd be scared for another reason,' Emma said. 'I'd think what I'd done to Sam's following, how many would stay away if they thought brazen Emma was trying it on with their preacher!'

Demelza thought about it. She could understand and sympathize with Emma's fears, but there seemed to be an element of illogic in the girl's attitude. Would not these objections have still existed if Sam had won his match and she had kept to the terms of the bargain? Perhaps not. Perhaps in some way Emma could have sheltered behind the compulsion to take the pressures off her attendance. And yet, for a young woman of her obvious boldness and determination . . .

Had she ever been going to see Sam this afternoon or had she just been desperately longing to talk it out with someone, and had luckily seen Sam's sister off blackberrying?

Reminded of her mission, Demelza began to pick again. Jeremy was well up the field now.

'Can I help ee, ma'am?'

'Thank you.'

They began to pick together.

'Tedn true, y'know, what they d'say about me.'

'What isn't?'

'What they say about me and men.'

'You've just said it yourself.'

'Aye but – tedn all true . . .'

'What isn't, Emma?'

'A man's never had me.'

Her own moral judgements being particularly sensitive these days, Demelza found herself uncomfortably and annoyingly reddening.

'How do you mean?'

'I let 'em take liberties. Always have. What do it matter? It d'give 'em pleasure. Me too sometimes. But – a man's never had me.'

Demelza lifted a maternal eye to Clowance, who had

wandered off with her basket among the corn stubble, but she was picking a few late poppies so there was no hazard in it.

Demelza said: 'Shouldn't you tell Sam this?'

'How can I? Anyhow, oo'd believe it? Every man d'talk – every man d'claim because they're shamed to confess they haven't, when others say *they* have.'

Demelza said: 'Sam would believe you. But maybe it wouldn't make so much difference to him . . . The – the greater the sinner, the greater the triumph . . . you know . . . more rejoicing in Heaven – what do they say?'

'That what I *hate*!' said Emma.

Jeremy gave a squeal of delight as a rabbit darted out of the hedge and made off across the field, white scut dipping and dodging.

'Are you happy at the Choakes'?' Demelza asked after a while.

'Yes, ma'am. Tis brave enough. Mistress Choake is a frail, vain little thing – begging your pardon – but she's kind. I d'get three pound ten a year and all found. And tea three times a day. Tis not hard, though the time off is but little.'

Demelza offered Clowance a blackberry to eat. 'Careful. Not the flower. Put it right in. There! Isn't that nice?'

'Blackle-burr,' said Clowance. 'Blackle-burr.'

'Dear of 'n,' said Emma absently.

Demelza was seeking for earthy wisdom but it did not come today. Sometimes she was happy to give advice and confident of her judgement. But this was a tangle she could not see through, and, in the present precarious state of her own emotional life, she would have been grateful not to have been asked.

She said: 'You *must* see Sam – have it out with him. For goodness' sake. A man and a woman, that is the only way it can be – between them, I mean. Nothing else – *nothing* else should matter except what he wants and what she wants. Don't worry what *other* people say, what they will say in the Connexion. Only worry whether you can suit *him*, and remember you can only suit him if you *belong*. And if you belong you'll have to accept. It can't be half-hearted; you see that yourself. That's all I can say. You see I can't help, Emma. I'm not helping at all.'

Emma stared over the sea. 'I did ought to go. There'll be a rare shine else.'

'You said just now you'd hate something,' Demelza said. 'Was it being saved – or just being thought a sinner?'

'Maybe both. Well, it's just the – the *feeling* that seems – it's so hard to face – something about it.'

'I think,' Demelza said, 'it would *have* to be clear cut. *Really*, Emma. One way or the other. Marry Sam and live his life. Or not. It would have to be definite, even if it meant doing something you – hated. You couldn't have part of both worlds.'

'That's it,' said Emma. 'That's what I'm afeared of. I've got to think. Though I've thought long enough.' She sighed. 'And pray. All by meself. I think I've forgotten how – if ever I knew . . .'

Demelza watched her walk off down the field, white hat tilted on the jet black hair, red cloak swaying. Soon she dipped out of sight and there were only the chimneys of Nampara to be seen, one lazily smoking where Jane prepared a broth for the children's supper.

CHAPTER VII

A letter arrived by hand in the first week in September from Mrs Gower and it was addressed to Ross.

'Dear Captain Poldark,

'I am sad to have to tell you that my nephew is now ill with a brain fever. He is quite lucid although very weak, and he has expressly asked to see you and your wife. I wonder if we could trespass upon your good nature to this extent? Pray come any day without notice, and spend the night here if your other engagements will permit. It is very grieving to us all to see Hugh so ill, and we daily intercede for his recovery. A new surgeon from Devonport, a Captain Longman, has been attending him this week and has certainly, I think, brought some improvement, but it is slight.

'Pray accept our kindest thoughts.

Frances Leveson Gower."

They were both in when the letter came. Ross looked across at Demelza as she was reading it.

He said: 'We can send a message back with the man. What's today? Monday? I could go Wednesday.'

'Any day you say, Ross.'

He went out and gave the message to the groom. When he came back she was examining a stain on a chair where Clowance had spilt some jam.

'I told him noon on Wednesday. I prefer not to spend the night, and we can have dinner with them and leave straight after.'

'Thank you, Ross.' Her face was hidden.

'Well, I don't relish the visit; but in such a matter one could hardly refuse.'

'All the same . . .'

He went to the window. 'When you went last time it was rather a false alarm, wasn't it?'

'He said so. Hugh said so. He made light of it. But I believe Dwight took a serious view.'

'It's odd,' Ross said shortly.

'What is?'

'When we brought Dwight and Armitage and the other man – what was his name? – Spade, in that boat from Quimper, I gave little for the chance of Dwight surviving. Hugh was the strongest of the three. Like a skeleton, as they all were, but one on wires. Now, it seems, while Dwight climbs slowly back . . .'

'I wonder if Dwight is no longer attending him? I wonder *why*?'

'It's a long way to ride. He couldn't do it every day. And rich people can call on anyone. It sounds as if this Captain Longman is staying in the house. Anyway, we shall see.'

They saw on Wednesday. It was a wet day, the first for two weeks. Rain fell in a weeping veil, the drops so fine and so dense that they penetrated the best protective clothing. When Tregothnan was reached they were both soaked, and Mrs Gower insisted on their having a room and a fire and dry clothing at once. Hugh was little altered, she said, though anxious to see them. Captain Longman was with him, and a nurse. As a precaution Colonel and Mrs Armitage, Hugh's father and mother, had been sent for from Dorset.

Rather irritably Ross wanted to let Demelza go in first to see the sick man, but she asked him to go with her. It was as well, for Hugh was almost unrecognizable. His head had been completely shaved and there were leeches working on his forehead. Blisters on his neck and the back of his head showed where the cantharides plasters had been lately removed. The nurse was bathing his face and hands with a mixture of gin and vinegar and water. There were obviously plasters on his legs from the canopy sheet above them and the pain with which he moved them. Captain Longman, a stout bearded man in his early fifties, with a great stomach and a stiff leg, supervised operations as a general will supervise the battle he is waging. He waved the visitors back and with the brisk movement of a conjurer removed the engorged leeches.

Hugh's eyes, however much they might be clouded with pain, however short and uncertain the distance they could see, were still the beautiful intent eyes he had focused on Demelza at that dinner at Tehidy only a year or so ago, the same eyes she had seen hazed with love and passion on the beach of the Seal Hole Cave. He saw her and smiled, and she pulled her hands away from her face, where they had flown in horror, to smile back at him. She and Ross sat on either side of the bed, and Hugh, moistening his lips, spoke to them slowly, some words coming through, some descending to inaudibility as he swallowed and hesitated with the effort.

'Well, Ross . . . it is a pretty picture, is it not . . . to cheat the Frogs and then oneself be cheated . . .'

'Hold hard,' said Ross. 'You must have seen many men as low in that camp. You'll be up and about again before long.'

'Ah . . . Who knows? And Demelza . . . Mon petit chou . . . You're kind to come . . .'

Demelza said nothing. Her throat had swelled up as if there would never be a passage through it again.

'. . . to come all this way. I have thought of you much . . . this lovely summer. But did you not get wet today?'

Demelza shook her head.

'Ross . . . my apologies to Dwight . . . He could not *live* here, and so my . . . my uncle thought . . . he being a rich man . . . that I should have – a resident physician.'

'Would you not wish to see Dwight now?'

Hugh smiled and shook his head.

'I do not think . . . it will make a great deal of difference, one doctor or another. Nor will these . . . little irritants applied to my body decide the battle.'

Captain Longman, who had not relished such remarks, said: 'These little irritants, my dear sir, though of only forty-eight hours' application, have brought down the fever, reduced the putrid humours and caused an intermission of the excessive action of the blood vessels. Already there is a distinct improvement. Another forty-eight hours will see a big change.'

They stayed a while, then Longman interposed to say his patient must not be tired. They rose to go, but Hugh's hand caught at Demelza's.

'Five minutes?'

Demelza looked at Ross and Ross looked at Longman.

'My wife will stay a few minutes more. I'll wait downstairs.' Ross turned to Hugh and patted his arm. 'Courage, my friend.' He smiled down at him. 'One of us will tire him less than two,' he said to Longman. 'That's good medical theory, I'm sure.'

As he left the room he saw the nurse moving round to his side of the bed to resume her ministrations. Demelza had reseated herself and Hugh was speaking again.

Ross went along two corridors to the room where they had changed. Their clothes were hung on a maiden before the fire but were not yet by any means dry. Being in another man's clothes always fretted him because they fitted ill and none of the pockets was where you expected it. He turned over Demelza's petticoat and stockings and then went out again and downstairs. There were a couple of servants but no sign of Falmouth or Mrs Gower or any of the children.

He went into the big parlour, but there was no one there except a Great Dane who came over to sniff at him, so he sat down in the least uncomfortable chair and patted the dog's head and stared out at the rain.

He did not know whether Hugh Armitage was going to have a long illness or quickly recover, but he was affronted by events, depressed, angry the way they were turning out. It disturbed and upset him to see Demelza so distressed; it upset him that she was so emotionally involved – and her face today in that sick room had betrayed more than it had ever done before. Yet his melancholy, his anger seemed to go even deeper than that. It was as if something in the dark weeping day, the big echoing cheerless house, his moment of utter loneliness now, were all symbolically pointing at him, at his life, at his family and achievements, and showing them up hollow and empty and without purpose or future. For what purpose had they if the centre were gone?

It was not merely his own life but all life that was equally empty and purposeless. People, countless thousands, were hatched upon the earth like maggots every day: they breathed and crawled and enough of them survived and bred to pre-serve the species; but within a space – the blinking of a few sunrises – some accident, some foul-smelling disease befell every one of them and they were thrust into the earth and hastily trodden down by the next generation. So it was Jim Carter a few years ago, and then Charles Poldark and Francis Poldark, and then Julia Poldark and Agatha Poldark, and this year it might be Dwight Enys or Hugh Armitage. Next year? Who came next? And did it matter? Did any damned thing matter at all?

There was a light cough behind him. A boy of about twelve was in the doorway.

'Good morning, sir. Uncle George was asking if you were down. I said I thought I had seen you come in here. He wants to know if you would take a glass of Madeira with him before dinner.'

II

Lord Falmouth was in his usual study and was wearing a banyan, in floral green, of Indian cotton, reaching to the knees. A cheerful fire was burning here and glasses and a bottle were on the table.

'Captain Poldark. I trust the suit is not too short. It belonged to my uncle, who was nearer your size.'

'It serves and is dry. Thank you . . . Yes, Madeira will do well.'

The amber drink was poured into fine crystal glass. Obviously any thought that there had been a conflict of opinion between them at their last meeting was not in his

Lordship's mind. Perhaps he did not remember any such difference. Possibly even his non-action over Odgers had been an oversight and not deliberate – not even worth being deliberate about. Beneath his notice, in fact.

'You – have seen Hugh?'

'Yes . . .'

'His parents should be here soon. I shall feel happier when they are able to take the responsibility.'

'The new doctor? Who is he?'

Falmouth shrugged. 'Attached to the Admiralty. He's highly esteemed and Gower recommended him.'

Ross sipped his drink.

'It's a new dry Madeira,' Falmouth said. 'Better before a meal . . .'

'When did Enys last see him?'

'Two weeks ago.'

'Do you think he should not be called again?'

'It presents a difficulty. Longman has been here scarcely a week and he says there is a distinct improvement in the last twenty-four hours. It's always a difficulty, Poldark . . . When my wife was so desperate ill we had the same problem. Either you trust a man and give him authority to carry out his treatment or you do not. When it goes well you are happy that you did so. When it goes ill you think, if only . . .'

'Yes, I do see that.'

'If his parents arrive tomorrow then the responsibility will be theirs. But no choice will come easy to them unless by then Hugh is clearly on the mend.'

Ross wondered if Demelza were still in the sick room or had returned to the room where they had changed. As if their thoughts ran parallel, Falmouth said:

'Mrs Poldark is with you?'

'Yes. I left her with Hugh.'

'That I think will be a comfort. Hugh thinks highly of your wife. He speaks frequently of her. I too think her an admirable woman.'

'Thank you.' Ross sipped again and watched his host over the rim of the glass.

Falmouth bent to poke the fire. 'It was she and Mrs Enys who helped, in their own way, to bring about a meeting between myself and de Dunstanville which has resulted in a new accord between us.'

'So I understand.'

'And a likely return of two suitably nominated candidates for Truro next week.'

'Next week? So near?'

'If the election goes well – and that is not yet certain – there will, of course, be added satisfaction to me in the fact that Mr Warleggan will lose his seat – a seat he has occupied with less than no distinction for only a twelvemonth.'

'If he loses his seat de Dunstanville will no doubt look after him elsewhere.'

His Lordship straightened up, his face flushed with stooping. 'Possibly.'

There was silence. Ross thought it over,

'But you think not, eh?'

'I think not?'

'Something in your tone suggested you were doubtful.'

'About Warleggan? Well, yes. At our one – er – meeting Basset gave me the impression that his admiration for his nominee was wearing thin.'

'Indeed.'

'Well, it seems that during the banking crisis Basset returned from London and found a situation here which much offended him.'

'Concerning George?'

'Concerning the Warleggans generally – of whom, of course, George is the most prominent. I gather that the Basset Bank and the Warleggan Bank have some agreement for working in accommodation with each other. Once or twice they have financed ventures jointly. But it seems that in February when the Bank of England suspended payment and every note-issuing merchant stood on the brink of disaster, Warleggan's Bank tried to use the crisis to bring down Pascoe's Bank; and in so doing involved Basset's Bank in an exercise which might be justifiable by some standards but which Basset, to his credit, considered highly unsavoury. He returned to Cornwall just in time to withdraw his bank from this manœuvre and to issue new credits to Pascoe's. He was only able to do this, of course, because the situation had eased in London; but he told me that it was likely he would limit further banking contacts of this nature.'

'From which you infer?'

'I do not think from the way he spoke that George Warleggan will be found any other seat that Basset owns.'

Ross stretched his legs towards the fire and then, feeling the seams pulling, withdrew them. 'Well, as I expect you know, my Lord, since everyone else appears to know it, I care for the Warleggans no more than you; so I shall shed no tears if George loses his seat next week.'

'It is by no means certain.'

'Not? But Basset has resigned as Alderman and has withdrawn his interest. That's what I understood.'

'Quite true.' His Lordship gestured with the poker. 'But as you will remember, there was a strong and wayward vote against me in the Council last year. Since then there has been bitter feeling and bitter words expressed on both sides. I do not suppose many who voted for Warleggan at the last election will change their allegiance, even though Basset has gone. It will be a very close thing.'

'Hm . . .' The thick rain was falling on the window without sound, as quiet as snow.

'There is strong feeling against the Government, you know. There is resentment against Pitt, distrust, even hatred.'

'In Truro or in the country?'

'In the country; but in most parts I know it to be in a considerable minority. Not in Truro, where local feeling against me is so much more important than mere dislike of Pitt.'

'Hm,' said Ross again. 'If he fell, who could lead us?'

'No one half so well. Not at this crisis in the country's affairs. But when a war is going ill the people must find a scapegoat, and who better to blame than the Prime Minister? The collapse of the Alliance, the shortage of food among the common people, prices ever rising, the mutinies in the Fleet, the run on the banks; we are alone in a hostile world and Pitt has led the country for thirteen years. So people, many people, believe he has led us into this.'

'Do you?'

'He has made mistakes. But who would not? And, as you say, who could take his place? There is no one of his stature in the country. Portland is a nonentity. Moira would be worse than useless.'

'What of the latest peace negotiations?'

'Foundering, like all the others. The Directory is making impossible conditions. With all Europe under their thumb they can afford to. The latest I hear is that they demand we shall give over to them the Channel Isles, Canada, Newfoundland and British India, as well as all our West Indian possessions.'

Ross finished his drink and got up, stood with his back to the fire.

'Pray help yourself.'

'Thank you.' Ross refilled both glasses. 'Well, there it is. So it's a pretty picture.'

'As dark as any in our history.'

Out in the hall young voices could be heard.

Ross said: 'I hope you will have good fortune with your Truro Members. But I suspect that on a national basis neither George nor Tom Trengrouse would differ much from Pitt on his war aims. They are no followers of Fox.'

Falmouth made no reply but sat staring contemplatively into the fire.

'Well,' Ross said restively. 'I'll see if my wife has returned from the sick room.'

'Of course,' Falmouth said, 'whatever happens to Hugh he will not be well enough to contest the election next Thursday.'

'No . . . of course not, alas. You will by now have had to choose some other candidate. A great pity.'

'I was considering,' his Lordship said, 'offering the nomination to you.'

III

Outside the window was a huge cedar, whose sweeping arms, crystal-grey and olive-green, out-curved in spreading crescents from lofty tip to ground level; and amid its dripping branches Ross saw a red squirrel sitting holding a nut between its front paws and nibbling earnestly. This was an animal they scarcely ever saw on the north coast; the trees were too sparse and wind-blown. He watched it for some seconds with great interest, its furtive, rapid motions, its bright eyes, its puffed nibbling cheeks. Then it spotted him through the window and in a flash was gone, up the tree and melting into the shadows, more like an apparition than a thing of flesh and blood.

Ross said: 'I don't suspect you can be serious, my Lord.'

'Why not?'

'We are usually in accord on the plight of England in war. But at our last meeting we were sharply at odds on everything related to the internal government of England. The function of Parliament, the way men are elected to it, the unequal distribution of power, the venality that exists . . .'

'Yes. But we *are* at war. As I have said before, I believe you have a greater potential than is realized by drilling some Volunteers and keeping your mine in profit. This is a way you might realize some of it.'

'As a Tory?'

His Lordship made a gesture. 'Labels. They mean little. Did you know, for instance, that Fox began his political life as a Tory and Pitt as a Whig?'

'No, I did not.'

'You see, times change. And alignments change. I don't know how much you have studied the course of politics over this century, Captain Poldark . . . But might I venture to offer you my views on the subject?'

'Certainly, if you wish.'

'Well, d'you know, it was the Whigs who, in 1688, saved England from domination by the Stuarts when King James turned away from our church to Rome – and all that that could imply. They brought over William of Orange; and then when Queen Anne died without issue they invited the Hanoverian to be George I. Remember, they were led by our finest aristocracy, who knew what it meant to preserve the liberty of the subject from extreme monarchy. My own family, I'm proud to say, supported them for many years, and secured that support by sending up the right sort of men to the Commons. Nobody believed then in the ideas you seem to have in mind, to change the electoral system which has been a part of our long tradition – nobody, that is, until that King George who is still with us, swayed by undesirable advisers, tried to take the reins of government too much into his own hands. Then the Whigs talked of liberty again – the rights of Magna Carta – and quite properly so.'

'But then – '

'Wait. But the excitable ones – Burke, and Fox and his friends – it went to their heads and they talked of "reform". Liberty to them came to mean equal representation and many of the other things you talk of. When the revolution in France broke out they were quite swept away – they thought Utopia had arrived. But disillusion came rapidly to many of them; especially to Burke; and indeed to the great majority of those who now accept the name of Whig. They didn't – they don't – believe in equal representation, Captain Poldark, any more than the Tories. (Consider your friend Basset.) Pitt is now a Tory, as I am; and I would remind you that in their time the Tories have stood up for religious freedom, for the old liberties of the smaller English gentry, for a greater distribution of power between king and nobles and lesser men. But be that as it may. When the war is won – or lost – we may all examine our allegiances afresh. Pitt is a man of advanced ideas – sometimes too advanced for me; but for the moment he has shelved those ideas because he knows – as all right-thinking men know – that France and its revolution would destroy us, and that is what immediately matters. Let me see, you have met my brother-in-law, Captain Gower, haven't you?'

'No.'

'He has been in the forefront in proposing reform within the navy. I think you would like him.'

Nothing stirred outside the window now except the drifting veils of rain.

'Good God,' Ross said impatiently. 'You offer *me* this? You have the pick of the country to choose from! And, apart from Armitage – relatives in plenty.'

'The answer to that, my dear Poldark, is very simple. I ask you because I believe you have the best chance of winning this seat. Your popularity in the town will, I believe, outweigh the resentment felt against me. Last time my candidate lost by one vote. There is always a certain additional influence attaching to a sitting Member, and Warleggan might still attract one or more extra to counteract de Dunstanville's withdrawal of support.'

'Thank you for your candour.'

'If you expected me to disguise my motives you would not be the man I supposed you to be. My other reasons for asking you I have already stated.'

'Why on earth d'you suppose I'd be likely to accept this offer after I turned down a similar one from Basset eighteen months ago?'

'Circumstances have changed. Times are more grievous. The country calls out for leadership. You know what Canning said last month? "Nothing," he said, "will rouse this nation from stupidity and sleep into a new life and action. We are now soulless and spineless." You admit to a frustration in your present life. One individual, you may say, can do little on his own. But a nation is made up of single individuals.'

Ross turned from the window, looked at his host. A cold man, at any rate in his business affairs, but at least not one you would ever have to mince words with. He decided not to mince them now. The general abrasiveness of his feelings lent an extra edge to his tone.

'You are inviting me, my Lord, to stand for a seat where an unwise use of your authority has alienated the normally amenable electors. Am I right? So, in effect, you're asking me to endorse not merely a system I don't like but a use of power I personally altogether reject. By standing as your candidate I should become a party to such contrivances and would be tacitly supporting them!'

His Lordship waved a dismissive hand.

'I inherited from my uncle an autocratic approach to the boroughs I control. In future I shall take a little more care for the sensibilities of the Council. So we may amend that a little more to your liking. What you may not amend is the electoral system as a whole. You must take it or leave it. Or work for its reform – outside or inside the House.'

He got up. 'But there are more urgent things to do, Captain Poldark. While all Europe is ranged against us.'

Ross said: 'I think my clothes will be dry. I should prefer to change them before dinner.'

'Just so. I'll not keep you now. But I must have your answer before you leave.'

'You shall have it.'

Falmouth put the bottle of Madeira into a cupboard and

locked it. 'Do not forget another advantage to your accepting.'

'What is that?'

'You may both at the same time do me a favour and War-leggan a disservice.'

IV

The young voices – and the young people – had gone from the hall. The house was very quiet, like the day, like the sick man upstairs, like the sickness and shallowness of life. Ross walked across the hall and heard a murmur from behind an open door and looked in. Demelza was talking to Mrs Gower. She looked strange in the borrowed frock, her face pale, her dark eyes thumb-printed with a heavier darkness; a half-stranger at least, not the young woman he had known for thirteen years, not quite his wife, someone withdrawn from him into a pool of her own spirit where not only the familiar emotions stirred.

They had not seen him and he did not go in, not wishing to break in on them, preferring his own dark thoughts. He went upstairs and missed his way, found himself at the foot of the spiral staircase leading to the cupola. He retraced his steps. A cheerless house, if ever there was one. Thank God he would never have the means or the ambition to enlarge Nampara more than he had done already. But the Bassets' was a cheerful place compared to this. Some people had a faculty for making a home.

He found the bedroom at the third attempt. His clothes were not dry but they would do. Lord Falmouth's uncle had had shorter legs, and it was damned uncomfortable.

The fire blazed brightly and he was glad of the warmth while he changed. After tying his cravat he moved some of Demelza's clothes nearer to make the best use of the heat. Her stockings were still wet and the hem of her skirt and underskirt would take half a day to dry.

As he moved the skirt a piece of paper fell out of the pocket and he stooped to pick it up and thrust it back. But the blue ink, which was unusual and distinctive, drew his attention, and before he could stop himself he was reading what was written there.

When I am gone remember this of me
That earth of earth or heaven of heaven concealed
No greater happiness than was to me revealed
By favour of a single day with thee.
If for those moments you should shed a tear
Proud I would be and prouder of your sorrow;
Even if no memory beyond tomorrow
In your sweet heart will empty me of fear.
Leave in the sand a heel mark of your crying,
Scatter all grief to silence and to air.
Let the wind blow your beauty ever fair
And leave me thus to occupy my dying.

CHAPTER VIII

The Warleggans returned to Truro from Trenwith on Sunday the tenth of September. It was earlier than customary, but George had to be present for the elections on Thursday, and Elizabeth decided to return with him. With no Geoffrey Charles and only her ailing parents for company, Trenwith offered no special attraction, and the hot lovely summer was almost over. The new parliament would re-assemble in early October, and she had decided to go up with George. Her last visit had brought her new experiences and new friends, and it was exciting to be at the very centre of things, so near the heart of power. And she would see Geoffrey Charles for a few days before he returned to Harrow.

She had consented to arrangements whereby he spent the whole summer with schoolfriends in Norfolk, knowing that this was for the best and that it might avoid a conflict between her son and her husband, and hoping that a whole year's absence would help to make the break between Geoffrey Charles and Drake complete. But life for her was not quite the same without him. The most important person to her had long been Geoffrey Charles. Valentine could not supplant him; he had never quite caught at her heart.

The day he learned of de Dunstanville's new accord with

Falmouth and his deal over the Truro and Tregony boroughs George had been like thunder: letter in hand he had ridden off to Tehidy the same morning. There some high words had been spoken; he had made his displeasure clear but had found his patron coldly, politely adamant – henceforward in the Truro borough Mr Warleggan must fend for himself. It was an unhappy interview, and some of the remarks he had made in his first moments of offended self-esteem he had soon regretted. Since the day he first met Basset he had made it his business to be agreeable to him and it had borne suitable fruit. He was too influential a man to be estranged from, and already George was making tactful efforts to heal the breach.

For, in fact, so far as his own seat in Truro was concerned George, after the first alarm, was not too gravely worried. After Basset resigned as Capital Burgess a battle raged within the Council as fierce as any that might happen at the election itself, for this could well *decide* the election. In the end the mayor, a Tory now, threatened with the example of a former mayor a few years before who had obstructed a majority and gone to prison for it, had given way, and the Whigs in triumph had been able to appoint Vivian Fitz-Pen, the scion of an ancient house now much decayed and him a good example of it, but a Foxite Whig who would not vote for a Boscawen candidate if the heavens fell.

So there was, as George explained to Elizabeth, now no political difference in the make-up of the Council from last year. Indeed he thought, he ventured to think, that certain steps he had taken to increase the obligation of certain councillors towards his family and himself would result in a larger majority than the very narrow one by which he had been elected last time.

It was the usual nasty journey home, bumpier than usual even, and dustier; but at least the extra riders who came with them were not needed to draw them out of the mud, and in spite of her sick headache, Elizabeth sent off a little card to Morwenna inviting them to supper on the Monday, and Morwenna replied that they would be delighted to come.

Elizabeth almost asked Rowella and Arthur as well; but somehow one just couldn't bring oneself to invite a librarian, not to supper at least, and she knew it would have made

George angry. Also of course she knew of the continuing, and puzzling, ill-will between the sisters.

When the guests arrived that evening George was absent, but she did have a few minutes alone with her cousin while her cloak was being taken, and she asked, first, of course, after the health of John Conan, and then, casually, after Rowella.

'I haven't seen her,' said Morwenna,

'Not at all?'

'Not at all.'

'You are lucky to live by the river. Truro has been very close and unhealthy, I expect. I trust she's well.'

'I trust so.'

'We shall be here about three weeks now before going to London, so I must ask her down to tea.'

'You must come to tea with me,' said Morwenna.

'Thank you, my dear. But will you not come and take tea with me when she is here?'

'Thank you, Elizabeth. I'd really prefer not.'

'My dear, you feel very hard upon her? She was very young and no doubt has erred in her judgement. But . . .'

'Dear Elizabeth, it is something I prefer not to discuss. If you don't mind.'

'But does not your mother write and ask you about Rowella – as she's not yet sixteen?'

'I believe Mama and Rowella correspond direct.'

'I have seen her husband in the library. He seems a courteous young man.'

'Yes, I believe he is.'

Elizabeth sighed. 'Very well, my dear. Let us go in, for Ossie will be all alone and feeling neglected.'

As they walked down the hall Elizabeth noticed that her cousin had not bothered even to pat her hair after taking off the crepe hood of her cloak. Her long frock of blue lawn with fichu at neck and lace at wrists was one Elizabeth had not seen before, but it was so creased the girl might have slept in it. Yet for all that she was not unattractive; it seemed as if she walked and talked with a new certainty which was no less becoming than the old shyness. Her face looked as if she had been through troublous times, but more men would look at her now than when she had been so young and innocent.

Ossie was indeed alone in the parlour and pondering a further strange and disturbing event in his life. Today, for the third time since they had parted, he had passed Rowella in the street. And this time, glancing at him obliquely through her lashes, she had half smiled. So difficult was the expression to interpret that it could have been a smile of derision, of triumph, of satisfaction, of would-be friendship or even of invitation. It had left Ossie hot and newly angry all over again and desperately aroused. It lent encouragement to his worst fantasies, and it had taken him all day to shake off the effects.

Now, however, he was himself again, and they drank canary and listened to his monologue on church affairs until George joined them.

George was not greatly pleased to have Osborne at his board today, nor in fact any day. Hardly a month went by but that Ossie wrote to George with some new request. His latest objective was the living of St Newlyn, which had fallen vacant; but everyone was turning a deaf ear to his pleas – in so far as anyone *could* turn a deaf ear to Ossie – the general feeling being that plurality for him had gone far enough for the time being. George would have borne with his importunities more patiently if his uncle, Conan Godolphin, had proved of more use to him in London. But Conan had turned out to be a fop, consorting with people of like mind, and although knowing and being often in the company of the Prince of Wales, peculiarly inept at introducing his new relative by marriage into any of the company that his new relative by marriage sought.

This evening George had come in directly from the office, where he and his uncle, Cary, had been looking over a number of account bills that were due and considering which might be renewed; and he was in no mood for idle chatter. This indeed eventually made itself perceptible even to Ossie, for, after a considerable silence because his own mouth was full, he noticed that no one else was speaking.

'How is it, Cousin George? You seem a thought down-in-the-mouth today. I trust you're not sickening of a summer fever. My man has had it; sweating like a pig he's been for three days; I've dosed him ten grains of jalap but he seems little improved. There's much of it about. I buried a girl last week who could not shake it off.'

'I have seldom felt better,' George said, 'so I don't think your official services are likely to be required.'

'Nay, no offence meant. Do you not think he looks a shade bilious, Elizabeth? Well, no doubt you've enough to occupy your mind, what with the war news no better and this coming election. It's time, I believe, our legislators made some move to put down unrest in *this* country before they continue the war in Europe. We cannot fight – indeed we cannot do anything – while so much revolution is being talked and bred on every hand.' He paused to stoke up, and again no one spoke while he chewed and swallowed, chewed and swallowed.

Morwenna said: 'It is the election on Thursday? But I thought almost everyone – '

Ossie said: 'It will be a hard tussle to gain re-election now Basset has gone. D'you think your new opponent will carry many votes on account of his so-called popularity?'

George looked up. 'Gower? I doubt it. I don't know who the other will be yet – '

'Oh, had you not heard? I heard from Polwhele this afternoon. You know how thick he is with the Boscawens? He supped with them last night. I went up this morning on church business. The Archdeacon, you know, is coming again, and I wish all my influential parishioners to be there at the Visitation dinner.' He stopped for another intake.

George sipped his wine. 'I do not suppose that Falmouth has – '

'It's to be Poldark,' said Ossie, swallowing. 'Poldark of Nampara. Myself, I should have thought him too much of a fly-by-night adventurer to be worthy of Falmouth's attention. But then you see – no doubt he conceits to turn his late notoriety to some account.'

For a while there was silence as supper proceeded. From below, outside, came the cupped clatter of horses' hooves, *tlot-tlot*, *tlot-tlot*, slow past the window.

George motioned to a footman.

'Sir?'

'Take this wine away. It is unpalatable. Bring a bottle of the vin de Graves.'

Ossie took a gulp at his glass. 'It's not the best, I agree. Maybe you've had it up out of the cellar too long. There's one thing I could do with at St Margaret's, a more adequate and cooler cellar. They say being so near the river one can hardly go deeper and remain dry.'

'Do you find the vicarage damp?' Elizabeth asked Morwenna. 'Of course, we too are on the river here, but it's less enclosed than among your lovely trees.'

'We have damp upstairs,' said Morwenna. 'When it rains. Where Rowella used to sleep. But not from the river, I believe.'

'We have damp in the *church*,' said Ossie. 'In the church-yard too. A great problem with the stones. The moss grows quick and the names quite disappear.'

'I was asking Morwenna about Rowella,' Elizabeth said to Ossie. 'Whether you had seen anything of her and if she is well?'

'*Nothing*,' said Mr Whitworth noisily. 'Nothing at all. For us it is as if she had never *existed*.'

'Forgive me, Ossie, but isn't that rather a harsh judgement on so young a girl for merely having married so much beneath her? She married precipitately – but for love, I presume?'

'I have no *notion*,' said Mr Whitworth. 'No notion *whatever*! Nor do I wish to *think* of it.'

The manservant came back with a new bottle of wine and fresh glasses. Anxiously he waited while George tried it; then, having received neither complaint nor approval, he proceeded to fill the other glasses. Presently it was done. Ossie tried the old wine again and then the new, and agreed that the new was better. Silence fell and endured.

'So Ross Poldark enters politics,' said George, looking across at Elizabeth.

'I never cared for the fellow,' said Ossie. 'But I suppose he'll draw a bit of water in the town.'

George said to Elizabeth: 'And as a Boscawen nominee. That's a cynical turnabout for a one-time rebel. To what desperate straits are some men driven to achieve respectability in middle life.'

Ossie said: 'He was very put out when that brother-in-law of his was flattened by your gamekeeper. That reminds me, I've had no reply from him to my letter about Sawle Church.'

Elizabeth, short of breath, said: 'Are you *sure* you have the person right, Ossie?'

'Oh, Gad, yes. Polwhele was somewhat entertained at the thought. Made a joke about it, if I remember. Said Poldark in parliament would provide more backbone than wishbone!' Ossie laughed, but no one joined in.

'He is not yet in parliament,' said George. 'Nor do I think he will get very far in seeking to further *that* ambition.'

No more was said on the subject over supper. Nor did any other conversation prosper.

II

Cary Warleggan scratched under his skullcap and put his pen down.

'It is – *totally* outrageous. Wait till your father hears!'

'Never mind about Father – he will hear in due time.'

Cary got up, his eyes a-glint, plucking at his bottom lip. The years had dealt less well with him than with most of the family. Chronic dyspepsia and stomachic gout had robbed him of the little flesh he had had, and his clothes hung on him as on an arrangement of bones. Yet he was seldom absent from the counting house, and often ordered what little food he ate brought to him there, rather than leave and disturb his industry. More than either his elder brother Nicholas or his nephew, he kept a finger on the pulse of all Warleggan enterprises. Whether it was arranging a shipment of pig iron from one of the foundries of Wales, or arranging for a clerk in the counting house to become secretary to a newly-formed joint stock company, it was Cary who attended to the details.

Though never dishonest, it was he who represented the less savoury side of Warleggan activity. It was he who had exerted the pressure in February and nearly brought Pascoe's Bank down, and, although this had been done with George's knowledge and tacit approval, George now held it bitterly against him because (a) it had failed, and (b) it had soured the relationship between their bank and Basset, Rogers & Co. Sometimes Cary could be too clever, too much the schemer; and George, who in earlier years had more often sided with his uncle than with his father, now saw more virtue in his father's scruples.

Of course Cary himself had certain standards which he now proceeded to air. Not everyone would have thought them inferior.

'It is absolutely monstrous that a man like Falmouth, who, whatever else, has inherited a peerage and vast estates, should ally himself with this good-for-nothing mountebank; a man with virtually a prison record and a –'

'No prison record, Uncle. You will remember, he was acquitted.' As always George seemed to appease his own enmity by fuelling Cary's.

'Acquitted against all the canons of justice! If not a record, then a history, of lawless escapades up and down the county. Having to leave England as a boy because of these episodes and clashes with preventive men, returning and breaking open a jail and taking out a prisoner! Concerned in the death of our cousin, in wrecking, in smuggling and inciting miners to riot! Now suddenly the idol of the county because of an equally dubious adventure, undertaken this time against the French! And this is the sort of man one of our premier viscounts considers suitable to represent this borough in parliament! It – it . . .'

'Our viscount,' said George, 'has no moral standards when fighting to regain a seat he considers his. He thinks Ross's popularity will sway the vote. We must see it does not.'

Cary wrapped his tail-coat around him as if he were cold. Since it was forty years old it was much too large for him and there was material to spare.

'We have attended to most of our supporters.'

'Yes, but let us go through the list again.'

Cary pulled open a drawer, took out a ledger, and opened it where a slip of paper was to be seen.

'Well, here they are. It all looks reasonable sound. I suppose you might put Aukett among the doubtful ones. And perhaps Fox.'

'Aukett,' said George, 'received a substantial loan in March.

It was advanced to him at three per cent interest with no question of a repayment date. He knows that no repayment will be demanded unless he shows independence in his voting opinions. It was understood. It was the purpose of the loan.'

'He was once a close friend of Poldark's, you know – in that copper-smelting venture.'

'Forget it. Or if you wish to underline the point, remind him. But friendships do not wax strong when a threat of the debtor's prison hangs over a man's head.'

'Fox also was in the smelting venture but less deeply involved – he drew out early. More recently he has had transactions with the Boscawens. Through them he received some contract for carpets; so he may be torn both ways.'

'Let us see that he is torn the right way.' George peered at the ledger over his uncle's shoulder. 'If it is a tug-of-war between obligation and indebtedness, then indebtedness should win . . . Yes, it must surely win. A letter tomorrow perhaps making his position plain, though in guarded terms.'

'No letter,' said Cary, pulling his skullcap down. 'A word is the thing. He lives distant. I'll send Tankard in the morning.'

A clerk knocked and came in with some enquiry, but George gave him a look and he shrivelled back out of the door.

'Polwhele?' said Cary.

'Hopeless. He's committed to the Boscawens and banks at Pascoe's.'

'Notary Pearce?'

'We shall take care of him.'

They went through the rest of the names. A few were Portland Whigs who nevertheless could be relied on to vote against Pitt, however much collaboration between the two groups there might be in the House. Others were Tories of the old school and equally pledged to the opposite side. Of the twenty-five voters, it boiled down to about ten who could sway the vote and could themselves be swayed.

It was past eleven o'clock and time to finish for the night, but they spent another half-hour in the dark little office discussing tactics. On a count yesterday they had made it out that George and Trengrouse would have a safe majority. Now that there was this added menace of the Poldark name –

and the added goad – they wished to be doubly sure. At the end – assuming that Aukett and Fox would toe the line – it really seemed to depend a lot upon two names, and two rather distinguished ones at that: Mr Samuel Thomas of Tregolls and Mr Henry Prynne Andrew of Bodrean. Both had dined with the Warleggans recently; both were very old friends of Elizabeth's parents; both had expressed themselves gratified at certain small favours George had been able to do them. If both these gentlemen voted for him, George counted on a majority of five. If one of the two chose wantonly to vote against him, he should have a majority of three. Even if by some extraordinary misfortune both defected to the other side, he would still get in by the single vote by which he had been elected before. It seemed safe enough. The point that waited decision was whether any form of request could be put to either of these two gentlemen, if so how it might be phrased, and whether there was the risk of its doing more harm than good.

It seemed certain that Falmouth would not leave them unregarded. But there was some story of Falmouth and Prynne Andrew having been involved in a dispute a couple of years ago over mineral rights.

Eventually, since Uncle Cary seemed to have no finesse in his nature which was not in some way connected with the manipulation of money, George put the sheet of paper back in the ledger and shut and locked the ledger away in the drawer.

'I will ask Elizabeth's advice. She's known them both since she was a child and will be more likely to know how far they would respond, and in what way, to a polite solicitation.'

Cary drew in his lips, as he usually did at mention of his niece by marriage – they seldom spoke. 'Why do you not invite *her* to ask them? They are old friends. Let her make the contact. Let her go and see them. Let her take a ride tomorrow afternoon – take tea with 'em, or whatever is the polite thing to do. Eh?'

George looked at his uncle without much favour. 'I'll discuss it with her. But nothing shall be done in haste. We still have a little time.'

CHAPTER IX

The dawn of September the fourteenth was brilliant, new-lit by the sun rising behind a sky as red as a wound. Gimlett said the weather would not last the day. The sea's darkness under the sun presaged the autumn. All the corn was in, and Ross had sent two of his farm men to Sawle to help draw in another catch of pilchards. Demelza's hollyhocks, dying hard in the warm and windless days, were flaunting faded colours from the last flowers.

Ross had told her that he had to be in Truro early and, lacking other information, she supposed it to do with the re-organization of the Volunteers.

It was a silent breakfast, Jeremy and Clowance still sleeping after being late to bed. Most meals had been silent recently and it had been a hard week. None like it since the last months of '93. Demelza was plainly grieving for Hugh Armitage, and waited all the time for a message of good or ill news. Ross, his feelings bruised but judgement half suspended, watched her anxiety and said nothing. If she wanted to speak about Hugh she could speak. If not, not.

He did not know the meaning of the poem he had read; it might mean that Demelza had been unfaithful to him, it might all be poetic licence. He had not asked her and would not ask her. What was plain during this week was that she was being unfaithful in spirit, her thoughts, her emotions, her heart, deeply engaged with another man.

And that man was gravely *ill*. How did a husband feel? Jealous and injured? Inadequate and angry? Sympathetic and understanding? Why did one's throat tighten at every other thought?

He left before eight, riding up the bare but smiling valley among the nut trees and the hawthorn, the bubble of the stream keeping him company. His land. Crickets sawed in the hedges, swallows were wheeling and swooping, cattle, his cattle, grazing in the fields. Wheal Grace smoked quietly and a couple

of tin stamps clanged. The countryside looked benign, as if
the summer had ripened every leaf and berry. It was all his —
his, changed from the overgrown worthless ruin he had come
back to fourteen years ago. But today there was no ripeness,
no contentment in him. So man set his hopes and endeavours
high and when he had achieved them they were so much dross
and clinker in his hands.

He was in Truro too early and left his horse at the Red Lion
and took a walk down to the quay. He had no wish to meet
anybody, neither his opponents nor his supporters, nor even
his sponsor until the required time.

The tide was in and water lapped close against the uneven
stone of the old quay. Here the last of the town fell down into
a huddle of warehouses and sheds and half-derelict, over-
peopled cottages. Littered about the quay among the wagons
and the hand-carts was the usual detritus of a small port:
rope ends and broken spars, rags of tarpaulin and sail-cloth,
broken jars and a dead seagull. A three-masted lugger was
being unloaded, and men were rolling barrels down a narrow
plank on to the shore. Farther on two other craft were moored
alongside, making the most of high water. Two beggar children
came whining to Ross but he waved them away: if you gave
to two there would soon be twenty. Women screamed at each
other from a window. A horse tossed its head in a nosebag to
reach the last of his meal.

Past all this you came to grassland and a sort of pool of
the river before it widened out towards Malpas and St Margaret's Church. Here it was utterly still, sun-lit, tree-sharpened
at the edges, a few river-birds skimming low. Near the bank
were four swans, almost stationary, moving so slowly that they
appeared only to be drifting with the tide. Each one was
mirrored, duplicated in the still water. It seemed sometimes
that they could see their own reflections and were admiring
themselves. Then one or another would break her reflection
by dipping a delicate beak. Graceful things. White things. Like
women. Unpredictable. Gentle. Fierce. Faithful or unfaithful.
Loyal or traitorous. God, who knew?

A gust of gnats moved around him, and he waved them
away like the beggar children. They departed as reluctantly.
Smell of wood smoke drifted on the air. Leaves were turning

colour early. In the massed trees of the other river bank copper
and ochre was staining the green.

The swans were separating little by little, inertly, more it
seemed by vagaries of the current than by design. The one
nearest the bank had a more slender neck and a more graceful
way of holding it, like a question mark. She drifted towards
him, wings a little elevated, head to one side, fate or errant
fancy bringing her. Then she suddenly turned away, foot lazily
moving, rejecting any interest she might appear to have shown.
He had made no movement either to entice or rebuff.

Four women in his life? Four with whom he had been
concerned this year? Demelza and Elizabeth, of course. Caroline? Who was the fourth? One of the swans had a damaged
wing, feathers awry and stained. On Sawle Feast day Ross had
been turning to leave his pew when Morwenna had smiled at
Drake, and he had caught a glimpse of the smile. The
damaged swan. Appropriate image. So she would stay while
she remained linked to that man. But who was to alter that
now? Whom God hath joined . . .

And his own marriage? And Elizabeth's? And even Caroline's? All in the melting pot? Certainly his own. This was the
worst of it, when he had thought his own the most deep-
rooted, the most secure. Like a rock. But the rock was on sand.
One man, a likeable man but in his own way unprincipled, had
come into their house and come between them. Now she was
part lost – or wholly lost – he did not know.

And why in God's name had he consented to come here this
morning to participate in this charade? What stupid and
inappropriate impulse had swayed him at Tregothnan a week
ago?

'I accept,' he had said, 'I accept your nomination on three
conditions. The first is that, irrespective of any directives you
may give, I may support Pitt in any measures to sustain the
war.'

'Of course.'

'The second is that I shall be free to support any Bill or
measure which in my view is likely to bring help or better
conditions for the poor.'

'Agreed.' There had been hesitation before this answer.

'The third is that I shall be free to support Wilberforce

against the trade in slaves.'

A further hesitation. 'Agreed.'

It had been settled like that, drily, a business transaction, little more said, neither of them attempting to specify the details. *Too* little had been said. It might be a small matter to the noble lord: it was not small to him; it involved half his future. If the details had been spelled out it might have enabled him to see over again the absurdity of the proposition, just as he had seen it when put to him by Basset last year. He would have had time to withdraw, to back out, to deride himself even for considering it.

There was still time . . . Well, hardly. The agreement had been made; it was a matter of honour to go through with it now. Honour? What had honour to do with it?

All the same he might well not be elected. During the week he had heard sufficient comment to know that the town council were still in a rebellious mood. Having only just thrown off the yoke of their aristocratic borough-monger, it seemed unlikely that they would meekly accept it again a year later. It would be much better if that happened. Then all the second thoughts, the rabid self-criticisms, the mental reservations would be unnecessary.

Ross kicked irritably at a stone. Fine. He would be defeated. So George Warleggan would be returned instead of him and go back to Parliament again. Was that what he wanted? Would this result enable him to live happily ever after? Another triumph over him for George – after all his other triumphs. Congratulations all round.

Better not ever to have stood than be defeated. Falmouth had put it to him bluntly, and, whether he cared to admit it or not, the circumstance of his being in opposition to George had influenced his choice. A bad reason, indeed an ignoble reason, but one that should not be evaded just because it was unsavoury.

The swans were moving away now, pale, dignified, enigmatical, out of his life for ever. Double mirrored in the soundless pool, they might have been representing some reverse side of their beings, like humans offering one image to the world and retaining another for private introspection. After all these years did he know or understand the mirror image of Demelza?

Not, it seemed, in anything but the shallowest of water. Did he even know and understand himself?

Starlings began to sweep the sky. The sun was disappearing in a watery mist. He took out his watch. Ten-thirty. He turned and walked back towards the town.

II

The council chamber was quite small, the numbers in it limited. Not all the voters had turned up yet, although it wanted only ten minutes to eleven o'clock. But it seemed improbable that any would fail to attend. Feeling ran high in the town. Mostly the elections in such a borough passed quietly enough and as a foregone conclusion. But from time to time storms blew up, and the by-election of last year had seen the biggest upset of them all. Fortunately it was unlikely that there would be endless – or even any – challenges as to the legitimacy of the voters, such as occurred at so many elections. The members of the corporation, the Aldermen and the Burgesses, had all been themselves truly elected and their election acknowledged, if grudgingly, by those who opposed them.

Ross was the last of the candidates to arrive. Lord Falmouth was already there, looking as usual like a prosperous farmer who had had a bad year. He was talking to the new mayor, Mr Warren. Captain Gower, a stocky dark-clad man of forty-odd, came across and shook Ross by the hand. Ross gave him an uncomfortable smile and glanced over at George Warleggan, who was talking to his fellow candidate, Thomas Trengrouse, who was a brother-in-law of the Cardews. It was the first time they had looked at each other, George and Ross, since the disputed wrestling match, and their glances were no warmer. Behind George was his father, and behind Nicholas the Reverend Dr Halse and Mr Hick, both life-long Whigs. Across the room was Harris Pascoe, who flushed when Ross moved to speak to him.

'So you see,' Ross said.

'Yes . . . yes I see.'

'It puts your conscience into more of a tangle than ever, this cross-fertilizing of so many pollens: friendship, loyalty to one's principles and the rest. If I were you I should have stayed away.'

'If you were I you w-would have come,' said Pascoe. 'Which is precisely what I have done.'

'To vote for me, I'm sure, and so ruin your standing as a leading Whig.'

'No more than I did last time.'

'Tell me, Harris, you have been at these occasions before; what is the polite procedure? Do I have to shake hands with my opponents as is obligatory at a wrestling match, or am I permitted to continue to eye them with enmity from the other side of the hall?'

'The latter, I think, is more customary. But I am interested, Ross, that you have decided to stand now, after last year refusing an invitation from the other side.'

'It might have made more sense if I had accepted then, mightn't it? Basset is more my style of man than Boscawen. Yet, really there's little to choose, as indeed there's little to choose betwixt the parties. Put my choice down to the way-wardness of fate and the contrariness of human beings. This is what makes the world the sad and wry place it is.'

Pascoe eyed his friend. Prosperity and the passage of a decade and a half had made little change in Ross from the days when as a bony, wounded young officer, he had returned from the American war penniless and the inheritor of a property overgrown and in ruins. Today, perhaps more than usually, he reminded Harris Pascoe of that young man. The high-strung disquiet was back at its most noticeable.

A bell rang. The clerk of the council, one Gerald Timms, had rung it to let the company know that it was eleven o'clock and time for business to begin. As he rose with a book in his hand, two more members of the council arrived. The clerk read the Proclamation, giving notice of the election, and then the Sheriff's precept. George Warleggan and Thomas Tren-grouse moved to take seats near him, and Captain Gower nodded to Ross to join him in doing the same. As they did this the clerk continued by reading the Act of George II.2, against bribery and corruption. He had a thin voice which squeaked on the high notes, and his breath was short. From the look of his teeth, Ross thought, it was likely to be foul also.

This done, another Act was read. When it was over the

mayor came forward and was sworn in as returning officer. He sat down and signed the book, pulled his glasses farther to the edge of his nose and waited.

George Evelyn, third Viscount Falmouth, rose from his chair, and as he was about to speak two more late-comers arrived. They were the last. Thereafter in the chamber was silence while Lord Falmouth put forward the two candidates he had to propose. He spoke first of his brother-in-law, Captain Gower, his work as Secretary to the Admiralty, his value to the town in obtaining certain contracts for supplies, his support of Pitt, his dedication to his duties both in and out of the House. He then commended his second candidate, Captain Poldark, who was new to politics but whom they all knew as a distinguished soldier and a brave one, whose daring exploit of '95 had resounded throughout the county and whose intimate and personal knowledge of mining and local industry as a whole would be invaluable to the town he would represent.

George Evelyn sat down, son of the late and great Admiral Boscawen (victor of Puerto Bello, Lagos and Cape Breton, the terror of the French). He had spoken with little effort and no emotion but in a manner which showed his long habituation to being heard. Nicholas Warleggan rose in his place, son of a blacksmith who still lived at an advanced age near St Day in a small house with two servants, whom he hated, to look after him. Only in the last twenty years had Nicholas become accustomed to deferential silence when he spoke, but twenty years is long enough, and to this he added an accent and a turn of phrase which his opponent lacked. He spoke of things current in the minds of all his listeners fifteen months ago when the by-election had been held; and, since he had now irretrievably quarrelled with the Boscawens, he did not hesitate to recall them or to mince his words in doing so. The squabble over the burial ground came up, the workhouse, stones from the quarry, and his Lordship's private and totally unjustified complaints that the borough was expensive for him to maintain and his frequent attempts to sell the seats to the highest bidder. Finally his treatment of the borough as a chattel to be disposed of at will and without the consent of the electors.

He made no apology for repeating these complaints, Mr Warleggan went on, since it was only because of the indigna-

tion of the council at being so treated that Mr George Warleggan had been persuaded to offer himself for the seat vacated
by the death of Sir Piers Arthur; and it was not out of disrespect for the Boscawen family but because of the council's
public-spirited and determined independence that they had
duly elected him. Since he had been elected Mr George Warleggan had faithfully served the town, as several merchants
and councillors of the town would no doubt be prepared to
attest. He would continue to do so; and many would agree
that it was a welcome change to have a local man to represent
them, a Member resident in the town, and a banker, with
a vast knowledge of local business affairs and needs, instead
of some up-country gentleman who served other interests,
mainly his own. Equally Mr Thomas Trengrouse was resident
in the town and a well-known and able attorney. Between them
these two gentlemen would make up a team such as had not
represented this borough in living memory, if ever before.
Both gentlemen, Mr Warleggan ventured to believe, were
greatly to be preferred to an Admiralty official whose time was
greatly taken up with naval matters or to a country squire
living far off on the north coast, a gentleman of narrow out-
look and unpredictable impulse, who knew little of commerce
– and what little he knew he tended to despise. In any event,
did the council still wish to assert this independence by elect-
ing two candidates who stood only to serve them, or did
they wish to bow to his Lordship, acknowledge their error
of last year, and accept his nominees who would thence-
forward do whatever he bade them do, in all matters civic and
parliamentary?

It was a good speech, not eloquent but meaningful and to
the point – a far better one than the one that had preceded it.
Ross had to admit that it half convinced him. Had it been any
other than a Warleggan speaking it and spoken of, he would
have felt like voting against himself. But then he knew, as
many others in the room must know, what the Warleggans
really stood for, in business, in banking, in the sort of
behaviour between man and man that he fundamentally and
passionately rejected. But how many of the two dozen
assembled voters, knowing what he did, *felt* as he did and were
prepared equally to reject it?

By the look in the eyes that had avoided his in the last fifteen minutes, Ross knew that not all his friendly acquaintances and well-wishers were going to vote for him. Had they been able to do so by letter and the letters kept private, it would have been a different matter. Some, he could see, were horribly torn, not for fear of offending him, for he had no stick to raise over them, but between incurring the anger of the Boscawens and the anger of the Warleggans. Basset with his lures and rewards was gone. But the choice was made no easier for that. The early indignation, the flashing heady independence which had occasioned the revolt last year had partly subsided. They had 'freely' voted then, and to the devil with the consequences. Now some at least of them had to vote under a conflicting duress.

The mayor was sitting rubbing his eyebrow with the feather of his pen. There was a long pause. No one wished to be the first to move.

The mayor said: 'Gentlemen . . .'

Nicholas Warleggan got up and walked to the table. 'I will vote for Mr Warleggan and Mr Trengrouse.'

There was another pause. Then a chair scraped. It was William Hick. 'Mr Warleggan and Mr Trengrouse.'

The Reverend Dr Halse followed him. He had been an enemy of Ross's ever since a card game in the Assembly Rooms many years ago. Perhaps even before that when he had tried to teach him Latin. 'Mr Warleggan and Mr Trengrouse.'

Moving rather quickly for him, as if anxious to prevent the appearance of a rout, Lord Falmouth moved to the table. 'Captain Gower and Captain Poldark.'

Harris Pascoe was behind him. 'Captain Gower and Captain Poldark.'

Lord Devoran came, blinking, as if surprised by the light. 'Captain Gower and Captain Poldark.'

A further pause. Some whispering. Footsteps. St Aubyn Tresize. 'Captain Gower and Captain Poldark.'

William Aukett, squinting more horribly than usual in his distress, stumbling over the words he had to say: 'Mr Warleggan and Mr Trengrouse.'

Scrapings at the back of the hall. Mr Notary Pearce, assisted by a servant, was now seen to be hobbling, pain-racked and blowing, towards the table. Mr Pearce had not slept at all well. His spinster daughter had been up and helping him to the close-stool repeatedly. The prime example of an elector torn both ways, he would gladly have pleaded illness and failed to turn up, had he not known that this way he would equally have offended both parties. But what was he to say? He asked his daughter and he asked himself. He was personally in debt to Cary Warleggan – not even to the slightly more impersonal Warleggan's Bank – yet he owed half his business to the Tregothnan estate, and Mr Curgenven, Lord Falmouth's steward, had made a point of calling on him yesterday to remind him of this. It was a dire fix, and the twist of his eyebrows as he walked, the sweat starting on his brow and under his bob-wig, were not solely the result of his physical infirmities.

He got to the table and an extra silence fell. The mayor looked at him over his glasses. Mr Pearce stuttered and then spoke.

'Captain Gower and – and Mr Warleggan.'

Someone tittered behind Ross as Mr Pearce staggered away. He had done his best, he seemed to say, making a gesture with his free hand; he had tried to please both sides. In fact both sides would be furious; yet they would be hard put to it to accuse him of betraying them. With an old notary's cunning he had made the best of an impossible dilemma.

Others were approaching the table more freely now, as if glad to be done with it. Polwhele and Ralph-Allen Daniell were for Gower and Poldark; Fitz-Pen, Rosewarne and Michell for Warleggan and Trengrouse. Then Mr Prynne Andrew stumped up. Elizabeth had been prevailed upon to call on him on Tuesday, much to her distaste, and had received what seemed a favourable answer.

'Captain Poldark and Captain Gower,' he said.

So that was a smack in the face. George's expression tightened but he made no comment to anyone, and his gaze was fixed elsewhere as Mr Andrew came past him.

Another man walked up, called Buller. He had a small estate and enough money to sustain it and owed nothing to anyone. He said: 'Captain Poldark and Mr Trengrouse.'

A second cross-vote, which could complicate the issue. The mayor looked down at his book and shook sand on it. There were nine more to vote.

Fox was the next, and Ross knew by the uneasy way he hobbled past that this choice would come from pressure and not preference.

'Mr Warleggan and Captain Poldark.'

Well. Pearce's example was catching. Fox had also obeyed his masters and defied them. It was a touching tribute to old loyalties.

Four more, including General Macarmick, voted conventionally, two each way. Then Mr Samuel Thomas of Tregolls. When he got to the mayor he seemed to hesitate, as if his mind still had to be made up, as if there were some conflict in his own thoughts deeper than mere obligation. Then he said firmly, 'Captain Gower and Mr Trengrouse.' George went white.

Three more to come. One was Dr Daniel Behenna, who, it might not be indelicate to say, had a finger in almost every pie. On him a lot might depend. But he had done his sums the night before. 'Mr Warleggan and Mr Trengrouse,' he said.

The last two were inoffensive men, one called Symons, a little dandy who always wore two watches. The other, Hitchens, was known in the town as Mister Eleven, from the thinness of his legs. Neither was susceptible to pressure, but while Symons was predictable, Hitchens was not. Symons in his mincing voice said: 'Captain Gower and Captain Poldark.'

Hitchens followed close behind in a dead silence broken only by the sound of Symons's little heels as he clicked away. Hitchens said: 'Captain Gower and Captain Poldark.'

A muttering growl instantly broke out, some crying one side, some the other. There was a scuffle in a corner as two men came to blows. Friends pulled them apart as the mayor, pen wagging while he counted, totted the votes. He went over it twice and then put down his pen, cleared his throat and looked down at the book before him.

'The voting has been as follows. John Leveson Gower, thirteen votes; Ross Vennor Poldark, thirteen votes; George Warleggan, twelve votes; Henry Thomas Trengrouse, twelve

votes.' George had lost his seat by the margin by which he
had been elected.

III

Amid the noise and argument which followed, Nicholas Warleggan could be heard challenging the validity of two of the
voters, on the grounds that their property was outside the
town boundaries; but in fact he knew it was no good – the
objections if they were to have been made should have come
earlier. The two men separated had fallen to fighting again;
councillors on the winning side were shouting their elation.
Harris Pascoe gripped Ross's arm and said: 'Good, good,
good. That is the b-b-best result.' Captain Gower shook hands
with Ross for the second time, his face flushed with relief.

The mayor gave the official return to the clerk to post on
the outer door of the chamber, so that the public might be
informed. Lord Falmouth had not come over to congratulate
the two winners. Nor had the two losers. Henry Trengrouse
was talking to Fitz-Pen and trying to hide the disappointment
in his face. (The Warleggans had been so sure.)

As for that other Warleggan, George was standing with his
hands behind his back, the icy sweat of anger and frustration
soaking through his shirt, so upset that he could hardly
memorize the way the voting had gone or which of his
expected supporters had let him down. Choking, hardly able
to see or speak, his fingers clenched and unclenched about
whitened knuckles. He knew, or thought he knew, exactly what
had defeated him. It was men like Andrew and Thomas and
Hitchens, who still looked on him as an upstart and had voted
for the so-called gentry. Even his partner Trengrouse, as a
solicitor, had not really had the standing. Privilege had closed
its ranks and chosen to forget all the illegal and near-illegal
misdemeanours of Ross Poldark's past, all his arrogant pretensions to be above the law, all his barely hidden contempt for
that society which people like Andrew and Thomas and
Hitchens were at such pains to preserve. A man like himself,
George Warleggan, who all his life had worked steadily
within the law, who had given money to appropriate causes,
who had been a conscientious magistrate for over three years,
whose businesses in the town and the county made him one

of the largest employers of labour, such a man was regarded
with patronage and contempt because his ancestry was inferior
to theirs.

It did not occur to him that other men in the county with
no more distinguished a pedigree than he had were in fact
totally accepted, and that in seeking an explanation he need
have gone no farther than the personalities involved, of his
own, of Ross's, of half a dozen of the voters. Lord Falmouth
had seen the issues clearly enough.

The doors of the chamber were now open and a few of
the councillors were leaving. Harris Pascoe said:

'There will be a celebration dinner?'

'I have no idea. I have not been in this situation before.'

'To t-tell the truth, Ross, half-way through the voting I
feared it would be the other side which would have cause to
celebrate.'

'When that cross-voting took place,' Ross said, 'I was never
more afeared in my life.'

'Why?'

'The prospect was opening up that George and I might be
elected together!'

Falmouth was at last coming across, with Ralph-Allen
Daniell beside him.

'Congratulations, Captain Poldark,' said his Lordship shortly.
'We have won the day.'

'Thank you, my Lord. So it seems. By an uncommon narrow
margin.'

'No margin is too narrow so long as it is the right way. And,
have no fears, the margin in this borough will now steadily
increase.'

'Indeed? . . .'

'There is to be dinner at the Red Lion, but I have asked to
be excused and have requested Mr Ralph-Allen Daniell to
take the chair in my place. In a few days there will be a ball.'

'Congratulations, Captain Poldark,' Daniell said.

'Thank you.'

'Later,' said Falmouth, 'in a week or two I want the council
to come and dine with me at Tregothnan. Naturally I hope
you will come.'

'Thank you.'

His Lordship coughed drily. 'At the moment I am not in a position to participate in the usual celebrations. I did not tell you, Captain Poldark, when we met before the election – there seemed no purpose in telling you then – but my nephew died last night.'

Ross stared. 'Hugh? . . .'

'Yes, Hugh. Nothing could be done. His parents were with him at the end.'

Falmouth turned away, and Ross was surprised to see that his eyes were full of tears.

CHAPTER X

It was after six before Ross was able to get away.

The day had clouded, but Gimlett's prediction of rain was not fulfilled. A dry chill breeze soughed over the moors. Sheridan, having worked off the surplus energy stored in a long wait in the stables by almost galloping up the steep hill out of the town, soon settled to a comfortable walking pace which Ross did not bestir himself to accelerate. He would get home in due course. He was not sure he wanted to get home.

It was quite likely, knowing their friendship, that someone from Tregothnan would have sent a message about Hugh to Nampara. He hoped so. But in any case it would be an impossible meeting.

Ross's sense of outrage over the last week or so had not yet been abated by his sense of shock. Of course he had seen Hugh to be gravely ill, but he had not quite believed there was a real risk that a man who survived twelve months in a hell-hole of a prison camp should die two years later from the after-effects. He was so *young*. At that age one had such recuperative power. At the back of his thoughts too, too ungracious to be given a conscious airing, had been a suspicion that a little dramatization of Hugh's illness had not been altogether absent in order to enlist Demelza's greater sympathy. And although he had liked Hugh, nothing he could ever do now could remove from Hugh's name and memory

feelings that arose from the normal instincts of a husband
seeing his wife captivated by another man.

But now his rival was *dead*, and the more he thought of it
the less he liked it. It was reasonable enough to regret the
passing of a young man of value to his country and his friends.
He was sorry – sorry for that and regretted it sincerely. That
was one thing. But what of the other? How could he ever feel
that he had won Demelza back from her infatuation in fair
contest? How combat a ghost? How fight a rosy memory,
the memory of a man who furthered his suit in stanzas of
tender verse? Hugh's death was a tragedy for them both. It
stood fair and square between them like a barricade to prevent
any true reconciliation, even if either of them should want it.

Sheridan half shied at something moving between two gorse
bushes at the side of the track. It was a he-goat, dark-eyed,
lantern-jawed, long beard trailing, chewing slowly. He looked
aggressive, randy, like some old devil come out of a bog. Ross
flicked his whip and the goat stopped chewing and watched
them but did not retreat. Sheridan stepped nervously past. This
being the breeding season, the smell of the goat followed them
on the chill breeze.

So if his affairs had been directed by some old he-goat out
of a bog, could they have been ordered more perversely? This
new adventure he had wrong-headedly embarked on had
drawn its cross-grained motives from all sorts of ignoble
sentiments, not least of them his estrangement from Demelza
and the feeling that if she were partly lost to him it were
better if he were more away. Nor had he altogether forgotten
Demelza's expressed opinion that such a position would not
suit him. Nor had he lost sight of the knowledge that the
position he was gaining was the one that George most hated
to lose. All exalted motives that would stand him in good
stead at the Day of Judgement. Generous and reputable man
that he was.

Ross reached the old gibbet at Bargus where four parishes
met. The Place of Death, as it used to be called. The tall
sinister post and bracket still stood – even the gypsies and the
vagrants would not venture to cut it down for firewood – but
it would probably never be used again. Nowadays they did
it more formally in Bodmin. From here the landscape stretched

away, barren and windy and dull: St Ann's, the drunken tower
of Sawle Church, St Michael, Carn Brea, the stooping trees, a
mine chimney here and there; everywhere the desolate moors.

He took a deep breath and tried to see his position more
objectively, pared away from the emotions of anger or disgust.
So far as the activities of this morning were concerned, it
clearly put an end to any hopes of a *détente* between the
houses of Trenwith and Nampara. A year or so ago he had
had hopes that by seeing little of each other, by encouraging
a slow growth of tolerance between them – because after all
they were unavoidably neighbours and relatives by marriage –
he and George could come to avoid that petty venomous
quarrelling which was so much more suitable to the young
than to the middle-aged. Not so now. George had prized his
position as a Member of Parliament more highly than rubies.
He had been deprived of it by Ross's intervention. The bitterness, the hatred, would become even deeper and ever more
enduring.

The clouds were frowning in the west. As he went on the
sun neared the horizon and the sunset flamed just as it had
this morning, as if the scabs had been pulled off and the ugly
red wound showed again. So the red sky at morning was to
be followed by a red sky at night. The shepherds couldn't have
it both ways.

Perhaps he, Ross, wanted it both ways – to justify himself
and to set George down. Yet, leaving Demelza temporarily
on one side, the essential ingredient for any even modest
satisfaction at this morning's work must be a positive and not
a negative one. Why deprive George of his seat if he were full
of doubts as to whether he really wanted it? He could not see
himself fitting in, either with his patron or with the society of
England's rulers in which he must now be prepared to spend
a part of each year. He had always played a lone hand. Could
he learn, would he be willing to learn, to give and take, to pull
in harness? Could he suffer fools gladly, or even silently?

And yet, men of high ability – *much* higher than his – could
do so. It was a matter of temperament, not talent. Demelza
thought he did not have such a temperament. Well, who knew,
perhaps he would show her – always supposing she continued
to be interested.

Who knew what the future was for them both now? Perhaps she would sail away, like those swans today, out of his life for ever. Perhaps she was the damaged swan, not Morwenna.

As home drew near Sheridan quickened his pace, and coming through Grambler village a number of men and women wending their way home called good night as he passed. His mind went back again to that October evening fourteen years ago when he had returned from America to find Elizabeth engaged to his cousin Francis, and he had left them at Trenwith, his life in ruins, and had ridden home like this, through this same village, down to Nampara House to find it in ruins also, and Jud and Prudie Paynter dead drunk in his father's old box bed. A different return tonight, with a house refurnished and rebuilt, clean, tidy and well cared-for, as many servants as he needed, a pretty wife, two lovely children. What a change! And yet, in one way, was there not a sinister similarity?

Just out of the village he overtook a single figure walking in the same direction as himself. The afterlight was in his eyes but he recognized Sam.

When he heard the hooves behind him Sam stopped to make way, but Ross reined in beside him.

'Are you going to the Meeting House?'

'Yes.'

Ross dismounted. 'I'll walk with you a few paces.'

They began to climb the rising ground together, Ross allowing the reins to trail behind him.

'There be no meeting,' said Sam. 'Twas just I thought to go tidy up and see all was clean for tomorrow.' His voice sounded flat and dull.

'You never stop working, do you?'

'Oh . . . I find it no trouble t'keep busy. Especially if tis about the Lord's business.'

'Except the Lord build the house . . .'

'Please?'

'Oh, it is some memory from my schooldays.'

The clump of wind-ravaged fir trees beside Wheal Maiden were outlined against the dying light. The blood had gone, and it was all black and white like a silhouette.

Sam said: 'You been Tehidy?'

'No, Truro.'

'Oh.'

'What made you think Tehidy?'

''Twas just in my mind.'

'Are you still thinking of John Hoskin?'

'No . . . I wasn't just then.'

'How is your group going?'

'Proper, thank ee. Two more partook of the Blessing last week.'

Ross hesitated. 'And Emma?'

Sam shook his head. 'No . . . not Emma.'

'If it is not my concern, pray say so; but what is to be done about Emma?'

'There's naught more as can be done, Brother.'

Ross hesitated. 'I have often thought of asking, Sam, but then thought perhaps I should not . . . Why did you lose the fight?'

Sam frowned and twisted his hands together. ''Twill seem like a presumption if I answer the truth.'

'Well, no other is worth speaking.'

'I thought, Brother . . . it come to me in that very moment when I was near victory . . . it suddenly come to me to think of Christ and – and of how He was tempted of the Devil and of Him being shown all the Kingdoms of the Earth . . . And He refused, didn't He? And I thought, if He refused; me in my humble way, I must try to follow where He led.'

They had come to the Meeting House. It was quite bright here, but in the valley dusk had already accumulated, like an advance guard of night.

Sam said: 'Emma come to me last Tuesday sennight. We talked and talked, just like we done before. And we come to a blank wall. She cann't pretend, she say. It might come, I say, and she say, yes, Sam, it might, but if it don't . . . I'd be riven from you and you from your Society.' He put up a hand to loosen his neckcloth. 'Some day, she say, some day I may feel different. All I know is I don't feel'n now.'

His voice halted as he cleared his throat. 'Well, Brother, that's how it is. I'd best be going in. And you'll be wanting to be home, like.'

'So she's not going to marry Tom Harry?'

'No, praise be. She's going away.'

'Away?'

'To Tehidy. They have want of a maid and she say, I'll go for a year, Sam. Tis a move up in money and in place for me, she say. She'll be comfortable there and – and not so much in the way of either one of us. Just for a year, she say. Demelza wrote for her.'

'Demelza did?'

'Yes. She wrote to Lady de Dun – whatever tis now – we always d'call her Basset still.'

'But what had Demelza to do with it?'

'Emma went to see her and asked for advice. Then Emma come see me. Then she went back see Demelza, and Demelza say, why not separate for a year, go further away so's your paths are not always crossing? A year from now, if so be as Emma still wish it and I still wish it, Sister will arrange for us to meet – see how it come out – see if there be any change.'

Sheridan, impatient, thrust his head over Ross's shoulder and clicked his bit.

Ross said: 'I hope there will be.'

'Thank, ee, Brother. I pray for Emma every day. I pray every day for the miracle.'

Ross said: 'So I have two brother-in-laws crossed in love. I wonder if Drake, too, prays for a miracle.'

Sam looked up sharply, as if that thought had not occurred to him and he found it vaguely shocking.

He said: 'Well, Brother, tis warming at least to know that you and Sister are so happy wed together. Tis a shining pleasure to me every time I come near your house. Even if tis not gladness in Christ, tis the gladness of two good people knit together in godly and compassionate love.'

'Thank you, Sam,' Ross said, and patted Sheridan's nose and walked off quietly and thoughtfully down the valley.

II

Lights burned in the old parlour but not in the new library. Generally speaking they still tended to live in the old part of the house and to keep the library for 'best'. Gimlett heard him coming and trotted round the house to take Sheridan.

'Is the mistress in the parlour?'

'No, sur, she went out two hours agone.'

'Out?'

'Yes, sur.'

He found Jeremy and Clowance in the parlour playing some very untidy game with Betsy Maria Martin, a pretty girl now of sixteen, who always blushed when she saw Ross exactly as her elder sister had done so many years ago.

'Sorry, sur. Twas supposed to be a game of moving furniture – '

Her explanations were drowned by the noisy welcome the two children gave their father. He swung them up and kissed them and teased them while Betsy hurriedly began to put the chairs and table to rights.

'Mistress is out, I hear?'

'Yes, sur. She went soon after dinner.'

'Did she say where?'

'No, sur. But twas not riding. I thought she'd be back before dark.'

Ross saw a crumpled note on the mantelshelf. He picked it up and read: 'My dear Mrs Poldark, It is with grief that I have to tell you . . .' and at the bottom 'Frances Gower'. While Clowance bubbled in his ear he thought: Well, she cannot have gone *there*, not walking. Where *could* she have gone? Anger welled up in him that was half anxiety.

'Did she leave a message?'

'Who, mistress? Nay, but she told Jane to see for the supper.'

'Did she say she would be back for supper?'

'I dunno, sur. Not to me she didn' say nothing.'

After a while he went upstairs to their bedroom. Her blue cloak had gone, nothing else. No scribbled message, as normally there was. He went down again and walked slowly round the outhouses. The two piglets, Ebb and Flow, already grown to substantial size, occupied their own special box next to the horses. But they were still pets and were let out to roam about the yard most days. They greeted him with snorts and snuffles of recognition and he gave them each a chunk of bread he had brought for the purpose. Sheridan, being just fed, was content with a pat and a stroke, as was Swift, though Swift, you could see, was restive for lack of exercise.

In the kitchen Jane Gimlett's head was over a pot of soup and Ena Daniel was cutting up some leeks. Screams of laughter and bangs on the stairs indicated that Jeremy and Clowance were making a slow way to bed. He went back into the parlour. It was all tidy again, except for a few things the children had dropped. He picked these up and put them in the basket behind the big arm-chair, poured himself a glass of brandy and drank half of it. Then he drew the curtains. A fire was flickering, almost lost in the great hearth, and he shovelled more coal on and watched the smoke balloon up the chimney.

The brandy had gone down like raw spirit, burning deep into his stomach; but it did not touch the other rawness within him. He was conscious of ever growing anger against his wife. There might or might not be good reasons for such anger, but this was not a rational thing. It sprang from deeper and more primitive sources. It seemed to him that *all* his rawness, *all* his distress, *all* his sense of disillusion and frustration and empti-ness sprang from her. Together they had had everything and she had flung it all away. Almost without a thought to what she was spoiling and soiling for ever. Demelza, whom he had dragged up and loved and worked for devotedly: a man had come and smiled at her and held her hand and she had weakly, sentimentally and wantonly fallen in love. Almost without a token resistance. From the moment Hugh Armitage set eyes on her she had been ready to melt into his arms. And had made no secret of the fact, even to Ross. 'Ross,' she had more or less said, 'this beautiful young man is after me and I like it. I can't help it. I'm going to give myself to him. A pity about our home, our children, our happiness, our love, our trust. Such a pity. A shame. Too bad. Goodbye.'

All the rest too, this involvement in parliament, the now unbridgeable and final breach with George, the . . . He swallowed his brandy and poured another.

And now Hugh was dead and now she was gone. Where the hell could she have gone? Perhaps she would not come back. Perhaps it was better that she should not. He could manage the children, Betsy Maria and Jane Gimlett could manage the house. To hell with her. He should have known better than to drag her out of the gutter, make a sham lady of her.

He gulped the second glass. He was strangely tired, an uncommon feeling for him. The day had been exacting in the wrong ways, the farce of the election, the stupid trumpery celebration dinner. He had eaten little at it and now felt hungry, yet had not the stomach to eat. He could be bothered with nothing.

As he finished the second glass of brandy a footstep at the door.

Her face was ashen, her hair blown as if it were windy out. They stared at each other. She dropped her cloak on a chair. It did not catch and slid slowly like a snake to the floor. She looked down at it.

'Ross,' she said in a flat voice. 'I'm sorry. I hoped to be back for you.'

'Where in hell have you been?'

She bent and picked up her cloak, smoothed it with a slow hand. 'Have you supped?'

'No.'

'I'll tell Jane.'

'I don't *want* it.'

After a moment she shook her head as if trying to clear it. 'You know?'

'About Hugh? Yes. I saw Lord Falmouth in Truro.'

She sat quietly in the chair, cloak on her knees. 'It was last night.'

'Yes.'

She put a hand up to either cheek and stared round the room. She might have lost her way.

'Demelza, where have you *been*?'

'What? Now? To – to see Caroline.'

'Oh . . .' That somehow did not seem so bad. 'You walked?'

'Yes . . . It – it was something to do. The – the exercise did me – it helped.' Her eyes went to the glass in his hand.

'You'd best have some of this.'

'No.' She shook her head again. 'I don't think so. I should only sick it up.'

Outside an owl was hooting in the dark.

He said: 'It's a long walk. You'd best have something.'

'No . . . thank you, Ross. But I went – I went in the wrong shoes. I forgot to change them.'

He saw she was wearing her house slippers. They were badly scuffed and the back of one was broken.

He went to pour himself another brandy.

She said: 'I went to see Caroline only because – because I thought she would know how I felt, how – how . . . She is so . . .'

'And did she?'

'I believe so.' She shivered.

He poked the fire, coaxing a reluctant blaze from the smoking coal.

'Did you – have a good day in Truro?' she asked.

'So-so.'

'How did you see Lord Falmouth?'

'He was at a meeting.'

'Did he seem upset?'

'Yes, very.'

'It's such a – such a waste.'

'Perhaps if Dwight had continued . . .'

'No. At least he said not. Perhaps he was being modest.'

'Was Dwight there when you talked to Caroline?'

'Oh, no. Oh, no.'

Ross stared at his wife and then went to the cupboard under the old bookcase – where she had once hidden from her father – and took out a pair of shoes she sometimes used on the beach, canvas and flat and comfortable. He brought them over and she made to take them from him.

'Look,' he said roughly, and knelt and took her slippers off, one after the other, and put the other shoes on. Her stockings were holed and her feet were bruised, and stained here and there with blood.

'You'll do well to wash them presently,' he said.

'Oh, Ross . . .' She put her hands on his shoulders, but he stood up and her hands fell back to her lap.

He said: 'The cattle sale was poor. People are trying to get rid of their thin cows for the winter, and no one wants to buy.'

'Yes . . .'

There was another long silence. She said: 'The little Trenéglos girl came over today – just to call to invite Jeremy to a party. She is badly marked. They have used rotten-apple water but it seems to have done little for her.'

He did not reply.

'I – *had* to talk to someone,' she said, 'so I went to Caroline. Although she is so different from me I know no one closer, more truly a friend.'

'Except me.'

'Oh, Ross.' She began to cry.

'Well . . . was it not so? Until this happened, was it not so?'

'It was so. It is so. *You* . . . I talk to you always, with *nothing* between us. No one has ever been so close. *Never*. But in this –'

'Until this.'

'But in this – over this, it is too much to ask – of me – of you. It has to be another woman. And even then . . .'

He said: 'Well, you have no need to confide in me more than you want. Just say what you want to do – now – tell me what you want, no more, no less.'

'Want?' she said. 'I want nothing.'

'Nothing?'

'Nothing more than I have.'

'Had.'

'As you please, Ross. It's just as you say.'

'No, my dear, it's just as *you* say.'

'Please, Ross, don't . . .'

'Stop crying, you fool,' he said roughly. 'It solves nothing.'

She wiped her sleeve across her eyes, sniffled and looked at him through a mixture of hair and wet lashes. He could have killed her because he loved her.

She said: 'What do you want me to do?'

'Leave or stay, just as you wish.'

'*Leave?*' she said. 'I don't want to *leave*. How could I possibly go away from here – from all, all that we have together?'

'Perhaps you should have thought of it before.'

'Yes,' she said, standing up. 'Perhaps I should.'

He bent again to stab at the fire.

'Well,' she said, 'if you want me to go I will.'

The words rose to his lips to agree that she should leave but they would not come out. They choked in his throat and congealed in a greater anger.

The door came open. Only Clowance stood there. She had become a stout little girl this year. Her great good health and contentment had given her a face with fat cheeks and arms with fat wrists, and the shape of her face was as broad as it was long. Her fair hair curled about her shoulders and a sort of fringe had grown unchallenged and stood out from her forehead. She was wearing a long white flannel nightgown.

She said: 'Mama! Where you was?'

'Yes, my love, what is it?' It was Ross who answered.

'Mama promised.'

'What did she promise?'

'To read me that story.'

'What story?'

Demelza incautiously raised her head. 'It was the – I've forgot the title – in that book – '

Clowance took one look at her mother's face and immediately let out a howl of intense anguish. The door from the kitchen opened and Betsy Maria came out.

'Oh, beg pardon, I didn't know – ' She picked up the howling Clowance. Demelza had turned quickly and was hiding her face by letting her hair fall about it as she bent over Ross's glass.

'Take her up,' Ross said. 'Tell her her mother will be up in a few minutes. Stay with her till then. Is Jeremy asleep?'

'I b'lieve so, sur.'

'Tell her she'll come to read the story in a few minutes.' The door closed.

Demelza wiped her eyes again and gulped some of Ross's drink. Ross picked up her ruined slippers and dropped them in the children's basket, took up her cloak a second time, folded it. It was not an instinct of tidiness.

'Tell me how you feel,' he said.

'You mean you don't want me to leave?'

'Tell me how you feel.'

'Oh, Ross, how can I? How dare I?'

'Indeed. But try.'

'What have I to say? I never intended. This crept on me unawares. I never thought – you must know I never thought . . . I am so sad. For – for all things.'

'Yes, well . . . Sit down here a minute and tell me.'

'What more is there to say?'

'Tell me what you feel about Hugh.'

'Really?'

'Really.'

She used her sleeve again. 'How can I say truthfully, when I am not sure myself? I tell you, it came on me unawares. It was the last thing I ever sought. Now my heart feels broken . . . But not in the way – not like at Julia's death. Now I weep tears, tears, tears, for so much youth and love buried into the ground . . . When Julia died I had no tears. They were internal – like blood. Now – now they stream down my face like rain – like rain that I cannot stop. Oh, Ross, will you not hold me?'

'Yes,' he said, doing it.

'Please hold me and never let me go.'

'Nor shall I, if you give me the chance.'

'Not till we die. Ross, I could not live without you . . . These – these are not the tears of a penitent – I may have reason to be penitent – but this is not that. I cry – it sounds silly – I weep for Hugh and – and for myself – and for – for the whole world.'

'Set some tears aside for me,' Ross said, 'for I believe I need them.'

'Oh, they are *all* yours,' she said and then choked completely and clung to him with great shaking sobs.

They sat for a while, crouched in an awkward attitude that neither noticed. Now and then he would free a hand to thrust it impatiently across his own nose and eyes.

After a long time he said: 'Clowance will be waiting.'

'I'll go in a minute. But first I must wash my face.'

'Drink this.'

She took a second gulp from his glass.

'You are very good to me, Ross.'

'Good *for* you, no doubt.'

'*To* me . . . Forgiving . . . But forgetting? I don't know.

Perhaps it's a mistake to forget. All I know is that I love *you*. I suppose that's all that really matters.'

'It's what matters to me.'

She shuddered and put a hand to each eye in turn. 'I'll wash my face and then go and read, and then if you want you can have a bite of supper.'

'I think,' said Ross, 'I'll come and read a while with you.'

The MS READ-a-thon needs young readers!

Boys and girls between 6 and 14 can join the MS READ-a-thon and help find a cure for Multiple Sclerosis by reading books. And they get two rewards—the enjoyment of reading, and the great feeling that comes from helping others.

For complete information call your local MS chapter, or call toll-free (800) 243-6000. Or mail the coupon below.

Kids can help, too!